RAVE REVIEWS FOR
ROBIN WELLS,
WINNER OF THE NATIONAL
READERS' CHOICE AWARD!

"Robin Wells is an author to watch. We will be hearing much more of her. [Her writing] is hilariously funny, tender and sensuous."

—*Rendezvous*

BABY, OH BABY!

"Fascinating characters, snappy dialogue and a swift pace round out this fantastic story. . . . *Baby, Oh Baby!* is a fun story that will have readers howling with delight!"

—*Romance Reviews Today*

"A dramatically touching romance. Ms. Wells adds the right mixture of wit to a serious story line and pulls off a passionate tale for readers to enjoy."

—*Romantic Times*

PRINCE CHARMING

"Ms. Wells's talent shines on every page of this terrific story. . . . A must read for connoisseurs of laughter and romance."

—*Rendezvous*

"*Prince Charming* is a funny, sexy, and charming Pygmalion tale. Highly enjoyable reading!"

—*Romantic Times*

"*Prince Charming* is an enjoyable and humorous contemporary romance that readers will fully enjoy. . . . Ms. Wells will charm readers with this offbeat novel."

—*Affaire de Coeur*

OOH, LA LA . . .

Kate rubbed her temple where a headache was gathering, trying to gather her thoughts as well. Why would Zack think she'd change her mind? She'd told him that the movie had to be completely factual or she couldn't work on it.

And then the events of the evening crashed down on her, thudding heavily into place. The warm, giddy sensation that had made the night seem magical degenerated into stomach-twisting nausea. How could she have been so stupid?

"She was right," she murmured.

"Who?"

"That woman with the car." She fixed Zack with an accusing gaze. "I *am* drunk, aren't I?"

He shifted his stance and shoved his hand in his pocket, refusing to meet her gaze. "There's, um, no reason you should be."

Outrage flamed in Kate's chest. "Oh, yes there is. You got me drunk sho you could make me shign this!" She waved the letter she'd found in front of him.

"Kate—it wasn't like that. I just wanted you to relax a little so we could discuss it. I never dreamed that one or two drinks would . . ."

Oh, dear Lord—that's what the kiss was about, too. Mortification flooded her soul. Mercifully, her sense of anger was stronger. "Everything about this evening was an attempt to get me to shign that letter."

OOH, LA LA!

ROBIN WELLS

LOVE SPELL   **NEW YORK CITY**

To Ken
Who puts the "Ooh" in Ooh, la la!

LOVE SPELL®

August 2002

Published by

Dorchester Publishing Co., Inc.
276 Fifth Avenue
New York, NY 10001

ISBN 0-505-52503-8

The name "Love Spell" and its logo are trademarks of Dorchester Publishing Co., Inc.

Printed in the United States of America.

Visit us on the web at www.dorchesterpub.com.

OOH, LA LA!

Chapter One

Marvin Goldman leaned back in his enormous black leather chair, the one rumored to be made out of bull scrotum, and fixed his pale, beady eyes on Zack. "I gotta say, Jackson, I admire your balls."

Zack Jackson fought the urge to protectively cross his legs. The movie mogul's testicle fixation gave him the creeps—which was exactly what Goldman intended. Everyone in Hollywood knew that the C.E.O. of Parapet Pictures had a nasty, sadistic streak, and his office testified to the fact. The walls and ceiling were lacquered a hellish black, the floor was paved in black marble, and the only light in the room emanated from the flame-shaped globes that topped the tall torchères along the walls. The old man's enormous glass desk sat on a recessed black pedestal, which made it appear to be levitating. All he lacked was a pair of horns and a pitchfork to complete the picture.

"Yessir, you've got a lot of nerve, showin' up here to pitch another movie after the way your last one tanked." The short, paunchy studio head pulled his ever-present uncut cigar out of his mouth and pointed the damp, turdlike end at Zack like an accusing finger. "You went ten million over budget, and you

1

didn't even deliver it in time for a holiday release."

It was an effort to sit still on the ergonomically incorrect metal bench, but Zack managed. Word had it that the slanted, bleacherlike seats in front of the movie mogul's desk had been deliberately designed to make people squirm, and Zack refused to give the old goat that satisfaction. He might have to grovel, but he'd be damned if he'd squirm.

Goldman waggled his cigar again. "What was that friggin' film called, anyway—*Up in Smoke?*"

Oh, hell—now he was going to have to play the old man's vicious little name game. "The title was *Trial by Fire.*"

Goldman's lips curled into an evil grin. "Oh, right. *Up in Smoke* was what happened to all our hopes for it."

It was classic Goldman. Zack waited until the old man's cackle had faded into a phlegm-filled cough, then forced a deliberate calm into his voice. "As you know, Marvin, the weather was a problem on that shoot."

Goldman made a low grunting sound. "Weather, schmeather. A good director shoots around it."

"It's a little hard to shoot around a flood when the movie's about a forest fire."

Goldman narrowed his beady eyes. "You sayin' I don't know my business?"

Damn—it was always a mistake to disagree with Goldman. The old man had the fattest ego in Hollywood but the thinnest skin, and he took the mildest dissent as a personal attack.

"Of course not, Marvin. No one knows the industry better than you do. I'm just saying some things went wrong on that picture."

"Yeah. The main one being that I green-lighted it in the first place."

The studio head leaned back in his chair and folded his hands over his bulbous belly. The man's odd physique had always reminded Zack of a child's drawing of a person—a large circle for the body, a smaller circle for his bald, round head, then short, skinny sticks for the arms and legs. His cartoonish appearance was enhanced by the fact that his chair back rose a good foot higher than the top of his head.

"The film before that fire fiasco was an even bigger flop." Goldman reinserted the cigar in his mouth and contorted his lips to speak around it. "You know the one—the one where everyone had microchips implanted in their brains. What the hell was it called? *Brain Truss?*"

The vile old goat was sub-human—a depraved, brutish, warped, malignant sore of a man, with a soul as black as the walls of his office. Unfortunately, he was also Zack's last chance of ever making another movie.

Zack unclenched his teeth just enough to answer. "The name was *Brain Trust.*"

"Oh, right. Must have been my brain in a truss, givin' that project the go-ahead." Goldman let loose another ragged cackle. "What's your excuse for that one?"

"Come on, Marvin—you know how things happen. There were a lot of unexpected delays and expenses on that shoot."

"Your job is to expect the unexpected."

"How could I expect that, halfway through the shoot, the leading man would have a car accident that would leave him in a body cast for three months? There were a bunch of other problems, too." Zack lifted his hand and ticked them off, starting with his thumb. "Special effects couldn't deliver as promised, the gaffers' union staged a strike, the set designer quit in a huff, and distribution screwed up the ship date."

"You left one thing out," Goldman snarled.

"What?"

"You forgot to mention it was a lousy movie."

Zack choked back the urge to dive across the desk and throttle the man. He pasted on a congenial smile. "I understand it's doing well in some of the foreign markets."

Goldman glared at him, clearly irritated to have any ray of sunshine injected into this black hole of a meeting. "Oh, yeah," he sneered. "It's a big hit in northern Siberia. And I hear it's got 'em linin' up for miles in Outer Mongolia." He leaned back in his scrotum-upholstered chair and shook his head at Zack. "Like I said, Jackson, you got guts, darkenin' my door again."

"Well, you've got guts, too, Marvin," Zack fired back. If he stroked the little ghoul's colossal ego, maybe he could turn things around. "That's why I came."

The old man's eyes narrowed suspiciously, all but disappearing in his face. "What's that supposed to mean?"

"Just that you trust your own instincts. You know a jewel when you see it, and you're smart enough to know that a diamond is a diamond, whether it's delivered in a blue box from Tiffany's or found lying in the dirt."

"You sayin' you've brought me some dirty jewels, Jackson?" Goldman's lips curled around his cigar. "What are they—your family ones?"

Christ. Didn't the S.O.B. ever give it a rest? "Sorry to disappoint you, Marvin, but I'm talking about a script. I've got a real jewel of a story, and since you have the option on my next movie, you get first shot at it."

The old man snorted. "First shot? Hell, I'm your first and your last, and don't think I don't know it." Goldman leaned forward and stabbed his stogie in the air. "You know what they're callin' you? Jinx. Jinx Jackson. Hell, I'm the only studio head in town who'll take a meeting with you, and the only reason I did was to see if you had the nerve to show up."

Bile, bitter and acidic, rose in Zack's throat. He knew how things were in this business. He'd been born into it—his grandfather had been an early film star, his father had been a big-screen hearthrob, and Zack himself had grown up in front of America, playing the precocious son of a small-town private eye in a popular TV series. He'd been in Hollywood all his life, and he knew it was an unforgiving town.

Unforgiving, and superstitious. No one wanted to be associated with a loser. You were only as good as your last movie, and if you bombed, it was hard to get a second chance. It was even harder to get a third.

But that was exactly what Zack needed—another chance.

And it was his lousy luck that his best shot of getting one was the miserable excuse for a human being sitting across from him. If Goldman took a pass on the project, it would be the kiss of death.

The old man's chair creaked as he leaned back. "I'm gonna give you a little advice. The Jackson name still has a lot of charisma, and you're not too bad lookin'. Maybe you ought to consider goin' back in front of the camera."

Zack shook his head. "Acting's not for me."

"You did all right for yourself as a kid."

Yeah, and he'd hated it. He'd hated waiting around, doing nothing more significant than trying not to wrinkle his pants, while all around him the real action took place. The power was in the decisions—big decisions, like what stories would be made into movies, which actors would play the roles, which footage would end up on the editing room floor and which would make it to the screen. Little decisions, like where the lights should be set, if the script needed tweaking, whether or not a scene needed another take. The public thought the actors were the key to a film, but Zack knew they were just paint and hubcaps.

The producer and the director were the ones who made it go. And in an increasing number of cases, the producer and the director were the same person. That had been Zack's goal from early childhood: to become a producer-slash-director. A producer/director had complete control of the picture from the first draft of the script to the final edit.

And more than anything, Zack wanted control. His childhood had been one long set of instructions. *Do this; do that—no, not that way, this way. Smile. Don't smile. Say this. Don't say that.* Like a poodle at a dog show, he'd been carefully groomed, trotted out on a leash, and judged on how obediently he followed orders. When he grew up, he'd promised himself, *he* would call the shots.

And that was exactly what he'd done. He'd made nine feature-length movies, and he'd made all the decisions for each of them,

5

from beginning to end. He'd found the stories, commissioned the scripts, sold the concepts, assembled the crews, directed the shoots, supervised the editing, and coordinated the distribution. Each film had brought a fresh set of headaches and problems, but Zack had loved every minute of it.

He loved the challenges, loved the creative process, loved the way each project completely absorbed him. Hell, he just flat-out loved movies. In movies, life made sense. People had clear-cut goals and motives, and it was easy to see the relationship between their actions and the outcome. Good was rewarded, evil was punished, and the characters got to live happily ever after.

Real life, of course, was nothing like that. In real life, love affairs always ended, friendships eventually fractured, and family ties—if they'd ever existed in the first place—inevitably frayed and severed. Zack sometimes wished he had the ability to con himself like the rest of the populace, but growing up in Hollywood, he'd learned the truth early.

Love and friendship were just gussied-up business arrangements. Like any business, they operated on the basis of supply and demand, and they only worked as long as both parties got an equitable exchange of goods or services. The fact of the matter was, people inevitably left you or let you down. Work was the only thing that could be trusted, the only thing that lasted, the only reliable source of satisfaction.

Unfortunately, Zack's ability to work was in the hands of the testes-obsessed gnome of a man squinting at him across the table.

Goldman sucked on his stogie, making the sound of a boot being pulled out of thick mud. "I'll tell ya what, Jackson—bring me a project that has you in it, and we'll talk."

"Nah. I'm no actor."

Goldman applied more suction to his cigar. "No director, either, judging from your last two pictures."

His last two pictures—were they all that counted? Didn't it

matter that all of the others had done well—damn well, considering the nature of the business?

Apparently not. Zack's stomach gnarled into a painful knot. Two strikes and it was all over. He wasn't even going to get a third swing of the bat.

A desperate, grasping-at-straws gamble formed in his mind. What the hell—he might as well go for it.

He rose to his feet. "Well, I won't waste any more of your time, Marvin. MGM wants a meeting, but I told them I had to talk to you first. Since you're not interested, I guess that frees me up." Zack strode to the door, his heart slamming hard against his chest. It was now or never. If Goldman let him walk out, his career was over.

His hand was on the doorknob when Goldman finally spoke. "Aw, hell. As long as you're here, you might as well give me what you got."

It wasn't the most encouraging invitation he'd ever received to pitch a project, but it was an invitation nonetheless. Zack loosened his death grip on the doorknob and slowly turned. "If you're not interested, there's really no point."

"Sit down, dammit, and give me your pitch," Goldman growled.

Zack strolled back to his seat, trying to pretend his entire future didn't hang in the balance, trying to ignore the way his stomach coiled like a cobra, trying to act calm and cool and nonchalant. He lowered himself on the gawd-awful bench, drew a deep breath, and plunged in.

"As the opening credits roll, we find ourselves inside a brothel called the Ooh La La. We're in New Orleans, and it's the late eighteen hundreds. The set is lush—velvet drapes, Aubusson rugs, lots of mirrors, nude sculptures, elaborate gold-framed paintings. We hear voices—a woman's laugh, the tinkle of crystal, piano music." Zack leaned forward. "The camera pans the room, picking up scantily clad ladies, expensively dressed men, and a blindfolded piano player banging out jazz. We see that the piano player's peeking out from under the blindfold. The camera goes in tight on his hands, and then we're in his point of view, seeing what he sees from under the blindfold."

Goldman stared at him, his expression as blank as a movie screen after the last credit rolls.

"We get little peeks of what's going on in various parts of the room," Zack continued. "We see a man's hand scooch up under some colored petticoats. We see a woman squeezing a man's behind as they dance in the corner. We see a woman bend over to pour a man a drink, and we get a close-up of cleavage—I'm talking *major* cleavage." Zack held out his hands, as if he were palming a pair of basketballs. "Our piano player throws back his head. We see a large, gaudy chandelier on the ceiling, and next to it, a ribbon-covered swing. The swing is being lowered from the ceiling by a squeaky pulley. And then we see . . ." Jake paused for effect. "A horse."

"A *horse?*"

Zack nodded. "A stallion. A man leads it into the room. Everyone steps aside and stops what they're doing—everyone except the piano player, who just keeps on playing. We're still in his point of view, so we're just getting little glimpses of the action."

Goldman pulled the cigar out of his mouth. That was a good sign. When Goldman took out his cigar during a pitch, it meant he was interested.

Encouraged, Zack continued. "First we see a close-up of the horse's face. Then we get a glimpse of a young woman as she sits in the swing. We get a peek of her leg as she peels off her stockings, then a colorful whirl of petticoats being tossed through the air. We see another close-up of the horse's face. We hear the swing being raised. We hear loud, bawdy voices. We see a close-up of a man, then a woman, then the horse."

Zack talked faster to convey the tempo. "The crowd gets louder. We hear murmurs of amazement. More close-ups of people's expressions—shock, disbelief, revulsion, fascination. Another close-up of the horse, this time looking wild-eyed. The music gets louder. We see the piano keys, see the player's fingers flying across them." Zack paused for just a heartbeat. "And then we hear a long, loud whinny."

Goldman sat perfectly still, the cigar between his fingers, his hands on his belly. "Hmm."

A triumphant thrill shimmied through Zack. Throw in a little deviant sex, and Goldman's interest level shot up like the thermostat on the back lot in July. The trick now was to keep him interested.

"The horse is led out," Zack continued. "The crowd applauds and cheers. The piano player's eye pans the room and lands on a brawny young delivery man in the back room, who's just set down several boxes of whiskey. He's staring through the doorway, stunned by what he's just seen. The man continues to watch as the madam, a buxom old dame dripping jewelry, steps forward and says something flowery like, 'The Ooh La La is pleased to present Salome and the dance of the seven veils.' "

Goldman leaned forward. "The delivery man is the hero?"

Goldman was asking questions—man, oh, man, he was taking the bait!

Zack nodded. "His name is Joe, and he's just come to New Orleans from the bayou. He falls in love with the dancer. Her name is Sadie, and it turns out she's working in the brothel as an indentured servant. She'd needed some quick cash for a noble cause—she paid for her grandmother's treatment at a tuberculosis sanatorium—so she agreed to work for the madam for three years in exchange for three thousand dollars.

"Joe wants to pay off her debt and marry her, but he doesn't have any money. He's in despair at the thought of having to wait until her time is up. And then he sees an ad for a big boxing match that offers a purse of ten thousand dollars. Joe decides to go for it."

Goldman sat perfectly still, his face inscrutable. Zack drew a deep breath and continued, "The man putting together the fight, see—his name is Drago—he controls all the gambling in town, and he's one bad dude. To make the point, we'll show a rigged riverboat race that ends in an explosion, a wild carriage chase

9

down Canal Street, and a huge gunfight scene in a French Quarter saloon. This guy will do anything—and I mean *anything*—to win."

"Drago tries to get Joe in his pocket when Joe starts winning all the preliminary fights, but our boy won't play. Drago starts to get rough, but Joe outwits him. There'll be a chase scene through the French Quarter, where Joe tries to escape two of Drago's thugs. There's another scene where Joe discovers that Drago's men have hidden broken glass in the bag of beans that Joe uses for a punching bag.

"Drago finds out about Sadie, and decides she's the ticket to talking Joe into dropping out of the fight. He tells her that if Joe doesn't back out, he'll be killed."

Goldman seemed to be listening intently. Encouraged, Zack went on. "Sadie realizes that she has to sacrifice her future to save Joe. There's a real tearjerker of a scene where she tells Joe she's calling off the wedding. She tells him that she doesn't love him, that she likes the fancy life. At first Joe doesn't believe her. She really needs to convince him, so she tells him she's become Drago's lover, and throws out a few details about how much he pleases her in bed.

"Joe is heartbroken, but instead of deciding to drop out of the fight, he's more determined than ever to get the best of Drago. He gets in the ring with Drago's man, who's a big, bad hombre full of tricks. He uses brass knuckles, then a hidden razor. Joe is taking a serious beating. Sadie can't stand it." Zack paused for dramatic effect.

"She makes her way up to the ropes and begs him to forfeit the fight. If he doesn't, she tells him, Drago will have him killed. Joe realizes she still loves him, that she said all that other stuff to save him. It gives him a reason to live. He gives it all he's got and against all odds, he wins."

Zack paused again. Goldman gave no reaction. "The crowd goes crazy. Drago reluctantly climbs into the ring to present the prize to Joe. Joe takes the money. He takes a bow. Then he takes a punch at Drago, knocking him cold. The crowd erupts in cheers.

"Later that evening, Joe and Sadie go to the brothel so Joe can pay off the madam. They plan to leave town and start a new life. Sadie says she needs to go upstairs to pack her stuff. Joe says she's never going up there again. She doesn't need a thing. She's making a fresh start with him, and he wants her to have everything new. And the first new thing he's going to get her is a new last name."

Goldman still sat perfectly still. Zack tried to read his face, but it was as expressionless as a potato. "I haven't even told you the best part. I saved the best for last."

Goldman's beady eyes drilled into Zack. "Well, let's have it," the producer said.

"The best part is, the story's true."

Goldman's bushy eyebrows flew up. "True?"

Zack nodded. "True. Joe and Sadie were real people. This really happened. You know how hot true stories are right now. Think *A Beautiful Mind*. Think *Erin Brockovich*. Think *A Perfect Storm.* "

Goldman leaned forward. "You own the rights to the book?"

"That's the beauty of it. There *is* no book. It's history, pure and simple. It's public domain."

Goldman's eyes narrowed. "If there's no book, where'd you get the story?"

"From an article." Zack slid a copy of a drab magazine across the desk, making sure not to touch the glass. Goldman went ballistic if anyone left a fingerprint on his desk.

The old man glanced at the black-and-white cover. "*Historical Research Quarterly?* What the hell is this?"

"A scholarly publication. You know—something professors and historians and other university types publish their papers in. I found it in the seat pocket on a flight to Chicago and started skimming through it. Anyway, the piece about Joe and Sadie was written by a New Orleans University history professor named Kate Matthews. Someone evidently donated Sadie's old

11

diary to the university, and the prof corroborated the diary's contents with other sources."

"This professor—isn't she going to be screaming copyright?"

"She can't. My attorneys checked. Our script is based on actual historical events, not the magazine article," Zack explained. "I sent a screenwriter to New Orleans to do some research. All of the documents mentioned in the article are available for public view. I've even got a copy of the diary, if you're interested."

"Who's the screenwriter?"

"Rich Bauer," Zack replied.

"Hmmph." Goldman gnawed his cigar. "He's a royal pain, but that's your problem. You got a script?"

"A preliminary one."

"Let me see it."

Zack passed it across the desk. Goldman slowly thumbed through it.

"This is all true?"

Zack shifted. "All the stuff about Sadie and Joe is. We jazzed up the bad guy's role to add more action."

Goldman continued to scan the script.

"This project has it all—sex, violence, jazz, and a couple of characters to really root for." Zack said. "And with its true-story angle, it has huge Oscar potential."

Goldman looked up. "Who do you have in mind for the leads?"

Excitement pulsed through Zack's veins. This was going well, really well. "George Talley—you know, that hot TV star on 'Emergency Central.' He's looking for a vehicle to make the jump to the big screen. He's seen the script, and he's itching for this role."

Goldman scratched his belly thoughtfully. "That could work. He's ripe for a crossover. You'll need a movie name for the leading lady, though, to keep it from looking like a M.O.W."

Zack nodded. No director wanted a major motion picture to look like a made-for-TV Movie of the Week. "I've sent the script out to Gwyneth Paltrow and Cameron Diaz. I haven't heard back from their agents yet."

"Send one out to Lena Brighton. She'd be perfect, and I hear she's looking for something."

Zack gave a measured nod, trying to suppress his excitement. The old man was going for it. He was actually going for it!

Goldman gnawed his cigar. "What's the budget?"

"About thirty-five." Zack tossed out the figure casually, as if he were talking about ones instead of millions.

"For everything? Post-production included?"

Zack nodded.

"Do it for twenty-five and we've got a deal. Same split as your last movie."

Zack's heart tripped like a snare drum. Goldman had made an offer! And it was a higher starting point than he'd dared to hope for, but he couldn't let Goldman know it.

Zack pulled his brows into a frown. "There's no way this movie can be made for that. It'll take thirty-three, at least."

"Thirty. And not a penny over."

It was just the figure he'd been aiming for. Zack rubbed his chin, pretending to mull it over. "Well, if we can get the talent for a reasonable salary, and if we're very conservative . . ."

"Oh, you'll be conservative, all right," Goldman snapped. "I want this movie on time and on budget, and I want it for the holiday season. It's got to be released before the deadline for Academy Award nominations."

Zack's mind raced. It was do-able, but production would need to start immediately.

"I intend to keep you on a short leash," Goldman continued. "I want to know when, where, and how you plan to shoot this thing, what your contingency plan is, and how much it'll cost. And once you're in production, I want a detailed weekly report. I want to know the second you hit any snags. And don't think I won't find out what's really going on."

Damn. The idea of Goldman looking over his shoulder and breathing down his neck stuck in Zack's craw. Under any other

13

circumstances, he wouldn't have stood for it, but as things were, he didn't hold any cards.

Goldman jabbed his cigar in the air. "I'm tired of throwing good money after bad with you, Jackson. If it starts to look like you can't deliver, I'll pull the plug and take my losses. This is your last chance—your *very* last chance. Capiche?"

Swallowing hard, Zack gave a curt nod. The old man wasn't exaggerating. If he screwed this up, his career would be history. And without his career, he'd have no reason to get up every morning.

"And one more thing."

Uh-oh. Goldman always saved the worst for last.

The old man picked the magazine back up. "It says here that this professor is the world's foremost authority on New Orleans's historic red-light district. We need to hire her as our technical adviser." Goldman stared at the magazine and curled his lips into what passed for a smile. "Yes, sirree. We're gonna build up this realism angle big time." He squinted at the picture. "Hell, we'll even use her as our spokesperson. We'll get the professor here all over the talk shows and magazines, talkin' about how authentic and historic this movie is. She's got the perfect look for it, too."

As far as Zack recalled, the grainy black-and-white picture above the byline showed a woman as plain as unbuttered toast. It was hard to tell much about her, aside from the fact that she looked to be about thirty and wore her light hair pulled back in a bun as serious as her expression.

"Hell, she coulda come from Central Casting. She's got that stuffy, nose-in-a-book kinda look," Goldman said, still looking at the photo. "Looks like a real intellectual. It's the perfect foil for someone talkin' about whores and horses and rigged boxin' matches." He set down the magazine and looked at Zack. "Hire her right away. She's our ticket to makin' this puppy fly."

Zack thought the public would be more interested in the movie's entertainment value than its historic merit, but if the professor floated Goldman's boat, what the hell. "All right." He reached for the magazine.

Goldman yanked it back. "On second thought, I'll have my people handle it. I want to put a clause in her contract about promotional appearances."

"Fine." Zack sat back and heaved an inward sigh of relief. A technical adviser—that was all Goldman wanted? Hell, that was nothing. For a moment there Goldman had had him worried.

Technical advisers never posed a problem. All they ever did was sit on their duffs and collect a fat salary. Give 'em a chair on the set and ask 'em a question now and then to make them feel important, and they were happy as clams.

A technical adviser. Zack breathed a sigh of relief. That was nothing—nothing at all. How much trouble could one little old female professor be?

Chapter Two

Kate Matthews punched the elevator button in the lobby of the Hyatt Regency, smoothed the brown gabardine of her below-the-knee-length skirt, and glanced at her Seiko. She was right on time. Zack Jackson expected her in his suite at two o'clock, and it was seven minutes till.

Just seven more minutes, and she'd be meeting with Zack Jackson. The thought made her stomach do a cartwheel. It was ridiculous to feel so nervous, she scolded herself. She knew New Orleans's history backwards and forwards, and she was an expert on Storyville, the city's old red-light district. She was farsighted, detail-oriented, hardworking, and intelligent. She was more than capable of handling this job.

But it wasn't her professional qualifications that had her stomach quaking like the San Andreas fault, and she knew it. It was the thought of coming face-to-face with Zack Jackson, the man who'd been her first love.

Not that she'd actually ever *met* him. Kate's love affair with Zack had been strictly one-sided and completely imaginary. She'd been only eleven years old when she'd fallen head over heels the first time she'd seen him on TV, in his role as Henley

16

Jones, the clever, crime-solving son of a detective on "Charlie Jones, Private Eye." For the next three years, she'd spent every Friday night glued to the tube, sighing over Zack's escapades and gathering fuel for new romantic fantasies.

She could still recall some of her favorite episodes. When Zack had helped his father find a kidnapped girl in an abandoned rock quarry, she'd pretended that she was the girl he'd rescued. When Zack carried an injured friend out of a burning building, she'd imagined she'd been the one in his arms. And when Zack had kissed a girl for the first time, Kate had lived on it for weeks, replaying it over and over in her mind, fantasizing that she was the lucky recipient of his affections.

She was ashamed to admit it, but when she'd finally received her real first kiss four years later from an awkward high school boy named Charlie, she'd closed her eyes and pretended he was Zack. It hadn't lived up to her fantasies, though. No kiss ever had.

Well, that just went to show how unrealistic her girlhood flights of fancy had been, she told herself, adjusting the strap on the large black bag on her shoulder. She'd long since abandoned the habit of spinning romantic daydreams. After all, she was no longer a starry-eyed adolescent, but a responsible adult with a child of her own.

Responsible—yep, that was the word that described her. The thought dampened her spirits like the March rain drizzling outside. She was responsible, all right—responsible for earning a paycheck, responsible for single-handedly raising an increasingly rebellious child, responsible for dealing with a neurotic, worrywart mother. She loved her family dearly, but sometimes the responsibilities of caring for them squeezed in on her like a garlic press, threatening to crush her under the pressure.

Especially lately, now that Skye was nearing thirteen. Kate's precocious daughter had always been a handful, but since she'd hit the rocky shoals of puberty, she was becoming impossible. The scary part was that Skye reminded Kate of herself at sixteen or seventeen—cocky and willful, certain that her hopelessly dorky mother was deliberately depriving her of a life of glamour and excitement, a life she just *knew* awaited her on the other side of all her mother's oppressive rules. Kate saw the parallels of Skye's life to her own, and it worried her to death.

Her family wasn't the only worry on her mind, Kate thought, staring at the lights above the elevator doors. The job that had always been her haven, the one place where she felt confident and serene, had recently turned into a headache of migraine proportions. The kindhearted head of the history department who'd hired her and mentored her had suffered a stroke five months ago, and the professor who'd been named as his replacement was her professional nemesis.

Kate and Dr. Compton had never seen eye to eye. Kate was interested in the history of people—how they'd lived, what they'd thought, what they'd felt. Dr. Compton thought that the only facts of any historical importance were dry, dusty statistics about economics and politics. Kate's specialty happened to be Storyville, New Orleans's old area of legalized vice and debauchery that had been the birthplace of jazz. Dr. Compton looked down his nose at the topic, calling it trashy and sensationalistic.

Their differences had come to a head two years ago when they'd vied for special funding for a research project. Kate had won, and Compton had never forgiven her for it.

In the two months that he'd been running the department, he'd become the bane of her existence. When she'd gotten the call from Hollywood a month ago, Kate had been so sure Compton would refuse to let her work on the project that she'd asked the studio executive to call the dean directly.

Sure enough, Compton's displeasure had been more than evident when he'd summoned her into his office three weeks ago.

"The dean has agreed to give you a three-month sabbatical to work on this—this *movie*." Dr. Compton had said the word as if it were a particularly nasty type of STD. "He seems to think the publicity will be good for the university's image."

"It can't hurt," Kate had said amiably.

Compton had frowned at her over the top of his outdated

plastic glasses. "I disagree. I think it will damage the university's reputation to have its name attached to such a salacious story."

Oh, brother. Here they went again. "The story is a part of New Orleans's history, Dr. Compton."

"Hmph." Dr. Compton's mouth puckered as if he'd bitten into a green plum. "We'd be much better served to focus on the history of our city's more upstanding citizens."

Oh, right. So you can wheedle the wealthy descendants of those upstanding citizens into donating money to the university, which will earn you brownie points with the college president.

Compton steepled his fingers together and eyed her with displeasure. "This all came about because of that vulgar article you published. You know, Kate, a professor on the tenure track would do well to devote her energies to more academic—and, might I add, less prurient—pursuits."

Kate's heart had sunk to the soles of her Easy Spirit pumps. It was just her luck to be up for tenure while Compton sat on the history department throne. As the department head, he'd chair the committee that would decide whether or not she was deemed worthy.

Kate had worked toward tenure for the past eight years, pouring her heart and soul into her work. She loved the study of history, loved the way over and over it proved that the human spirit could surmount any obstacle, loved the way it showed how the efforts of just one person could change the lives of many. Tenure would be validation of her ability to pass on the lessons of the past, proof that her efforts were of value, evidence that she'd succeeded. But most of all, tenure would mean security. History departments were shrinking at universities all over the country, and New Orleans was no exception. If she lost her job, another position would be hard, if not impossible, to find. Even if she could find another post, it would probably involve a move, which would mean uprooting Skye and abandoning her mother. As much as Kate loved her work, her family was her top priority.

"The dean approved my involvement in the movie," Kate had told Compton.

"Yes, but you're putting yourself in a very precarious situation." Compton's voice had held an ominous, almost threatening tone. "If this movie is historically inaccurate in any way, you'll embarrass the university. I don't need to tell you what repercussions that could have on your career."

No, he didn't need to tell her. If she botched the movie, she could kiss any chance of tenure—and maybe even her job itself—good-bye.

But there was no need to worry about that. She *wouldn't* botch the movie. If there was one thing she was sure of, it was her skill as a historian. She would use the same care on the movie that she used on her research papers and lectures. She would do such an impressive job that the dean and the tenure committee would be eager to make her a permanent member of the university's staff.

"Perhaps you'd like to reconsider," Compton had said.

"I've already given it plenty of thought," she'd replied, giving him her sweetest smile. "I'm looking forward to the challenge."

And she was. How many history professors got the opportunity to actually bring a piece of history to life? This was the chance of a lifetime, and she wasn't going to let the old coot scare her out of seizing it. Besides, Parapet Pictures was paying her more than a year's salary for three months' work, and she could definitely use the money. This movie would give her a chance to make some financial headway.

Not to mention a chance to meet Zack Jackson in person.

The last thought sent a fresh skitter of nervousness frisking up her spine, and she jumped as the elevator chimed its arrival. The brass doors slid open, and Kate stepped inside, along with two middle-aged women wearing convention badges. As the elevator whisked upward, she tugged at her jacket and smoothed her chignon, wishing she'd worn something more colorful and maybe done something different with her hair. When she'd talked to that nice Mr. Goldman on the phone, though, he'd told her they wanted her to look scholarly and professional, just like she had in that published photo. Part of her job would be talking to the media about the history of the movie, and the studio wanted her to look like an intellectual heavyweight.

Well, that was no problem. Kate usually geared her appearance to being taken seriously, and her closet was full of serious clothes. The only frivolous items in her wardrobe were her undergarments, and no one ever saw those.

Nor was anyone likely to, she thought ruefully. She'd all but given up on Mr. Right putting in an appearance, and she had no desire to go another round with a Mr. Wrong. Her experience in the romance department was limited, but from what she'd seen it was highly overrated.

Still, she really ought to get out more. If she had a more active social life, maybe she wouldn't be in such a lather over meeting the object of her adolescent adoration.

The elevator stopped on the fourteenth floor and the two convention attendees stepped out. As the door slid shut behind them, Kate fingered the buttons on her jacket, debating whether to open it or leave it closed. She was being ridiculous, she told herself. Zack Jackson wasn't likely to care what she wore or how she wore it. She wasn't coyote ugly, but she wasn't beautiful like the actresses he dated in Hollywood, either.

The elevator stopped on the twenty-seventh floor. Clutching her bag in a white-knuckled grasp, Kate stepped out and followed the room number signs past the concierge desk and down the hall. She hesitated in front of a set of mahogany double doors for a moment, trying to calm her pounding heart, then drew a deep breath and knocked. The door swung open, and there he was.

Oh, my. It was a shock, looking straight into the dark eyes that had played the lead role in all her pubescent fantasies. In some ways, he was just as she remembered—he still had thick, black-brown hair, still had a dimple in his right cheek, still had an unexpectedly sensual mouth—but now he also had defined

21

cheekbones, a strong jaw, and a deep cleft in his chin.

Her gaze traveled down, taking in the muscular body clad in faded jeans and a blue-and-gray-striped knit shirt. His body had matured as handsomely as his face; his shoulders were wide, his stomach was flat, and his chest looked hard and muscled. His biceps bulged as he rested his hands on the doorjamb.

Kate tried to swallow, but her mouth was too dry. She'd known he was no longer a boy, of course. He was probably three or four years older than she was, and she'd just turned thirty-one. She'd glimpsed him on TV a couple of years ago, escorting a beautiful actress to the Academy Awards, so she'd known he'd grown into an attractive man.

She just hadn't realized *how* attractive. He had more than physical appeal, he had an indefinable presence. He exuded a raw, masculine energy that left her weak-kneed and slack-jawed, unable to do anything but stand numbly in the doorway and stare.

He flashed straight white teeth in a smile. "Miss Matthews?"

His voice was just as she remembered, but an octave lower. She managed a smile and pulled herself together enough to stick out her hand.

Zack enfolded it in a firm, warm grip. "I'm Zack Jackson."

As if she didn't know. Her hand felt hot and tingly in his, and by the time he released her hand, she felt hot and tingly all over.

"Nice to meet you," he said. "Come on in."

He opened the door wider, and she hesitantly stepped into a small entryway, her heart pounding so hard, she was afraid she'd hyperventilate.

Get a grip, she silently ordered herself. You're here as a professional, not a lovestruck groupie.

She drew a deep breath and followed him into a large parlor. Deliberately pulling her gaze from Zack, she looked around. The elegant room was filled with Regency-style furnishings in rich shades of green and burgundy and gold. A pair of gold damask sofas sat facing each other in front of a faux fireplace. To the right was a wet bar, and at that far end sat a long table strewn with papers, surrounded by ten tall-backed chairs. A thin, thirty-something man with round metal glasses and a narrow, Back Street Boys–type goatee sat at one end, tapping on a laptop computer. Zack gestured toward him. "This is Rich Bauer, our chief screenwriter."

The writer waved a greeting without looking up. Kate lifted her hand and self-consciously waved back.

Zack gestured toward the table. "Have a seat, Miss Matthews."

"Actually, it's *Doctor* Matthews," Kate replied automatically.

Zack's eyebrows quirked up. "Well, well, well—a doctor. How about that, Rich?"

"Fascinating," the writer muttered, sounding as if he found it anything but.

"I could sure use a doctor," Zack said. "Ever since I found out how closely the studio is going to be monitoring this shoot, I've had terrible pain back here." He rubbed the rear pocket of his jeans.

"Oh, I'm not that kind of doctor," Kate quickly said. "I'm a Ph.D."

The writer snickered. Zack folded his arms and grinned.

A rush of heat flooded Kate's face. He was teasing—any fool would have known that. He probably didn't even care that she held a Ph.D., although Mr. Goldman had certainly been interested in her credentials.

Oh, dear—why did she always act like a prissy dork whenever she got nervous? It was a horrible disorder to have, getting all wooden and overly serious. She wished she could just get sweaty palms like other people.

Zack pulled out a chair and swept his hand toward it, his lips twisted in a smile. "Well, *Doctor* Matthews—we're happy to have you on board."

She stiffly lowered herself into the chair, feeling the worst kind of fool. "I, uh, usually only use my doctoral title in academic circles. I prefer to be called Kate."

"Great. You can call me Zack." He pulled out the chair next to Kate, then turned it around and sat in it backwards. His legs sprawled on either side of the seat, his arms resting on top of the chair back.

"Rich and I were just discussing how glad we are that you'll be joining us—weren't we, Rich?"

"Yeah. Right." Rich's lack of enthusiasm clearly said otherwise.

Zack smiled at Kate encouragingly. "I understand you're a real expert on New Orleans's history."

"Well, I've done quite a bit of research into the antebellum period through the First World War," she replied modestly.

"Why, that's perfect, isn't it, Rich?"

"Yeah. Perfect."

Zack flashed that smile again. "What kind of research have you done?"

"Well, I did my Masters thesis on the impact of Storyville on New Orleans's society, and my doctoral dissertation on the evolution and demise of legalized vice there. I've also published numerous research papers about various individuals involved in Storyville-based businesses."

Oh, mercy—even to herself, she sounded as boring as one of Dr. Compton's lectures. Zack must think she was duller than dirt.

Not that it mattered, she sternly told herself. She was here to do a job, not to impress him with her sparkling wit and breezy personality. Mr. Goldman had said they needed an authority who could be taken seriously, and that was the only role she was here to fill.

Still, a traitorously unreasonable part of her, the part that couldn't quit staring at Zack's mouth and remembering how he'd kissed that girl on TV, hated to think that Zack would find her boring.

He didn't act as if he did. He gave a low whistle. "Wow. That's really impressive."

"Yeah. Impressive," Rich echoed in a monotone.

"We're certainly lucky to have someone with your credentials on our crew." Zack gave her a dazzling smile as he rose from his chair. "Can I get you a glass of wine? Or a beer?"

"Oh, no, thank you."

"You want something else? We've got a fully stocked bar."

"No thanks. I don't drink while I'm working." Crimony. Why did every word that came out of her mouth have to sound like some prim old school marm?

"Well, this is more of a get-acquainted session than actual work. I'm going to have a beer. Won't you join me?"

She didn't want to be rude. Her tolerance for alcohol was two shades shy of nonexistent, but just because she accepted a drink didn't mean she actually had to drink it. "Well, all right. Thank you."

"Good." Zack strode to the built-in bar halfway across the parlor and pulled three cans of beer from the small fridge. Returning to the table, he slid one to Rich, then pulled the tab off another one and handed it to her. It was a small but chivalrous gesture, opening her can for her, but it struck Kate as incredibly sexy. His hand touched hers as he passed it to her, and she felt a shocking, shooting heat.

She really needed to get a life, she told herself. It was ridiculous, the way just the brush of his hand set her pulse to racing. She busied herself by pulling a notebook and pen from her tote bag, figuring that the best way to control her thoughts was to steer the conversation to the topic of work. "How much of the movie do you plan to shoot in New Orleans?"

Zack sat down backwards in the chair again, propping his arms across the top of the back. "All of it. We're in something of a time crunch, so instead of shuttling everybody and everything back to Hollywood, we'll just shoot it all here."

"When do you plan to start filming?"

"In three weeks."

Kate's eyebrows rose. "That soon?"

"Yeah." Zack rubbed his head ruefully. "We've had to move everything up because of the schedules of our male and female lead. We've cast George Talley and Lena Brighton, you know."

Katie knew who Lena Brighton was—a beautiful blond actress who was rapidly rising to super-stardom. George Talley was the star of a popular medical show on TV, but since Kate seldom watched television, she'd never actually seen his program.

"We only have a six-week window to shoot all the scenes with the two of them together, so we're likely to pull some long days." Zack took a sip of his beer. "You'll have full access to the set during the shoot. We even intend to see to it that you have your very own chair." He smiled, as if the chair was a big bonus.

"Great," Kate said, wondering if a chair shortage was usually a problem on a movie set.

"Our pleasure. Now, I'm sure you're wondering what we'll need from you."

"Well, actually, the contract from Parapet spelled it out explicitly."

Zack waved his beer in a dismissive gesture. "Oh, that's all a bunch of legal mumbo-jumbo. Here's what it boils down to— our wardrobe department has lots of resources, but it would be a big help if you could get us some pictures of the clothing people wore in New Orleans back then. And the prop department will need your guidance with details on the set."

A beep of alarm sounded in Kate's brain. Surely Zack didn't mean that was *all* they'd need from her. Surely he meant that was just what they'd need *first*.

"I understand you've already sent in some photos," Zack was saying.

Kate nodded. "I mailed them to Parapet with my signed contract. I brought copies." She pulled four thick plastic folders out of the black bag on her lap and handed him the pink one. "This one shows women's apparel, including sleeping attire and undergarments. I've included examples of what was worn by the upper and lower social classes."

Zack thumbed through the pictures. "Terrific."

She passed him a blue folder next. "I've done the same with men's clothing in this one."

He rapidly rifled through it. "Great. This is just what we need."

"And here are photos of boxing attire and paraphernalia, along with a sketch of what boxing rings looked like back then." She passed a yellow folder to him. He flipped through the pages, nodding appreciatively. When he set it down, she handed him the last folder, appropriately colored scarlet. "This last one contains photos of Storyville's sporting palaces, showing both the interiors and exteriors."

Zack glanced through it as well. When he looked up and smiled, a rush of heady pleasure shot through Kate. *I'm sitting here with Zack Jackson, and he's smiling at me.* She suppressed the urge to pinch herself.

"Professor, you do good work. I must say, I'm impressed."

She'd impressed Zack Jackson. Another thrill pulsed through her. It was so nice to work with someone appreciative for a change. Zack was absolutely charming—even nicer than he'd appeared on television.

Not to mention sexier. Kate quickly tried to banish the inappropriate thought.

He slid the folders across the table to Rich, who ignored them and continued to stare at his laptop screen. Zack treated Kate to another brilliant smile. "Well, Professor, it looks like you've bought yourself some free time."

Another beep sounded in Kate's brain, this time a little louder. "What do you mean?"

"Well, you've already given us everything we need, so you don't have to do a thing until we start shooting."

He seemed ready to dismiss her, and they hadn't even talked about anything important. Kate pulled her brows into a frown and leaned forward. "Excuse me, but it's my understanding that I'm supposed to be much more involved."

"Oh, you'll be plenty involved." His tone was smooth and reassuring. "We'll have you right on the set so you can answer any questions that might come up. We'll even get your name on your chair."

27

There he went with that chair again. Kate was worried about getting tenure, not a spot to rest her buns. The warning beep in her brain escalated to a full-scale red alert.

Zack took another sip of his beer. "Do you have any questions?"

"Well, yes. A whole list of them, in fact." Kate opened her notebook. "When do we discuss the script?"

Zack brushed his hand in the air. "Oh, that's Rich's department. You don't have to worry about that."

"I'm afraid I do."

Zack's eyebrows rose questioningly. Kate once more reached into her bag and pulled out a bound copy of the script encrusted with dozens of Post-It notes. "You see, I've read it, and it contains several very serious errors."

The writer at the end of the table jerked up his head. "Hey!" He glared at Kate, bristling with indignation. "That's some of my best work."

"Oh, I didn't mean it isn't well written," Kate said quickly. "It is. It's very interesting, too. But according to the contract I signed with Parapet, I'm responsible for the historical accuracy of this movie, and I'm afraid this script is far from historically accurate."

Zack smiled to hide his aggravation. Whoever had handled hiring this dame had screwed up royally. He should have insisted on doing it himself, instead of leaving it to the suits at Parapet. Why the hell had they sent her a script? It was always a mistake to give a technical adviser too much information. It made them think they could start meddling with things that were none of their business.

He gestured toward the document in her hand. "What you've got there, Kate, is just a preliminary script. They weren't supposed to trouble you with that. I'm sure that any little discrepancies you've found will be fixed before we begin shooting."

Kate pressed her lips together. They were nice lips, Zack thought absently—or at least they might be, if they weren't all pursed up like a little old lady's knitting bag. She might even be attractive, but it was hard to tell, with her hair bound back in that tight-ass twist and her body swaddled in that awful brown suit.

"I'm not talking about a few little discrepancies," she was saying. "I'm talking about major plot points that are completely wrong."

Zack shot a glance at Rich. The writer's scowl was so intense that his eyebrows were close enough to tango. Rich didn't take criticism well under the best of circumstances, and he wasn't likely to accept it graciously from the likes of Kate.

"What plot points?" Rich growled.

"Well, for starters, that scene with the paddle boat race," Kate said. "Paddle wheelers were disappearing from the river by 1898. This was the era of steamships. And there were no recorded ship explosions of any sort in the New Orleans port that year."

Kate obviously didn't understand the rules of the game. Zack nodded with feigned patience. "We put in that episode to demonstrate the ruthlessness of our villian—to show that he was crooked enough to destroy a boat in order to win a race."

"That's called artistic license," Rich snipped.

"Well, I'm afraid it's also called factual inaccuracy. And it's not the only error, either." Kate thumbed through her copy of the script with unnerving sureness.

Zack peered over at it. Christ—she not only had the pages marked but color coded!

"In fact," she continued, "all of the events that involve Drago—the carriage race, the gunfight, the man being tarred and feathered . . . All of those events are inaccurate."

Those were the action scenes, the highlights of the movie! Zack's fingers tensed around his beer bottle. He glanced at Rich and could practically see the steam coming out of the writer's ears. Zack silently counted to five, willing his voice to remain calm. "By inaccurate, what do you mean, exactly?"

"I mean they never happened."

Little Miss Priss here was turning into a major pain in the gluteous maximus. Zack gave his most cajoling smile. "Now, Doc—I mean, Kate—the medium of film is less literal than books. Movies need drama, and those scenes are a good way of dramatically illustrating Drago's character. Besides, to be perfectly blunt, we need some action to jazz things up a little. We can't worry about keeping every little detail absolutely factual."

"Oh, yes, we can. That's why I'm here." Kate dove into that apparently bottomless bag of hers, pulled out a clump of legal-sized papers, and pushed them in front him. Zack glanced down at what appeared to be her contract with Parapet. She leaned forward, tracing a line in the document with a neatly trimmed, unpolished nail. "See? It says right here that I'm to oversee the historical accuracy of the entire movie."

The professor was beginning to really get on his nerves. "It doesn't really mean that. You're not supposed to take that literally."

"Oh, yes I am." Her gaze was disarmingly direct and earnest. "Mr. Goldman was quite specific about it when we spoke on the phone."

Zack froze. "You've talked to Goldman?"

"Why, yes."

Goldman never talked on the phone. Not that Zack knew of, anyway. He summoned people to him, and he didn't care if they were halfway around the globe, in the middle of a shoot, or checked into a rehab center. Zack narrowed his eyes. "Goldman himself? Marvin Goldman?"

Kate cocked her head, her blue eyes quizzical. "Sure."

Zack squinted at her, trying to gauge whether or not she was telling the truth. "What did he call you about?"

"Well, actually, I called him."

Goldman *took* a phone call? That strained credibility even further. "May I ask what about?"

"My work on the movie, of course. I wanted him to know that if I were to take the job, the movie had to be completely factual. My professional reputation will be attached to it, and my reputation is my career. I've worked too hard for too many years to jeopardize it now."

You're not the only one, lady. "And what did Goldman say?" Zack asked carefully.

"That he understood completely. He said he wouldn't dream of asking me to misrepresent the truth. He was very supportive. He said he wants the movie to be entirely factual, too, and he's counting on me to make it that way. He was very nice."

Goldman was *nice?* Now he *knew* she was lying. She was awfully good at it, though. Her face was the picture of sincerity.

"He said he wanted me to be comfortable going on TV and vouching for the movie's truthfulness."

Zack pushed out of his chair and strode to the window, too agitated to sit still. Whether or not she'd actually talked to Goldman, he obviously needed to educate her about how Hollywood handled true stories. He shoved his hands in his pockets. "Yeah, well, there's truth, and then there's truth. It's like everything else—it comes in varying degrees."

Her brow knit in a disapproving frown.

A fresh rush of irritation shot through him. "Come on, Doc. Truth is relative. If there are five different witnesses to a car wreck, you'll get five different versions."

"Maybe so, but they'll all agree there *was* a car wreck." She tapped the script and looked up at him with reproachful eyes. "You've got things in here that never happened."

Little Miss Goody Two-shoes was turning into a serious problem. Zack braced his hands on the table and leaned across it toward her. "How do you know? They *could* have happened. Not everything is written down."

"An exploding riverboat would have been written up in the local newspaper. So would a gang of men shooting up a saloon, or a prominent citizen being dragged through the streets looking like a half-plucked chicken. You can't just invent major events like that and call them the truth."

Zack's fingers curled tightly into his palm. "I sure as hell can."

Where did she get off, telling him what he could and couldn't do? This was his movie, damn it!

"Well, I can't very well go on TV and say things happened when they didn't."

"You won't have to." Zack pushed off the table and resumed pacing. "This doesn't have to be an all-or-nothing proposition. You can vouch for the parts that are accurate, and say that some events were changed or added for dramatization."

"That's not what I agreed to."

"Well, that's the way it is."

Her chin tilted up at a stubborn angle. "Perhaps I should call Mr. Goldman and let him settle this."

"Yeah. You do that." She was bluffing. She'd never be able to get the old goat on the phone. Hell, she probably hadn't even talked to him in the first place.

Kate pulled a cell phone out of her bag of tricks, unfolded it, and daintily punched in a single number.

Yeah, right. She expected him to believe she had Goldman on her *speed-dial?*

She lifted the phone to her ear. "Mr. Goldman? Hello. This is Kate Matthews."

Nah. No way. She couldn't have gotten Goldman on the phone that easily. She was probably talking to her answering machine at home. Zack fixed her with his darkest scowl. "Hey, now, Doc, if you think I'm gonna fall for some cheap, juvenile stunt . . ."

"Oh, just fine, thank you," Katie was saying into the receiver. Another pause. "Yes. In fact, I'm with him right now. We seem to have run into a bit of a problem, Mr. Goldman, and we need you to clarify a few things."

She no more had Goldman on the phone than he had smoke rings coming out of his undershorts. "Cut the bull, Professor," Zack growled. "That's not Goldman, and I know it."

She continued as if he hadn't spoken. "I was telling Zack that you wanted the movie to be factual, and he said that certain parts didn't have to be. There are several parts of the script that disturb me, and . . ." She paused.

"You're making a real fool of yourself, there, Doc," Zack snapped.

"Oh, of course," she said into the mouthpiece. She held out the phone to Zack. "He wants to talk to you."

Zack's eyebrows shot up. Man—this dame was quite an operator. She must have lined up a co-conspirator in advance in case she didn't get her way. He shook his head in disgust. "You know, I've worked with some devious people in my day, but you take the cake. Who is this—your brother, maybe, or your husband? Or—oh, wait, I get it." He shot her a knowing smirk. "It's some wannabe actor friend of yours, huh?"

"I told you. It's Mr. Goldman."

"Yeah, right." Zack snatched the phone from her hand. "Listen up, Bub—if you think I'm gonna fall for this kind of cheap audition stunt, you're in for a hell of a disappointment."

"Jackson?" snarled a familiar voice through the phone. "What the hell's the matter with you?"

Oh, damn. That vile rasp was unmistakable. "M-Marvin?"

"No," Goldman bellowed. "It's the friggin' Easter Bunny. Who the hell did you *think* it was?"

"I-I thought . . ."

"I don't care what you thought. I only care what you do, and you're gonna do what I say." A wet, nasty sucking sound assaulted Zack's ear. "Now listen up and listen good, 'cause I'm only gonna say this once. The professor there is our ticket to marketin' this movie. I had to sweet-talk the hell out of her to get her to sign on, and I want you to do whatever it takes to make her happy. Got it?"

Zack cut narrowed eyes to Kate. She curved her mouth into a prissy little smile.

Hell, but he wanted to strangle her. He turned on his heel and carried the phone into the bedroom.

"Come on, Marvin," he said, closing the door behind him with more force than necessary. "She wants to cut all the good stuff—all the violence and chases and explosions. If all the nuts and bolts are factual—the brothel stuff, the boxing match, and the love interest—I don't see why we can't use a little creative license on the rest. That's what they did with *Perfect Storm.*"

"You're not gonna cut a damn thing from the script unless you replace it with somethin' better."

"But she says it all has to be factual!"

"Yeah, I know. I had to promise her that to get her to sign on. It's your job to convince her otherwise."

"And how the hell am I supposed to do that?"

"That's your problem." Goldman made that disgusting wet vacuum noise again. "Look—I don't give an ant's patoutie where you two draw the line on what's a fact and what's not. I only care about two things: you making this movie so freakin' exciting that the theaters'll need to install seat belts, and you making the professor so happy she'll stand up and swear on her mother's grave that it's all true. She's got the final word, Jackson. We can't have her gettin' on TV and changin' her tune. I want to see her initials on every draft of the script you send me."

"You're practically making her co-producer," Zack ground out through clenched teeth.

"Hey, you're right," Goldman shot back. "An' that gives me an idea. If I have any more complaints from you or any more calls from Kate askin' me to set you straight, that's just what I'll do."

Zack's fingers tightened around the phone so hard it was in danger of shattering. Man, what he would give to tell this S.O.B. where to go and what to kiss when he got there! Why, he'd give his right arm, his eye teeth, his firstborn child . . .

But would he give up his future as a director and producer?

Damn, damn, and triple damn. Zack painfully swallowed around the boulder in his throat, drew a deep breath, then blew it out in an exasperated sigh. "All right, Marvin. We'll revise the script."

"Wise choice." Zack could hear Goldman's smirk. "Now put the professor back on."

Zack reluctantly strode back into the parlor. Without a word, he thrust the phone at Kate.

"Yes?" she said into the receiver. "Oh, good. Thank you for straightening that out." She listened for a moment, then glanced at Zack. "Oh, he hasn't been *that* difficult." Another silence. "I'll be sure and let you know. Thank you again. Good-bye."

She flipped the phone closed, looked up, and gave him a conciliatory smile. "Well, I'm glad that's settled."

Zack suppressed the urge to bang his head against the wall.

Rich leaned forward, anxiously stroking his goatee. "What did he say?"

Oh, hell—Rich was sure to pitch a major fit. The screenwriter had two speeds: quiet and sullen or outspoken and anguished. He had to be told, but damn, Zack hated to do it.

Kate spared him the effort. "He said the script needs revising."

Rich clutched the arms of his chair as if it were about to rocket into space, tilted his face to the ceiling, and yowled like an injured cat.

Kate stared at him, then at Zack, her eyes wide with alarm. "Is he all right?"

"He will be. Just as soon as he recovers from getting kicked in the groin."

"Oh, dear—I didn't mean to offend him." Kate's brow wrinkled and her eyes filled with an annoyingly sincere look of concern. "I just want the movie to be accurate."

Zack had seen some ball-busting power plays in his life, but the professor's took the cake. And then she had the nerve to sit there and act all innocent! Well, she might have won this round, but he'd be damned if she'd tell him how to make his movie. It was high time he seized control of the situation.

Zack lowered himself into a chair at the head of the table, reached for two copies of the script from the pile of papers in the middle of the table, and shoved one at the screenwriter. "Come on, Rich. Let's go through the script and let the Doc tell us what needs tweaking."

"I'm afraid it's going to need more than a tweak." Kate gave

35

a polite, apologetic smile. "Several scenes will have to be taken out or changed completely."

Rich slumped, dropped his head to the table, and moaned.

What needed to be changed, Zack thought grimly, wasn't the script, but the professor's mind. He needed to convince Little Miss Historical Accuracy here to lighten up and let him make this film the way he wanted.

He wondered what her hot button was. Well, he intended to find out, and when he did, he'd push it until she cried uncle.

Chapter Three

"She's butchered my script," Rich groaned half an hour later, his head in his hands, his elbows propped on the long table.

Kate turned worried blue eyes to Zack. "All I did was point out a few historical inaccuracies."

Rich lifted his head enough to cast a woeful gaze at Zack. "She's butchered it. She's gutted it, bled it dry, and cut every shred of meat off the bones."

Rich was nothing if not poetic, Zack thought grimly. Unfortunately, he was also right. Doctor Truth-and-Righteousness here had just ripped every shred of action out of the movie. The script was covered with so much red ink, it looked like the victim in a slasher movie.

"She's reduced it to a skeleton," Rich moaned. "A skeleton in Death Valley. One that the vultures have picked clean and the dogs have gnawed. One that's been bleached by sun for a thousand years until it's nothing but crumbs and splinters."

Christ. No one did angst quite as eloquently as Rich. Unfortunately, Zack was in too dark a mood to provide much in the way of consolation. He needed to get out of here before he slipped up and told the professor exactly what he thought of her and her historical accuracy. He raised his arm and made a show out of looking at his watch, then pushed his chair back from the table. "Sorry to run, but I promised my location scout I'd look at a site she recommended."

"I'll come with you," Kate said quickly.

Oh, hell. "No need. My location scout is a real pro, and if she says a place is perfect, I'm sure it is. Besides, it's Friday afternoon and I'm sure you're anxious to start your weekend."

"Well, I'll need to look at the locations sooner or later to make sure they're historically accurate."

Damn—this dame was harder to get rid of than a case of head lice. But he sure didn't want her getting on the horn to Goldman again. Zack ran a hand down his face and blew out a hard breath. "Get your stuff together while I call for the car."

Kate gathered up her things and precisely tucked them into the various pockets of her enormous bag. As Zack hung up the phone, she walked over to the writer, held out her hand, and smiled. "It was very nice meeting you, Rich."

Hell. You'd think she was leaving a tea party instead of a blood-letting.

Rich refused to look up, much less shake her hand. For the last half hour, the writer had refused to speak to her, addressing all of his comments to Zack. Instead of talking to her now, Rich lay his head on the table and covered it with his arms in classic crash-landing position.

Zack strode to the entryway, yanked open the door to the hall, and tapped his foot impatiently. "If you're coming, come on."

Kate hurried to the door, then cast another worried glance at Rich. "Is he going to be all right?" she whispered.

"Yeah."

"He's really upset." Kate turned her eyes on him. They were disconcertingly blue, as blue as a pair of jeans. "You are, too, aren't you?"

To put it mildly. Zack gave a noncommittal grunt, then closed the door a little harder than necessary.

Kate scurried alongside him as he strode down the hall. "I didn't mean to cause any problems. I just want the facts to be correct."

"Yeah, well, we just want the film to be seen by more than the editing crew."

Kate dodged an unattended maid's cart. "Mr. Goldman thinks that the historical accuracy of the movie will attract viewers."

Zack didn't want to send her scrambling for her cell phone again, but she was really working on his nerves. "Goldman also thinks the movie is going to contain chases and gunfights and explosions." He jabbed at the elevator button. "This film was supposed to appeal to both men and women. Men like action. You just eliminated half the potential audience."

"Well, boxing is action."

Zack gave a dismissive snort. "Stallone more than covered it. Besides, that's not what this film needs. It needs scenes that develop Drago's character, that paint him as a ruthless villain. Without that, this movie is just a namby-pamby romance."

"Well, what's wrong with that? Men like romance."

He cast her a derisive look. "Men like sex, Doc. There happens to be a difference."

Not that she was likely to know, Zack thought, jabbing the brass-plated elevator button again with irritation. If she were half as rigid in the bedroom as she'd just been in that meeting, it would take a crane and a crowbar just to get her into position.

A middle-aged couple sauntered up to the elevator bank. Zack was glad to see them, because it meant he didn't have to talk to Kate on the ride down. When the elevator opened on the first floor, he let Kate precede him out the door, then stalked silently beside her through the lobby and out the brass doors into the cool, humid air.

"Where's your car?" Kate asked.

Zack silently gestured to a black Lincoln Navigator at the curb. The parking valet took Zack's receipt, then followed them to the car and opened the passenger door for Kate.

She climbed in. As she sat down, her brown wool skirt rode

up and the slit in the side of it fell open. Zack did a double-take. Her leg was slim and unexpectedly shapely, but that wasn't what made Zack drop his jaw. It was the startling discovery that under her drab suit, the precise, overly conservative professor was wearing lace-top stockings and a black garter belt.

Hell's bells—who would have guessed that the no-nonsense professor shared a secret with Victoria? It was so unexpected that Zack stood stock-still and stared, unable to tear his eyes away until the uniformed valet closed her door.

He rapidly pulled out a dollar, thrust it at the parking attendant, and circled to the driver's seat, irritated at himself and even more irritated at her. Hell. The professor wasn't his type—not in the least. Up until now, he hadn't given her undergarments any thought. If he *had* speculated about her underwear, though, he would have figured her for the plain, white, three-to-a-pack type.

Zack scowled as he pulled the vehicle away from the curb. Blast it all—now that he knew her taste ran to black lace and garters, he couldn't help but wonder what else she was or wasn't wearing.

"Where are we going?" Kate asked as he turned the car onto Poydras Avenue.

"To a house my scout says is perfect for the bordello exterior."

"Great. What's the address?"

Zack reached into his pocket, pulled out a piece of paper, and handed it to her. From the corner of his eye, he saw her eyebrows pull up into another one of her disapproving frowns. Aw, hell. She wasn't going to throw a wrench into the location plans, too, was she?

She was. His stomach balled up like a paper wad.

"The two thousand block of Prytania?"

"Yeah." Zack pretended he hadn't heard the incredulous note in her voice. "Tell me which way to turn to get there."

"But . . ."

Zack drew a deep breath and counted to ten. "But what?"

"But I'm pretty sure all of those homes are Greek Revival."

Zack felt a nerve twitch in his jaw. "Let's just go look at the place, all right?"

"Well, all right, but if the house is Greek Revival, it won't work. Most of the sporting palaces were narrow, three-story buildings that looked like large Victorian town houses. Besides, the homes on Prytania all have beautiful trees and lawns, and the Storyville brothels were lined up right by the sidewalk."

Zack's fingers gripped the steering wheel in a death choke. "You know, Doc, you don't have to find fault with everything. You're not getting paid by the ix-nay."

Her eyes grew large. "I-I'm not trying to find fault. I'm just trying to do my job."

"And just exactly what do you think your job is, Doc? To kill this movie before it even gets shot?"

Her voice turned defensive. "Of course not."

"Well, that's exactly what you're doing, Doc."

"That's certainly not my intention. I wish you'd quit acting as if I'm deliberately causing problems." Her tone was as icy as a Sno-cone. "And I'd appreciate it if you'd quit calling me Doc."

"Yeah, well, I'd appreciate it if you'd quit ruining my movie."

"But I'm just trying to—"

If he heard her say "historical accuracy" one more time, he'd jump off the Mississippi River bridge. "Yeah, yeah, yeah," he cut in. "I know all about your fixation with facts."

Her chin tilted up. "It's not a fixation. It's what I'm being paid to do."

He had to put a stop to this. Zack abruptly swerved onto a side street, pulled to the curb, and slammed on the brakes. Jamming the car into park, he twisted around on the seat to face her. "Look here, Professor—you and I need to talk. Can we have a private conversation, or is everything I say going to get back to Goldman?"

She shrank back against the passenger door and eyed him with alarm.

"Can you and I talk, off the record?" Zack repeated.

"Well, of—of course."

"Good. Because I want to lay things out for you." He draped his arm over the top of the steering wheel and angled his body more fully toward her. "This whole business about historical accuracy—it's all a bunch of bull. Goldman doesn't care about that."

"But he said—"

"I don't give a rat's furball what he said. The truth is, he's only interested in packaging and marketing. True stories are really hot right now, and the only thing he cares about is that you're willing to go on TV and vouch that this movie is factual. Now, I know you're a professor, and this is your field of expertise, and you want everything hunky-dory and picture perfect, but that's not the way things work. As soon as Goldman sees the revised script, he's going to kill the whole movie. Then you'll be fired and I'll be fired, and that'll be the only historically accurate fact about this whole friggin' project. So you and I need to work a few things out."

She regarded him as if he were a rabid skunk. "Work out what things?"

"Well, hey, I'm sure you're not doing this for your health." He drummed his fingertips on the steering wheel. "You're being paid for your time, but you can probably use a little extra cash, right? So, I want you to know that I'd be more than willing to compensate you for a little cooperation."

Her eyebrows rode high on her forehead. "Are you offering me a *bribe?*"

"Well, now, I wouldn't call it that."

"But that's what it is, isn't it?"

"Oh, come on. I'm not asking you to do anything illegal. I'm just asking you to be a little more flexible." Zack leaned toward her. "Here's the situation: I need to make a movie that's going to sell at the box office. My last two haven't done so well, and this is my last chance before everyone starts slamming doors in my face. This film is really important to me, and I'm sure you can use some extra cash. So why don't we cut a deal? I'll pay you, say, five Gs, and you start being a little more cooperative."

She drew back, her expression offended. "You're offering me five thousand dollars?"

"Okay, okay. I'll make it ten."

She stared at him, her eyes round with disbelief.

Zack lifted his shoulders. "What the hell. I'll go as high as fifteen, but that's my final offer."

She shook her head, her expression incredulous. "You must think I have no backbone at all."

"Damn." Zack heaved a heavy sigh. "Man, I didn't want to go this high, but okay. I'll make it twenty."

Her eyebrows drew down into a hard frown. "You just don't get it, do you? This isn't about money."

"Come on, Doc. Everything is money."

"Not to me, it isn't."

"Well, then, what do you want? A part in a movie? An introduction to someone? You name it, and I'll try to make it happen."

"Is this how you usually operate?"

"What do you mean?"

"Do you always try to buy people off if you don't get your way?"

Oh, hell. Here she went with that self-righteous act again. "No," he growled. "Usually I just fire them and hire someone else."

She straightened her spine and tilted her chin at a stubborn angle. "Well, then, maybe that's what you ought to do with me."

Believe me, Doc, I'd love to. Unfortunately, Goldman thought she was going to lay a golden egg. Zack forced his lips into what he hoped passed for a cajoling smile. "Oh, come on now, Professor. Why is it so hard for you to just bend a little?"

"You mean, aside from the fact that I happen to have some ethics?"

Zack's mouth curled in displeasure. "Yeah, Doc. Aside from that."

"Because I've spent years building my professional reputation—years of studying and teaching and lecturing, years of

43

writing and doing research and trying to make history come alive for my students. My career is based on my knowledge and my integrity, and I'm not going to throw it all away just so you can cut a few corners."

Hell—she made it sound as if *he* was the one who was being unreasonable! He jammed a hand through his hair, then drummed his fingers impatiently on the steering wheel. Maybe she needed some time. Maybe if he backed off and gave her some space, she'd think things over and come around. He forced himself to unclench his jaw and soften his tone. "Look. There's no need to give me an answer right now. Go home, think about it over the weekend, and talk it over with your husband."

"I don't have a husband."

No husband. The memory of her garter-clad leg filled his mind. So, who was the fancy underwear for? He deliberately pushed the thought away. "Well, then, take some time and give it some thought."

"There's nothing to think about. My integrity is nonnegotiable."

Great. Just great. He'd ticked her off, insulted her, and made her think he was a total sleaze bag in the bargain. *Good going, Jackson.* Just when he'd thought things were as bad as they could possibly get, he proved himself wrong.

Blowing out an exasperated breath, Zack put the Navigator in gear and pulled away from the curb. Plan A was a bust. Time to move on to Plan B.

Unfortunately, he didn't have one. There had to be *something* she wanted—something that would make her see things his way. He just had to find out what it was.

"This is it," Zack said fifteen minutes later, slowing down in front of a large, white-columned home on Prytania Street.

Kate's fingers tensed in her lap. Greek Revival—just as she'd feared.

Oh, dear—this project wasn't going at all as she'd envisioned.

Goldman had led her to believe that Zack would welcome her input. She'd thought she'd get to be a valued member of his team, not a problem so severe he would bribe her to go away.

Kate worried her bottom lip. She'd known Zack had been unhappy about the script revisions, but she'd still been shocked that he would offer her a *bribe*. It was disturbing, seeing him in this light.

What was even more disturbing, she thought ruefully, was the realization that she'd secretly expected him to be as virtuous in real life as he'd been on TV. She was a grown woman, and she knew the difference between fiction and reality. It was ridiculous to think he'd be like his TV character. Still, she was disappointed to learn that he cared more about making money than portraying the truth.

Well, she had no intention of compromising *her* principles. She'd been hired to make sure this movie was accurate, and that was exactly what she was going to do. And if Zack Jackson disliked her for just doing her job, well, so be it. He wasn't turning out to be the Prince Charming she'd always imagined, either.

"So, what do you think?" Zack asked, jerking his thumb toward the stately home. "I think it's perfect."

She drew a deep breath. "Apparently your scout didn't receive the photos I sent. This is all wrong. It's nothing like the brothels in Storyville."

His lips hardened into a grim line. "This is exactly what people expect a New Orleans cathouse to look like."

"It might be what they expect, but it's not historically accurate."

Zack muttered something unintelligible that Kate was glad she couldn't quite hear.

"I can show you some houses that are architecturally similar to the ones in Storyville, if you're interested," she offered.

His brow gathered like a thundercloud. "What I'm interested in, Doc, is making this movie, and it's going to be damn difficult if you insist on changing every gnat's ass of a detail."

Kate cringed inside, but she was determined not to show it. If he knew she was intimidated, he'd run over her from here on out. "This is a major point, not a detail. And I'm not trying to be difficult," she continued firmly. "In fact, I'm doing my best to be helpful." *And civil, but you're making it darn near impossible.* "Now, do you want to look at the houses that might work or not?"

A vein bulged in Zack's neck, and his glare was so hot he looked as if he were about to self-combust. Kate nervously gripped the seat, bracing herself for an angry tirade. Her fingernails had nearly cut through the leather upholstery when he finally faced forward and put the vehicle in gear.

"Hell." Reluctance dripped from his voice. "Let's go take a look."

Relief flooded Kate's veins. "Fine."

"Which way?"

"Straight ahead, then turn right at the first light."

They'd traveled several blocks in awkward silence when Kate's cell phone rang. Digging it out of her bag, she flipped it open and put it to her ear. "Hello?"

A loud sob reverberated through the receiver. "M-M-Mom!"

Kate's heart nose-dived to her stomach. "Skye? What's the matter, honey?"

"I-I—" Skye's voice dissolved into tears.

Alarm hurled through Kate like a fastball. "Are you hurt?"

"N-no."

Zack cast her a quizzical look. Kate hunched over the phone, holding on to it with both hands. "Where are you?"

"At the po—po—" Sobs obscured her voice.

"Skye, calm down, sweetheart. Take a deep breath and tell me where you are."

Kate heard the faint rumble of a man's voice in the background. There was a shuffling sound, and then a deep baritone came through the line. "Ms. Matthews? This is Sergeant Wilks with the NOPD. Your daughter is with me here at the Vieux Carre station."

Kate's blood roared in her ears so loudly that she wasn't sure she'd heard correctly. "My daughter is at a police station?"

"Yes, ma'am. We picked her up for truancy and loitering."

"Truancy? Loitering?"

"Yes, ma'am. On Decatur Street. We need you to come down to the station to get her."

"Of—of course. Is she all right?"

"She's fine. She's just scared. Do you know where the station is?"

"I'm not sure . . ."

"It's on Royal, between Conti and Dumaine."

"I-I'll be right there." She hung up the phone, her thoughts tumbling over each other like a troupe of Chinese acrobats.

"I take it we have a change in plans," Zack said flatly.

She looked over to find his gaze fixed on her, his expression inscrutable. At least he was no longer scowling. "I-I need to go to the French Quarter. My daughter . . ."

"I heard. What's the best route there?"

Twenty minutes later, Kate charged through the door of the police station like a lioness on a cub rescue mission. Zack looked around as he climbed the marble steps behind her. Wedged between stylish art galleries and expensive antique shops, it was an unlikely site for a police station, and the building itself seemed too refined for its function. The doors were topped with fanlights, the ceiling was triple crown-molded, and several large chandeliers lit the large room. A built-in desk stood in front of the entrance. Only New Orleans could make a police station look like a Cecil B. DeMille set.

Kate made a beeline for the uniformed middle-aged woman behind the tall desk. "I'm here to get my daughter."

The woman pushed her glasses up on her nose. "What's her name?"

"Skye Matthews."

Skye. It wasn't the kind of name Zack would have expected the straitlaced professor to give her daughter. But then, he hadn't expected her to have a daughter at all—especially a daughter old enough to be picked up by the police. Unless she were a lot older than she looked, Kate must have been a teenaged mother.

Now that didn't fit the mold of a rigid, conservative, morally upright scholar. Zack eyed her curiously. Apparently there was more to the doc than met the eye. The image of her garter-belted leg flashed through his mind. Yessiree—a whole lot more.

Zack watched Kate bite her bottom lip as the officer slowly typed on her computer. This unexpected side trip meant the afternoon was shot, but hopefully it wouldn't be wasted time. With any luck, it would help him figure out a way to convince the professor to relax her historical standards.

She was plenty upset, that was for sure. Her skin was at least two shades paler than it had been earlier, and her eyes were dark and troubled. Right now she didn't look like a prickly stickler for accuracy who was single-handedly ruining his movie. Right now she looked vulnerable and scared and badly in need of moral support.

What the hell—he might as well provide it. Maybe it would even help resolve their standoff. Zack stepped up beside her and placed his hand on her back. She jumped at the contact and looked up questioningly.

Zack gave her a reassuring pat. "Hey—it's going to be okay."

She tried to smile, but her lips trembled and she looked like she was about to cry.

She really cared about this kid of hers. Against his will, the thought eased his animosity toward her. Zack wondered if the kid had any idea how lucky she was, having a mother who cared. Neither of Zack's parents had ever given a damn.

He watched Kate nervously twirl a strand of hair around her finger. Little wisps had come undone from her topknot, softening her features, and her lips were red where she'd bitten them. Her jacket was unbuttoned, and he glimpsed the swell of small breasts visible through her tailored white blouse. Well, what do you know—when she wasn't buttoned down, slicked back, starched up, and standing like she had a broomstick for a spine, the professor wasn't a bad-looking woman. Not bad at all.

The officer peered at the computer screen over her glasses. "Matthews—here it is. Your daughter's thirteen?"

"Twelve. She won't turn thirteen for another two months."

The officer turned her back to them, picked up a phone, and punched in some digits. When she hung up, she turned again to Kate. "You can go on back. Third door on the right."

Zack walked through the large double doors with her, not waiting to be invited. The corridor was narrow and lined with small offices. The rumble of men's voices, the squawk of a police radio, and the slow peck of an old-fashioned typewriter seeped out from behind the closed doors. The acrid smell of coffee that had sat too long on the burner hung heavy in the stale air.

The third door on the right was open. Zack followed Kate in, then nearly bumped into her as a long-haired girl hurled herself into Kate's arms.

"Mom!"

Kate wrapped her arms around her daughter, stroking her dark hair and holding her close as the girl wept uncontrollably. The child—if you could call her that—was nearly as tall as her mother. When her sobs finally quieted, Kate pulled back and looked at her, hands on the child's upper arms.

"Skye?" Kate stared at the girl, her eyes huge and disbelieving. Her lips parted and moved, but no further words came out.

It was a sight to leave you speechless, all right, Zack thought. The girl was dressed in a black tank top, a black vinyl miniskirt, torn black fishnet stockings, and black army boots. She sported a tattoo on each shoulder, a spiked leather choker that looked like a dog collar around her neck, and what appeared to be a pair of manacles on her wrists. Her skin was coated with Morticia Adams–pale makeup, her eyes were ringed with heavy black eyeliner, and her mouth was painted jet black. Thanks to

49

her sob-fest, her face sported more tracks than the Union Pacific Railroad.

"My Lord, Skye!" Kate gasped. "W-what happened?"

"We found her on Decatur Street," said a heavyset, balding officer behind a gray metal desk. His chair groaned as he hoisted his heft to his feet. "Hangin' out with the Goths."

"The Goths?" Kate echoed blankly, her eyes still fixed on the incredible sight of her daughter.

The officer nodded. "Yeah. Short for Gothics, I guess, since they all dress in black. They're a bunch of older teens—runaways, mostly—who panhandle and turn tricks in the Quarter."

"Turn tricks?" Kate's face lost another shade of color, making it nearly as pale as her daughter's.

The cop nodded. "Some of those kids'll do anything for a fix."

Kate gazed at her child, her eyes wide and shocked. "My God, Skye—what on earth were you *doing*? What were you *thinking*?"

The girl stared down at her black-painted fingernails. "I dunno."

Her brow creased with anxiety, Kate tenderly cupped the girl's face in her hands. Her voice dropped to a ragged whisper. "Honey—were you running away?"

The girl looked up in surprise. "No! I was just hangin' out."

"She was standing on a street corner with a group of them when we found her," the officer volunteered. "She looked awfully young and scared, so we picked her up."

"I wasn't scared," Skye said belligerently. "I was upset. A girl stole my book bag."

"Oh, Skye, honey . . ." Kate reached for the girl's shoulders. Her fingers froze over the matching red-and-green roses that festooned her daughter's skin. Kate's hands flew to her mouth in horror as a low, anguished moan escaped her lips. "Oh, baby—you've gotten yourself tattooed!"

Skye rolled her racoonlike eyes. "They're not real, Mom. They'll wash off."

"Thank heavens!" Her gaze traveled over her child, checking

for permanent damage. "Did anyone hurt you? Or—or give you drugs?"

"Jeeze, Mom—I'm not stupid enough to take drugs!"

Just stupid enough to skip school and hang out with kids who do, Zack thought wryly.

"Did anyone hurt you?" Kate repeated.

"No. But a girl stole my book bag with my school uniform in it."

Kate fingered a strap on Skye's tank top. "Where on earth did you get these clothes?"

"I bought them with my allowance money. There's a real cool thrift shop on Decatur Street."

"But, Skye—you're miles from your school. How did you get here?"

"I took the streetcar."

"You skipped school?"

The girl studied her scuffed boots. "I went to my morning classes. But they were having a stupid pep rally this afternoon." She looked up, her jaw tilted at a familiar stubborn angle. Like mother, like daughter, Zack thought. "I didn't want to stand around and cheer for a bunch of stupid jocks. They don't cheer for *me* when I ace a science test."

Kate gazed helplessly at her daughter, apparently at a loss for words.

The professor looked like she could use some help. Zack turned to the policeman. "Are you filing any charges?"

The officer shook his head. "We'd have to take her to juvenile hall to do that. Since it's her first time, we'll just let you all handle it."

"So we're free to go?" Kate asked.

The policeman nodded. "I'll need to see your ID."

Kate pulled her wallet out of her bag, flipped it open, and handed it to the cop.

Skye looked at Zack as if she were seeing him for the first time. "Hey—are you one of the movie people?"

51

Sheeze, but her face was a mess. Zack couldn't help but grin. "I guess you could call me that."

"Oh, wow! Have you ever met Freddie Prinze, Junior?"

"Well, as a matter of fact, I have."

"For real?" Skye's face grew animated under her Gene Simmons makeup, and she seemed to drop five years off her age.

Zack's grin widened. "For real."

The policeman held Kate's driver's license at arm's length and squinted at it. "Okay." He handed it back to her, then turned to Skye, a stern expression on his bulldog face. "You were lucky, young lady, that you only had your book bag stolen. It could have been a lot worse—a whole lot worse. You don't even want to know some of the things I've seen happen to girls like you." He shook his head solemnly, then wagged a beefy finger at her. "I better not catch you in the Quarter again without a parent or guardian. And the next time you're caught skipping school, you won't get off so light."

Skye nodded, her expression somber.

"I want your word that you won't do it again," he said sternly.

"Okay."

"Okay, what?"

"Okay, I won't skip school or go off on my own again."

"All right. You're free to go."

"Thank you, Officer." Kate wrapped an arm around her daughter and led her out of the office. Zack followed them down the corridor and into the entry hall, then opened the front door for them. The wail of a saxophone drifted on the damp March air as they stepped outside.

"I'll give you a ride home," Zack said. "Where do you live?"

"Uptown," Kate said. "But my car's at the hotel."

"We'll worry about that later. You look too shaken up to drive."

For the first time since he'd met her, Kate didn't disagree with him. She walked quietly beside him, her arm still around Skye, down the block to the parked Navigator.

Skye climbed into the backseat, directly behind Zack. "I can't believe you know Freddie Prinze, Junior. What's he like in person?"

"Don't change the subject, young lady," Kate told her sternly. "We're not through talking about your behavior."

Skye sighed and sat back to fasten her seat belt. "Guess I'm grounded, huh?"

"For the rest of your natural life." Kate twisted around to look at her. Her eyes softened, and so did her voice. "Skye, honey, what on earth were you thinking?"

"I dunno." Zack started the engine, then glanced in the rear-view mirror as he pulled away from the curb. The girl's face was drawn and sullen. "I sure wasn't thinking I'd get caught."

Zack suppressed a smile at the honest reply.

"Did you really think I wouldn't find out?" Kate demanded.

Her daughter squirmed uneasily. "Well, I was gonna change back into my uniform before I went home."

Kate shook her head. "Skye, I just don't understand. Why did you do this? Why would you want to hang around with a bunch of drug addicts?"

"I didn't know they were into drugs. I saw them on our class field trip, and I thought they looked cool."

"And you wanted to be cool, too?"

She lifted her shoulders, then sank down in the seat. "I just wanted to see if I could fit in. I sure don't at school."

"Oh, Skye, honey . . ." Kate's voice trailed off. She glanced away, looking lost and bewildered.

"Why don't you fit in?" Zack couldn't resist asking.

" 'Cause I'm not rich and cute, and everyone thinks I'm a brainy nerd."

"She's very intelligent," Kate explained. "She's in the gifted classes. She tried acting dumb last year, but her teachers called her on it."

"I *hate* school," Skye said sullenly. "It's such a waste of time." She gazed sulkily out the window. "I wish I could move away and live with my dad."

Kate's back stiffened. "You know that's out of the question."

The abrupt tone of her voice made Zack glance over. "Why's that?"

"Because he . . ." Kate paused and swallowed. "He travels all the time. He can't take care of a child."

"I'm not a child anymore," Skye said.

It was none of his business, but Zack's curiosity got the best of him. "What does he do?"

"Oh, he's got a really important job," Skye volunteered. "He travels everywhere, preserving endangered species of animals."

"Sounds interesting." Zack shot a glance at Kate. "Is he with the National Park Service?"

"No." Kate's eyes were fixed on her lap.

"The Wildlife Federation?"

"No." Kate picked an invisible piece of lint off her skirt.

"The Sierra Club?"

She shook her head, her eyes still downcast. "It's a, uh, private foundation."

It was odd, the way she refused to meet his gaze. She obviously hated to talk about her ex. Zack wondered why.

He glanced in the rearview mirror at Skye as he braked for a stoplight. "Do you see your dad very often?"

Skye made a rude snorting sound. "More like never."

He'd evidently hit on a very sore subject. He tried to smooth things over. "Well, I'm sure he sees you as often as he can."

"Are you kidding? I don't even know what he looks like. He sends packages on my birthday and at Christmas, but he never even telephones. And it's all Mom's fault."

Zack glanced at Kate. Her face was turning scarlet.

"That's enough, Skye," she said.

Not for Zack. This was just getting interesting. "What do you mean, it's your mother's fault?"

"Mom did something to him that was so terrible, he's still mad at her. He doesn't call or come around because he doesn't ever want to see her or talk to her again. Mom won't say what she did, but it must have been truly, truly awful."

"Skye!"

The girl leaned forward, ignoring Kate's protest. "I think maybe Mom dumped him for another man—maybe even his best friend."

Zack sneaked a curious glance at Kate. She didn't seem to be the type, but then, looks could be deceiving. He wouldn't have figured her as the mother of a teenage daughter, either.

"That's *enough*, Skye," Kate said sharply. "I won't stand for you speculating about me in such a disrespectful fashion."

"Well, if you'd just tell me what happened, I wouldn't have to speculate."

"Young lady, you're in enough trouble already. Don't make things any worse."

Skye stuck out her chin. "How can it get any worse? I'm already grounded for the rest of my life." She turned her attention back to Zack. "So, did you work on a movie with Freddie or what?"

Man, this girl was a real piece of work. Zack looked at her ridiculously made-up face in the mirror and grinned. "We've never worked together. I've just run into him at some social functions."

Skye's eyes grew wide. "Wow, you must be pretty important if you party with Freddie! Are you famous?"

Zack shrugged. "Not really."

"What's your name?" Skye pressed.

"Zack Jackson."

"Oh, wow! You're the guy Mom has a major crush on!"

Zack glanced over at Kate. Her face was a flaming shade of fuchsia, and she refused to meet his gaze. He grinned into the rearview mirror. "Is that right?"

"Yeah. She's nuts about you!"

"You'd never know it from the way she treats me."

Kate cleared her throat. "I, uh, used to be a fan of your TV show when I was about Skye's age."

"Grams said Mom was bonkers over you," Skye volunteered. "She used to have posters and pictures of you all over her room. Grams thinks she's still got a thing for you."

"Is that a fact?" Zack sneaked another glance at Kate, the memory of her garter-belted thigh flashing through his mind.

"Skye Marie Matthews, that is quite enough!" Kate's voice was stern, but it held an odd squeakiness.

"Yes, Mom," Skye said obediently. She leaned forward and whispered in Zack's ear. "Know what? I think Grams is right. I can tell, because Mom's acting all strict and starchy. She gets like that when she's nervous."

Well, now, this was certainly an interesting bit of information. Very interesting, in fact. Zack looked at Kate, who was staring out the side window. Her face was averted, but her slender neck was bright pink.

Hmm. He hadn't been able to get to the professor through her pocketbook. Maybe he'd have better luck with her heart. If he gave her a little of the moonlight-and-roses treatment, maybe he could sweet-talk her into dropping her historical accuracy requirements.

It was worth a try. Yes, indeed, it was certainly worth a try.

Chapter Four

Zack glanced over at Kate fifteen minutes later as he steered the SUV into a quiet residential neighborhood. Maybe Skye was wrong. Nothing in Kate's behavior or demeanor indicated the slightest bit of romantic interest. As Skye had prattled on about Freddie, Jr., Kate had sat perfectly still, her hands folded primly in her lap, her spine rigidly aligned against the buttery leather of the seat, her eyes fastened straight ahead. She looked stiff as a two-day-old corpse.

He was used to women smiling and flirting and sending clear signals of interest. Kate's body language didn't purr, "Come here. I'm interested." It shouted something more along the lines of, "Don't move or I'll shoot."

Women usually pursued *him*. Not that he thought it was Zack Jackson, the person, they wanted; he was enough of a realist to know it was Zack Jackson, the package, they were after. Everyone sugarcoated sex and romance, but the truth was, relationships were deals. Like any other deal, it all depended on what you brought to the table. It just so happened that Zack was lucky enough to have the goods most women wanted—money, fame, and a presentable physical appearance. Connections and a prestigious family name didn't hurt his case, either.

Unfortunately, none of those things seemed to hold much sway with the professor here. If she had a thing for him, she was sure keeping it under wraps.

A jerk on the back of his car seat pulled Zack out of his thoughts.

"Do you get to pick who's in your movies?" Skye asked.

"Most of the time."

"So, can I be in this one?"

"Sure. I'll find you a spot as an extra."

"Oh, wow!" Skye sat back and bounced on the seat. "Really? Wow!"

Zack glanced over to see Kate's forehead pucker in a frown. Uh-oh. Looked like he'd better backtrack. "If, um, it's okay with your mother, that is," he quickly added.

In the rearview mirror, Zack saw Skye clasp her hands prayerfully together. "Please, Mom?" she begged. "Pleeeease?"

"I just picked you up at the police station," Kate said. "This is not the time to be asking for favors."

"Ahh, Mom!"

"You're grounded, remember?"

"But, Mom . . . this is the chance of a lifetime! I promise I'll be good. Please? Pleeeease?"

"We'll discuss this later."

"Mom!"

"Not now, Skye," Kate said firmly. "We'll have to see."

"Aww! That usually means no." Skye flounced back against the seat. In the rearview mirror, Zack saw her fold her arms across her chest and scowl. "You're just like Gram. You never want me to do anything!"

A wounded look crossed Kate's face. "You know that's not true."

Hoo boy. It sounded like he'd really stepped in it. Zack shot Kate an apologetic look. "Sorry. I should have asked your permission before I said anything. I just thought—"

"You need to turn left again at the next intersection," Kate said curtly, cutting him off in mid-sentence.

She obviously didn't want to discuss this anymore in front of her daughter. Zack didn't have a clue how to win Kate over, but he was pretty sure that ticking her off wouldn't help. He turned the car as she indicated, guiding it onto a quiet street of modest, well-kept homes that looked like they belonged on a historic register somewhere.

"It's the second house on the right."

Zack squinted against the setting sun. "The one with the police car in the drive?"

"Oh, great," Skye groaned from the backseat. "Grams is at it again."

"At what?" Zack couldn't resist asking.

"Calling the cops. She always thinks she's seeing criminals."

Zack was beginning to wonder if he'd fallen down the Alice-in-Wonderland rabbit hole. He glanced over at Kate. "This is your mother we're talking about?"

Kate nodded.

"She lives with you?"

"No. Across the street."

"But she's always at our house," Skye piped up. "It's just like she lives with us."

As Zack approached the house, a uniformed policeman carrying a small brown paper sack strolled to the squad car and climbed in. "Looks like he's got some of Grams's homemade cookies," Skye observed. "She always gives the cops a treat so they'll be willing to come back next time."

Kate shifted uneasily. "I'm sure Mr. Jackson isn't interested in all the details of our lives, Skye."

"But I am," Zack said. "It's very interesting."

And it was. Fascinating, in fact. Besides, the more he learned, the more he'd know about how to persuade Kate to see things his way. He braked by the curb and let the police car back out of the drive. Kate and Skye both waved to the officer, and he waved back as he drove off down the street.

Zack pulled the SUV into the driveway and turned off the engine. He hopped out and rounded the vehicle to open the door for Kate, but she'd already done it herself. He reached out to help her down, and she hesitantly accepted. Her hand felt small and warm in his, and when their eyes met, a jolt of electricity shot through him. The fleeting look of surprise on her face told him that she'd felt it, too.

She quickly looked away. "Thank you," she said primly.

"No problem." He couldn't help but glance at her skirt, and felt a stab of disappointment that it didn't fall open as it had earlier.

A slender, fifty-something woman in jeans and a red sweat-shirt that said PROPERTY OF THE F.B.I. stood on the porch, a camera dangling from around her neck. Her gray-streaked, light-brown hair swirled around her head in short, chaotic curls, and her features were so similar to Kate's that he didn't need to ask her identity.

The woman hurried down the porch. "Kate, I'm glad you're home. I was getting worried about you."

"I'm a big girl, Mom," Kate replied. "And it's not even dark yet." Skye clambered out of the vehicle, her boots thudding loudly on the cement.

The woman's eyes grew round as Moon Pies. She pressed a hand to her cheek. "My Lord! Skye, is that you?"

"Yeah, it's me." The girl plodded up the steps to the porch.

"Skye, go to your room and change clothes," Kate directed.

The older woman's face twisted into a worried, almost panic-stricken frown. She stepped into Skye's path, forcing her to stop. "Dear heavens, child—why are you dressed like that? And what is that stuff all over your face?"

Skye looked down at her black-painted fingernails. "It's a long story, Grams."

The older woman stared at her, her eyes full of distress. "You look just like a girl I saw on TV. She'd been kidnapped by a cult, and they tried to brainwash her. The first thing they did

60

was change her appearance to isolate her from her family and the rest of the world."

Skye looked back at Zack and rolled her eyes, then turned back to her grandmother. "Gee, Grams, what a coincidence—that's just what happened to me!"

The older woman stepped back, clutching both hands over her chest.

"Yeah, it was really awful." Skye's face was poker-straight, her eyes innocent. "I was abducted by a cult of crazed tourists. They grabbed me and forced me to the Macy's makeup counter, and I had to endure a really, really bad makeover."

Zack burst out in a loud laugh. When he saw Kate's stern expression, he quickly disguised his amusement in a fit of coughing.

"Skye Marie, stop baiting your grandmother and go upstairs this minute," Kate ordered. "While you're there, I want you to write a two-page essay about why it's wrong to skip school, and another two-page paper about why you shouldn't go to the French Quarter alone. You're confined to your room until they're finished."

"Aw, Mom!"

"Go on," Kate ordered.

The girl clomped to the front door and disappeared inside.

The older woman watched the door close, then turned to Kate, her blue eyes anxious. "Was she really kidnapped?"

"Of course not, Mom." Kate's voice had the weary edge of someone who was tired of making explanations. "She played hooky from school and went to the French Quarter."

"Hooky? She told me she was staying after school to work on a science project." The woman ran a hand through her hair, her eyes bewildered. "Where on earth did she get the weird getup?"

"She bought it at a thrift store. Everything's okay, Mom. I'll tell you all about it later." Kate turned to Zack, looking eager to change the topic. "Mom, this is Zack Jackson. Zack, this is my mother, Ruth."

"Pleased to meet you," Zack said.

Ruth's face softened with a smile as she extended her hand. "I feel like I already know you, as often as you've been in my living room. On TV, I mean." She pumped his hand up and down enthusiastically, making the camera on her neck sway against her chest. "Katie used to live for your show. Why, she had pictures of you taped all over her bedroom, and—"

Zack was amused to see Kate's cheeks turn bright pink. "I think he gets the picture, Mom."

"And to think that now she's working with you on a movie!" Ruth shook her head just as vigorously as she'd just shaken his hand. "It's a small world, isn't it?"

"Getting smaller all the time," Zack agreed. Not to mention weirder. He shoved his hands in his pockets. "I couldn't help but notice that there was a police car in your driveway. Did you have some kind of problem?"

Ruth leaned forward, as if she were imparting a confidence. "A car drove by with a suspicious-looking man in it."

"Suspicious-looking how?"

"He was going at a snail's pace, looking at the houses, as if he were casing them. And I thought he looked like one of the mug shots I saw down at the post office." She patted her camera. "So I took several pictures and called the police. Officer Michaels came by to take my statement and my roll of film." She looked at Kate and shook her head woefully. "He said they're not going to be able to give me back the pictures anymore. I'll have to get them developed myself from now on if I want to keep the prints."

Kate lifted her shoulders. "Well, you know what they say, Mom—all good things must come to an end."

Ruth gave an indignant sniff. "Well, you'd think they could at least pick up the tab for my film, since I'm helping them do their job. They've always done it before."

"So, this happens pretty often?" Jake couldn't resist asking.

"Oh, yes," Ruth said. "Criminals are everywhere. People just don't realize it because they don't know what to look for."

But I bet you do. The lady was clearly a pancake short of a stack. "I didn't realize New Orleans had such a bad crime problem," he said politely.

"Oh, it's not just New Orleans." Ruth's eyes were as blue as Kate's, and just as earnest. "Crooks are everywhere, and they keep moving around so they won't get caught. That's why I study the WANTED posters and never miss an episode of 'America's Most Wanted.' And I always keep my camera with me. You never know when you're going to get the chance to capture a bit of evidence."

Zack glanced at Kate. She lifted her shoulders in an embarrassed little shrug.

Ruth's eyes suddenly narrowed. "What happened to your car, Kate?"

"It's at the Hyatt."

"Oh, you shouldn't leave it there overnight, especially on a weekend. It might get stolen."

Kate blew out a hard sigh. "It'll be fine, Mom."

Ruth made a tsk-tsking sound. "You can't be sure of that. There was a story about a car theft ring at the Superdome just last week. That's right next to the Hyatt."

Zack saw an opportunity to get Kate alone. "I can take you back to get it," he offered. "I'm heading to the hotel now."

"Well . . ." Kate hesitated. "All right. Thank you." She turned to Ruth. "Would you mind keeping an eye on Skye?"

"Not at all. But it'll be getting dark soon. Do you have your phone with you?"

Kate sighed. "It's in my bag."

"Be careful!"

"I always am, Mom."

"Hey, Mr. Jackson!" Zack looked up to see Skye waving from an upstairs window. "Try to talk my mom into letting me be in your movie."

Zack cast a dubious glance at Kate. "I don't know that I can talk your mom into anything."

"I bet you can. Remember what I told you."

*　　*　　*

If his slow, sidelong smile was any indication, Zack remembered, all right. Boy, oh boy—when she got Skye alone, that child was going to get a piece of her mind. It was bad enough having her girlhood crush trotted out and discussed in front of Zack, but it was downright mortifying to have it declared still in effect.

"That's some kid you've got there," Zack remarked.

"She's something, all right."

Zack opened the door of the SUV and Kate stepped up. Too late, she realized the slit in her skirt had hiked up and spread apart, exposing a flash of white thigh above a lace-topped stocking. Kate quickly whipped her skirt together, hoping Zack hadn't noticed.

No such luck. He was staring at her legs. His gaze pulled up and collided with hers. The impact was like two Mack trucks in a head-on crash. "Sorry," she mumbled, tugging at the skirt again.

Awareness, crackling and carnal, pulsed between them for a hot, shocking moment.

His gaze seemed to see right through her, to see the mad thumping of her heart. His mouth curved in a wicked smile. "Don't be. I'm not."

He closed her door and circled the SUV. She leaned back against the headrest, her blood roaring in her ears, her face flaming with embarrassment. She averted her eyes as Zack climbed into the vehicle and started the engine, praying that he wouldn't say anything further about her choice of undergarments.

Unfortunately, he seemed to have an uncanny knack for doing the very thing she feared.

"Your legs are sexy as hell." He cast her a sidelong smile as he backed the vehicle out of the driveway. "Especially in those stockings."

Oh, mercy—she wished she could crawl under the seat and disappear. If he continued to talk about her unconventional taste in hosiery, she'd die of humiliation.

She had to change the topic, and fast. "I'm sorry I ruined your plans for the afternoon. Thanks for taking me to the police station."

"No problem. Glad to help." He shifted the vehicle into drive. "I gotta say, though, I was surprised to learn you have a daughter who's nearly a teenager. You must have been just a kid yourself when you had her."

It wasn't a subject she wanted to discuss, but it sure beat talking about her undergarments. "I was eighteen."

"Were you just out of high school?"

She swallowed hard and gave him the standard lie. "I, e-e—um, *eloped* in the middle of my senior year." Even after all these years, it was still hard to get out the untruthful word.

His brow shot up in surprise. "Wow. I didn't know anyone ever really did that." He slowed for a bicyclist. "Who was the guy? Someone you went to school with?"

Kate shook her head. "Wayne was seven years older than me."

"So what did he do?"

"He asked me if I wanted to share his table at a really crowded McDonald's."

"Wow, a smooth operator." He angled an amused smile at her. "But I meant what did he do for a living."

Of course. Something about Zack made her feel as if her brain were swaddled in cotton. "He wanted to be an actor. He was working odd jobs and trying to save up money to move to New York City."

"That's where you went when you eloped?"

Kate nodded. "Somebody told him he'd have better luck breaking into show business there than in L.A." She gave a rueful grin. "He should have tried L.A."

"So how did he make the leap from acting to animal preservation?"

Kate's throat constricted; the way it always did when she had to lie. "I—I'm not sure. That was after we, um"—she swallowed—"we divorced."

65

Zack's gaze rested on her curiously. "How long were you married?"

"Not long." She averted her eyes and stared out, the side window.

What happened?"

She lifted her shoulders. "It just didn't work out."

"I gather he's not very involved in Skye's life now."

Kate squirmed on the seat, a sense of anxiety clutching her chest. She hated talking about Wayne. Maybe discussing her underwear wasn't so bad after all.

"Why isn't he?" Zack pressed.

"He just isn't."

The professor was awfully prickly on the subject of her ex, Zack thought—not to mention tight-lipped. She hadn't even told her daughter the reason for their breakup, except that her ex was still mad at her. What could have happened to create that kind of bad blood? He was curious as hell.

"What about you?" Kate asked. "Have you ever been married?"

Oh, hell. She was turning the tables. "Nah."

"Why not?"

Zack hesitated. If he was going to use romance as a means of persuasion, he needed to let her know the rules of the game. He never got involved with a woman without making things clear from the very beginning. "I don't believe in marriage."

Kate tilted her head. "What do you mean, you don't believe in it? Marriage isn't the tooth fairy."

"It's close. 'Happily ever after' only happens in fiction."

"Wow. That's a pretty cynical take on society's most basic institution."

"Maybe so, but it's honest. 'Until death do us part' is an unrealistic expectation." He clicked on the blinker to make a left turn. "When the newness wears off, people get disillusioned and romance hits the skids. That's why I always like to set an expiration date at the outset of a relationship."

Her eyes widened. "An expiration date? Like on a carton of milk?"

Zack nodded. "Most relationships are naturally self-limiting anyway. They end when a movie's wrapped, or the holidays are over, or a location shoot is finished. Instead of going through a lot of angst and awkwardness, it's easier to just agree upfront that you're going to enjoy your time together, then go your separate ways when it's over."

"What if the deadline arrives and you don't want to go your separate ways?"

He shrugged. "You do anyway. That way, you have pleasant memories."

Kate stared at him. "You're not kidding, are you?"

Zack shook his head as he braked for a stop light. "Nothing lasts forever."

"Well, then, how do you account for all the people who stay married for a lifetime?"

He shook his head. "Some people prefer the evil they know over the evil they don't."

"Love as an evil. Gee, I'm glad to see you're not too jaded on this topic."

"Hey, I'm a realist. But that's not to say I'm not also a romantic." He reached out and rubbed the back of her neck. The strands of hair that had come loose from her topknot were soft over his knuckles, and her skin was like warm silk.

Kate's lips parted in surprise. They were nice lips, he thought distractedly—full and ripe and naturally pink. He wondered how they'd taste if he kissed her, wondered how she'd react if he tried. Would she go all stiff and wooden, or would her response be as surprising as her choice of legwear?

Damn, but he couldn't get those stockings out of his mind.

He pulled back his hand as the light changed. She reached up and self-consciously smoothed her hair. "Well, I think you're wrong."

"You don't think I'm romantic?"

Her cheeks colored. "That's not what I'm talking about. I

know for a fact that people can stay in love for a lifetime, because my parents' marriage was like that. They positively doted on each other. When dad died, it was like part of mom died, too."

So her mother was a widow, not a divorcee. He'd automatically assumed she was divorced. But then, he always assumed any single, formerly married person was divorced. Funny, how one interpreted things based on one's own experience. "Well, there's always an exception to every rule."

"My grandparents' marriage was like that, too. They were married for fifty-five years, and they still held hands and called each other 'darling' like a couple of teenagers."

Zack lifted his shoulders. "Maybe there's a marriage gene. If so, it doesn't run in my family."

Kate's gaze was warm on his face. "Your parents divorced when you were young, didn't they?"

Zack nodded. "I was three."

"And you lived with your father, as I recall."

He shot her a sly grin. "Hey, you're pretty up on this stuff."

"I used to read a lot of movie magazines when I was a teenager." She gave an embarrassed smile. "I loved your dad's spy movies. He always seemed so cool, sophisticated and clever. Was he like that in real life?"

Zack shrugged. "You'd have to ask one of his wives or girlfriends. I didn't really see much of him."

"Oh. I'm sorry."

She said it in the tone one might use if someone had died. Zack's fingers tightened on the steering wheel. How the hell had they gotten on this topic, anyway?

"What about your mom?" Kate asked. "Did you see her often?"

Zack lifted his shoulders. "Only at Christmas. She moved to New York and had an awfully busy schedule."

And she never penciled him into it. When he was eleven, he'd realized that she only wanted him at Christmas as a décor item, like a Christmas tree or a holiday wreath. You had to have a kid around to create the perfect setting. The memory gave him a painful twinge. After all this time, it still hurt. Maybe a person never got over not being loved by his mother.

"You must have been lonely," Kate murmured.

"Not really. I was never alone." If there was one thing Zack couldn't stand, it was poor-little-rich-kid pity. He flicked on the turn signal and changed lanes. "I always had one nanny or another. And when I started acting, I had a tutor and an agent. I even had my own accountant. Dad made sure I had everything I needed."

He could feel her warm, soft gaze again. "Everything except a parent."

Hell. Why had he ever opened his mouth? It was way past time to change the subject.

"Yeah, well, my folks wouldn't win any Parent-of-the-Year awards, but they introduced me to the film industry, so I owe them for that."

"Sounds like you really like your work."

"I love it."

"No expiration date on that love affair?"

"I'm afraid there might be." He shot her a solemn look. "If this movie doesn't do well, I'm all washed up. And without the action scenes, it doesn't stand a chance."

Her eyes grew large and sympathetic. "I'm sure we can find a way to solve this."

Hope swelled in Zack's chest, but he was careful not to show it. "I don't see how."

"Well, maybe I can find some actual events to use in place of the ones we deleted."

Aw, hell. He didn't want some weak substitute action. He wanted Kate to change her mind so he could use what he already had. "You're not likely to find anything as exciting as an exploding riverboat or a buggy race down Saint Charles Avenue."

"Maybe I'll find something even better."

Oh, right. Fat chance of that. But he couldn't flat-out refuse her offer without insulting her.

What the hell—let her look. In the meantime, he'd work on softening her up and convincing her to let him use the existing script.

"I guess it couldn't hurt for you to take a shot at it." He turned onto the long drive that led to the Hyatt Regency's entrance, then braked behind a car unloading luggage.

"It'll take me a couple of days to look through all the resources," she said. "But I'm sure I'll turn up something."

"That would be great." He placed his hand on top of hers and gave it a squeeze.

Her hand tensed under his. She cleared her throat nervously. "Sure. And thank *you* for the ride."

She started to pull her hand away, but he caught it and cradled it between his palms. "It's Friday night. Let me take you to dinner."

She blinked in surprise. "I—I can't. My family's expecting me."

"Tomorrow night, then."

She hesitated.

Zack poured all of his considerable charm into a pleading smile. "Please. We got off to a bad start, and I want to make it up to you."

Her eyes were uncertain. "Well . . ."

"If you turn me down, I'll think you're still mad at me."

Her lips tilted in a small smile. "You make it hard to say no."

"That's the whole idea. Come on. I'll pick you up at seven."

The doorman opened Kate's door. "All right," she conceded.

"Great! So it's a date."

She froze for a brief moment, then pulled her hand free and scrambled out of the vehicle, tightly clutching the slit in her skirt.

Chapter Five

It's a date. It was absurd, the way those three simple words had twirled in her mind for the past twenty-four hours, swirling through her thoughts like leaves in a whirlwind.

They'd kept her awake late into the night; then they'd teased and taunted her all day. And now, as she stood staring at the contents of her closet, trying to decide what to wear to dinner, she could practically hear Zack say those words again.

It's a date.

She was behaving like a silly schoolgirl, she chided herself. He'd only meant it in a platonic way. She wasn't fool enough to believe that Zack Jackson thought she and he would . . . That they'd . . .

Kate impatiently pushed aside another clothes hanger, trying to push aside her disturbingly sensual thoughts, as well. She was making way too much of this. The fact that it was Saturday night—traditional date night—was nothing but a coincidence.

This wasn't a real date—not the kind with romantic possibilities, anyway. Zack dated movie stars and models, not plain-Jane history professors.

Still, something had flashed between them—something elec-

71

tric and exciting and distinctly sexual, something that made her blood run hot and fast through her veins. The thought of it sent a shiver up her spine, a shiver that had nothing to do with the fact that she was still damp from her shower and wearing only a large pink towel.

She shoved aside another hanger, then paused at a black jersey dress, one she'd bought on sale but never worn. Lifting it from the rack, she held it in front of her and gazed into the mirror mounted on the back of her closet door. It wasn't her usual style at all. It was tighter, shorter, and lower cut than anything she'd ever owned, and she never would have bought it if her friend Samantha hadn't insisted that she looked gorgeous in it.

"You need a fabulous dress for when you meet a fabulous man," Sam had said.

The dress was better suited to Samantha's life as a flight attendant than Kate's, but she'd bought the dress because she wanted to buy into the fantasy. The truth was, there were no fabulous men in Kate's life, nor were there likely to be. The men who routinely crossed her path at the university and Skye's school functions were either too old, too young, too married, or too weird. If she *did* run into an eligible man, he was usually looking for someone along the lines of Samantha rather than a fade-into-the-woodwork historian.

Still . . . she *did* look pretty good in the dress. Should she wear it tonight?

"Don't be ridiculous," she muttered, jamming it back on the rack. She and Zack had a business relationship, and an adversarial one at that. The man had tried to bribe her, for heaven's sake! She needed to spend the evening convincing him that New Orleans's history didn't need any fictional embellishment, not nuturing an old school-girl fantasy. Snatching her navy pantsuit off the rack, she laid it across her bed and padded back to the bathroom to dry her hair.

She'd just picked up the blow dryer when the doorbell chimed. Oh dear—Zack was early! She wasn't dressed, her hair was dripping wet, and she didn't have any makeup on. The thought of leaving him at the mercy of her mother and Skye made her throw herself together in record time.

Stepping into a pair of navy sandals and grabbing her purse, she hurried downstairs and followed the sound of voices to the kitchen. She stopped in the hallway and surveyed the scene. Zack was seated at the breakfast table, scribbling something on notepaper, while Skye leaned over his shoulder and Ruth talked a blue streak.

". . . And by the time the police found the body, there was nothing left but teeth and a hank of hair," her mother was saying.

Oh, no. Kate stepped into the kitchen. "Mom, I'm sure Zack isn't interested in hearing your gruesome stories."

The camera around Ruth's neck swung as she turned toward the doorway. "But that crime happened in California, where Mr. Jackson lives."

"Still, Mom, I don't think . . ." Kate lost her train of thought as Zack rose to his feet, smiling. There it was again—that hot, breathless surge of attraction that made her stomach tighten and her tongue feel glued to the roof of her mouth.

"Hi, Kate."

Why did being in the same room with him make her brain turn to mush? "Hello," she managed.

His gaze traveled over her, warming her skin. "You look great."

Skye glanced up, then turned her attention back to the pile of papers in front of her, apparently unimpressed. "She looks the same as always." She slid another stack of notepaper in front of Zack. "Here, sign a few more."

Kate peered over Skye's shoulder. "What on earth are you doing?"

"Getting his autograph."

Kate leaned forward and riffled through the pages stacked on the round oak table. "Looks like you already have a couple dozen."

Skye lifted her shoulders. "So? I want a few more."

"I don't mind," Zack said, bending over the table and picking up the pen.

Kate eyed her daughter suspiciously. "Why do you need so many?"

"I'm gonna sell them."

Zack grinned up at Kate. "She's turned me into a regular cottage industry."

Kate regarded her daughter with dismay. "Skye!"

"What?" the girl asked, imbuing the word with an inflection that simultaneously said *I'm not doing anything wrong* and *you're a clueless moron.* "The more autographs I get, the more money I can make. Mother's Day is coming up, and his autograph would make a good gift. Since you had a crush on him, I figure other kids' moms did, too."

Kate fought the urge to crawl under the blue-and-white hooked rug under the kitchen table.

"I hate to break the news, but I wasn't exactly a teen idol," Zack told Skye. "I was more like Opie than David Cassidy."

Skye looked at him quizzically. "Who were they?"

Zack laughed. Kate placed her hand on her hip and eyed her daughter sternly. "Skye, I won't allow you to take advantage of Mr. Jackson."

"It's okay. Really." Zack scrawled another line across the paper and smiled up at Kate. "I love to be taken advantage of."

She felt her face heat. Her mother laughed, then peered worriedly out the kitchen window. "It's getting dark. Most crime happens after sunset, you know." She turned to Zack. "Why don't you stay and have dinner here?"

Oh, great. Kate heaved an impatient sigh. "We'll be fine, Mom. Nothing is going to happen."

"That's what everyone thinks. Do you think the person who got shot downtown last week thought that was going to happen?" Ruth turned to Zack and fixed him with a pleading smile. "Let me make you a nice dinner. I've got a lovely piece of liver, and—"

"Ugh!" Skye stuck her finger in her mouth and made a retching sound. "You guys better bring me a doggie bag."

"That's very kind of you, Mrs. Matthews." Zack smiled at the older woman so warmly that for a moment, Kate feared he was about to accept. "But we have reservations at Arnaud's. Don't you worry, though. I promise I'll take very good care of your daughter."

He turned and gave Kate a smile so sexy she wondered what kind of care he had in mind. Fortunately, Ruth's attention was drawn to something outside the window. Lifting her camera to her eye, she clicked off a shot.

Zack's eyebrows rose. "Another criminal?"

Ruth lowered the camera but continued to squint out the window. "You never know. I got the license plate just in case."

Zack nodded somberly, as if the explanation made perfect sense. Skye rolled her eyes. "Grams, criminals are *not* cruising up and down our street! There hasn't been a crime in our neighborhood in ages."

"All the more reason to keep an eye out." Ruth kept her gaze fixed out the window. "You can't beat the odds forever."

Skye made a little circle next to her head and pointed at her grandmother's back, then slid another paper in front of Zack for him to sign. Propping her elbows on the table, the girl rested her head in her hands. "Do you just know movie people, or do you know rock stars, too?"

He scrawled his name across the paper in fast, bold strokes. "I know a few people in the music industry."

Skye's face grew eager as a puppy's. "Do you know Britney Spears? I just loooove Britney Spears!"

"Sorry. Never met her."

"Oh." The syllable was imbued with complete disillusionment. A second later, her face brightened again. "Well, what about 'N Sync? Or the Back Street Boys? Have you met any of them?"

"Afraid not."

Skye slumped in her chair. "I guess you just know musicians who're old like you, huh?"

"Skye!"

"I didn't mean he was *old*-old. I just meant middle-aged. Like you."

Zack burst out in a loud laugh. Kate shot her daughter a threatening look, but Skye's gaze was fixed again on Zack. "Hey—what about Cristina Aguillera? Do you know her?"

"Young lady, that's quite enough," Kate ordered. "Leave Mr. Jackson alone."

"He doesn't mind. And he likes to be called Zack. I asked him."

Kate needed to get out of here before her urge to throttle her daughter overrode her protective motherly instincts. She pulled her purse up on her arm and looked pleadingly at Zack. "We'll lose our reservation if we're late."

"Right. We'd better go." Zack signed one last signature and rose from his chair.

"Wait!" Ruth scurried across the kitchen, yanked open a deep drawer, and pulled out a huge red flashlight. She thrust it at Zack. "Here. Take this."

He gripped the flashlight, clearly puzzled.

"Crooks hate light," Ruth explained. "If you suspect that someone is following you, just whip around, shine it straight in his eyes, and shout, 'Back off or else!' It works like a charm."

"I'll bet it does." The corners of Zack's mouth were quivering, but to his credit, he managed not to actually laugh.

"Grams did that at my school's open house." Skye gave a disgusted sigh. "The man turned out to be my principal."

Ruth lifted her chin and sniffed. "Well, he had no business following us out to the parking lot."

"He wasn't following us, Grams. The meeting was over and he was going to his car."

Kate needed to get Zack out of here before he decided to have them all committed. Taking the flashlight from him, Kate placed her other hand on his arm and tugged him toward the door. "We don't want to be late."

To her alarm, he placed his hand possessively over hers, trapping her palm against the warm steel of his jacket-clad arm. Zack gave a gallant smile to Ruth. "It was nice to see you again. Thanks for the iced tea. And thanks for the loan of the flashlight." He grinned at Skye. "Good luck with your autograph sales."

Kate tugged him toward the door.

"How about Jennifer Lopez?" Skye called as Kate ushered him to the porch. "I bet I could get a ton of money for her autograph. Do you know her?"

"Sorry," Zack called over his shoulder.

"Awww!"

The door closed firmly behind them, mercifully cutting off Skye's baleful whine. Kate drew a deep breath. The evening was warm, and the twilight sky was the deep purple-blue that came just before true dark. It was the time of day that Kate had always thought was the most perfect, romantic time on earth.

But she had no business thinking of romance right now—especially since her hand was still trapped against Zack's left biceps and the feel of it made her insides all fluttery. He was close enough that she could inhale his scent, a heady blend of shaving cream and soap and something fainter. Probably testosterone, she thought. That would account for the acute sexual awareness she felt whenever she was near him.

She cleared her throat. "I apologize for Mom and Skye."

"Why? They're terrific." He stopped by the passenger door of the SUV. "They're real originals."

"Is that code for certifiable?"

Zack laughed and released her hand to open her door. The heat from his touch stayed with her while he circled the car, climbed in, and started the engine.

"I hope you'll excuse Skye," Kate said. "She can be awfully pushy."

"She's persistent. That's a good trait to have." He shot her a grin. "I thought I could eke out a few more years, though, before I qualified as middle-aged."

"Skye thinks everyone over twenty-five is ancient. It drives Mom crazy." Kate gave a dry smile. "Not that Mom is exactly sane to begin with."

Zack looked over curiously as he backed out of the drive. "What's the story with her, anyway? She seems awfully concerned about crime."

Kate gave a rueful grin. "Oh, you picked up on that, did you?"

Zack laughed. "It would have been hard to miss. I thought she wasn't going to let me out of there unless I strapped on an Uzi and a few rounds of ammunition."

Kate laughed. "You got off easy, all right."

"So what's the story?"

Kate shook her head. "I'm afraid a long one."

"Hey, I've got all night."

Kate could think of a lot better ways to spend it than discussing her mother's eccentricities, but since Zack had been treated to a full range of them, she owed him some kind of explanation. "It all started after my father died."

"When was that?"

"I was ten, so let's see . . . twenty-one years ago."

"What happened to him?"

"He had a heart attack while he was driving back from the Northshore. His car went off the bridge and he drowned in Lake Pontchartrain."

"Wow. That must have been rough."

Kate nodded. "It was. I was devastated, but Mom was nearly destroyed. She became terrified that something was going to happen to me, too, and she didn't want me out of her sight."

"Oh, I'll bet you really loved that."

Kate gave a rueful grin. "It was really fun when I hit my teens."

"Is that why you eloped?"

A twinge of discomfort shot through Kate, the way it always did when the subject came up. "That had a lot to do with it," she admitted.

"I'll bet your mom wigged out when she found you gone."

Kate nodded. "That's when she started focusing on crime."

Zack frowned. "I don't get the connection."

"I didn't, either, until a friend of mine who's a psychology professor explained it to me." Kate angled more fully toward him. "Mom thinks crime is something she can control. She realizes she can't control accidents, and she can't control me, but she thinks that if she's vigilant enough, she can control whether or not we're victims of crime."

"Wow. That's fascinating." The Navigator bumped over the streetcar tracks as Zack steered around Jackson Circle. "That's got the makings of a movie."

"What would it be—comedy or horror?"

"Probably a little of both." He grinned and looked over as he braked for a stoplight. "Have you tried to get her professional help?"

Kate nodded. "She's in complete denial. She says she doesn't need it, and she gets upset if you mention the topic. My psychologist friend says it's useless to try to change her if she doesn't want to change." Kate looked out the window. "As neuroses go, Mom's is pretty harmless. And Skye and I are used to it." Kate lifted her shoulders. "So I let her give me flashlights, then just leave them in the car."

"Aw, don't tell me you're going to leave it in the car." Zack frowned in mock chagrin. "I was hoping I'd get to see your 'back off or else' technique."

Kate smiled. "Maybe I'll give you a private demonstration later."

"Oh, I hope not." Zack's mouth curved. "I was hoping for a private demonstration of a whole other kind."

His eyes locked on hers, and it was as if Kate had stepped on a downed powerline. Electricity, hot and powerful, zapped between them. The temperature in the vehicle suddenly shot up by several degrees. Kate knew she should look away, but she was completely unable to pull her gaze away from Zack's.

A honk sounded behind them. Kate jerked her eyes forward to discover that the light had changed.

How long had they been sitting there, just staring at each other? As Zack turned his attention back to driving, Kate gazed out the window, trying to calm her pounding heart. Never in her life had she experienced such intense attraction to a man. For a moment there, it had seemed as if their eyes were doing something carnal.

Oh, dear—this had to stop. How was she going to protect her professional credibility and stand up to Zack on historical issues if she got all addle-brained every time he looked at her?

She couldn't allow him to rattle her.

In fact, this dinner was the perfect opportunity to tell him all about New Orleans's history, to swing him around to her way of thinking. Once he learned how rich and colorful Storyville's past was, he'd realize it didn't need any fictional embellishment. Instead of acting like an enamored teenager, she needed to focus on convincing him that truth could be as entertaining as fiction. And, for the rest of the evening, that was exactly what she would do.

Chapter Six

". . . and since Federal law stated that a house of ill-repute couldn't operate within five miles of a military installation, Storyville was closed at the beginning of World War One."

"Is that a fact." Zack smiled politely, but he couldn't help shifting restlessly. They were sitting at a candlelit table at Arnaud's, one of the city's oldest and most romantic restaurants, but the evening had been far from romantic. Kate had chattered on about the history of New Orleans throughout the last three courses, and she was still talking about it as they waited for dessert to be served. How the heck was he supposed to romance her when she never gave him a chance to get a word in? Every time he tried to steer the conversation to a more personal topic, she brought up a new historical fact.

The tuxedoed waiter who'd anticipated their every need all evening appeared at their table. With a smile and a flourish, he set a dish in front of each of them. "Bread pudding for madame, and crème brûlée for monsieur. Enjoy."

Kate picked up her spoon. "Have you ever tried bread pudding?"

"Can't say that I have."

"Well, then, you have to taste it." She pushed her dish toward him. "It's an old New Orleans specialty that can be traced back to the early eighteen hundreds. It originated as a way of using up stale bread."

"Hey, don't oversell it."

Kate grinned. "Give it a try."

Zack reluctantly dipped his spoon into Kate's dish and tasted it. To his surprise, a rich, delicious flavor filled his mouth.

"It's good, isn't it?" Kate prompted.

"Delicious. What's the stuff on top?"

"Whiskey sauce." Kate dug into the bowl. "In the old days, whiskey was only served by the wealthy, so it became something of a status symbol. The more whiskey in the pudding, the wealthier the host. It became the height of fashion to serve sauce strong enough to give your guests a buzz."

"Is that how this is prepared?"

"No. Nowadays, it's cooked until the alcohol evaporates."

Too bad. If he could get a little alcohol into Kate, maybe he could get her to loosen up and drop the history lectures. He'd ordered champagne, but she'd only taken a few tiny sips.

"I'm not much of a drinker," she'd told him. "One glass, and I start feeling tipsy."

She might not be much of a drinker, but she was sure one hell of an eater. Between her discourses on local history, she'd managed to devour an order of oysters Bienville, a house salad, and a generous serving of pomparo en croute and now she was attacking her dessert with the same enthusiasm.

Zack couldn't help but smile as he watched her. Most of the women he knew acted as if food was an enemy. It was refreshing to see a woman with an appetite—refreshing, and somehow provocative.

Provocative. It wasn't a word he'd expected to apply to the professor, and yet it fit. Under her no-nonsense suits and severe hairstyle was a hidden sensuality. Kate had a whole other side, a side that wore black lace garter belts and gazed at him with enough heat to melt the tires off his Navigator—a side that intrigued the hell out of him.

But that wasn't the reason he was here with her tonight, he reminded himself, at least, not the *only* reason. He had a letter in the pocket of his navy blazer that he hoped to persuade her to sign, a letter to Marvin Goldman stating that she'd changed her mind about the script needing major changes, that it was just fine as it was.

It was hard to keep that purpose in mind, though, as he watched her slide another spoonful of pudding between her lips and close her eyes, a look of pure ecstasy on her face. Was that how she'd look during sex? The image of Kate lying under him, wearing nothing but that look on her face, flashed through his mind with vivid clarity, sending a surge of heat to a lower region with a mind of its own.

He leaned forward. "You know, Kate, you've told me a lot about the history of Storyville, but you haven't told me much about your personal history."

She gave a rueful grin. "After meeting Skye and Mom, I'm afraid you know far too much already."

Zack grinned. "Ah, but I don't know the pertinent stuff. Such as whether or not you're seeing anyone."

Their eyes met, and a flash of undeniable sexual awareness surged between them. Kate looked back down at her pudding. "I really don't see how that's pertinent," she said.

Zack grinned. "It's not. It's impertinent. So, is the answer yes or no?"

A tell-tale blush brightened her cheeks. "I'm not dating anyone right now." She took another bite. "What about you? Do you have a pending expiration date?"

He shook his head. "I haven't been involved in quite a while." Too long a while, if his reaction to the professor was anything to go by.

"Why not?"

"I haven't met anyone I was interested in." He smiled. "Not until yesterday."

Kate gave a wry smile. "Sorry. I only like expiration dates on my luncheon meat and dairy products."

"The concept isn't as cold as it sounds. The way I see it, romance is a lot like bread pudding—sweet and delicious and intoxicating. And while it lasts, it should be savored to the fullest."

"You're talking about infatuation. With love—real love—there's no bottom of the bowl."

"Sounds great in theory. And it looks good in movies."

"It looks good in real life, too," Kate replied. "You should have seen my grandparents rocking together on their porch swing like two lovebirds. Or my parents, slow dancing in the living room when they thought I was asleep."

A familiar wistfulness tugged at Zack's chest. It was the same on-the-outside-looking-in feeling he used to get as a boy when other kids' parents showed up at Little League games and school plays, and no one came to cheer for him. He pushed it away. "I guess you're looking for that kind of relationship, too, huh?"

"Sure. If Mr. Right ever comes along." She looked at him curiously. "Haven't you ever thought about making a relationship permanent?"

"Once. When I was young and foolish."

"What happened?"

"It ended anyway." He took a sip of champagne, but it suddenly tasted sour. He needed to turn the conversation back to Kate. "What got you interested in history?"

"My dad was a historical architect. He specialized in restoring buildings and homes to their original condition. I couldn't help but wonder about the people who used to live and work in those buildings. I caught the history bug early."

"Which do you like better, teaching or doing research?"

"Teaching. I try to make history come alive, to give my students a taste of what it was like to live in the 1800s. They do a lot of studying outside the classroom. In fact, I just finished taking my rural Louisiana history class on a living history lesson."

"Yeah? To a place like Jamestown or something?"

"They wish." Kate gave a wry smile. "Every spring I take the class to an old fishing cabin in the swamp that has no running water, no electricity, no modern conveniences at all. The only concessions to the twenty-first century are insect repellant and toilet paper. For two days, the students have to catch and gather their own food, collect their own wood, haul their own water, cook their meals over a wood stove, etc. If they don't want to sleep on the floor, they have to collect Spanish moss and stuff their own mattresses with it. It gives them an appreciation of history that you can't get from a book."

"You sound like a really good teacher."

"I love what I do. I feel very fortunate to have a career I really care about."

"We're a lot alike that way," Zack proposed. "I feel the same way about mine."

Kate smiled. "Well, then, I'm sure you can understand why it's so important to me to make sure things are done absolutely right in this movie."

Hell's bells. He wasn't making any headway at all. Suppressing a scowl, Zack tucked several large bills inside the leather folder the waiter had left on the table.

At this rate, there was no way he was going to get her to sign that letter. If he could get a drink or two into her, though, maybe she'd loosen up enough to at least discuss a compromise.

"Let's get out of here and walk around a little," he suggested.

"All right," she agreed. "I'd love to show you some of our historic landmarks."

"But there's nothing really historically significant about Pat O'Brien's," Kate protested as Zack steered her down the narrow sidewalk two blocks away from Bourbon Street.

"Sure there is. It's a New Orleans landmark."

"If you want to see more landmarks, there are plenty others around. I haven't shown you the old U.S. Mint or Preservation Hall or . . ."

"I'm thirsty," Zack said. Besides, it was high time to change the way the evening was going. Kate had dragged him around the French Quarter for the last two hours, explaining the history of just about every building they passed. It was all very interesting, but it wasn't advancing his cause.

"There it is." Zack pointed to a rustic red brick building with a green and white sign that said PAT O'BRIEN—HOME OF THE FAMOUS HURRICANE.

"This is nothing but a tourist trap," Kate said.

"Maybe so, but it's a legendary tourist trap." Zack took her elbow and ushered her through the door, into a long, brick-lined foyer. Piano music and raucous laughter spilled out of a room on the right. "Are Hurricanes as good as everyone says?"

"I wouldn't know. I've never had one."

Zack's eyebrows rose. "You live here and you've never had a Hurricane? Well, that's an oversight we need to correct."

"I don't think . . ." Her voice was drowned out by the din as Zack steered her into the darkened barroom. The room vibrated with the sound of not one but two entertainers banging out "Way Down Upon the Swannee River" on matching copper-topped baby grand pianos. An elderly man stood on the stage between them, wearing thimbles on every finger and thumping on something that looked like a metal tray. To make matters worse, at least half of the patrons in the crowded room were belting out off-key lyrics, and the other half were attempting to talk over the ruckus.

Zack led Kate to a table near the stage, placed an order with a passing waiter, then sank down in the chair beside her.

"It's awfully loud in here," Kate remarked.

Pretending not to hear her, Zack scooted as close as possible, draped his arm across the back of her chair. "What did you say?"

The scent of soft perfume and herbal shampoo invaded his senses. Damn, but she smelled good. He could just bury his nose in her neck and breathe in her scent all night.

"I said they're awfully loud." Her breath on his ear sent a delicious shiver down his spine.

His hand fell from the back of her chair to her shoulder. "Yeah. Isn't it great?"

Great was not the word she'd had in mind, but the feel of Zack's hand on her shoulder eclipsed every other thought. Her pulse pounded in her head like syncopated sonic booms, and the music no longer seemed to be the loudest thing in the room.

It was ridiculous, the effect Zack had on her. Every time he touched her, her body went bonkers—and he seemed to touch her with alarming frequency. It must be an L.A. thing, she decided. People from the West Coast were just more touchy-feely than she was accustomed to.

A lot more flirtatious, too. If a local man had given her half as many come-hither looks as Zack had this evening, she'd think he was seriously interested in her. Which was absurd. Zack was probably one of those men who flirted with every woman he met.

The waiter returned with two tall, curved glasses topped with fruit and umbrellas, and set them on printed napkins on the copper-topped table. Kate breathed a relieved sigh when Zack removed his arm from her shoulder to pull out his wallet.

The crowd erupted into cheers and applause as the piano players mercifully drew their song to a close. When the roar receded to a rumble, Zack lifted his drink. "I propose a toast. Here's to making *Ooh, La La!* a blockbuster."

Kate lifted her glass. "To a blockbuster." She clinked her glass against Zack's, then took a teeny, tiny sip.

Zack's eyes reproached her. "Hey, you've got to drink the whole thing."

"I beg your pardon?"

"It's an old Hollywood tradition. You have to drink the whole glass after a toast. It's bad luck not to."

"But . . ."

Zack's brows knit in a stern frown. "You don't want to jinx the movie, do you?"

"Oh, come on. You don't believe in jinxes."

"Sure I do. Everyone in Hollywood is superstitious." He lifted his glass. "Come on, now. Drink up."

"But this is huge!" she protested. "And I don't handle alcohol very well. I don't think . . ."

Jake held up his hand, stopping her in mid-protest. "Don't worry. I ordered a virgin Hurricane as well as the regular kind."

"Oh. Well, that's different."

"Come on, then." He raised his glass and gazed at her expectantly. "Bottoms up."

What the heck—it couldn't hurt to comply with his silly superstition. She lifted her glass and clinked it against his again, then slowly downed its contents. She peered over the rim to make sure he was doing the same.

They set down their empty glasses at exactly the same time. Zack blew out a satisfied sigh. "Man, that was good."

Kate nodded. "Delicious. I can see why they're so popular."

"Want another one?"

"I don't think . . ."

"Oh, come on," he urged. "I'm going to have another. Don't make me drink alone."

What could it hurt? It was nonalcoholic. And it *was* awfully good. "Okay. That sounds lovely." Very lovely. In fact, the whole evening seemed to suddenly be taking on a lovely rosy hue, as if it were bathed in fairy dust.

Zack scooted back his chair. "Our waiter is nowhere in sight. I'll go place our order at the bar."

The room seemed to have gotten quite a bit warmer. Kate fanned herself with her napkin and leaned back in her chair. "All right-y."

Zack shot her an amused smile, as if she'd said something clever, then rose from the table. Kate leaned back in the green leather chair, feeling loose-limbed and relaxed, and watched him thread his way through the crowd.

He cut an impressive figure as he sauntered away—broad shoulders, narrow waist, and the sexiest tight-muscled tush she'd ever seen. The thought made her giggle out loud. Men's backsides were not the kind of thing she usually noticed.

It was funny—she'd always thought her sex drive was on the low end of the scale. Ever since she'd met Zack, though, it seemed to have revved into high gear. She'd always found sex to be disappointing, but being around Zack made her want to do some more research.

Uh-oh. She covered her mouth with a giggle. She wasn't supposed to think about Zack in sexual terms, but she couldn't remember exactly why not. She frowned, trying to gather her wisps of thought into something concrete.

Historical accuracy—that was it. Professional credibility. She was supposed to keep the movie factual, and whenever she thought about Zack in personal terms, she forgot about facts and drifted off into the most distracting feelings. She needed to stay clearheaded, and Zack made her feel all foggy and breathless.

She sure didn't feel clearheaded now. Her brain felt pleasantly fuzzy and blurred, as if everything was in soft focus. The only thing that seemed perfectly clear was that even from across the room, Zack was one heck of a hunk.

She wasn't the only person in the place who thought so, either. Several other women in the room were watching him, too, their eyes surreptitiously fastened on his profile as he waited, his foot on the brass bar rail, for the bartender to mix their drinks.

He didn't seem aware of the attention he was attracting. Maybe he didn't even know how good-looking he was. After all, men didn't praise other men for their appearance—not straight men, anyway. And the women Zack dated were all models and actresses, women accustomed to being on the receiving end of compliments, the kind who wouldn't say anything nice about a man's appearance because they were playing hard to get.

The piano players began banging out a rowdy version of "Dixie," and Kate turned her attention to the stage. At the next table two heavyset men wearing convention badges started belting out lyrics.

Kate's foot tapped under the table. Funny—she'd heard this song a million times, but she'd never before realized it was such a catchy tune. Her fingers drummed on the tabletop. Before she knew it, she was humming along.

Drinks in hand, Zack headed back to the table to find Kate singing at the top of her lungs, "Oh, I wish I waa-aas in the land of cotton . . ."

Zack winced. She had a voice like a strangled chicken, but that didn't seem to inhibit her in the least. She hadn't been kidding about having a low tolerance for alcohol.

He sat down hesitantly. "How are you doing?"

"Great. Come on—you should shing along to thish shong."

Oh, Lord. She was completely snookered. He felt a twinge of conscience and tried to reason it away. He hadn't lied to her, exactly; he *had* ordered one virgin drink and one regular one. What he'd failed to mention was that *he* was drinking the nonalcoholic one.

"Look away . . . look away . . . look awaaaay . . . Dischieland."

Hell—he'd wanted to get her relaxed, not completely blitzed. He'd never dreamed that one drink would affect her like this—especially after she'd put away a full meal. Well, one thing was for certain: She sure didn't need any more booze. He surreptiously shuffled the drinks on the tabletop, sliding the nonalcoholic one in front of her.

Kate caught him in the act. Narrowing her eyes, she wagged her finger at him. "Uh, uh, uh! I saw that."

"Saw what?"

"You tryin' to shwitch drinks on me."

"I was making sure you got the nonalcoholic one."

"Let's shee." She took a sip of the drink in front of her, then frowned. "Thish doeshn't taste like the last one." She leaned forward, drew the other Hurricane toward her, and took a long pull on the straw. "Ah! Thish one's more like it."

He watched her take another long slurp. Hell—from the way she was guzzling that thing, you'd think she was a camel that had just trekked across the Sahara. He'd intended to get her relaxed, not pickled. He couldn't ask her to sign the letter when she was in this condition. The moment she sobered up, she'd accuse him of trickery, and she'd be more opposed to the script than ever.

Kate stared up at the empty stage. "Oh, darn. The penises are taking a break."

Zack's lip twitched. "I, uh, think you mean pianists."

"Yeah." Kate gave an apologetic snicker. "Shorry." She reached for the drink again.

He had to get her out of here. "Why don't you show me the French Market?"

"It'sh closed at night."

"You can still show me where it is and tell me about it."

"Well . . . okeydokey."

At least she was a congenial drunk. She wobbled a little as he helped her to her feet, then bent forward and reached for her glass.

"Let's leave that here."

"But I want it. It's a shouvenir glass."

"It'll be a nuisance, lugging it around."

"No, it won't."

Zack sighed. "Well, then, I'll carry it for you." *And ditch it the first chance I get.* Holding her arm, he steered her out of the bar and onto the sidewalk, where a line of people waited to get into the place.

"I'm getting thirshty," Kate said a block later. "Can I have my Hurricane?"

He couldn't let her drink any more. Borrowing a scene from an old movie, Zack feigned a stumble and poured the drink on the pavement. Kate grabbed him around the waist, thinking he was about to fall.

"You okay?"

91

Her arm was warm and soft against him. Her eyes were that way, too—all concerned and worried. Looking into them did something funny to his chest. "Yeah. I stubbed my toe on a crack in the sidewalk, that's all."

"Maybe you had too much to drink."

Boy, was that the pot calling the kettle black. He grinned. "I'm all right."

"One of the shigns of being tipsy ish not knowing that you are."

"Is that a fact."

She nodded. The movement made her sway, and he put his arm around her to steady her. "That'sh why I don't drink."

"That's undoubtedly a good policy."

"Yesh."

Her hip bumped against his as they made their way down the sidewalk, away from the lights and noise, into a quiet part of the French Quarter. The delicious scent of her filled his nostrils, and he tightened his hold on her waist.

They turned onto a deserted street. Zack spotted a trash can and dropped in the glass.

"Hey—that was a shouvenir!" she protested.

"It was all sticky. I'll buy you another one."

She smiled up at him again. "You know, you're very gentlemanly."

"Is that a fact?"

"Yesh. Hash anyone ever told you that before?"

"Can't say that they have."

She nodded sagely. "I figured you didn't get many compliments. Want to know shomething else I bet no one's ever told you?"

"What?"

She stood on tiptoe and whispered in his ear, the words coming out in warm little puffs. "You have a very sexy tush."

He burst out with a laugh. Sheeze, she was wasted.

"It's true." Her eyes were bright and sincere. "And I'm not the only one who thinks sho. Half a dozen other women were ad-

92

miring your buns while you were shtanding at the bar."

"Gee, maybe I better check and see if I have a hole in my pants."

"No." She looked up at him, her eyes doing that honest, earnest, guileless thing again, as if it were important she convinced him. "They thought you looked good. You didn't shee them because they looked away when you turned around. Women do that, you know. Sho I got to thinking . . ."

Uh-oh. Any thinking in her current condition was bound to be warped.

". . . that maybe no one ever gives you a compliment on your appearance."

The corners of his mouth quirked upward. He wondered if she'd remember any of this in the morning. "Well, thanks for filling that void."

"Not that you don't *desherve* compliments," she explained. "I just figured everyone prob'bly thinks you're complimented all the time, sho they don't do it, sho they won't sheem like everyone else, but then you don't get any compliments at all because that'sh what everybody thinks."

"I can tell some deep thought went into this."

She nodded. "People that sheem to have everything lots of times don't, because other people don't give them things they think everyone else gives them. Sho shometimes the people that you'd think have plenty miss out on compliments and invitations and friendship and stuff."

She underestimated the suck-up factor in Hollywood as far as compliments and invitations went. But when it came to friendship, she was dead right. He had lots of acquaintances, but very few people he could actually call friends. There was no one he could just hang out with, no one to go with to a Lakers game or out for a beer.

He looked down at Kate as they strolled past an ornate, wrought-iron street lamp. The expression in her eyes was so warm and sincere that he got that tight, funny feeling again.

"Well, thanks. You've got some very attractive features, too."

93

"Don't feel like you have to return the favor."

"I don't. And anyway, I couldn't. You've had your tush covered by a jacket both times I've seen you."

"My tush is actually quite nice," she confided, her expression dead serious. "It's the rest of me that doesn't meet your shtandards."

"How do you know what my standards are?"

She lifted her shoulders. "You date very beautiful women."

"You're beautiful, too."

She made a snorting sound. "Nice try, but I know what I look like."

"Evidently you don't." He placed a hand on her face, tipping it to the side, then turning it back toward him. "You have beautiful eyes. They're kind of a cross between Gwyneth Paltrow's and Meg Ryan's and Bette Davis's in her heyday." It was absolutely true. Her eyes were huge and bright and expressive, rimmed with feathery dark lashes, and they were staring up at him, so wide and surprised that it made him grin. He moved one hand up and touched her cheek.

"Your skin is beautiful, too . . . soft and smooth and flawless." His finger trailed down her jaw. "And then there's the matter of your mouth." He ran the pad of his thumb over her bottom lip. Her mouth opened slightly. "Do you have any idea how many actresses spend big bucks on collagen injections, hoping to make their lips look half as sexy as yours?"

"My lips are . . . sexy?"

The total lack of guile in her voice made him smile. "Very."

He wasn't lying. They were sexy as hell. The lips in question tipped up in a pleased grin. Zack ran his thumb over them again, then lowered his head and covered them with his own.

Soft—soft as satin, as silk, as a cloud. The sensation washed over him, tugging at him like undertow. Damn, but her mouth was something—hot and Hurricane-flavored and incredibly, exquisitely textured.

He angled his head and deepened the kiss. With a little moan, she wrapped her arms around his neck and flattened her breasts against his chest. He slid his tongue between her lips, tasting her, exploring the inner softness of her mouth.

She moaned again and moved closer, standing on tiptoe to fit her pelvis against his. A painfully hard erection immediately strained against his fly. Damn, but her mouth was sweet. It had been a long time since a kiss had kindled this kind of fire inside him.

It was his last coherent thought. Standing on one leg, Kate wrapped her other leg around him. She gave a little moan and rubbed herself against him, and the next thing he knew, a blindingly hot, urgent haze of desire consumed him. He cupped her bottom and lifted her off the ground. Clinging to his neck, she curled her other leg around his hip, so that both legs were wrapped around his body.

Need flamed through him, searing off all rational thought. Carrying her, Zack lumbered forward and set her down on the hood of a white car parked at the curb. Her thighs climbed higher to lock around his waist, and she pulled him down as she lay back against the hood, all the while doing things with her lips that drove him wild.

His mouth mated with hers, his tongue plunging in again and again, doing to it what he ached to do with other, more intimate body parts. Her breath huffed out in hot little spurts, and hungry, whimpering sounds escaped from her throat. Her hands unlocked from his neck and wound around his back, reaching lower and lower until they tightened on his buttocks.

Dear Lord in heaven—she was driving him crazy. When she raised her hips to align herself more closely against his erection, he burrowed his hand under her waistband and caressed the soft, silky skin of her bottom, his fingers moving slowly across her skin. She didn't appear to be wearing any underwear, Zack thought hazily. No, wait—the professor was wearing a thong!

She moaned and tipped her hips higher, urging on his fingers. Zack was more than eager to comply. In fact, he was ready to rip off her slacks right then and there, and unzip his own, and . . .

He heard an odd click, and then Kate started glowing. He opened his half-closed eyes more fully. Kate wasn't lit up; it was the inside of the car.

"Look, Henry—there's someone on our car!" warbled a high-pitched woman's voice behind him.

Zack pushed himself up. Kate tried to pull him back down, tightening her legs around him.

"Hey, there—what do you think you're doing?" demanded a man's voice. Zack swiveled his head to see a gray-haired couple standing on the sidewalk beside the car. The man held a small remote control in his hand, which he'd apparently just flicked to unlock his Taurus.

Good God in heaven—what was he thinking, making out on the hood of a stranger's car on a public street? He must have taken leave of his senses. Kate's kisses had drained all the blood from his brain and funneled it to a part of his anatomy not known for level-headedness.

"We've got to move, Kate," Zack croaked.

She opened her eyes and gazed at him uncomprehendingly, like a person awakening from a trance. Zack disentangled her arms and legs from around him, pulled himself off the hood, then helped her to her feet. She swayed unsteadily. Zack put his arm around her to brace her.

"Sorry," Zack muttered to the gawking couple as he steered Kate toward the sidewalk.

"Get a hotel room, for God's sake!" the man snapped.

Kate stumbled on the curb as she stepped up to the sidewalk. Zack caught her before she fell.

The elderly woman planted her hands on her hips and glared at Zack. "You ought to be ashamed of yourself, taking advantage of a woman in that condition."

Zack tried to hustle Kate away, but she stopped and turned to the woman. "Whatta you mean, in my condition?"

"Why, you're falling down drunk!"

"Am not!" Kate bristled with indignation. "I don' drink."

"Don't argue with her, Hazel," the older man urged, opening

the passenger door and urging her in. "Let's just go."

Good idea. "Come on, Kate." Zack tightened his arm around her and urged her down the street.

"I can't believe she'd think that about me." Kate stumbled and pitched forward.

Zack caught her before she fell all the way to the pavement. "Shorry," she murmured. "I'm feeling a little dizzy."

You're not the only one, Zack thought. That kiss had made his head spin like Linda Blair's in *The Exorcist.* He was still reeling from the effects of it.

Just how the hell had it happened? He prided himself on his ability to stay in control. Somewhere along the line, though, he'd forgotten everything except the taste of her lips and the sweet heat of her body.

"I just lost my shandal."

"I'll get it for you."

Kate sat down on the curb as Zack reached for the shoe. A paper fell out of his jacket and floated to Kate's feet. Before he could reach for it, Kate picked it up. "What's this?"

Alarm skittered through him like a rat through a sewer. "Nothing." Zack stretched out his hand to take the paper.

But Kate was on her feet, staring at it, her forehead wrinkled. "It has my name on it."

Zack's stomach took a sudden dip. "It—it's just some paperwork."

Turning away from him, she lifted the paper up to the light of the street lamp.

Zack placed a hand on her arm, trying hard not to give away the sense of panic rising in his throat. "Come on now, Kate—"

But she was reading aloud. " 'Dear Mr. Goldman: After careful conshideration, I agree with Zack that adding a few fictional details would enhance the shtory without harming its integrity.' " Her brow knit in a hard frown. " 'The script has my full approval, and I will vouch for the movie's complete historical accuracy as we agreed. Shincerely, Kate Matthews.' "

She stared at him. "What's going on?"

Oh, hell. Zack lifted his shoulders and struggled to appear nonchalant. "It's nothing. Just something I wanted to have handy in case you changed your mind."

Kate rubbed her temple where a headache was gathering, trying to gather her thoughts as well. Why would Zack think she would change her mind? She'd told him that the movie had to be completely factual or she couldn't work on it.

And then the events of the evening crashed down on her, thudding heavily into place. The warm, giddy sensation that had made the night seem magical degenerated into stomach-twisting nausea. How could she have been so stupid?

"She was right," she murmured.

"Who?"

"That woman with the car." She fixed Zack with an accusing gaze. "I *am* drunk, aren't I?"

He shifted his stance and shoved his hand into his pocket, refusing to meet her gaze. "There's, um, no reason you should be."

Outrage flamed in Kate's chest. "Oh yes there is. You got me drunk sho you could make me sign this!" She waved the letter in front of him.

"Kate—it wasn't like that. I just wanted you to relax a little so we could discuss it. I never dreamed that one or two drinks would . . ."

Oh, dear Lord—that's what the kiss was about, too. Mortification flooded her soul. Mercifully, her sense of anger was stronger. "Everything about this evening was an attempt to get me to sign that letter."

"Kate, it wasn't like that."

"Oh, please." Kate's hands knotted at her sides. Anger must have burned the alcohol out of her system because she no longer felt the least bit inebriated. Instead, she felt furious. "It's bad enough that you made a fool of me. Don't make it worse by lying."

"I swear, Kate, it wasn't like that. I didn't mean to get you drunk."

"Yeah, right." Kate turned and started to walk away, only to realize that Zack was still holding her sandal. She whipped back around and held out her hand. "Give me my shoe."

"Not until you hear me out."

"No way." Kate yanked off her other sandal and strode barefooted toward St. Peter Street.

Zack hurried after her. "Kate, I'm sorry. Here. Take your shoe."

Kate snatched it from his hand but didn't pause to put it on.

Zack strode beside her on the sidewalk, his gait almost crablike as he turned his body toward her. "Come on, Kate. At least let me take you home."

"I'm not getting in a car with you." Her voice shook with anger. "Heaven only knows what you'd try next. Besides, you've been drinking."

"Actually, I haven't."

She whipped around and glared at him, her hands on her hips, a sandal in each hand. "Great. Just great. You got me drunk as a skunk while you stayed nice and sober." Kate raised her hand to hail a passing taxi.

"Oh, hell—it wasn't like that, Kate. You make it sound so smarmy."

"That's because it *is* smarmy. And I'm sure Mr. Goldman will think so, too."

Zack's heart plummeted to the sidewalk. "If you'd just let me explain . . ."

The cab stopped. Carrying her shoes, Kate stalked barefoot across the street and climbed in.

Zack followed her. "Kate—wait!"

She slammed the door in his face. He stood and watched as the cab turned at the intersection and disappeared from view.

Just like his career would, if Kate called Goldman.

"Damn it all," he muttered. How had he managed to screw

things up so badly? And there was no way to fix it tonight. She was too angry to listen to reason.

Oh, Lord. He could only hope she wouldn't call Goldman while she was still half-drunk. He'd give her a chance to cool down, then go see her first thing in the morning. He'd throw himself on her mercy and beg forgiveness. He'd grovel at her feet, if that was what it took. He'd do anything—anything at all—to keep her from making the call that would end his career.

Chapter Seven

Steam drifted off the coffee cup in Ruth's hand, fogging the middle pane of her kitchen window. Plucking a paper towel from its holder on the gray counter, she wiped it away and peered across the street, squinting against the morning sun. It was eight o'clock, and no one had stirred at Kate's house yet. Kate's Sunday paper was still in the driveway.

Ruth's newspaper was still outside, too, lying on her front lawn beside the flowerbed that blazed with hot pink azaleas. When Pete was alive, he used to go out and bring it in, and they'd spend cozy Sunday mornings poring over it, reading interesting tidbits aloud to each other, talking and laughing over hot beignets and coffee. Dear heavens, how she missed her husband! Twenty-one years had gone by, and she still longed for their Sunday morning ritual.

The plastic bag around the thick, folded paper glistened with dew, beckoning her in the sun. Ruth longed to go out and get it, but first she'd have to shower and get dressed. She refused to set foot outside until she was fully clothed. She'd hate to be kidnapped or murdered in nothing but her pajamas and her old terry-cloth robe. You never knew what might happen when-

101

ever you set foot out of your home. Crazy people were everywhere—crazy people and criminals. All you had to do was turn on the TV or read the newspaper to know it. The news was filled with crime stories—murders, rapes, armed robberies, burglaries, assaults, car-jackings. They happened every day, often in places that appeared safe, to people who least expected it. It was a dangerous world. She hadn't realized just how dangerous.

She wished she could convince Kate to take more care. Kate ran around oblivious, staying out till all hours, taking all kinds of chances. Just last night she'd come home in a taxi. Had she stopped to think that the taxi driver might be a serial murderer? Of course not. The possibility hadn't even entered her mind.

Ruth shook her head and took another sip of coffee. Zack Jackson had promised to take good care of her, but had Kate stayed with him? Noooo. She'd apparently stormed off on her own after they'd had some kind of disagreement. Kate had come home looking rumpled and upset, and she'd refused to tell her mother anything.

A movement out the window caught Ruth's eye. She rapidly set down her coffee cup and reached for the camera around her neck, then lowered it again. It was just Kate's next-door neighbor, Mr. Hendrix, waddling down his front stoop in blue-and-white-striped pajamas so tight his pale belly gleamed through the button gaps. He reminded her of a fat walrus, with his portly build and drooping gray mustache. The nasty-looking thing completely covered his upper lip and half of his bottom one, and most of the time it looked like he'd just used it for a soup strainer. She wondered how his wife could stand to kiss him.

She used to love to kiss Pete. Ruth closed her eyes and let the memories wash over her. She'd loved the way his jaw had always felt just a little bit rough after he'd shaved. And the gentle way he'd sometimes tug on her lower lip with his teeth—that had always made her melt. And the look he'd get in his eyes when they were making love—so hot and tender and intimate and intense . . .

Ruth abruptly opened her eyes. Unfolding her arms, she

picked up her coffee cup and stared back out the window, trying to will away the stab of pain in her chest. Pete had been dead for twenty-one years. After all this time she should know better than to allow her thoughts to drift in that direction. People had told her that the memories of him would comfort her, but they were wrong. The sweeter the memories, the more they hurt.

She watched Mr. Hendrix bend down to pick up his newspaper, his bald head glaring in the sun like a tanning bed reflector, and she deliberately focused her thoughts on the here and now. Mr. Hendrix certainly wasn't very observant, Ruth thought disapprovingly. Why, he didn't even look up when a gray minivan drove by. For all he knew, it could have been filled with terrorists pointing machine guns at him. He might have been mowed down right in his driveway, wearing nothing but those ridiculous, too-tight pajamas.

Well, it would serve him right. Mr. Hendrix was president of the neighborhood watch association, yet when Ruth called him about suspicious cars prowling the streets or bogus-looking plumbing trucks in people's driveways, he never did a darn thing. In fact, he'd had the nerve to tell her that unless she saw someone actually waving a gun, forcing a door, or breaking a window, he didn't want her to bother him anymore.

"Idiot," Ruth muttered as she watched him shuffle back toward his house. By the time any of those things happened, it would be too late.

Prevention—that was the key. And the only way to prevent becoming the victim of a crime was to practice constant vigilance.

Ruth curled her fingers around the coffee cup and sighed. She hadn't always felt so vulnerable. Back when Pete was alive, she'd always felt safe and secure.

Boy, had she been naïve. Back then she hadn't known how life could turn on a dime, how suddenly everything you took for granted could just be swept away. One moment her biggest worry was what to fix for supper. The next, she'd found herself a widow with a young child to raise, terrified that something awful was lurking around the corner, ready to snatch her child away, too.

Well, she wasn't naïve any longer. Now she knew that every breath was tentative, every heartbeat precarious, every good-bye potentially final.

A large black SUV turned into Kate's driveway. Fear, heavy and smothering and all too familiar, seized a stranglehold on her, making it impossible to breathe. She reached for her telephone, and then she remembered that it was the vehicle Zack had been driving last night. Ruth placed a hand on her chest and murmured a prayer of thanks.

She watched Zack open the door, climb out, and stride purposefully up the porch steps. What was he doing at Kate's so early on a Sunday morning? And what on earth was that dark red thing in his hand? Ruth grabbed her camera and peered through the telephoto lens to get a better look.

Oh, my goodness—flowers! He was carrying a bouquet of red roses. They were the kind they sold in grocery stores—wrapped in cellophane, with a small packet of flower preservative visible through the thin plastic. It was probably the only place one could purchase flowers on a Sunday morning.

"Well, well, well," Ruth muttered with a smile. A man didn't show up at a woman's house at the crack of dawn on a Sunday morning with red roses after a business disagreement. The argument must have been personal—very personal, if the roses were any indication.

Kate and Zack Jackson. Ruth lowered the camera and picked up her coffee cup, her lips curving in a smile. What an interesting turn of events. Ruth had been wanting Kate to get out and see people. Of course, she wanted her to do it during the day in a safe part of town, while taking every possible precaution and remaining aware of who was around her at all times, but she did want Kate to have a social life. Her daughter was too young to spend all her time holed up at her office or at home. To Ruth's way of thinking, Kate was missing out on the best part of life.

Kate needed a husband, and maybe another child or two. Ruth had seen the way she looked at babies. Just the other day, a young woman had been pushing a stroller down the sidewalk while Kate worked in her front yard flowerbed. Kate had sat back on her heels and watched them, her eyes wistful and sad, until they turned the corner and disappeared from sight.

Kate was usually standoffish with men, but she was different around Zack. Maybe he'd be able to climb the wall she'd built around her heart after that no-good jerk she'd run off with had broken it into a thousand pieces. Ruth didn't know the whole story, but when Kate had come home from New York, she'd been like a Coke bottle flattened by a bulldozer. Time had melted down the pain and reshaped Kate into a new woman, a woman who was smarter and stronger and tougher, but Kate's recycled life lacked a key element: a loving relationship with a man. She said she had no time for it, but Ruth knew better. Kate made no space for it.

And it was all Ruth's fault. Guilt pressed down on her chest like a trash compactor. If she hadn't been so restrictive, Kate never would have left. She'd only wanted to protect her child, but it had all backfired. In trying to shelter her daughter, she'd driven the girl away.

Of course, it was impossible to entirely regret the whole episode, because Skye had come out of it. The thought of her granddaughter brought a soft smile to Ruth's lips. That child was a handful and a half—bright and creative and curious, and full of a youthful sense of invincibility. More and more, as Skye grew older, she needed the steadying influence of a father figure. She'd certainly taken to Zack.

Wouldn't it be something if things worked out between Zack and Kate?

After all, Kate had always had a thing for him. Kate thought Zack was out of her league, but she underestimated her own appeal. When Kate let her hair down, both literally and figuratively, she was a beauty.

Maybe Zack was just what she needed to drag her out of her

rut. Of course, he lived in California, and if anything serious developed between them, that meant Kate and Skye would probably move, but love would overcome obstacles like that. And there was no reason Ruth couldn't move with them.

Ruth turned the coffee cup in her hand. She'd read that Zack was a committed bachelor, but that didn't mean anything. All men were committed bachelors until they found the right woman. Pete had been like that when Ruth had first met him. Her lips turned up at the memory. It was funny, the way love could change what a man thought he wanted.

Ruth watched Zack punch the doorbell. He ran a hand through his hair, then shifted the bouquet from his right hand to his left.

He looked anxious—nervous, almost.

Ruth grinned. Good. If he was nervous, that meant he cared. In all too many relationships, there was a Carer and a Caree. That had been the case in Kate's first relationship; Ruth was sure of it. Although her daughter had never said so. Kate had never said anything about Wayne, though, and she looked so emotionally pained whenever his name was mentioned that Ruth had never pressed. All Kate had ever said was that things hadn't worked out. It made Ruth's heart ache, the way her daughter's bright eyes dimmed whenever the subject arose. Whatever had happened, it had wounded her so deeply that to this day, Kate wouldn't talk about it.

Well, she was going to have to talk about it soon, though. Skye's curiosity about her father was intensifying every day. What kind of man could have a daughter and not want to see her? Kate had assured Skye that her father loved her—that the only reason he didn't come around was because he was angry with Kate—but Ruth didn't buy it. No disagreement in the world would have kept Pete from *his* child. No, there had to be more to it than anger with Kate, but Ruth tried hard not to pry. She'd driven her child away once, and she didn't want to do it again.

Ruth took another sip of coffee and watched Zack fidget on

Kate's porch. It was funny, how Kate would take risks with her physical safety but guard her heart like Fort Knox. To Ruth's way of thinking, Kate had it all backwards.

Zack punched the doorbell again. Kate had said she was an early riser, so he'd come over as soon as the sun was up. He'd barely slept a wink all night for worrying about her calling Goldman.

He owed her an apology—big time. He couldn't believe how badly he'd mismanaged the situation. Not only had he misjudged Kate and her tolerance for alcohol, but he'd practically made love to her on the hood of a car on a public street, then let her see that blasted letter. He couldn't blame her for thinking he was a lower life-form than plankton.

She was unlikely to believe the truth: he'd only intended to get her relaxed, not blitzed. It was even more unlikely that she'd believe he hadn't intended to convince her to sign the letter while she was drunk. And as for that kiss . . . What the *hell* had he been thinking?

He hadn't been thinking—that was the problem. The explosiveness of Kate's response had knocked him for a loop. When she had wound her legs around him, his brain had quit functioning and lust had taken over. Pure, hot, hungry, unbridled lust.

His behavior bewildered him. She had an excuse—she'd been drunk. What was his excuse? He never lost control—especially not in public. Even in bed, he prided himself on his restraint and self-control, on his ability to ensure that his partner had as good a time as he did.

What was it about this woman that sent him into such a frenzy?

It probably wasn't even anything about her; it probably was just the fact that he hadn't been with a woman in several months, and he had a backlog of hormones just rarin' to go.

He'd chalked his lack of libido up to a preoccupation with work. He'd been pouring all his energy into trying to save his career from the big trash heap in the sky, and he figured he was just too stressed out to have much interest in sex. Now that his career was back on track, it was natural for his sex drive to return as well.

Well, the doc was exactly the wrong person to release it on. His mind must be playing some sort of masochistic trick on him, making him lust after an uptight, suit-clad bun-headed brainiac intent on ruining his career.

He'd made a terrible mistake, and he was here to plead or beg or do whatever it took to convince her not to call Goldman. He prayed that she hadn't already done so.

Zack glanced at his watch and wondered if he'd come too early. Kate was likely to have one hell of a hangover this morning. Maybe she was sleeping in. Maybe this wasn't the best time to pay a call. Maybe he should come back later.

He'd decided to do just that when the door squeaked open. Skye stood in the doorway, wearing a bulky yellow terry-cloth robe over blue flannel pajamas and huge pink slippers that looked like lop-eared bunnies. Her face lit in a big grin. "Hey!"

"Hey, yourself. Is your mother up?"

"Sure. She's in the shower." Skye stepped back and opened the door wider. "Come on in. Want some Froot Loops?"

"No thanks. But I'd take some coffee if you have any."

"I think we still have some. Mom made a full pot this morning, but she's been gulping it like crazy. She said she had a headache."

I bet she does. Zack followed Skye's bunny feet into the kitchen. The girl opened a cabinet and pulled out a mug printed with the message YOU'VE GOT TO KISS A LOT OF TOADS TO FIND A PRINCE. She handed it to Zack, then gestured to a Mr. Coffee machine on the white formica counter. "Help yourself."

"Thanks." Zack set down his tissue-wrapped bouquet.

Skye picked it up and sniffed the roses as Zack poured his coffee. "Did you and Mom have a fight or something?"

Zack's fingers tightened on the cup handle. "Why? Did she say we did?"

"No. But you're bringing her roses . . . and when I asked her if she had fun last night, she said she didn't want to talk about it, and her face got all weird."

"Weird, how?"

"Well, her brow got all frowned up and her mouth got pinched and her eyes looked like they were shooting lasers or something."

Not a good sign. Zack poured himself a cup of coffee. "Do you happen to know if she made any phone calls last night or this morning?"

"I don't know. Why? Who do you think she might have called?"

"Oh, nobody."

"Grown-ups." Skye rolled her eyes. "And you guys think kids are weird."

Zack grinned and took a deep sip of coffee.

Skye hopped up on the counter and dangled her bunny feet. "So, did you talk Mom into letting me be in your movie?"

Oh, no. He wasn't going to get into *that* discussion again. "That's between you two. I was out of line to make the offer without clearing it with your mother first."

"You've *got* to talk her into it. She won't listen to me."

"What makes you think she'd listen to me any better?"

"She likes you."

"Don't bet on it," Zack muttered.

"Skye, have you seen my black bra?" called a familiar voice from the hallway.

Zack saw Kate at the same moment she saw him. They both froze. He heard her sharp intake of breath—or maybe it was his own. She stared at him, her lips parted.

Zack stared back. She was clad in a green towel and apparently nothing else. Her hair was wet, her face was pink and freshly scrubbed, and her legs . . . Zack swallowed. Good Lord. Her legs were enough to give a man hot chills and cold sweats. Long and slender and smooth, they had a soft sheen to them, as if she'd put some kind of lotion on them. The mirror in the hallway behind her afforded him a view of her back. Her shoulders had that sheen, as well. The thought of Kate slathering lotion all over her naked body made it suddenly hard to breathe.

"What are *you* doing here?" Kate demanded, taking a step back and drawing the towel tighter around her.

He jerked his eyes away from her legs. "I, uh, came by to apologize."

"I knew it!" Skye crowed triumphantly. "I *knew* you guys had a fight!"

"Kate, we need to talk," Zack said.

Her spine grew straight and her chin stubbornly tilted up. "There's nothing for us to talk about."

"Oh yes there is."

"I disagree. And this is a most inopportune moment."

Christ. Who said things like "most inopportune"?

"In case you hadn't noticed," Kate continued, "I happen to be half-dressed."

Zack couldn't help but grin. "Oh, I noticed, all right."

"Sheeze, Mom, you're nowhere *near* half-dressed," Skye chimed in. "Heck, you're not dressed at *all!*"

Kate shot her a near lethal look.

"Why don't you throw on some clothes and I'll take you somewhere for coffee," Zack suggested.

"What's wrong with the coffee here?" Skye asked.

Kate's eyes flashed at Zack. "I thought I made myself clear. I have nothing to say to you, here or anywhere else. Now, if you don't mind, I'd like you to leave."

"Mom, that's rude!"

"Stay out of this, Skye. This doesn't concern you."

"But you always told me there's no excuse for rudeness. And you said that if I have a disagreement with a friend, we should try to talk things out. You're breaking two of your own rules."

Kate's gaze faltered. Zack could see her wavering between setting a good example and sending him packing.

Skye shot him a surreptious look, then turned back to her mother. "If you don't take your own advice, why should I?"

Oh, man, the kid was good. Kate was beginning to cave.

"You know, Mom, I always try to follow your example," Skye added.

Kate heaved a defeated sigh. "Oh, all right." The look she fired at Zack said she was only doing this under duress, and that she didn't intend to give an inch. "Let me get on some clothes."

"You're forgetting something, Mom." Skye ducked into the laundry room and reemerged with a lacy black bra dangling from her finger. Stretching it out like a slingshot, she fired it across the room.

Kate reflexively reached out to catch it, loosening her grip on the towel. She clutched it as it unwound, barely managing to keep her front covered. The bra landed at her feet.

Skye took one look at her mother's murderous expression and gave a sheepish grin. "Well, I guess I'll go get dressed, too." The girl hurried past her mother and down the hall, the fluffy tail on the back of her bunny slippers flopping with every step.

"Here. I'll get that," Zack said. Stepping forward, he bent and picked up the lacy bra. As he straightened, he realized that the hallway mirror gave him a perfect view of Kate's naked backside.

Good Lord. He froze, unable to move, completely transfixed by the reflection. She was a work of art, all fair skin and sculpted curves. The smooth expanse of her back nipped in to a slender waist, then flared provocatively to gently rounded hips and a perfect, peach-shaped bottom.

Kate gingerly reached for the bra. It took all his willpower to pull his eyes from the mirror and hand it to her.

"Thank you." Her tone was cold enough to cause frostbite. Clutching the bra along with the towel, Kate rapidly backed down the hall, careful to keep her front toward him, unaware that he'd already gotten an eyeful.

And what an eyeful it was. Zack braced both his hands on the counter after she'd gone and drew a ragged breath. It was ridiculous, the way Kate aroused him. He'd bedded some of the most gorgeous women in the world. He'd calmly directed totally nude actresses in steamy love scenes. So why did a forbidden peek at the professor's fanny stir him like nothing had in years?

Kate reappeared in the doorway less than five minutes later, wearing blue jeans and a black knit top, her damp hair cascading to her shoulders in fat, moist curls. She looked a lot different with her hair down, Zack thought. Younger. Prettier. More accessible.

Zack wondered if she was wearing that lacy black bra under her shirt, then immediately scowled at the thought. He had to cut this out. Thinking along those lines had gotten him into this mess in the first place. He jammed his hands into the pockets of his chinos. "Can we go somewhere and talk?"

Kate's chin tipped up to an obstinate angle. "Whatever you've got to say, you can say right here."

A clomping sound heralded Skye's descent down the stairs. She appeared in the kitchen, wearing an orange T-shirt emblazoned GIRLS RULE. BOYS DROOL.

Plopping into a chair at the breakfast table, her gaze swiveled from Zack to her mother and back again. Her eyes were bright and expectant, as if she were waiting for a World Federation Wrestling match to begin.

"Skye, why don't you go clean your room?" Kate suggested pointedly.

"I cleaned it yesterday. It doesn't need it."

"Well, your closet does."

"Aw, Mom! You're just trying to get rid of me."

"Bingo."

"Why can't I ever stay for the good stuff?" Skye's chair screeched on the tile as she reluctantly scooted it back.

She huffed out the door of the kitchen, but the sound of her footsteps stopped in the hallway.

"It's rude to eavesdrop," Kate called. "Go on upstairs."

"Aww!"

Zack listened as the girl clunked up the stairs. "Are you sure you don't want to go somewhere else?"

"I'm sure."

"Well, then, I'll get right to the point." Zack pulled his hands out of his pockets and drew a deep breath. "Kate, look—I apologize. I acted like a jerk."

She folded her arms across her chest. "No kidding."

"It was never my intention to get you drunk."

"Right." Scorn dripped from her words. "I suppose that alcohol jumped in my drink all by itself."

"I know it looks bad, but honestly, Kate, I never intended to get you loaded. I just thought a drink or two might help you unwind."

She arched an eyebrow. "My, aren't you considerate."

"Come on, Kate. You were all rigid and uptight, and you wouldn't even consider a compromise. I thought that if I could just get you to relax . . ."

She fixed him with an icy glare. "That what? I'd relax my standards? Or did you think you'd have to take me to bed to accomplish that?"

Christ, she made him feel like subterranean worm larvae. He shoved his hand through his hair. "Kate, it wasn't like that," he said for the millionth time.

"No? Well, then, perhaps you'd like to explain exactly what it *was* like."

Zack shifted his stance uneasily and weighed his options. If she suspected he was B.S.-ing her again, she'd never give him another chance. He had to level with her. "Okay—I admit that I thought that maybe if we flirted a little and had a good time, it would be easier for us to talk things out and reach an agreement."

"So you got me drunk and put the moves on me."

"No!" This wasn't going well. Not at all. He was trying to tell the truth, but the truth sounded so . . . sleazy. He blew out a breath between his teeth. "Look, maybe it sort of started out that way. But damn it, Kate—that's not how it ended up. When I kissed you . . ."

113

She stared at him, her gaze cold enough to freeze cryogenic holes in him.

He swallowed hard. "Look—I didn't expect things to get all out of control like they did. I didn't count on the chemistry that . . . that I . . . that we . . ." He shoved his hands into his pockets again, then abruptly pulled them out. "Dammit, Kate—there was a certain biological response that I couldn't have faked if I'd wanted to, and you know exactly what I'm talking about."

She knew, all right. She'd been shamelessly rubbing against it. Kate felt her face flood with heat as memories, vivid and tactile and excruciatingly detailed, rushed in. The sweet-salty taste of Zack's mouth. The delicious weight of his body pressing her back against the hood of that car. The clean, soapy, shaving-cream scent of his skin. Never in her life had she experienced anything like the sensations Zack had stirred in her last night—pleasure and hunger and a need so all-consuming that she'd lost track of time and place.

And then, when she'd seen that note, she'd felt sick with humiliation. She'd lain awake most of the night, castigating herself for being such a fool, wondering how she could have been taken in so easily. Her world had temporarily stopped turning on its axis, but for him, the whole episode had been nothing more than a calculated attempt to get her to sign off on his script.

And yet, he had felt *something*, because he'd unquestionably been aroused.

"From the way you're blushing, I gather you know what I'm talking about," Zack said.

It was true—he couldn't have faked his physical response. The kiss might have started out as an intentional ploy, but it had rapidly turned into something more—on his part as well as hers. The thought cheered her immensely.

All the same, his behavior was inexcusable. She eyed him sternly. "All I know is that you've tried to bribe me, you've lied to me, you've deliberately gotten me drunk, and you've tried to

114

emotionally manipulate me. I obviously can't trust you." She tightened her arms across her chest. "I don't see any way we can work together."

He took a step toward her. It was all she could do not to step back. The closer he got to her, the harder it became to think.

"Come on, Kate," he said softly. "Give me another chance."

She shook her head. "Too late. Your chances are now officially over."

His body tensed. "You mean you've already called Goldman?"

"No, but I'm going to—as soon as it's a decent hour in California. I'm withdrawing from the project."

He took another step toward her, his eyes pleading. "Please, Kate—don't." He placed his hands on her upper arms. His thumbs caressed her skin. "This movie is my last chance. My whole future hangs on it."

How could she form a coherent response when he was touching her like this and gazing into her eyes with such an imploring expression? He was using that coercion-by-seduction trick again. Well, it wouldn't work a second time.

Kate pulled away. "My future hangs on it, too. I'm up for tenure, and if this movie is inaccurate, I won't get it. There's a good possibility I could even lose my job."

"You hadn't told me that."

"You hadn't asked."

He looked at her with open chagrin. "I don't want you to lose your job." His gaze was so direct, his voice so sincere, that she almost believed him.

"I think it would be best for everyone if I just withdraw from this project."

"If you do that, Goldman will cancel the whole movie."

Did the man never run out of ploys? It irritated her that he thought her so gullible. "That's ridiculous."

"Yeah, I know."

"Mr. Goldman could just hire another historian. Why would he cancel the whole film?"

"Beats the hell out of me. For some reason, he's got it in his

115

head that you, and only you, are the key to marketing this film. He made hiring you a condition of funding the movie."

You're the key to marketing this film—the words sounded eerily familiar. Oh, dear—that was exactly what Mr. Goldman had said to her!

"You're the top authority in the country on this stuff," the elderly man had rumbled through the phone in their initial conversation, "and you've got a real nice, intelligent, respectable kinda look goin' on. No one can do this but you."

At the time, Kate had thought the movie mogul was just flattering her. Now she wasn't so sure.

"Yep, if you back out of your contract, Goldman will dump the whole project." Zack rubbed his jaw and cast her a rueful look. "I'll be washed up in Hollywood, and everyone who signed up to work on this movie will be out of a job."

It was unfair, the way he was laying all this guilt on her—but she already knew Zack didn't fight fair. She blew out an exasperated breath. "I'm not going to pretend something is factual when it isn't. And I didn't sign on to work on a film that's half fact, half fiction."

"I understand. And I was wrong to try to get you to." He looked like he meant it. He wore a remorseful, hang-dog expression that weakened her resistance. "But the other side of the coin is, Marvin won't approve the script if it doesn't have any drama in it."

Frustration boiled inside her. "I started looking through the records to see if I could find some actual events to put in the script, but you didn't give me time to find anything."

"You've got time now," he said quickly. "I'll use anything you come up with. Heck, even a dogfight would be better than nothing."

Could she trust him? He certainly looked sincere, but then, he'd been an actor.

The real question, she thought reluctantly, was whether or not she could trust herself. Zack had amazing powers of persuasion—as was shown by her even considering this offer!—

and he could make it awfully tempting for her to twist the truth.

"Give me another chance, Kate." He took a step toward her, his eyes dark and imploring. "I promise we'll do things your way from here on out."

Oh, mercy—she wanted to believe him. She longed for the opportunity to bring Joe and Sadie's story to life, to prove Compton wrong, to do such a great job that she'd sail through the tenure process. And there was another reason, a reason she could barely bring herself to acknowledge: She wanted to spend time with Zack.

"One more chance." She fixed him with her sternest look. "But that's it. If I get the slightest hint that you're trying to double-cross me or rewrite history, I'm finished."

"Thanks, Kate." Grinning widely, he hauled her against his chest in a tight embrace. "Thanks."

The faint roughness of his jaw against her cheek, the clean male scent of him, the hard warmth of his chest—a slew of impressions invaded her senses. He pulled back just far enough to look down at her. His eyes were warm and smiling, and she found herself smiling back.

His hands slid down her arms. The moment stretched and lengthened, and his smile deepened into something else. Kate knew she should step back, but her feet seemed cemented to the floor. The next thing she knew, he was bending down, and his lips were on hers.

Sweet. Hot. The two sensations registered simultaneously as his mouth moved over hers. His hands strayed to her back and he drew her flush against him, flattening her breasts against his chest.

It was happening again—that exciting, swirling, warm, melting, drifting sensation, that sense of being transported somewhere else, to a place where nothing mattered but being close and getting closer. His mouth moved over hers, gently at first, then surely, more intimately, pulling her under until she was drowning. His hand slid slowly, slowly down her spine. The universe was shrinking to just the span of his arms around her.

Her muscles seemed to have melted and her thoughts were slow and fuzzy. She was vaguely aware that her sense of reason was drifting away. If she didn't grab it soon, it would float right out of reach.

She called upon her last remaining shred of logic and pulled away. "I-I don't think this is a good idea."

"I think it's an excellent idea." Zack's eyes were gleaming in a way that sent hot shivers racing through her.

Space. She needed to put some space between them or she'd succumb to him again. She abruptly turned and crossed the room under the pretext of getting some water. Her hand shook as she opened the cupboard and pulled out a glass. "We need to lay down some ground rules if we're going to work together."

"Such as?"

"No more of . . . that." She waved her hand, then turned and filled her glass at the faucet. "It's a bad idea to mix business and pleasure."

Zack leaned against the counter and gave a slow, seductive smile. "I've always found them to be perfectly compatible."

Kate shook her head. "I don't want to cloud my judgment or jeopardize my objectivity."

"You think I make you less than objective?"

"I know you do."

"Come on, Kate. There's some incredible chemistry between us."

"That's exactly the problem."

Attraction pulsed between them for a long, tense moment. At length, Zack let out a sigh. "Okay," he said reluctantly. "You make the rules. I'll keep my distance until you tell me otherwise."

"Don't hold your breath."

"Too late, Kate." His lips curved in a smile that turned her joints to jelly. "I already am."

Chapter Eight

"I have to book the pyrotechnics company by this afternoon or they're not going to be able to meet our timeline." Zack's executive assistant drew her eyebrows together over her close-set eyes, making her pug nose wrinkle. "I need to know if we're going to want them or not."

Zack sighed. Deb not only looked like a bulldog; she was as tenacious as one. Usually that was a positive quality. As his assistant, she handled the mechanics of making arrangements, and it was her job to nail things down. Her constant nattering about all the unresolved issues on this film, though, was driving him crazy. He didn't need any more reminders that things were out of control. "We'll know by this afternoon."

Deb tucked a stringy lock of limp hair behind her ear and peered down at the clipboard propped against her ample belly. Zack headed across the hotel suite, hoping to escape any further badgering, but she trailed after him. "The indemnity insurance people want a rundown of all the equipment that we need covered."

Zack stopped and refilled his cup from the coffeemaker at the bar. "They'll get one."

"They need it tomorrow."

"All right, all right."

"Deb's not the only one who needs some answers," piped up Andrea from her perch on a barstool. The forty-something location scout with the anorexic body and expensive choppy haircut scowled over the lipstick-stained rim of her Pellegrino bottle. "I can't believe that history freak is making us change the brothel location."

"I'm more worried about cutting the action scenes." The film's director of photography, Fritz Gibson, looked up from the script he was studying by the window. With his gray ponytail, grizzled bear, professional wrestler physique, and propensity for wearing Harley Davidson t-shirts, he looked more like a member of Hell's Angels than one of the best cinematographers in the world.

The best, in Zack's opinion. It was just a matter of time before Academy Award nominations started raining down on the man like water from a shower massage. Fritz had a gift for knowing just the right angle, just the right lighting, just the right way to shoot a scene for maximum effect. He was also one of the nicest people in Hollywood, although few people knew it because he was as reclusive in his personal life as he was demanding on the set.

"I was really looking forward to shooting that riverboat explosion," Fritz said.

"Me, too," Zack admitted.

"We've got way too many loose ends to be just three weeks out." Deb trailed after Zack as he paced the room. "We've cut things close before, Zack, but this is really making me nervous."

"You're not the only one," Zack muttered. "We don't even have a script."

"Hey! I revised it like you asked." Rich lifted his head from his prone position on one of the sofas. "Have you looked at the latest draft?"

"Yeah."

"And?"

"It sucks. Big time."

Rich folded his hands behind his head and smirked. "Told you."

The little weasel resented having his work tampered with, so he'd deliberately made the script as lame as a three-legged dog, Zack thought darkly.

"It's not my fault," Rich continued. "I was working with less than nothing. Lizzie Borden did less damage to her parents than the professor did to my script."

Zack raised his hands. "All right, all right. Hopefully she'll bring us some usable stuff when she gets here."

"Since when does a technical adviser start calling all the shots?" Rich asked.

"Yeah," chorused the others.

A nerve ticked in Zack's jaw. "Since Marvin Goldman said so."

"So when is this Historian from Hell coming by?" asked Andrea.

"Sometime this morning. She said on the phone that she'd uncovered some great events."

"Oh, I can hardly wait," Rich sneered. "What do you think she's found—a quilting bee or a tea party?"

Great. On top of everything else, the crew seemed ready to either mutiny or make Kate walk the plank. Zack sighed. "Come on, Rich. She said it was exciting."

Rich gave a scornful grunt. "The professor wouldn't know excitement if it jumped up and bit her on the butt."

"Give her a break. When you get to know her, she's really—"

"—a sanctimonious, time-warped, fusty-musty geckette who can't tell a movie plot from a burial plot," Rich cut in.

Snickers and groans filled the room.

"The professor's such a tight-ass, I bet her butt cheeks have lockjaw," Rich continued.

Deb gave a discreet cough and cut her eyes meaningfully toward the door. Zack turned around. Oh, hell. Kate stood in the doorway, wearing the stunned expression of someone who'd just been slapped.

Zack's stomach sank. This was not the fresh start he'd hoped for. "Kate!" He strode toward the door, forcing a wide smile. "Come in, come in. We've been expecting you."

"So I heard." She stepped into the room and gave Rich a dry smile. "I'm no authority on anatomy, Rich, but I believe that lockjaw of the posterior is a physical impossibility."

Zack shot the writer a withering look, then turned back to Kate. "Pay no attention to him. He's suffering from lockjaw of the brain. Let me introduce you to everyone." He took Kate's arm and steered her into the room. "This is my assistant, Deb. She's a one-woman wonder who keeps track of about a million things simultaneously."

Kate smiled and held out her hand. "It's nice to meet you."

"Likewise." Deb's eyes clearly said otherwise. She looked at Kate with a mixture of distrust and dislike, and reluctantly gave Kate's hand a single, unenthusiastic pump.

"Nice T-shirt," Kate said. "You must like animals."

Deb glanced down at her oversized shirt, emblazoned with the words ANIMALS ARE PEOPLE, TOO, but she didn't rise to the conversational bait. "Yeah," she muttered, looking down at her clipboard.

Zack waved his hand toward the photographer. "That's Fritz by the window. He's our director of photography."

Fritz lifted his hand like a wooden cigar Indian.

"And this is our location scout, Andrea."

Kate smiled. "Hello."

Andrea rose from the barstool and smoothed her tight black slacks, looking Kate up and down with dismissive disdain. "I understand you don't like the location I selected for the brothel."

"It's not a matter of not liking it," Kate said, her expression earnest. "It's a lovely house. It's just not representative of Storyville."

Andrea's lipsticked mouth curved in an expression that could only be described as a sneer.

"Well, let's get started, shall we?" Zack waved a hand toward the conference table.

Zack pulled out a chair for Kate as the others made their way to the table. Seating himself in front of his laptop computer, Zack watched Kate extract a stack of papers from her enormous Mary Poppins bag. Her hair was pulled back, but not as tightly as before. Little wisps escaped at her temple and at the nape of her neck in a way he found very appealing. No chance of seeing a flash of leg today, he noted with disappointment. She was again wearing a pantsuit, this one in severe gray. She looked scholarly and professional, and her expression was all business. So why did he feel an odd buzz of attraction?

He must be getting kinky, he decided dourly, opening his laptop. Next thing he knew, he'd develop a thing for elderly women in nun's habits.

"So, Kate," he said when everyone was seated, "you came up with some authentic events for the script?"

"As a matter of fact, I did."

Rich sniffed haughtily. "Little old ladies knitting doilies won't quite fit the bill."

She cast Rich a patient smile. "Doilies are crocheted, not knitted."

"Oh, pardon *moi*." Rich rolled his eyes. "That will be *much* more exciting."

"That's enough, Rich." Zack flashed him a warning glance, then turned back to Kate. "Tell us what you've got."

Kate lifted her first piece of paper and held it up, as if she were presenting Exhibit A to a jury.

"This is a photocopy of an 1898 newspaper," she said. "As you can see, there's a front-page story about a fire at a New Orleans bank that summer."

"So?" Rich demanded. "We need events that can be tied to Drago."

Kate ignored him, keeping her gaze on Zack. "The fire was

123

arson. The bank had turned down Drago's request for a loan to construct two new brothels—and the banker's wife was the leader of a local ladies' group trying to shut down Storyville."

Zack leaned forward. "So Drago torched the bank?"

"The police could never prove it, but everyone was sure he was responsible."

"A fire." A surge of adrenaline filled Zack's veins. "Hey, that's not bad. That's not bad at all." He glanced at Fritz. "What do you think?"

The older man grinned. "I think you're back in business."

Zack nodded, an expansive sense of relief filling his chest. This was exactly the kind of big action he was looking for. And staging a fire would cost half as much as the riverboat stunt.

"This is great. What else have you got?"

Kate picked up the next set of papers. "Well, Drago owned racehorses, and he wasn't above tipping the odds in his favor. That summer he staged an off-track race between an untried filly and a champion racehorse from Kentucky. The Kentucky horse stumbled and broke a leg. After the race, it was discovered that a series of holes had been dug on the inside bend on the last stretch. Drago's people claimed they were gopher holes, but observers noticed that Drago's rider steered clear of that spot, even though it was the shortest route."

"What happened to the hurt horse?" Deb asked, creasing her forehead like a worried pug.

"It had to be shot."

"Wow, that's terrific!" Zack exclaimed.

Deb stared at him, horrified. "Not about the horse," he quickly added. "I mean it'll make a great scene."

"Hey, I know a trainer who specializes in horses." Fritz chimed in. "They know how to die like nobody's business. It'll make you think they're doing the death scene from *Romeo and Juliet*."

"Great. Give his name to Deb." Zack turned and beamed at Kate. "Way to go, kiddo!"

Rich gave a derisive sniff. "We still don't have a chase scene."

"Actually, we do." Kate lifted the last set of pages in front of her. "I found an incident in the police ledger about a wild chase through the French Quarter. Apparently two of Drago's thugs tried to shake down a man who owed some gambling debts. He ran upstairs and out a window, and they chased him from balcony to balcony. The man ducked into the bedchamber of a young lady. She screamed bloody murder and her father ran in, brandishing a revolver. The man raced back out onto the balcony, where the thugs cornered him. Desperate to escape, the man jumped and broke both legs. The two thugs carried him away. The man's body washed up on the riverbank twenty miles downstream two days later."

"Wow," breathed Deb.

Zack pushed back his chair and rose, his pulse pumping with excitement. "Kate, this stuff is great!"

Rich's chin rose to a belligerent angle. "It won't translate into a script nearly as well as the original events."

"Yes, it will," Kate replied.

"Oh, so now you're a screenwriter?" Rich demanded.

"No, but . . ." Kate stopped and looked questioningly at Zack.

"But what?" Zack prompted.

Kate threw Rich an apologetic look. "Well, I put the information I have into scene format and inserted it into the script where I thought it should go, and . . ."

"Oh, great." Rich threw his hands in the air.

Zack ignored him and kept his gaze focused on Kate. "Let me see."

She dug into her bag, pulled out the script, and handed it over. Rich tapped his pencil in a rapid, impatient stacatto on the table while Zack perused it.

After a few moments, Zack looked up and grinned. "Hey—this isn't half bad. Not bad at all. Take a look, Rich." He slid the script across the mahogany table toward the writer.

Rich flipped through the pages, his lips pursed like a drawstring bag. "You're right, Zack—this isn't half bad." His tone sharpened to outright disdain. "It's completely *dreadful!* It's drek. It needs a total rewrite."

"Well, then, you'd better get to it."

Rich snatched up the script and the photocopies and stalked huffily out the door. "If anybody needs me, I'll be in the bar drinking strychnine."

Kate frowned worriedly as she watched him go. "I didn't mean to step on Rich's toes."

Zack shot her a surprised glance. After all of Rich's rude remarks, she was worried about hurting his feelings? The professor sure had a generous nature.

"Hey, you did him a favor. You'll have goaded him into doing his best work." Zack looked around the table. "And speaking of work, let's get to it. Deb, get the name of that animal handler from Fritz and see if he's available. And we'll need a flammable prop for the fire scene. Get with Kate about what the bank exterior looked like and get it out to bid."

Deb nodded and bustled away. Zack turned to the sullen brunette. "Andrea, we'll need sites for these new scenes."

"City Park is perfect for the horse race," Kate volunteered. "And I know just the spot in the French Quarter for the chase scene."

"Terrific! Take Andrea to see them. And show her the place you have in mind for the brothel exterior while you're at it."

Zack scrolled down his laptop. "Let's see . . . while we're on the topic of locations, where are we on the scene where Joe takes Sadie to a cabin in the swamp for the night?"

"I've a found a site at Lake Pontchartrain," Andrea said.

Kate's eyes grew dismayed. "But the lake is nothing like a swamp!"

"We'll make it work." Andrea waved a manicured hand dismissively.

"But there aren't any fishing cabins like the one Sadie described in her diary."

Andrea shrugged. "So we'll rig one up. That's the magic of Hollywood."

126

"But wouldn't a real one be better? I can take you to an authentic cabin in a real swamp."

"Where?" Zack asked.

"About an hour and a half drive from here, near Houma. You have to take a pirogue or an airboat out to it, but it's the perfect setting."

"Sounds horribly inconvenient," Andrea said.

"What's the cost of renting this place?" Zack asked.

"Nothing."

"Nothing?"

"Actually, it belongs to me. It used to be my grandfather's."

"Is this the place you were telling me about, where you do your—what did you call them?"

"Living history lessons. Yes, this is the place."

"We could save a lot of money if we didn't have to build a set," Zack said thoughtfully. "I think we should take a look at it."

"If you want, we could stay overnight and turn the trip into a mini lesson," Kate offered. "It would give you a better idea of what life was like for Joe and Sadie. All of you could come."

"That's not a bad idea." Plus it had the bonus of reassuring Kate that he was serious about adhering to historical accuracy from here on out. "Fritz is leaving this afternoon and Deb is tied up here, but Rich, Andrea and I can go. Set it up."

"I'm afraid I can't make it either," Andrea said quickly. "I have to be in L.A. by Saturday morning."

"This is just Wednesday." Zack looked at Kate. "Can we do it tomorrow?"

Kate nodded.

"All right, then. Tomorrow it is." Zack pushed back his chair and looked at Kate. "Can I see you a moment?"

"Sure."

Kate followed Zack through the tiny vestibule and into the room on the other side. It was a bedroom—a bedroom dominated by an unmade king-size bed. The thought of Zack sleeping between

127

those rumpled white sheets made her stomach do a funny flip. She wondered what he wore to bed. Probably nothing. He didn't look like the type for pajamas.

Not that it was any of her business, she silently reprimanded herself.

Zack closed the door and turned toward her. "Kate—that stuff you found is great. It's better than the fiction Rich wrote in the first place. I owe you an apology. I really underestimated you."

The look in his eyes warmed her. She lifted her shoulders in an embarrassed shrug. "We lucked out."

He took a step closer. He was near enough that she could see the pupils of his eyes, see the individual whiskers on his chin. "I'm so happy I could kiss you. Too bad I promised I wouldn't."

His mouth was still smiling, but his eyes darkened, and the heat in them sent a fevered chill through Kate's muscles. "You could still kiss *me*, though," he murmured.

The memory of how his mouth tasted, how his body felt, how his skin smelled, poured over her in a sudden rush. The air between them seemed to sizzle with possibilities. He was standing close, so close that it would only take one step to be flush against him. Then she could reach up and pull down his head and . . .

And what? Have a three-month fling? She had a hard enough time thinking straight around him as it was. How much worse would it be if she were sleeping with him?

And then there was the fact that the press would be swarming around once the shoot got underway. The university would have a cow if one of its professors made tabloid headlines for having an affair with a Hollywood celebrity.

Not to mention how it would undermine her credibility as the watchdog of historical accuracy.

There were too many reasons that this was a bad idea. She drew herself up and put her hand on the doorknob, then mustered a cocky smile. "In your dreams, Jackson."

"I'll see you there, all right."

Unfortunately, Kate was afraid she'd see him in hers, as well.

Chapter Nine

Ruth gave a sigh of relief when she saw her daughter's car pull into the driveway, then she rapidly ducked away from the window before Kate caught her watching. Her daughter scolded her for worrying so much, but Ruth couldn't help it. Worry held her like the strings of a marionette, limiting her movements, controlling her actions, jerking her emotions up and down. A single thought obsessed her whenever Kate and Skye were away from home: What if they never came back?

She just couldn't rest easy when they were away. They couldn't live their lives locked up at home; Ruth knew that, and when she thought about it rationally, she didn't want them to. She wanted them to be safe, but she also wanted them to experience the best life had to offer—love and joy and a sense of accomplishment, a sense of belonging to the world and making a contribution to it. She wanted their lives to be wonderful, as wonderful as hers had been before Pete died.

But she couldn't keep from worrying, and couldn't keep from feeling an extraordinary sense of relief whenever Kate or Skye returned home. She heard the garage door close and busied herself at the stove, a wooden spoon in her hand, as Kate walked through the kitchen door.

"Hi, honey," Ruth said, replacing the lid on the pot and turning around. "How did things go today?"

Kate hung her black bag and keys on a wall hook by the door. "Depends on which things you're asking about." She inhaled a deep breath of spice-scented air. "Mmm. Something smells good. What are you making?"

"Jambalaya."

"Yum." Kate crossed the kitchen and lifted the lid on the large pot simmering on the stove. "Looks delicious."

Ruth watched her daughter pull a spoon from the drawer and dip it into the fragrant mixture of rice, spices, sausage, chicken, and shrimp. "So, did Zack like the new information you found?"

"Yes." Her face lit with a wide smile. "In fact, he loved it."

She ought to smile like that more often, Ruth thought. Kate was beautiful when she smiled. She was too serious for her own good.

"That's wonderful, honey."

Kate nodded and slipped the spoon in her mouth. "Mmmm. So is this jambalaya."

"So, what happened that *wasn't* so wonderful?"

"The whole rest of the day." Kate put the spoon in the sink, leaned against the counter, and sighed. "I spent it with the location scout, and she found fault with every single site I suggested. The places she wants to use are picturesque enough, but they're not representative of the time period."

"Oh, dear."

"You can say that again. And her attitude is horrible. She resents the heck out of me."

"Why?"

Kate lifted her shoulders. "I guess she thinks I'm taking over her turf and telling her how to do her job."

"So, how are you going to handle it?"

Kate gave a rueful grin. "By taking over her turf and telling her how to do her job."

Ruth laughed.

"She wants to use Lake Pontchartrain as a swamp setting. Can you imagine?" Kate shook her head. "She said they'd build a fishing shack and make it look authentic, but from the sketches she showed me, her idea of a fishing shack is more like a lodge. So I convinced Zack to take a look at Granddad's place. It'll be much more authentic than anything they could rig up, and it'll cost less money."

The fishing cabin. She and Pete used to go there all the time. They'd spend long lazy weekends there, fishing and playing poker and just soaking up the beauty of God's creation.

Kate opened a drawer and pulled out three blue-and-white-checked placemats and napkins, then crossed the room and placed them on the table. "That reminds me, Mom—will you look after Skye tomorrow night?"

"Of course." Anxiety started its ugly crawl up Ruth's skin. She struggled to keep it out of her voice. "You've got plans?"

Kate nodded. "I'm taking the scout, the screenwriter, and Zack down to the camp to spend the night."

Fear clutched Ruth in a tight fist, the way it always did when Kate went on an overnight trip. "Do they know how primitive it is?"

"That's the whole point. I'm giving them a living history lesson."

"No telling what criminals and outlaws might be hiding in the swamp, Kate."

Kate gave her one of those looks, the kind that said she was going to do what she darn well pleased and Ruth might as well save her breath. "We'll be just fine. Skye and I have never had any problems, and I've never had a problem when I take a class. You used to go there all the time, too, and you never saw a bogeyman, did you?"

"The world's a lot more dangerous than it used to be. For all you know, some fugitive from justice might have broken into the cabin and is living there right now."

Kate opened the flatware drawer and pulled out three knives, forks, and spoons. "Jean-Pierre's been looking after it, Mom. I called him today and he said it's in great condition. In fact, he's meeting us at the dock and taking us to it in his airboat."

Jean-Pierre was a Cajun fishing guide who lived near the cabin with his wife, Marie. Ruth smiled at her old friend's name. "How is Jean-Pierre? And how's Marie?"

"He sounded good. He said Marie is as fat and happy as a blue crab."

Ruth laughed. "He always knew how to flatter a woman."

Kate placed the flatware at each place setting. "He said they both miss seeing you."

Ruth absently tore a leaf of romaine lettuce into a brown ceramic bowl, her thoughts drifting back. When Pete was alive, the two couples had enjoyed many an evening together on the fishing porch, eating gumbo or fresh-caught catfish, playing cards and laughing at Jean-Pierre's tall tales.

"Marie would love for you to come for a visit," Kate said. "When this movie's over, maybe you and Skye and I can go down to the camp for a weekend."

"Oh, I don't know, Kate." Ruth ripped the lettuce harder and faster. She hated the thought of leaving her home unguarded for a whole weekend. She had a high-powered alarm system, but that would only thwart a stupid burglar. A clever crook could easily disarm it.

Her home was her refuge. Truth be told, her home and Kate's house were becoming her whole world—the only places she felt relatively safe and secure. She'd gotten to the point that she hated to even go to church or the grocery store or the post office, although she forced herself to do so. Those were about the only places she went alone anymore, unless she needed to pick Skye up or drop her off somewhere.

It was funny; she could go out if Skye or Kate were along, but if she went out by herself, she sometimes had awful spells. Terror would clutch her in its claws and squeeze her until she couldn't breathe. Her heart would beat so hard and fast that it was a wonder it didn't bruise her ribs, and her head would feel light enough to float away. A couple of times she'd actually passed out.

"It would do you good to get away, Mom," Kate said.

"Get away from what?" Ruth said brightly. "I've got everything I need right here."

"You know what I mean." Kate gave her a pointed look that made Ruth feel as if she were the child and Kate were the parent. "You need to get out more."

Kate didn't know about the spells, and Ruth didn't intend to tell her. Kate already thought she needed to see a mental health therapist.

And she didn't. There was nothing wrong with her. Absolutely nothing.

Ruth realized she'd shredded the lettuce into confetti. "Speaking of getting out, Kate, you need to get Skye out of her room. She's been holed up in there since she got home from school."

Kate's brow furrowed with concern. "Is something wrong?"

"She dragged in with the longest face and saddest eyes you've ever seen. I asked her what was wrong, but she didn't want to talk about it. She just wanted to be left alone. She didn't even want any homemade chocolate chip cookies."

"Uh-oh. If she's passing up your cookies, she's in a really bad way." Kate set down the last fork and turned toward the door. "I'd better go up and see her."

Funny how life came around full circle, Ruth thought as her daughter headed for the stairs. Now it was Kate's turn to deal with a recalcitrant child. It wouldn't be easy, trying to guide Skye through the awkward, stormy teenage years ahead, trying to protect her without driving her away.

She only prayed that Kate could do a better job of it than she herself had.

Kate knocked softly on her daughter's bedroom door. "Skye?"

"Go away," came the muffled response.

"Honey, I'm worried about you. Can I come in?"

Silence. Kate hesitantly opened the door and eased into the dim room. The last rays of sunlight streamed through the dormer window, illuminating the poster of Britney Spears that hung on the yellow wall, between posters of 'N Sync and the Back Street Boys. Skye lay sprawled across the daisy-print comforter on her bed, her face hidden by her arm. The mattress squeaked as Kate sat down beside her. "What's the matter, honey?"

"Nothing."

"Looks like a mighty sad nothing." Kate soothingly stroked the girl's dark hair. "Did something happen at school today?"

Skye lifted her shoulders.

Kate interpreted the gesture as a yes. "Want to talk about it?"

Skye shook her head, her face still buried against her arm.

"You'll feel better if you get it off your chest," she prompted gently.

"No, I won't."

Kate's hand moved through Skye's hair, her fingers sifting through the silky strands. She'd stroked her daughter's hair like this many times over the years—to soothe her when she skinned her knee, to reassure her after a bad dream, to console her after her guinea pig died. Up until now, Kate had always been able to calm and comfort her, but Skye was growing beyond her ability to help. She was bigger now, and she moved in a larger world. Her hurts were bigger, too—too big to be soothed away by her mother's touch.

Kate's hand stilled on her daughter's head. She couldn't force her way into Skye's confidence. She'd have to wait to be invited. "Well, I'm here for you if you want to talk."

"I don't. I just want to be left alone."

"Okay." Kate rose from the bed and headed across the room. She was about to pull the door closed behind her when Skye burst out in a sob and abruptly rolled over. "Tiffany's having a sleepover tomorrow, and all the girls in my homeroom class are invited except me!"

"Oh, sweetie." Kate quickly crossed the room and gathered her daughter in her arms, her heart aching.

"Not that I would have gone to her dumb old party anyway," Skye blubbered. "But I wanted to be *asked*."

Kate rocked her child, searching for the words to comfort

her, feeling completely inadequate in the face of her pain.

"Nobody likes me," Skye sobbed. "I'm just a big fat loser."

"Oh, honey, that's not true." Kate held her close, inhaling the soft, familiar scent of her hair. Skye's best friend had moved away two months ago, leaving Skye the only girl in the gifted class. She'd felt left out and lonely ever since. "There are so many wonderful, lovable things about you! You're bright and funny and kindhearted and beautiful . . ."

"Oh, yeah, right." Skye's tear-choked voice dripped with sarcasm. "That explains why everyone treats me like toenail fungus."

"Baby, you've got to give people a chance to get to know you. Sometimes you act all aloof and defensive, as if you don't need anybody, and that pushes people away."

"That's because I don't want them to think I care what they think."

"But what you're doing, sweetheart, is rejecting them before they can reject you," Kate said softly.

Skye stared at her mother for a moment, then fresh tears sprouted in her eyes.

"I don't know how else to act."

"Don't act at all, honey." Kate stroked her hair. "Just *be*. Be yourself, and stop worrying about projecting an image."

Skye gave an inelegant sniff. Kate grabbed a box of tissues off Skye's nightstand, and the girl blew her nose. "I wish I could start over somewhere else. I wish I could go live with my father."

"Honey, you know that's not an option."

"You just don't *want* it to be an option." Skye's eyes were red and accusing. "You don't want me to see him."

Guilt clutched at Kate's gut, and her heart thumped hard. "That's not what we're talking about here."

"You *never* want to talk about him."

"Right now, honey, I'm concerned about *you*. And a change of location won't change the things that are bothering you. You need to change the way you relate to people."

"How can I relate when no one wants to talk to me? Once

135

you're labeled a nerd, no one ever gives you a chance to prove you're not. The only thing that's cool about me is my dad."

A sharp pang of fear stabbed Kate's heart. She struggled to focus her thoughts as Skye twisted her tissue into a paper tornado. "Well, sweetie, maybe you need to find some opportunities to get to know some girls outside of school."

"How am I supposed to do that?"

"You take up an activity and get to know some kids who have the same interest."

"You mean like soccer or basketball?"

"Exactly."

"Come on, Mom! You know I'm a klutz at sports."

"There are things beside sports. There's debate team, or French club, or you could take ballet lessons . . ."

Skye rolled her eyes. "Give me a break!"

"There's the school chorus . . ."

Skye stuck her finger in her mouth and made a retching sound.

"Well, what about drama club?"

Skye's eyes lit up momentarily, then her shoulders sagged again. "It's too late. They've already assigned all the roles for the spring play and they've been in rehearsals for weeks."

"Well, maybe that's something you can do next year."

Skye's eyes filled with fresh tears. "So, what am I supposed to do in the meantime?"

"Honey, the world is your oyster. What do you want to do?"

"Be in Zack's movie." Skye looked at Kate, her eyes hopeful. "That would be *so* cool—maybe even cool enough to un-nerd me with the kids at school!"

Apprehension shot through her. "Skye, sweetie, it's always a bad idea to do things just to impress other people."

"I'm not. This is something I really, really, really want to do. I'd want to do it if everyone in the whole world thought it was geeky." Skye's eyes were bright and hopeful. "Please, Mom? Pleeeeease?"

Kate hesitated. Having a small role as an extra would probably be good for Skye's self-esteem—and there was no real reason not to let her. No reason at all, except that Skye's father had been an egocentric jerk who longed for the spotlight, and Kate hated the thought of Skye following in his footsteps.

All right," Kate relented. "But you're not going to miss more than two days of school, and you'll have to make up any schoolwork you miss."

"Deal!" Skye jumped off the bed, her eyes bright, her face excited. "Oh, I can't wait. This will be the coolest thing I've ever done in my life." Skye twirled around the room, then squeezed Kate in a big hug. "Thanks, Mom. You're the best mom in the whole wide world!"

Would that it were so. Kate's heart ached as she returned Skye's hug. When Skye was younger, she'd felt pretty competent in the motherhood department. Lately, though, she'd felt more and more like a clueless neophyte. A gulf was widening between them. Kate knew that separation was a necessary part of the growing up process, but she hadn't known how it would hurt.

How much worse would it get when Skye learned the truth about her father? Kate's palms grew damp at the thought. She couldn't continue to hide it much longer. How on earth was she going to explain to her daughter that everything she'd ever been told about her dad was a lie?

Chapter Ten

"Ow!" Andrea whirled around and glared at Rich as she stepped aboard the small airboat Thursday afternoon, her hand covering her just-slapped shoulder. "What the hell are you doing?"

"Killing a mosquito the size of an Apache helicopter." The writer climbed onto the boat behind her. "There are two more on your right leg."

Andrea bent to swat them, lost her balance, and stumbled forward, causing the boat to rock like a cradle.

"Christ!" Rich lurched onto the long bench that ran the length of the small boat and gripped the side of the craft, his face as white as his knuckles. "Don't drown me just because I'm trying to keep you from catching malaria!"

"Watching the two of them is like watching an episode of 'Gilligan's Island,' " Kate murmured to Zack from the dock.

Zack shot her a grin. "Yeah, except the characters on that show managed to actually board a boat."

Kate laughed. During the long drive from New Orleans, she'd found herself increasingly attracted to Zack. They shared similar taste in books and music, and an easy bantering rapport.

All of which made it harder to keep a professional distance.

When she was near him like this, she was acutely aware of his every gesture, every glance, every body part. The light dusting of masculine hair on the back of his hands, the muscle of his jean-encased thighs, the hint of dark hair at the unbuttoned collar of his maroon polo shirt—everything about him fueled her growing sense of attraction.

"Seet down, *cherie,*" Jean-Pierre told Andrea. The swarthy fishing guide with a dark, contiguous eyebrow stood at the front of the boat, wearing dirty jeans, a blue-and-yellow plaid shirt, and red suspenders. "Gators bite worse zan mosquitoes."

Andrea promptly plunked herself beside Rich, her eyes wide and terrified. Rich's face paled another shade. "Are there really alligators in this water?" he asked.

"*Mais oui.* Many, many gators."

Rich swallowed audibly. "Can they get in the boat?"

Jean-Pierre's dark eyes nearly disappeared in his creased face as he grinned. "Not unless eet teeps over."

"Which is practically impossible, since it's flat-bottomed." Kate stepped into the boat and sat on the bench opposite Andrea and Rich. "Jean-Pierre loves to tease."

Andrea slapped at another mosquito and muttered a most unladylike word.

"You should have put on insect repellant like Kate suggested," Zack said as he climbed aboard and lowered himself beside Kate.

"I refuse to cover my body with toxins," Andrea retorted.

The muscular Cajun grinned. "You prefer to be covered with mosquitos, *cherie?*"

The brunette gave a haughty sniff. "I would *prefer* to be someplace less bug-infested."

And I'd prefer you quit complaining, Kate thought. Andrea had complained throughout most of the road trip, citing reason after reason why the lake location she'd selected was superior to a real swamp. It was the same song and dance they had heard about every other site Kate had suggested. Andrea was deliberately making things difficult, and Kate was tired of it.

139

"Where are the life jackets?" Rich demanded.

"Don' worry. Zee water, eet ees not deep." The Cajun grinned, showing several missing teeth. " 'Sides, zee gators would eat you before you could drown."

Rich's face took on a greenish tint.

Jean-Pierre unlashed the rope from the mooring, then jumped back in the boat. A second later, the engine rumbled and the large fan on the back of the boat whirred to life.

"Aren't there any seat belts?" Rich called out over the noise.

"No. But don' worry—I don' lose too many passengers."

Kate leaned forward reassuringly. "He's joking."

Rich grimaced. "Yeah, well, I hope he's not waiting for a call from Leno."

The boat began to move forward. "Watch out for low branches," the guide called. "And snakes. Sometimes zey drop out of zee trees."

"Another joke?" Rich asked.

Kate hesitated. "Well . . ."

"Oh my Gawwd," Rich groaned. He slid off the seat and cowered on the bottom of the boat, covering his head with his arms.

"It's very rare," Kate said, leaning forward and patting Rich's back.

Jean-Pierre guided the boat into a clear stretch of open water, then gunned the engine, making conversation nearly impossible. The small craft skimmed across the top of the bayou. Rich hunched toward his knees in crash position, while Andrea held on to her hair as if it were a hat about to blow off.

Zack stretched his arm along the back of the bench, just grazing Kate's back. The touch made her heart rate quicken.

Rich and Andrea were maddening, but Zack was the one who was driving her crazy.

Zack shifted on the bench and glanced at Kate. She was casually dressed in jeans and a denim-blue chambray shirt, and her hair was pulled back in a ponytail. Tendrils of it had blown free, and the loose strands waved around her face. Her cheeks and lips were rosy from the wind, and in the outdoor light, her eyes were as blue as the Caribbean on a sunlit day.

It was funny—the more he was around Kate, the more beautiful she seemed. He didn't recall thinking she was gorgeous when he first met her, but now he wondered how he could have overlooked it.

The airboat slowed and quieted as Jean-Pierre guided it into a narrow bayou overhung with Spanish moss–draped branches.

"It's lovely, isn't it?" Kate asked.

It sure is. But Kate was talking about the swamp. Zack pulled his eyes away from her face and studied his surroundings. "This is incredible."

It was even better than he'd imagined. He mentally started planning shots—the old, weathered trees with vines and Spanish moss dangling from their limbs like Christmas tinsel. The fat clump of purple irises jutting out of the water. Green and white water hyacinth floating on the still, black water. They could put a stationary camera on the solid land to the left, and a camera in a boat, to give the feeling of movement. Fritz could open the scene with something really creative—a tight shot on a reflection in the water or something. Fritz would have a field day out here.

"Look over there." Kate pointed to a knobby brown tree stump. As he watched, what had appeared to be the top of the stump lifted off and flew away.

"What was that?" he asked.

"A brown pelican. Louisiana's state bird."

"Wow, he was really well camouflaged."

Kate nodded. "Just about everything in the swamp is like that. You have to look beyond the obvious to see what's really there."

A lot like Kate, Zack thought.

"See those knobby things sticking up from the water?" Kate asked. "Those are cypress knees."

"What are they for?"

"They help the trees get oxygen. They're part of the root system."

"They'll look great on film." In fact, this whole place would look great on film.

"Oh, my Gawd!" Andrea clutched her chest with one hand and pointed to the left with the other. "There's a giant rat swimming over there!"

Kate smiled. "That's not a rat. It's a nutria. And that thing that looks like a stick is a heron."

"This place has unbelievable wildlife shots," Zack said.

"Speakin' of wildlife, a beeg gator eez right beside us." Jean-Pierre pointed to the water.

"Where?" Rich's voice was tinged with panic.

Zack peered off the side of the boat. "All I see is a submerged log."

"That log is the gator," Kate explained. "The front bump is his head. If you look closely, you can see his eyes."

"Son of a gun," Zack murmured.

"The next lump is part of his back, and the last one is his tail."

"You weren't kidding about how things are camouflaged out here." Zack gazed over the side of the boat. "How big is he?"

"Prob'ly seex or seven feet," Jean-Pierre volunteered.

The alligator slid underwater as the boat went past. Rich's face turned a lighter shade of pale. "How much longer until we get to dry land?"

"We're nearly there," Kate said. "The cabin is just around the next bend."

"Thank heavens." Andrea scratched first one arm and then the other. Large red welts dotted her skin. "I can't wait to take a cool shower."

Kate gave her an apologetic smile. "Oh, I'm afraid there's no running water at the cabin."

"What?"

"We have a cistern to catch rainwater, and there's a pump about a quarter mile away."

"There is a bathroom, isn't there?"

"Well, there's an outhouse."

The look of horror on Andrea's face made Zack grin. He quickly suppressed it.

"Actually, an outhouse was a luxury a hundred years ago," Kate said. "Most folks made do with the woods or a slop bucket."

Andrea closed her eyes and shuddered.

Kate pointed to the right. "There's the cabin now."

A weathered shack with a rusty tin roof stood on stilts at the end of a rickety dock, looking no more stable than a pile of toothpicks. It spoke of poverty and a hard life. It looked primitive and rustic and worn. It looked . . .

"Perfect," Zack murmured. "It's perfect."

Kate beamed. "I thought you'd like it."

"I didn't realize you wanted such a rundown shanty." Andrea's defensive tone was tinged with disdain. "I suppose it'll do for an exterior, but I doubt we can use the inside."

Zack shrugged. "If we can't, we'll shoot that part in a studio. That's what we've planned anyway."

Jean-Pierre turned off the engine and let the boat glide to the dock. The quiet was so deep it was jarring.

"Listen," Zack murmured.

"I don't hear anything," Rich said.

"Exactly." As his ears grew accustomed to the silence, though, Zack realized it was far from complete. The titter of birds, the buzz of insects, the gentle lap of water against the hull of the boat filled the humid, heavy air with nature's music.

Jean-Pierre expertly threw a rope onto a weathered wooden post, pulled it taut, then climbed out of the boat, extending his hand to help his passengers onto the dock.

"I unlocked zee place theez morning, and Marie, she swept it out," he told Kate as he helped her onto the rickety dock.

"That was very kind of you." She set her large duffel bag on the rough bench, unzipped it and pulled out a bottle of fine bourbon. "I brought this for you and Marie for all your help."

Jean-Pierre's eyes lit up as she handed it to him. "Oh, merci! But you shouldn't have."

"If he doesn't want it, I could sure use a snort." Rich looked at the cabin with undisguised dismay. "You expect us to spend the night in *this*?"

"Sure," Kate said. "Come on. I'll give you the grand tour." She gestured toward the tiny stretch of boards rimmed by a rough-hewn rail that jutted out over the water. "This is the fishing porch. It's where we'll catch our supper."

"Are you sure it's not where the alligators will catch theirs?" Rich asked.

Kate smiled. "It's several feet above the water. You'll be perfectly safe." She led the way through a plank door into the dim cabin. A primitive table with two benches sat at one end, next to an old wood-burning stove and a rustic cupboard filled with tin plates and cups. A lumpy bed covered with a faded quilt sat against the far wall.

Zack looked around, taking in the uneven floor and the tin ceiling. A thrill raced through him, the way it always did when he anticipated shooting a perfect scene. "This is terrific."

Andrea sniffed. "It's awfully dark."

"That's good," Zack replied. "We can light it just the way we want."

Andrea sat on the bed and gave a test bounce. "This is a horrid mattress."

"It's better than most were back then," Kate replied. "It's made of Spanish moss instead of horsehair."

"Where are the other bedrooms?" Rich asked.

"There aren't any. We'll sleep on the floor."

"In sleeping bags?" Andrea's carefully plucked eyebrows rose in alarm.

"No, they didn't have those back then. We'll gather Spanish moss and stuff mattress covers."

Rich stared at Kate. "This is a joke, right?"

Kate shook her head. "The only way to really understand history is to experience it yourself."

"I can just see it," Zack murmured, crossing the room. "Lena in a homespun dress, cooking something on the stove. George

bringing in a string of fish. This is going to be realistic as hell."
He turned to the writer, excitement pulsing through his veins.
"Hey, Rich—let's tweak the script to take advantage of this
place. Let's have Joe and Sadie fishing on the porch. They get
to laughing and joking around, and Sadie almost falls in. Joe
grabs her. The laughter stops as they look at each other, and
they kiss. He carries her in here, and lays her on the bed—and
then we'll have the big scene where they make wild, passionate
love."

Kate's forehead scrunched. "But they didn't make love."

Zack's eyebrows rose. "What?"

"They didn't make love here. According to Sadie's diary, Joe
just held her through the night."

"Yeah, right," Andrea said scathingly.

Rich gave a derisive snort.

"Really," Kate insisted. "It's in the diary."

Oh, hell; just when he thought everything was all ironed out,
here she went again. "I read that diary, Kate, and that's not the
interpretation I got from it."

"I thought it was quite clear. Joe wanted to wait until Sadie
had left the brothel."

"Well, maybe so, but that doesn't mean—"

Jean-Pierre cleared his throat. "*Excusez-moi*, but I must go.
What time should I come in zee morning?"

"Nine or nine-thirty," Kate said.

"D'accord." The Cajun turned to go.

Andrea grabbed his arm. "Wait!" Jean-Pierre stopped, his
mono-brow raised questioningly.

Andrea turned to Zack. "I'll go back with Jean-Pierre."

Zack frowned. "I thought we all agreed this would be a good
way to deepen our understanding of Joe and Sadie."

"I don't need to understand them. If this is the site you want,
fine; I'll work out the details. But my work is done. I'll find a
hotel in town."

What the hell. At least he wouldn't have to listen to Andrea
gripe all evening. Zack lifted his shoulders. "Suit yourself."

"I'm going with Andrea," Rich said suddenly.

"Wait just a friggin' moment." Zack glared at the writer. "We're giving you an opportunity most writers would kill for— the chance to experience firsthand what your characters went through. Think of the insight you'll gain, of the richness this can add to your work. You don't want to throw all that away, do you?"

The pointy beard on Rich's chin jutted up belligerently. "I've written about aliens sucking out people's brains, and I didn't have to actually experience *that.*"

"Are you sure?" Zack growled. "That could explain a lot."

"Very funny."

"Come on, Rich," Kate urged soothingly. "It'll be fun."

"Gee, I'd really love to, but I'm allergic to outhouses and Spanish moss."

"I bet you'll be more allergic to unemployment."

"Hey, there's nothing in my contract about sleeping in the boonies. And I'm sure the screenwriters' guild has some kind of rule against forcing a member to endure unnecessary hardship and risk."

Hell. Rich was just the type to file a lawsuit. Even more likely was the possibility that he'd retaliate by writing a lousy script and holding up production while he did rewrites.

Besides, Zack abruptly realized, there was a bright side to all this. If Rich went back in the boat with Jean-Pierre and Andrea, Zack would be alone with Kate.

The evening was suddenly looking up. Way up.

"Well, hell—go ahead." He handed the keys to his SUV to Rich. "Just be sure and come back to the dock to pick us up in the morning."

Jean-Pierre looked at Kate. "So you two, you ees stayin'?"

Kate cut a nervous glance at Zack. "Well, under the circumstances, maybe we should—"

"Of course we're staying," Zack interrupted. "There's no better way to understand the characters than to walk a mile in their shoes, and I, for one, am not about to pass up that opportunity.

After all, we want to make this movie historically accurate, don't we, Kate?"

She gave a wan smile and a weak nod.

Jean-Pierre looked from Kate to Zack, then back again, his lips curved in a speculative smile. "Well, zen, we'll see you een zee morning."

Andrea, Rich, and Jean-Pierre clambered aboard the boat. Jean-Pierre unfastened the mooring rope and pushed the boat away from the dock with his foot. The Cajun waved as the engine rumbled and the fan on the back of the boat whined to life. *"À demain!"*

"Till tomorrow!" Zack echoed. He glanced over and caught Kate looking at him. She immediately turned her gaze back to the boat and lifted her arm in a wave, but not before he saw her cheeks flush scarlet.

A jolt of pleasure shot through Zack. He finally had Kate exactly where he wanted her: all to himself, all night long.

Chapter Eleven

Kate watched the airboat disappear around the bend, feeling all her composure disappear with it. Dear heavens—how had she ended up in this situation? Spending the night alone with Zack wasn't at all what she'd had in mind when she'd suggested a living history lesson.

Zack didn't seem the least bit chagrined. He looped his arm around her shoulders and shot her a slow, sexy grin. "Looks like it's just you and me, Doc." His hand slid down her arm in what felt suspiciously like a caress. A hot, unbidden shiver passed through her.

"Just the two of us," he repeated. "Just like Joe and Sadie."

Kate abruptly pulled away and crossed the porch to pick up her duffel bag. "They didn't do it, you know."

"Didn't do what?"

Kate felt her face heat. Why had she brought *that* up? Now he'd know she was thinking about sex. "You know. It." She turned away and riffled through her duffel bag, wishing desperately that it could somehow swallow her whole. "What we were talking about earlier."

From the corner of her eye, she could see Zack's grin widen. "You mean they didn't have sex?"

The amusement in his voice made her face burn even hotter.

"Is that what you meant?" he pressed.

She gave a quick nod, pretending to be completely absorbed in the contents of her bag.

Zack leaned against a wooden rail and watched, standing far too close for comfort. "Well, now, that's an interesting thing for you to bring up the moment the two of us are all alone, Professor."

"No, it's not." Oh, mercy—why did she have to sound so defensive? She cleared her throat and tried again. "We were talking about it earlier, and it never got resolved."

"There you go with that *it* again." He cocked his head and grinned at her, his brown eyes dancing. "Is this the same *it* we just clarified, or a different one?"

She pulled herself to her fullest height and forced herself to meet his gaze. "The same one. The one that you and I aren't going to be doing, either."

He threw back his head and laughed. "You sound awfully sure."

"I am."

"About Sadie and Joe, or about us?"

"Both."

"When it comes to you and me, Professor, you hold all the cards. As for Joe and Sadie, though, I thought the diary was pretty clear."

She pulled a stack of stapled papers out of her bag and handed them to him. "I brought a copy of it. Take another look. They didn't consummate their relationship that night."

His teeth flashed in a grin. "I just love it when you talk dirty, Doc."

"*Consummate* is not a dirty word."

His low laugh told her she'd been suckered again. "You're right. Come to think of it, it's not even sexy. It sounds more like two people making soup than making love."

He was impossible—not to mention maddeningly sexy and more than a little amusing. She couldn't help but grin.

"Come on, Kate. What do you think they did all night? Watched 'I Love Lucy' reruns?"

"If you don't believe me, look in the diary." She tapped the pages in Zack's hand.

He frowned down at the top page. "This isn't the transcribed version, and I can't read this flowery handwriting. You'll have to read it to me."

She strongly suspected that he was just saying that to make her read it aloud. No doubt he thought it would embarrass her. Well, she'd show him.

"All right." She sat down on the bench with all the dignity she could muster. He sat down, too, disconcertingly close beside her, so close she was sure she could feel heat radiating from his body.

"You'd better read the whole entry, so we can keep it in context," Zack said, stretching his arm on the rail behind her.

"Fine." It was hard to concentrate with him so close. Kate drew a deep breath and flipped through the pages until she found the one she was looking for.

" 'Monday, April 15, 1898. The cabin wasn't much to look at,' " she began. " 'Just a one-room shack standing on stilts above the water. It leaned to one side and looked like a strong wind might blow it away, but I thought it looked like paradise, 'cause I would finally get to be alone with Joe.' "

"Sounds a lot like this place," Zack remarked.

And a lot like this situation. Kate pushed the thought aside and resolutely read on. " 'We spent the day fishing and picking blackberries, and we had a grand time, talking and laughing together, but I thought he never would get around to kissing me. When the sun got low, we cooked dinner together and ate outside. Oh, it was a beautiful night—God really outdid Himself that evening. The locusts and crickets and tree frogs were chirping and humming, and the sky was so clear it looked like you could just reach up and pluck a star. I said something about the night being so lovely it almost hurt, and Joe said it wasn't nearly as lovely as me. And then he kissed me.' "

Kate could feel Zack's gaze on her. Her skin grew hot and her mouth grew dry. She swallowed and forced herself to continue. " 'It was a real gentle kiss, but at the same time, it was real powerful. It made me feel things I'd never felt before. My chest felt like a big bird was trapped under my ribs, flapping its wings. My stomach felt all jumpy. And then . . .' "

Oh, mercy—Kate felt as if she were reading about herself, baring her soul to Zack. But she couldn't stop reading now. She wouldn't give Zack the satisfaction of knowing how profoundly he disturbed her.

" ' . . . and then all kinds of feelings moved lower—warm, nice, good feelings. I sure never felt anything like *that* before. I've been with lots of men since I been working at the Ooh, La La, but I'd never known what it was like to want to be with one, not until then. I wanted Joe so bad I ached for him. I longed to get as close to him as a man and woman can get, and I told him so.

" '*Not yet,* he says. *Not until you're out of that brothel. When I make you mine, I intend for you to belong to me and only me for the rest of our lives.*' "

Kate put down the manuscript and looked up triumphantly. "See? I told you they didn't."

"That isn't the end of the entry," Zack said. "Keep reading."

Kate sighed impatiently but decided to humor him. " '*I already belong to you and only you,* I says. *You have my heart. Those other men, they don't touch any part of me that really counts.*'

" 'I thought he was going to cry. He kissed me again and again, real tenderlike, and told me he loved me. He held me all night long. It was the sweetest, most lovely night of my life. I stayed awake all night because I didn't want to miss a single second of being in his arms."

"Ah ha!" Zack said. "They slept together."

" 'Sleeping together doesn't mean they had sex. It just says he held her."

151

"Of course he held her," Zack said with exaggerated patience. "After they did the wild thing."

She impatiently thwacked the pages down on her lap. "You are such a cynic!"

"Oh, come on. Why do you think he brought her all the way out to the swamp in the first place?"

"Because he loved her and wanted to spend some time with her."

"Doing what?"

"Just enjoying her company."

"Get real, Kate. She was a *hooker!*"

"But Joe didn't see her that way. He saw her as the woman he loved, and he wanted to be the one man who loved her for herself and not just for her body."

"Just because he said they should wait doesn't mean that's actually what they did. Do you have any idea how many people say that, then do just the opposite?"

"Joe wasn't like that. He was a man of principle."

"He was a *man*, Kate. A man in bed with an attractive woman who'd flat-out asked him for sex."

Kate rose to her feet, too irritated to sit still. "You make it sound as if it's impossible for a man to control himself."

"Well, in that situation, it just about would be."

Kate propped her hands on her hips. "So you're saying a man couldn't say no to a woman under those circumstances?"

Zack rose from the bench and leaned on the railing. "Well, it would depend on the woman."

"Let's say it was someone attractive. Let's say Lena Brighton."

"I can't speak for every man in the world, only for myself."

"And?"

"I could say no to her." Zack took a step toward her, and his eyes took on a look that made her pulse roar in her ears like the airboat motor. "But you . . . well now, that would be a whole different story."

Kate felt as if the air had been sucked from her lungs. *Fool,* she scolded herself. It's flirtatious banter, nothing more. But the hungry look in Zack's eye said otherwise.

"Very funny," she managed to say.

"I wasn't trying to be funny." Sure enough, his eyes held no hint of laughter. They were dark and smoky, and when they locked on hers, electricity arced between them like lightning between two clouds. He took yet another step toward her. "There's some amazing chemistry between us, Kate. When you kissed me . . ."

Adrenaline flooded Kate's veins. "That wouldn't have happened if you hadn't gotten me drunk." Oh dear—she hadn't meant to bring that up, but she needed to throw up some kind of shield against the all too potent memory.

"I didn't mean to. I'm very, very sorry about that."

Zack remorseful was even worse than Zack deliberately seductive. It made him seem less threatening, made the possibilities more . . . possible.

Zack took another step closer and lifted her hands. "Look— when I first met you, all I could see was a know-it-all professor out to ruin my last chance in this business."

Tension coiled inside her. She made another stab at changing the course of this rapidly spiraling-out-of-control situation. "How very flattering."

"Does it help to know that's not how see you now?"

No. It doesn't help at all. It's not one bit helpful. In fact, it's just about the most unhelpful thing you could say.

She had to stop this. Things were rapidly heading in a direction that scared her to death. She tugged her hands free and stepped back.

"Look, I think we should let bygones be bygones." She struggled to make her voice sound calm and matter-of-fact. "From here on out, I'll treat you with respect and professionalism, and I expect the same from you." She turned and rummaged through her backpack until she found three burlap bags. She handed him two. "Well, we'd better get busy. We have a lot of work to do if we want to eat tonight."

He gazed at the bags, then looked at her questioningly. "What are these for?"

"One is for gathering the stuffing for your mattress. The other is for gathering your dinner."

"And what might that be?"

"Dandelion greens."

He raised his eyebrows. "Lawn weeds?"

"You'll be surprised how good they are. And blackberries, if we can find some ripe ones."

"Is that all we're going to eat?"

"Not if we have any luck fishing." Kate dug back into her bag, pulled out an empty coffee can, and passed it to Zack.

He turned it in his hand. "What's this for?"

"Bait. We'll need to dig for worms."

"I'd hoped you had a cooler full of steaks in that bag of yours."

"Sadie and Joe wouldn't have had steaks. I only brought a few supplies that they would have had on hand—cooking oil, salt and pepper, corn meal, coffee, that sort of thing. I want you to have a real taste of what Joe and Sadie experienced in the swamp."

His eyes got that look again. "I can think of other things they experienced that I'd like to try."

She held up her hand and shook her head. "Oh, no. I'm not getting into that again. We've already covered that topic."

"We haven't begun to cover it, Professor." His grin was slow and full of wicked promises. "Not by a long shot."

That's what I'm afraid of, Kate thought. *That's exactly what I'm afraid of.*

"You're pretty good at this hunter-gatherer business," Kate said two hours later as they stepped through the doorway of the cabin, which was as dark as a theater. It took a moment for Zack's eyes to adjust.

He thumped his chest and lifted his bag of greens as if it were a trophy. "Tarzan find food for Jane."

"Great. Now Tarzan bait hook and catch fish."

Kate turned and headed to the back door. Grinning, Zack carried the can of worms out to the fishing porch and watched her pick up two fishing poles propped near the door. He couldn't remember even enjoying a woman's company as much as he'd enjoyed Kate's this afternoon. They'd talked about old movies and music and books and current events. They'd discussed Mardi Gras and the San Andreas Fault and whether or not there was life on other planets. They'd joked and teased and bantered. Through it all, an undercurrent of sexual tension had stretched between them, growing stronger every time they brushed hands or made eye contact.

Those undercurrents were at full tilt now as dusk approached. Zack sat beside her on the bench at the end of the porch and untangled a hook from the line.

Kate gave a contented sigh and gazed out at the water. "I always forget how quiet it is here."

Zack pulled out a worm and threaded it on the hook. "It reminds me of the quiet in the Sierras. After every movie, I go backpacking there for two or three days to clear my head."

He threw the line into the water, then handed the pole to Kate. She looked at him, her eyes dark in the waning light. "Two or three days—is that all you ever take off?"

He shot her a grin as he pulled the other pole toward him. "That's pretty much all I can handle before I go into withdrawal."

"You really love your work, don't you?"

He nodded.

"What's the best part?"

"Whatever part I'm working on at the moment." He swung the pole and cast the cork on the water. It landed with a soft plop, setting off a chain reaction of ever widening circles. "There's something incredible about creating a world that the audience can enter, a world that seems so real that for two hours, they forget their troubles and get caught up in what's happening on the screen. It's a rush to make people laugh and cry and think and feel." He leaned back against the bench.

155

"When I finish a movie, I always feel really drained, but after a couple of days of peace and quiet in the great outdoors, I'm ready to go again."

"Did you spend a lot of time outdoors as a child?"

"Not until I was ten and went to summer camp. That was the greatest." Zack smiled at the memory. "I spent four whole weeks just being a regular kid, hiking and swimming and canoeing and riding horseback. Man, I loved it. Until the last day, anyway."

"What happened the last day?"

"Everyone went home." His mouth curved in a wry grin, but underneath, an old pain ached. "Everyone but me."

"What do you mean?"

Zack jerked his line, as if it were a fly fishing rod instead of a bamboo pole. "I mean nobody came to get me."

"Your parents got the date wrong—or they each thought the other one was picking you up?"

He shook his head. "Neither one even knew where I was. The nanny had made all the arrangements, and she was on vacation."

"Oh, Zack!" Kate's eyes grew wide and sympathetic. "How horrible!"

"That's pretty much the way I felt." Not to mention abandoned. And forgotten. And unloved. And unwanted. "Especially after all the other kids left and it started to get dark. The camp director called my dad and even my mother, but he only got their answering services."

Kate sat perfectly still, thinking of all the plans and back-up plans she made for Skye. Her child's well being—not to mention her whereabouts—was her top priority. She couldn't imagine a parent not knowing where his child was for four entire weeks.

"What finally happened?"

"The staff had to stay for the weekend to take the camp down, so I just stayed, too. It was weird, being the only kid and watching the place fold up around me. And then the counselors all went home. I think the director was about to call the authorities when he finally located my dad's agent. He sent a limo to come get me."

"Wow." Kate's voice was low, her heart flooded with sympathy. "What a traumatic experience."

"Yeah, well, I learned from it, so it's no big deal."

Kate was afraid to ask, but she did anyway. "What did you learn?"

Zack lifted his shoulders. "The way things are."

"Meaning . . . what?"

"Not to expect things from people. Once you learn that everyone's out for themselves, you quit relying on folks and they lose the power to hurt you. Everything's okay once you realize you're basically alone."

Kate gazed at him, her heart aching. No wonder Zack didn't believe in long-term relationships; he didn't want anyone to ever get close enough to hurt or abandon him again. It was a survival technique he'd learned at all too young an age. It was his way of protecting his heart.

Zack abruptly leaned forward. "You've got a bite."

Kate felt the pole jerk in her hand. The next thing she knew, Zack's hands were over hers, holding the pole, and her senses were invaded by his nearness. The smell of his skin, the firm pressure of his hands, the soft heat of his breath on her cheek—a dizzying onslaught of sensual sensations blazed through her. Oh, dear—*her* heart needed protection, too.

"Steady," he murmured, and it took her a moment to realize he was talking about her grip on the pole. She tried to concentrate on the cork being dragged under the water, but it was her heart that felt like it was on the line, being tugged and towed to a place far more dangerous than the swampy waters.

The oil lantern cast long shadows across the cabin later that evening as Kate rinsed the last of the dinner dishes and handed it to Zack. He wiped it with the cotton cloth and added it to the stack on a rough-hewn shelf. "Wow—that was delicious. Where did you learn to cook like that?"

157

"Right here." Kate's hair gleamed like spun gold in the flickering light. "My grandmother taught me to cook the way *her* grandmother used to cook." The old ache kicked in again. After all this time, you'd think it wouldn't bother him to hear about close-knit families.

"That's really something, having roots that go back that far."

"Want to go out on the porch?" Kate asked.

"Sure."

The door squeaked as Zack held it open for her.

"What a night," Kate murmured.

It was, indeed. The moon hung low over the cypress trees, incredibly huge and orange. The air was soft and unseasonably warm, filled with the rich, earthy scent of the water. A chorus of tree frogs trilled in rhythmic swells.

Kate sat on the bench and inhaled deeply. "It's like Sadie described in her diary. A night so beautiful it almost hurts."

Kate was so beautiful it almost hurt. Her hair was loose around her shoulders, her face tilted up as she looked at the stars. Zack sat down beside her.

"I used to sit out here as a child with my grandparents," Kate said. "Grandpa would play the fiddle, and my grandmother would tell stories."

"What kind of stories?"

"Fairy tales, mostly. She used to say the swamp became enchanted during a full moon. The fairies would come out of their homes under the water hyacinth and dance in the air. If you caught one, they had to grant you a wish."

Kate grinned. "I spent a lot of my childhood chasing fairies. Every time I thought I'd caught one, though, it turned out to be a lightning bug."

Zack laughed. "Your grandmother would have made a good screenwriter. Are your grandparents still around?"

"No. When I was twelve, they died within three weeks of each other." Kate's face took on a sad smile. "After Grandma passed away, the doctor said Grandpa died of a broken heart."

She turned to him. "What about you? Did you know your grandparents?"

"Just my father's father, but not very well. He died when I was five or six. I mainly know him through his movies."

"Do you have any other family?"

"No." Zack stretched his arm along the back of the bench. His hand brushed against her hair. "What about you?"

"Just Mom and Skye."

"What about Skye's father?"

He felt Kate tense beside him. "He's not a member of the family," she said.

"He's a member of *her* family." Zack shot Kate a pointed look. "Why isn't he in the picture?"

She averted her eyes and stared out at the swamp. The Spanish moss hanging from the branch of the cypress in their line of vision swayed like a ghost as a faint breeze stirred the air. "He's just not."

"Was he ever?"

She wrapped her arms protectively around herself. "This isn't something I talk about."

"With just me, or with anyone?"

"With anyone."

"Not even with your mother?"

Kate shook her head.

"Well, you're going to have to talk about it to Skye pretty soon."

Kate heaved a sigh and stared out at the inky water. "I know."

"Maybe you should practice by telling me."

159

Chapter Twelve

"When you bury a secret too long, you can start thinking it's a lot worse than it is," Zack prompted. "If you want to get it off your chest, I promise it'll go no further than me."

Kate sat perfectly still, staring out at the water. Loneliness filled Zack's gut, the deep, orphaned-child kind he was so used to. He knew it was irrational, but it bothered him that she wouldn't confide in him.

Not that he'd given her any reason. "I guess I can't blame you for not trusting me."

She glanced at him, then looked back at the water. "That's not it. It's just a sore subject."

"Why is it sore?"

Kate sighed. "Because I made some really stupid choices, and I feel like a fool."

"Everyone does that. It's part of being human." Zack stretched his arm across the back of the bench. "What if I tell you something first?"

Kate's brow shot up quizzically. "Like what?"

"I don't know. Anything you want to know."

Her mouth curved up. "What is this—Truth or Dare?"

"More like Truth or Truth."

She studied him for a long moment. "Okay," she said at length. "You said you thought about getting married once. What happened?"

Oh, man, she really knew how to go for the jugular. "You promise you'll tell me about your ex if I answer?"

"That's the deal."

Zack leaned back against the bench and watched the stars blink against a midnight sky. The darkness seemed to wrap a blanket of intimacy around them. Bit by bit, the memories slithered out of their dark snake hole. "Her name was Tanya, and I met her when I was a junior at U.C.L.A. I was nuts about her, the kind of nuts only a starry-eyed kid can get—so nuts that I started thinking about marriage and kids and white picket fences."

Kate gazed at him, her expression intent.

"She was a big fan of old movies and she wanted to meet my dad, so I took her to a party at his beach house one weekend," Zack continued. The memories started to break over him, cold as Pacific waves. "It was a huge party. People were everywhere—in the house, on the deck, in the pool, walking down some rocky trails to the beach. Dad was already half-crocked when we got there. I got trapped in a conversation with an old windbag producer, and Tanya kind of drifted off. When I went to look for her, she wasn't anywhere around. I got worried, thinking maybe she'd wandered off and gotten lost."

Kate's eyes shone with concern. "Did you find her?"

"Oh, yeah." Zack's face twisted in a mirthless smile. "In bed with my dad."

Kate's hand flew to her mouth. "No!"

"Yes." The image was seared into his mind like a cattle brand. Time had scarred it over, but it was still there, vivid and hideous.

"Oh, Zack . . ." Kate's hand touched his arm. "What did you do?"

"Well, I was too upset to stick around, but I was too upset

161

to be driving, too. I took a curve too fast, went off the road, and flipped the car."

"Were you hurt?"

He lifted his shoulders. "I had a concussion, a broken arm, and a couple of broken ribs." He'd barely felt the pain. The hurt in his heart had been too acute.

"What did your father do?"

"He showed up at the hospital, all contrite. He said Tanya came on to him, that he didn't even know she was with me."

"Did you believe him?"

"Yeah. It fit his M.O." Zack had chosen to accept his father's explanation, needing to believe his dad had at least that much regard for him. "Knowing Dad, he probably never even asked her name before he took her to bed."

"What did Tanya say?"

"I refused to talk to her after that, but she sent me a letter. I was going to throw it away unopened, but curiosity got the best of me."

"What did it say?"

"That Dad was a big movie star and she'd always had a crush on him and I shouldn't take it personally." Zack shook his head. Even after all this time, a bitter taste welled in his throat. "Shouldn't take it personally. Can you believe that?"

"No." Her eyes were large and perilously moist, as if she were about to cry. A funny mix of surprise and warmth pulsed through him. No one had ever cried over him before. No one had even cared that much.

"You must have been heartbroken," she murmured.

It was disconcerting, this feeling of closeness, this sense of being understood and cared about. Like a diver who had gone too deep, he felt disoriented and eager to return to the surface. He lifted his shoulders. "Yeah, well, you live, you learn." Zack stretched his hand behind the bench, close to her shoulders. "Okay now. I've told you my deepest, darkest secret. Your turn."

Kate pulled her bare feet up on the bench, wrapped her arms

around her calves, and rested her chin on her knees. "I don't even know where to begin."

Zack burrowed his hand under her hair and began to rub her neck. Her blond locks spilled over his hand in a silky waterfall. "The beginning is usually a pretty good place."

Kate drew a deep breath and leaned back against his fingers. Her neck was soft and warm.

"You told me you met Wayne at a McDonald's near your school," he prompted.

Kate nodded. "I went there for lunch with my friend Samantha. I wasn't even supposed to be there; Mom didn't want me to go anywhere without her."

"Anywhere?"

Kate nodded. "It was like being in prison. I couldn't go to the movies or on a date or to a dance or to a friend's house. She was terrified something was going to happen to me like it had to Dad. So when I met Wayne, I guess I saw a chance to escape." Kate gave a grim smile. "He was good-looking, and he knew how to turn on the charm. I was flattered that such a sophisticated older man was interested in me. Looking back on it now, I can see a lot of red flags I couldn't—or wouldn't—see back then."

"Like what?"

"Like the fact that he started really pursuing me after he learned I'd inherit a small trust fund from my dad's estate when I turned eighteen."

"Ah, hell."

Kate gave a rueful smile. "I was ridiculously naive and gullible. He painted all these exciting pictures of how wonderful our lives would be in New York. He'd make it big as an actor, and we'd get married and have a fancy apartment and go to all these great parties, and he'd support me while I went to college. All we needed was a little seed money to get to New York."

"So you agreed to finance things."

Kate nodded. "My mother's sister, who lived in northern Louisiana, came to New Orleans for some medical tests shortly after my eighteenth birthday. I decided to leave while she was staying with us, so I wouldn't be leaving Mom all alone. I withdrew all my money from the bank account and sneaked out of my bedroom window at night, leaving Mom a note that said I was eloping."

"Did you use a ladder?"

Kate's grin was sheepish. "I'm afraid so."

Zack shook his head in amazement. "You really followed the classic script."

"Except for one little detail." Kate looked away. "We never got married."

Zack's eyebrows rose.

"I figured that if Mom thought I was married, she wouldn't come after me. And I honestly thought we *were* going to get married. So when I called her from New York the following night, I told her we already were."

"What happened in New York?"

Kate blew out a hard sigh. "The money started to go fast. After a couple of weeks in a hotel, we rented a tiny one-room dump of an apartment, which required a huge deposit and was incredibly expensive. I insisted on saving the last thousand dollars, so I took a job as a hotel maid and Wayne worked as a waiter, but he never lasted long at any restaurant. He signed up with an agent, who made a lot of promises and charged a small fortune for processing fees, but he never even got Wayne an audition."

"A shyster."

Kate nodded. "Wayne enrolled in an acting class. He said he was auditioning and going to plays and workshops at night, but he always came home half-drunk, reeking of booze. Money was tight and we were arguing a lot, and then . . . well, I found out I was pregnant."

Zack's fingers moved slowly down her back. "Let me guess. That didn't fit in with Wayne's plans."

Kate nodded. "He said he wasn't ready to be a father, that he didn't want to settle down, that it was all my fault I was pregnant

164

in the first place. He wanted me to get rid of the baby. I refused, and we had a big argument. When I got home from work the next day, all his stuff was gone, and so was the rest of my money."

A rush of anger shot through Zack. "Man, that's low."

"I kept thinking he was coming back. I couldn't believe he'd really take the last of my money and leave without a word. I thought that after a while he'd think about it and cool off and come back. I waited and waited and waited. By the time I finally accepted the fact that he wasn't coming back, I was visibly pregnant."

"What did you do? Did you go home?"

"I should have, but I was too ashamed—or maybe too proud, I don't know. I didn't want my mother to know I'd lied. Besides, it turned out that her sister had cancer and was terminally ill. Mom was taking care of her, and I didn't want to be an extra burden. So I just let Mom think I was happily married and thrilled about being pregnant."

Zack shook his head. It was hard to imagine a pregnant 18-year-old with no money trying to fend for herself in New York.

"I had a bad time, trying to make ends meet—especially after the baby came. I got a job as a housemaid at a rich old woman's apartment so I could take the baby to work with me. But then I got sick and couldn't work for a month, and, well . . . No work, no money. But the bills just kept coming and the baby needed clothes and diapers and formula. I was finally ready to ask Mom for help, but then her sister died, and I just couldn't bring myself to give her more bad news."

"Oh, man."

"About two weeks later, the electricity got shut off. There were days when I went hungry so I could buy baby formula. And then the landlord locked me out of my apartment because I hadn't paid the rent, and suddenly the baby and I had no place to stay."

Zack felt a strange tightening in his chest. Unsure what to say, he simply put his arm around her.

"I hit bottom. I was afraid that if I went to a shelter, Social Services would take Skye away from me. I had no place to go. I spent a night wandering around, scared to death. I knew I couldn't go on like that, that it wasn't fair to the baby. So the next day I called Mom."

"How did she take it?"

"Well, I couldn't bring myself to admit I'd been lying all along. So I told her that Wayne and I had just divorced, and that I was broke and had no place to live. She bought me a plane ticket home. She was so glad to see me and so taken with her grandchild that she didn't ask too many questions. Skye bridged the gap between us. I earned my G.E.D., then went to college. Mom cared for Skye while I was in class."

Zack caressed her arm. "And you've never told your mother or Skye the truth?"

Kate shook her head.

"Did you ever hear from Wayne again?"

"No. But I saw his picture in the newspaper when Skye was four or five. He'd been convicted of credit card fraud and grand larceny. He'd evidently stolen the wallets from the dressing rooms of some Broadway actors while they were on stage." Kate gave a tight grin. "The headline said 'Thief breaks into show business.' "

Zack tried to imagine Kate as a teenager, tried to imagine what she'd seen in this jerk. The thought of Kate caring for the guy made his blood boil. "Did he serve time?"

"The article said he was sentenced to twelve years, but he'd be eligible for parole in eight. It said it was the third time he'd been arrested." Kate looked down at her lap. "I had no idea he'd ever be in trouble with the law. I guess I never really knew him at all."

Eight years in the penn. Plenty of time to turn him into a hardened criminal, capable of only God knew what.

"He's a convicted criminal, and Skye thinks he's this great guy who works with animals." The irony in Kate's voice didn't hide the undertone of anguish.

166

"That's what you told her?"

"Yeah." Kate gazed at her clenched hands in her lap. Her hair hung along the sides of her face like a curtain, obscuring her expression, but he didn't need to see it to feel her shame. "I had good intentions. When Skye was four, she came to me in tears because one of her friends told her that her daddy didn't love her. Skye wanted to know what she'd done to make her daddy mad. I couldn't bear for her to think that, so I said her daddy was mad at me. The reason he wasn't around was because he was helping animals far, far away. At the time, it didn't seem like much more of a lie than Santa Claus or the Easter Bunny."

Kate sighed. "On her next birthday, I bought her a present and wrapped it up with a card that was signed 'Daddy.' Then I sent it to a friend who's a flight attendant, and she mailed it to Skye from overseas."

Poor, misguided kid—Kate had only wanted to spare her daughter pain. The funny feeling in Zack's chest intensified.

"Skye was so thrilled. And then came Christmas and her next birthday, and then the next Christmas, and the whole thing took on a life of its own. Once I started sending gifts, I didn't know how to stop." Her head was still bowed. A wet blotch fell on her thigh, darkening the worn denim of her jeans, and Zack realized she was crying. "I'd created a monster. To have the presents just abruptly stop seemed cold and cruel. And now . . . well, so much of her identity is tied up in the idea that she's the child of this great guy. And I don't know how to tell her I lied."

Zack's arm tightened around her. "She's a bright kid. She'll understand that you only wanted to spare her feelings."

Kate shook her head. "I don't know. She's gotten awfully attached to the idea that she has this cool, politically correct father."

"Who has never been there for her," Zack added. "Kids know who loves them and who doesn't. Twice-a-year presents can't compare with a mom who's been there all along. Believe me, I know."

Another tear fell onto Kate's lap. "This whole situation is eating me up. I'm basically a truthful person, but here I've lied to Mom about getting married, to Skye about her father. I've made such a mess of things."

"You did it from a kind place in your heart."

Kate looked at him, tears pooling in her eyes. "Do you think Skye will forgive me?"

"Hey, I would have forgiven my parents anything if they'd acted like they halfway cared about me." He ran the back of his fingers against her cheek. "Skye's an awfully lucky kid, having you for a mom."

"I don't think she'll see it that way."

"She'll see it. Maybe not right away, but she will."

Hope and something that looked a lot like gratitude shone in her tear-soaked eyes. Kate wiped her wet lashes with the back of her hand and gave a tremulous smile. "I can't believe I just told you all that."

"I'm glad you did."

"You're awfully easy to talk to."

"So are you."

Their eyes caught and held, and physical awareness blazed between them. Attraction, so intense it was almost palpable, hung in the air like smoke.

"There's some mighty strong chemistry between us," Zack said.

Kate shifted nervously. "We probably confided in each other because we know we'll never see each other after the movie is over," she said. "Maybe that makes us feel safe."

"Safe." Zack reached out and touched her chin, tipping her face toward him. "Is that how I make you feel?"

His touch was light, but Kate felt it all the way to her bones. The air seemed to quiver with expectation. The tree frogs and cicadas thrummed a low, rhythmic chorus, waiting for her answer.

Before she knew it, a whispered word slipped out: "No."

"Why not?"

"Because . . ." Unbidden, her gaze fell on his lips.

"Because of the electricity between us?" he prompted.

The current that had charged between them all day was now at full voltage. Wordlessly, she nodded.

His hand slid down her arm. "Kate—I can't stop thinking about kissing you. The memory of it is driving me crazy."

Kate swallowed, her mouth dry, her palms damp.

His eyes were dark and smoky and full of heat. "We've got two months together, Kate. Let's make the most of them."

"Oh, I don't think . . ." She looked away, her heart pounding hard. When he looked at her like that, it was hard to remember the reasons she needed to keep her distance. "I—I can't." Even to her own ears, she sounded unconvincing.

"Why not?"

"It's just not . . . not wise."

His finger traced a slow, languid trail from her shoulder to her neck. "I'll tell you what's not wise—it's not wise to waste a night like this. And if you expect me to keep my distance, it's definitely not wise to be sitting here in the moonlight with me, because I want to kiss you so bad I can almost taste you."

Kate couldn't move. She couldn't think. She could barely even breathe.

"I promised I wouldn't make a move on you again unless you wanted me to, so the ball's in your court, Kate." Zack's finger moved back down to her shoulder. Her heart pounded so loudly she was sure he must be able to hear it. "Say yes, Kate," he murmured. "Please say yes."

The heat in his eyes melted away all of her resistance. Before she could stop herself, her hand was on the back of his head and she was pulling his mouth to hers.

The kiss started out soft, as gentle as the flutter of butterfly wings. And then Kate wrapped her arms around his neck, and the kiss exploded. Sensation rocked through her like a bolt of lightning—electric, jarring, scorching, shocking. Zack's tongue plundered her mouth, and she moaned aloud, wanting, needing more.

He hauled her into his lap. She flung her leg over and twisted around so that she was facing him, her arms around his neck, her legs straddling his.

"Kate . . ."

He breathed her name against her lips. She pressed her mouth to his and shifted against him, aligning the seam of her jeans with his fly. Angling his head, he kissed her until they were both panting and breathless. His hands roamed down her back, cupping her buttocks, pulling her tight against him.

Desire spread through her like melting butter. It pooled low in her belly, dissolving all ability to reason. So *this* was passion. *This* was what all the songs and books and poems were about. She'd felt desire before, but never with this intensity, this urgency, this aching, throbbing need.

"Kate." The word was full of hunger and yearning, and it set her blood aflame. "Kate—are you sure?"

She was sure that she wanted him in a way she'd never wanted anything or anyone. She was sure she'd never felt this way before and quite possibly never would again. She was sure that she was beyond caring about anything except this night, this man, this moment.

"Yes," she whispered. "Yes."

Clutching her tightly, he rose to his feet, his mouth still on hers. She wound her legs around his hips and clung to his neck. He wrapped his arms under her fanny and carried her to the weathered screen door, holding her with one arm as he opened it.

Striding to the bed, he gently set her on the old, quilt-covered mattress. The room was dark, illuminated only by the moonlight through the window and the flickering light of the lantern on the table. A soft breeze blew through the screen door and the cabin's lone window, but Kate's skin was hot, fevered with a desire unlike anything she'd ever known. She didn't want to turn loose of him, didn't want to break the sweet, intimate alignment of their bodies, even for a second. Her legs still wrapped around him, she pulled him down on the mattress with her.

He leaned over and kissed her again and again, his tongue tantalizing her, filling her with the taste of him. At length he shifted onto his side and reached for the buttons of her shirt. She reached up to help him, but he stilled her hand.

"Let me," he murmured. "I've wanted to undress you ever since we met."

The words set her on fire. A throbbing ache burned low in her belly as slowly, slowly, he unfastened first one button, then another, stopping to kiss the exposed skin each movement revealed. His breath fanned over her skin, warm and moist and tantalizing, down, down, down until the last button gave way and her shirt fell open, revealing her sheer black bra. He reached for the clasp between her breasts and gently unfastened it.

"Beautiful," he murmured. "So beautiful."

Beautiful. The word sliced through Kate's haze of passion, making her tense. Beautiful wasn't a word that applied to her. Beautiful described models and movie stars, the kind of women Zack was accustomed to. It was a word reserved for the busty, naked women in men's magazines—the ones Wayne had always criticized her for not looking like. How much more lacking would she seem to Zack, a man who dated some of the most glamorous women in the world?

She drew up her arms and covered her breasts.

Zack pulled back. "Kate, honey—what's the matter?"

She drew a shaky breath and looked away. "Y-you said I was beautiful."

"And that upset you?"

"I know what I look like." She kept her face averted. "I'm nothing like the women you're accustomed to."

"You're right about that." Zack leaned up on one elbow. "You're genuine and smart and sexy as hell, and you turn me on more than anyone has in years." *Maybe ever.* Zack pushed the thought away.

"I'll just disappoint you."

He stared at her quizzically. "What are you talking about?"

She closed her eyes, a look of shame covering her face. "I—I'm not very good at sex."

"Not very good?" He pushed up higher. "Where'd you get an idea like that?"

"From Wayne." A tear trickled down the side of her nose. "He—he said I'm not responsive."

It wasn't enough that the sorry SOB had used Kate to finance a move to the Big Apple, stolen her money, and abandoned her when he got her pregnant—he'd also seen fit to give her a major inferiority complex. "Wayne's an even bigger idiot than I thought." Zack leaned over her and looked directly into her eyes. "Kate, honey—you are a beautiful, desirable woman, and the only thing you're not good at is selecting men to get involved with."

"But the whole time I was with him, I never had . . . I mean, I never could . . . I never a-a-achieved . . ."

"You never had an orgasm?"

She threw both arms over her head.

Zack wanted to look her in the eye, but her face was covered with elbows and forearms. "And he blamed you?" Muttering an oath, he shook his head. "Honey, surely you've learned from other men that Wayne was the one with the problem."

A soft sob sounded from under her arm, followed by her muffled voice. "There haven't been any other men." No sex in more than thirteen years—and the only sex she'd ever had was with a jerk who didn't know or care how to please her. Wow. She was less experienced than most virgins.

"Sugar, for an educated woman, you sure have a lot to learn." He gently pulled her arms off her face and waited until she opened her eyes.

Tears leaked out of the corners of her eyes. "But Wayne said other women always climaxed with him."

Yeah, right. They probably faked it to get the insensitive oaf off them as fast as possible.

"I tried and I tried, but I never could."

"That was probably the problem. Sex isn't about trying to

172

reach a goal. It's about giving and taking pleasure and losing yourself in the moment."

He gently brushed a tear from her face, along with a wayward strand of hair. "I'd like to propose a solution."

She parted her arms enough to peek through them. "What?"

"Just for tonight, I want you to try *not* to have an orgasm."

"N-not to have one?"

"That's right. Let's remove the goal so there's no pressure. You are hereby expressly forbidden to climax. Just lie back and enjoy yourself, and tell me what you like and what you don't like. Agreed?"

"But—but what about you?"

"Don't worry about me, sugar. I'm going to enjoy this plenty. Now lie back and relax."

Kate lay back against the soft pillows. Zack leaned over, putting his lips close to her ear, and brushed kisses along the side of her neck. "Do you like this?" he whispered.

The warmth of his breath sent delicious shivers chasing through her. "Oh, yes." Kate's arms wound around his back, and he stretched on top of her, supporting his weight on his elbows. He kissed her until she was once more on fire, her breath coming in hot, urgent puffs. His five o'clock shadow rasped deliciously against her skin, giving her a thrilling rush of goose bumps.

His kisses trailed to her collarbone, and he eased her shirt open again.

"You need your shirt off, too," she murmured.

He sat up and pulled his shirt over his head. The sight made her breath catch in her throat. His shoulders were broad and well muscled, his chest covered with dark masculine hair that narrowed to a thin line down his hard belly.

His biceps bulged as he tossed the shirt aside and bent back over her. His mouth blazed a white-hot path of pleasure from her throat to her breast. His fingers languidly followed, cupping her breast as his mouth claimed a pebbled tip.

173

Kate gasped. A live wire seemed to run from her breasts to the juncture of her thighs, carrying a current of heat and pleasure. She moaned as his mouth worked erotic magic, moving from one breast to the other, grazing the tips with his teeth, stimulating nerve endings she'd never known she had.

His mouth slid down, stringing kisses along the underside of her breasts, moving lower across her belly. His beard-shadowed chin grazed a soft-rough trail across her skin, all the way down to the waistband of her jeans. He unfastened the top button and slowly, slowly, pulled down her zipper.

"Just relax," Zack whispered. "Just relax and enjoy."

He sat up on the bed and tugged off her jeans.

"You, too," she murmured.

He smiled, his teeth a flash of white in the dark. "All right." He stood beside the bed and shrugged off his jeans. He wore cotton knit underwear, the designer kind that was half boxer, half brief, but the fabric and cut were not what riveted her attention. It was the enormous, unmistakable evidence of his arousal.

Her heart stampeded against her chest. "Oh, my."

His eyes glittered as he climbed back in bed and resumed where he'd left off, sliding kisses across her stomach. His fingers slowly worked their way up her outer legs, then danced a sweet, slow waltz across her skin, gliding to the sensitive flesh of her inner thigh. Heat pooled inside her, heavy and languid and luscious, as his fingers teased the edge of her panties. She let out a little moan and arched against him.

"Do you like that?"

"Oh, yes. Oh, I want . . ."

"Yes?"

She raised up on her elbows and looked down at him. "I want to do something for you."

"Believe me, honey, you are." His lips curved in a sexy grin as his fingers continued their sweet torment. "Just lie back and let me."

With a contented sigh, Kate lay back and surrendered to the

pleasure he was stirring within her. At last, at long last, he slid a finger softly down her center, pressing the silk of her panties against her flesh.

She moaned and moved against the pressure.

"Just relax," he murmured. He caressed her through the fabric for several long moments, then slowly peeled her underwear down and off her legs.

He moved lower on the bed and gazed at her. "You're so beautiful—so very beautiful."

This time, she believed him. He made her feel wonderful and sexy and desired.

He brushed her soft triangle of hair for a long moment; then his fingers moved inward, intimately caressing her with slow, inciting strokes, teasing but not entering, making her ache to be filled. His fingers moved up and down her desire-slicked womanhood, circling her swollen nub, until her breath was coming hard and fast and her hips strained toward him. When he touched her with his tongue, she stiffened.

"Let me, Kate," he pleaded. "Let me taste you."

Never had she dreamed that such pleasure existed. A taut cord of tension tightened within her, a tension that was exquisite and excruciating. Her fingers curled into Zack's hair as the pleasure mounted to unbearable intensity.

"Please," she murmured, not even knowing exactly what it was she craved, but craving it with all her being. "Oh, please."

"Just relax," he whispered. "Just relax and feel."

His mouth resumed its delicious torture, driving her beyond words, beyond thought. Just as it seemed she could take no more, her universe imploded, collapsing down to nothing but this man, this moment, this incredible, amazing gift of pleasure he was giving her. She shuddered and shattered and gave herself over to the moment, to the pleasure, to him.

He moved up the mattress and held her in his arms.

"That was . . ." She searched her mind, but words failed her. "That was . . ."

"That was an orgasm," he said helpfully.

She returned his smile, her heart bubbling with emotion. "I thought I wasn't supposed to have one."

He trailed a fingertip down her chest, his eyes warm. "There are no supposed-to's in lovemaking."

"You tricked me."

"Do you mind?"

"I don't guess I do." She smiled into his face, and he smiled back. Tenderness, full and sweet, saturated the moment. Emotion swelled in her heart, along with the need to give him some of the joy he'd given her. Her hand slid down his chest to his belly, then lower.

He gasped as Kate's fingers closed around his manhood.

"I want to feel you inside me," she murmured.

It was all he could do to form a thought, much less words. "Me, too," he managed. He couldn't remember ever wanting anything as much in his life.

He reached down, dug in the pocket of his jeans, and pulled out the small plastic packet he always kept in his wallet. After he'd donned protection, he leaned over her. Claiming his mouth in a kiss, she pulled him down and wrapped her legs around his waist.

That was all he could stand. The thought of those legs around him had been driving him crazy ever since that night in the French Quarter. She tilted her hips, and he slowly eased his way in.

"Oh," she moaned.

He paused, suddenly remembering that it had been thirteen years since she'd had sex. He gazed down, worried. "Am I hurting you?"

"No. Oh, no." She shifted against him, driving him deeper. "It feels sooooo good."

"You ought to feel it from my side," he whispered.

A soft smile lit her face. Zack gazed into her eyes and slid all the way home. The pleasure was so intense he nearly lost it immediately. She was slick and hot and tight, and she met him thrust for thrust. He slowed the tempo, struggling to hold back, wanting to give her another release.

He gazed down at her, taking in her parted, panting lips, the curved sweep of her lashes, the soft sheen of sweat between her breasts. Emotion, as baffling as it was intense, swelled in his chest, fueling his passion. Just as it reached a fever pitch, Kate cried out and contracted around him. Her pleasure drove him over the edge. He dove into a honeyed place deep within her, a place of sweet release and completeness, a place that felt like home.

Chapter Thirteen

Kate awoke slowly the next morning, clinging to the wispy remnants of a dream. The content escaped her, but the colors remained—blazing, glorious colors, mouthwatering shades of raspberry and peach and plum, warm tones of sunshine and fire and burnt umber. The colors had wrapped around her and embraced her, then seeped inside and saturated her, leaving her with a bone-deep sense of contentment.

She wondered why she'd never dreamed in color before. The dream was starting to fade, but the delicious, cozy feeling of being embraced lingered. Mercy, but her bed felt good this morning. The covers were deliciously warm and solid.

She gave a languorous stretch, then froze. Her eyelids flew wide open.

That wasn't a blanket wrapped under her breasts; that was a large masculine arm. And her back wasn't pressed against a pillow, but a solid, hairy chest. Most alarming of all, the hard thing draped between her legs wasn't a twisted sheet but a muscled masculine leg.

All of those Y-chromosome body parts could only belong to one person—*Zack*.

Her heart fluttered wildly as the events of the night before flooded her in complete, excruciatingly intimate detail. She closed her eyes against the onslaught of emotion, then opened them abruptly as a thought shot an arrow of terror straight through her heart. *Oh, my stars—I'm falling in love with him.*

No. She couldn't fall in love with him. It was an impossible situation—worse than impossible. She'd promised herself that she'd never again give her heart to someone who didn't love her back, and Zack didn't even believe in love. How could she fall for someone who believed love affairs should have expiration dates?

Besides, she and Zack came from entirely different worlds. He went to A-list Hollywood parties and Academy Awards ceremonies. She went to the grocery store and junior high PTA meetings. They weren't even on the same side of the fence when it came to the historical accuracy of this movie. There was no way she could fall in love with him. It was insane. It was a heartache waiting to happen. She absolutely, positively refused to get emotionally involved with him.

But she already was. What, oh what, was she going to do?

He shifted his heavy arm more tightly around her. She could hear him breathing, feel the warm rhythmic puffs of air against her hair. To her alarm, his fingers curled around her breast, cradling it in his hand. His thumb slid across her nipple. She thought he was still asleep as an unmistakably aroused, very male part of his anatomy pressed against her backside. But then he nibbled on the top of her ear. "Good morning, sugar."

A sense of panic flooded her veins. "G-good morning." She scooted to the edge of the bed and started to climb out, only to realize she was completely naked under the sheet.

"Where're you going?"

Back to a place where her heart was safe and her life made sense and her emotions weren't fried and scrambled. Except she had no idea where that might be, or how the heck to get there. She needed some time to think. "I need to, uh, visit the, uh, facilities." She grabbed the old faded quilt off the end of the bed and wrapped it tightly around her.

Zack leaned up on one elbow and grinned at her. "No need to wrap up like a mummy. I've seen you naked, you know."

Kate's face flamed. She tugged the quilt higher around her breasts. "I'm sort of bashful."

"You weren't last night."

Kate's cheeks blazed hotter. "Well, I'm not accustomed to strolling around naked."

Zack gave her a wicked grin. "We'll work on it. By the time the shoot's over, you'll be walking around like a regular nudist."

By the time the shoot's over. Oh, dear—that would be their expiration date. He'd go back to Hollywood and she'd go back to the university, and life would go on just as before.

Except it wouldn't be like before. She'd be abandoned and devastated and brokenhearted, just as she'd been with Wayne. If she cared for Zack now, how much more would she care after weeks of sharing his bed?

Tears gathered behind her eyes. She turned away, not wanting him to see them. "I-I'll be back in a moment." Tightly clutching the quilt, she grabbed her duffel bag and held it in front of her as she hurried to the door, wishing she had something to shield her heart as well.

She stood outside the cabin a few minutes later, fully dressed and fully resolved. Drawing a deep breath, she pushed open the squeaky screen door and stepped inside. The room was dim after the bright light of the outdoors, but not so dim that she couldn't see Zack, propped against the old metal headboard of the bed, his hands behind his head.

The sight made her heart clatter against her ribs. It was unfair that he should look so sexy. The muscles of his arm stood in prominent display, and his tanned skin made a stark contrast to the white sheet riding low across his flat belly. His hair was tousled, his chin dark with stubble, and his eyes glittered with sensual promises as he grinned at her.

"I can see we need to get right to work on your bashfulness."
He reached out his hand toward her. "Come on over here."

All she had to do was take three steps—four at the most—
and she'd be back in his arms. Good heavens, but it was tempting. The memory of the sensations he'd stirred in her last night
made her knees feel like wet noodles. He'd not only touched
her body, but her heart. Making love with Zack had been the
most moving experience of her life.

Which was exactly why she didn't dare repeat it. Kate nervously moistened her lips and stiffened her spine, hoping to
stiffen her resolve as well. "We need to talk, Zack."

"No, we don't. We need to make love." His voice was low
and sultry, and it did dangerous things to her body temperature.

She braced herself on the back of the old wooden chair.
"That's what we need to talk about. Last night was—"

"Fantastic," Zack cut in. The hot look in his eyes gave her
shivers. "Absolutely amazing. *You* were amazing." He gave her
a slow grin.

"It was a mistake."

He sat up more fully in bed, his eyebrows raised, his forehead
creased in consternation. "You didn't enjoy it?"

"No. I mean, yes! Yes, of course I did." Oh, dear. It was so
hard to keep her thoughts collected when he smiled at her like
that, his eyes all wicked and knowing and seductive. "But en-
joyment isn't the issue here."

"So, would you mind telling me what is?"

Panic spilled through Kate's veins. She couldn't very well tell
him that she was afraid of falling in love with him; that would
be mortifying, knowing that he didn't even believe in love. She
needed to come up with a rational, unemotional reason that
would allow her to retain a modicum of pride so she could work
with him for the next two and a half months.

Work. That was her answer. "Look, we got carried away last
night. But mixing work and pleasure isn't a good idea. Being
involved with you could compromise my judgment. And I have
my reputation to consider."

181

"Your reputation? You're not in high school, Kate."

"Universities are like big high schools. They tend to frown on their professors having high-profile love lives, and you're not exactly a low-profile person. Besides, if word gets out that you and I are involved, my objectivity would appear to be compromised, and that could put my tenure in jeopardy. My boss is looking for any excuse to discredit me."

"We can be discreet, Kate."

"According to Mr. Goldman, the press will be swarming around this movie. I can't afford to end up on the front page of the *National Enquirer.*"

"We can avoid that."

"I can't take that chance. I won't endanger my whole future just for a couple of months of—of—of . . ."

"Great sex?"

There was no denying it. Kate gave a reluctant nod. "Look— we lost our heads—maybe because of the moon or swamp fairies or something," She tried to smile, but her lips refused to cooperate. "In any event, this is a brand new day, and I think we should just put it all behind us and pretend it never happened."

Zack's eyebrows quirked up. "In other words, just forget about it?"

"Yes."

Zack leaned back, his hands behind his head. "I don't think I can. Last night was pretty memorable."

"Look, I just want to go back to how things were before."

"Before, things were leading up to this."

She straightened her spine. "Well, it's not going to happen again."

Zack's eyes held hers in a stranglehold. "You sure, Kate?"

No, her heart murmured. *Not at all.*

The sexual tension in the room was thicker than gumbo and twice as hot. She averted her eyes. "I'm sure."

He blew out an exasperated breath. "Come on, Kate. You're making too much of this."

And you're not making enough of it. To you, this is just another location fling. To me, it's a one-way ticket to heartache.

"I think I'm in a better position to judge the potential consequences," she said stiffly.

"We can be careful. Nothing's going to happen to your career."

"You're darn right nothing's going to happen, because nothing further is going to happen between us." She turned on her heel and crossed the room, pausing before the screen door. "Jean-Pierre will be here soon. You'd better get dressed."

Zack watched the door bang shut behind her, then peeled back the sheet and rose from the bed, mumbling an oath under his breath.

She was like a female Jekyll and Hyde—beautiful lover by night, prim and proper professor by day. He snatched his jeans off the floor and shoved a foot into them. He didn't need this kind of aggravation in his life.

Here she was, all worried about people thinking she was compromising *her* standards, when *he* was the one who was actually in danger of doing that. Another session or two like the one they'd shared last night and he'd turn the movie into a documentary on earwax if Kate said he should.

He yanked on his T-shirt so hard it nearly ripped. Good Lord, but the sex had been incredible—beyond incredible. Mind-blowing. Stupendous. Hell, he wouldn't be surprised if there were scorch marks on the sheets. Even now he wanted to pull her back into bed, peel off all her clothes, and make wild, tender, hot-and-bothered love to her until she made that sweet, surprised cry of release. The woman should be classified as an addictive substance.

But damn it all—He didn't need a complication like this right now. He didn't need anything or anyone diverting him from his movie.

If he had any sense at all, he'd be grateful she'd called things off.

The problem was, he *didn't* have any sense when it came to Kate. And gratitude was not among the dark tangle of emotions that knotted his gut as the approaching whir of Jean-Pierre's airboat signaled an end to their stay in the swamp.

Chapter Fourteen

"Is this the movie queen of New Orleans?"

Kate cradled the kitchen phone against her ear and smiled at the sound of Samantha's voice. "It depends. Am I talking to the Duchess of Delta Airlines?" A flight attendant based in Atlanta, Sam was her oldest and dearest friend—and aside from Zack, the only person who knew the truth about Wayne.

"None other."

Kate laughed. "Thanks for returning my call, Sam."

"Sorry it took so long. I had a layover in Paris. I got back last night and gave you a call, but Skye said you were at the grocery store."

"I go to the grocery store, and you go to Paris," Kate said wryly. "Where's the justice in that?"

Sam's laughter tinkled through the phone. "Look who's talking! I'm not the one working on a movie with Zack Jackson. So, how's it going?"

"Okay, I guess." Holding the phone against between her shoulder and her ear, Kate loaded another plate into the dishwasher.

"Okay? You can do better than that," Sam chided teasingly.

"Skye told me you've been spending a lot of time with Mr. Dreamboat. She said he's been over to your house and taken you to dinner, and that you two had a fight. She said you'd even taken him camping!"

"It wasn't exactly camping," Kate hedged.

"Well, then, what was it?"

Kate hesitated. Sam knew all her deepest secrets, but for some reason, Kate didn't want to talk about that night in the swamp. If she didn't talk about it, maybe she could pretend that nothing had happened.

Yeah, right. As if she didn't think about it every other second. The truth was, she'd thought of little else in the past two weeks. Thank heavens she hadn't had much contact with Zack during that time. She spent most of her time at the university library or the New Orleans Historical Collection, digging up details for the props department. When she'd seen Zack at meetings, he'd treated her with polite professionalism.

It was exactly what Kate wanted, and yet it left her perversely depressed. She'd been relieved when Zack had flown back to California five days ago.

"It was just a trip to the fishing cabin. They're going to use it as a location."

"An *overnight* trip, from what Skye said."

"I've really got to talk to that kid about talking so much."

"Come on, Kate," Sam urged. "Dish!"

"There's really nothing to tell."

"*Nothing* happened?"

Kate hesitated.

"Aha!" Sam said triumphantly. "Something *did* happen!"

There was no point in pretending. Sam could read her like a book. Besides, it suddenly seemed unbearable, keeping it all to herself.

"Yes, something happened. But it's not going to happen again." Kate had meant to sound determined, but her voice cracked on the last word.

"Kate, honey—you sound upset. What on earth . . ."

186

"Oh, Sam." Kate's words poured out in a rush. "He doesn't *do* relationships. Not long-term ones, anyway. He puts expiration dates on all his affairs, if they were packages of sliced bacon. And I didn't intend to get involved, I really didn't, but we had such a good time together, and we talked and talked, and I told him stuff I never talk about, and there's this incredible chemistry between us, and, well . . ."

"So, things got physical."

"Yes."

Samantha lowered her voice. "How was it?"

Kate choked back a sob. "Oh, Sam, that's the worst part."

"It was bad?"

"No! It was amazing. Incredible. Better than anything I ever imagined. I saw rockets and stars and meteor showers."

"Not to mention a guided missile," Sam interjected dryly.

"Sam!"

"Sorry."

Kate's words tumbled out in a teary rush. "I'm falling for him, and there's no future in that. I'm only going to end up with a broken heart."

"So, what are you going to do?"

"Nothing. I told him we'd made a mistake, that it was always a bad idea to mix business and pleasure, and that if word got out that we were involved it could jeopardize my career at the university. I said I wanted to forget anything had ever happened and go back to having a professional relationship."

"And?"

"And he's doing it!" Kate fought a fresh onslaught of tears.

"Aww, honey, you've got it bad, don't you?"

"Not as bad as I'd have it if I continued to sleep with him."

"Do you have to be around him much?"

"He's been out of town for the past few days. He comes back tomorrow, and then the shoot starts. I'm hoping that we'll both be too busy to see much of each other." Kate shifted the phone to her other ear, suddenly anxious to shift the topic as well.

"If that's what you want . . . well, I hope so, too." Sam's voice sounded dubious. "Skye said he's really nice. She said he's going to let her be in the movie."

"She's going to be an extra. She's thrilled beyond words."

"I could tell. She sounded so grown up, Kate."

Kate sighed. "I know. She's growing up too fast."

"She's got a birthday coming up soon, doesn't she?"

A knot of guilt formed in Kate's throat. "That's why I called. I want to send you a package to mail to her."

A long pause sounded over the phone. "She's getting a little old for this, isn't she?"

The lump grew larger. "I know, I know. I've got to tell her soon. It's just that things have been really hectic, and Skye's having problems fitting in at school, and she's going through a pre-teen identity crisis. . . . I just hate to shake up her world right now. I thought I'd let her have this one more birthday and then tell her this summer, after school is out and I'm finished with this movie."

A long silence stretched between them. "Please, Sam," Kate urged. "Just one last time."

Sam's sigh whooshed through the phone. "Okay," she said reluctantly. "But this is the end of it, okay? When we started, she was just a toddler and there didn't seem to be any harm in it, but the last few years . . . I don't know, Kate. I feel like I'm in on some kind of conspiracy to suppress the truth or something. It doesn't feel right anymore."

"This will be the last time, Sam, I promise. I just want to see her through this rough spell. I'll tell her as soon as things settle down."

"Do it soon, Kate. The longer you wait, the harder it'll get."

"I know." Fear blew through her like cold needles of sleet. What if she'd already waited too long? Skye had reached a difficult age, an age when emotions were volatile and the parent-child bond was becoming tenuous. What if the news devastated Skye? What if Skye hated Kate for deceiving her? What if the confession destroyed all of Skye's trust in her?

But it would be worse if Skye found out the truth on her own. Kate had to tell her, and she had to do it soon.

Zack stepped over a tangle of cables as he entered the musty French Quarter bar, squinting against the bright lights. Tomorrow was the first day of the shoot, and his crew was busy preparing the site for the first scene. Fritz was directing the placement of a light in the corner. Two members of the prop crew were arranging tables, and a third one was carefully pulling bottles from the back of the bar. Deb stood in the center of it all, talking on a cell phone, her clipboard in her hand. She waved and headed toward him, finishing her conversation as she picked her way through the maze of cables.

"How're things going?" Zack asked.

"Everything's coming together. When did you get in?"

"Just now. I came straight from the airport." Zack looked around, his eyes searching the room. "Where's the professor?"

"Rounding up some authentic glasses and an antique beer spigot."

He shoved his hands in his pocket, deliberately keeping his tone casual. "I hope she hasn't been driving everyone crazy."

Because she's sure been doing that to me. The whole time he'd been in L.A., Kate had prowled through his thoughts like a burglar. He'd thought about how beautiful she looked when she smiled, and how her chin tilted up at that obstinate angle when she dug in her heels on an issue. He'd thought about how she wore outrageously sexy lingerie under her severe clothes. He'd thought about the way she got all stiff and starchy whenever she was nervous.

He'd thought about other things, too—like how hard it must have been for her, her being all alone and pregnant in New York. He'd thought about the way her eyes got all tender when she talked about her family, and how they glowed with passion when she talked about history.

And speaking of passion—oh, Lord. The memory of how her legs had felt around him had been driving him to distraction.

He thought about the way she'd looked stretched out naked in the lamplight. He'd recalled the creamy, smooth texture of her skin, the silk of her hair, and the way her flowery herbal scent made him want to burrow his nose in her neck and stay there. He'd thought about the way she tasted, about her soft moans of pleasure, about her sweet, surprised cry of release. He couldn't remember ever before having had sex that hot in his life.

He'd tried to convince himself that it was because he hadn't had sex in a long while, but he could no longer use that excuse. He'd had plenty of opportunities to be with other women in California—beautiful, desirable women who were more than willing to satisfy any and all of his urges—and he'd had no interest in any of them.

"You know, I really misjudged Kate," Deb was saying. "I thought she was going to be an obnoxious know-it-all, but she's been terrific. She not only knows what we need but where to find it. Then she goes out, makes all the arrangements, and brings the stuff to us. She's saved us a bundle by convincing antiques dealers to loan us stuff in exchange for a credit."

"Good. Glad to hear it." But for some reason, he wasn't. The fact that Kate was making herself useful unsettled him.

"Here she comes now."

Zack turned to see Kate coming through the door, carrying a large cardboard box. She halted in the doorway when she saw him. Their eyes locked, and for a second, it seemed as if they were the only people in the room.

Zack's heart pounded hard. "Hi."

Kate resumed crossing the room. "Hello."

"Need a hand with that?"

"No. It's not heavy." She made her way to the bar, then set the box on top of it. "When did you get back?"

"Just now." He strode toward her as she pulled up the top of the box. "I understand you've been going above and beyond the call of duty, gathering up authentic props. Thanks."

Kate pulled out a large wad of newspaper and carefully un-wrapped an old glass. "Just doing my job."

"We have props people who can do that for you, you know," he said.

"The owners of the antiques stores feel better if they know I'm personally handling their stuff."

Zack smiled. "I don't blame them. I felt better when you were personally handling me."

Her fingers stilled. "Zack . . ."

He hadn't meant to start in, to say that, but he couldn't seem to help himself. He cut her off before she could voice her pro-test. "I've been thinking about you, Kate. A lot."

She kept her head down. Her hand shook as she pulled an-other newspaper-wrapped object from the box. Good, Zack thought. She was driving him crazy, so it was only fair that he could at least make her nervous.

He stepped closer, close enough to smell the soft scent that had been haunting his thoughts, close enough to feel the grav-itational pull she seemed to exert on him. "I've missed you. Will you have dinner with me tonight?"

"I can't. I have plans with Skye." She continued to unpack the box with businesslike efficiency. "And anyway, you agreed we should keep things platonic between us."

"I never agreed to any such thing."

Her hand froze on a glass and her spine stiffened.

"You're the one who wanted it that way. I was hoping that you'd change your mind."

She resumed unpacking the box. "I haven't."

Zack shoved his hands in his pocket, pretending not to be as disappointed as he felt. "Well, can we at least be friends?"

"Sure."

Zack searched for a friendly kind of question. "So, how's Skye?"

Kate paused a moment, then let out a sigh. "Fine."

"You sure? You hesitated before answering." Zack picked up a wrapped glass and began peeling off the newspaper. "She hasn't gotten picked up by the police again, has she?"

"No, nothing like that." Kate placed an old whiskey bottle behind the bar. "She's just been kind of blue. She wasn't invited to a party last week that all the girls in her homeroom class were invited to, and she's really been down about it. She found out yesterday that another girl is having a swim party this evening, and she just feels really left out of things." Kate carefully unrolled a glass. "But I told her that she can be in the movie."

"Good for you."

"She's dying to see how a movie's shot. She can't wait."

"She doesn't have to. She's welcome on the set anytime. In fact, she can come this afternoon if she wants."

Kate looked up. "Really?"

"Sure."

"That would sure take the sting out of the party snub." Kate's face softened into a smile. "I'll call Mom and ask her to bring Skye down after school."

"Your mom is welcome to stay, too."

"I'll pass that along, but I doubt she'll take you up on it. She doesn't stay out of the house much."

"Because of 'crime'?"

Kate nodded. "She's becoming something of a hermit. The more she stays in, the more she wants to stay in. But she doesn't mind driving Skye places. She'll be happy to pick her up at school and bring her down here. She's been worried about her." Kate smiled, her eyes warm. "This is great, Zack. Thanks. Thanks a lot."

"My pleasure." And it was. Making Kate smile like that made him feel good all the way to his toes.

Their eyes caught and held.

"Hey, Zack," Deb called. "Are you ready to block this scene?"

"Sure." He turned back to Kate. "The dinner offer stands. Any evening you feel like taking me up on it, I'll be more than ready."

Chapter Fifteen

"Come *on*, Grams. Park the car, already!"

"I can't just stop in the middle of the street." Ruth braked as a taxi bullied its way in front of her Toyota. "I have to find a parking place."

Skye peered out the window. "But we're here! They've got the street blocked off and everything. Just stop, and I'll get out." She started to unfasten her seat belt.

Ruth stretched out her arm, as if she were restraining an infant. "Not so fast, young lady. You're not going anywhere in the French Quarter alone."

"Awww! At this rate, they'll be finished before we even get there."

"Patience is a virtue." Ruth made a right turn and headed down Conti in search of a parking spot. "I suggest you work on cultivating it."

Skye rolled down the window as they cruised by two young men with blond Mohawk haircuts. "Hey! Are there any parking garages around here?"

One of the young men pointed. "Halfway up the next block."

Skye waved. "Thanks!"

A surge of alarm rushed through Ruth. She abruptly hit the window button.

Skye raised up along with the sliding glass to talk through the narrowing opening. "Hey, I like your hair!"

"You can't just talk to strangers on the street!" Ruth admonished.

"Why not? I found out where we can park." Skye pointed to the left. "There it is."

Ruth frowned as she steered the car into the garage entrance. Skye had no idea of the danger out there—no concept of the horrible things that could happen in the blink of an eye. She was still fretting about it as as she stopped the car.

Skye rolled her eyes as her grandmother carefully removed her car key from her key ring. "You don't need to do that. Just give them the whole key chain."

"So they can make copies of my house key while we're gone and burglarize my house any time they feel like it? I don't think so."

"How would they even know where you live?"

"With most people, they'd only have to look in the glovebox to find the registration papers." Ruth unlocked her glovebox, pulled out a large white envelope, and stuffed it in her purse. "I don't believe in giving strangers access to that much personal information."

"Jeeze, Grams, you're paranoid. You really oughta see a shrink."

Ruth bristled. It wasn't the first time Skye had implied that she was mentally ill. And Kate kept hounding her to get some kind of counseling. Neither one of them knew what they were talking about, though. Neither one of them had ever been inside a mental institution or seen a *real* mental case, or they wouldn't make the insinuation so lightly. "There's nothing wrong with me. I just believe in using common sense and caution, that's all."

Ruth handed the single key to the attendant, took the ticket, then followed Skye out to the street. She carefully looked in both directions. "Stay close to me and keep your eyes peeled," she warned.

But her granddaughter was already striding down the sidewalk, straight toward two unkempt men in dirty jeans. Ruth hurried to catch up with her. "Let's cross the street," she whispered urgently.

"But we need to be on this side."

"Just do as I say."

"Because of those two guys? Grams, they aren't going to jump us."

"You can't be sure of that."

"Jeeze!" Skye huffed out an exasperated sigh but strode across the street with Ruth. The minute the men were past, she darted back across the street.

Ruth was glad she was wearing sneakers and jeans, because otherwise she would have had a hard time keeping up with her granddaughter. Skye hurried down the next half-block, then headed straight into the midst of a crowd that had formed outside a barricade. Ruth followed as she edged her way to the front and started to climb over.

A large, burly policeman stepped in front of the girl, his barrel chest blocking her way. "Hey—you can't come in here."

"Yes, I can. I'm going to be in the movie."

The policeman's bushy right eyebrow rose over his sunglasses. "Oh, yeah?"

Skye tilted her head up in an unconscious imitation of Kate. "Yeah. Right, Grams?"

Good heavens—she needed to sit that child down and give her a serious talk about the correct way to speak to people in authority. Ruth gave the officer a conciliatory smile. "As a matter of fact, Officer, we were invited here by Mr. Jackson."

The officer's mirrored glasses turned in her direction. Ruth smoothed a wayward lock of hair in the reflection.

"What're your names?" he asked in a gruff voice.

"I'm Skye Matthews."

"And I'm Ruth. Ruth Matthews."

"Wait here." The officer took a few steps away, pulled a walkie-talkie from his belt, and mumbled into it. The crackle of static could be heard over the murmur of the crowd.

"Are you really in the movie?" A teenage boy standing by the barricade asked Skye.

Skye nodded.

"Wow. Are you anyone famous?"

"Not yet," Skye said confidently.

The officer turned back to Ruth with a diffident smile. "Come right in, Ms. Matthews. Mr. Jackson said he's expecting you." The barricade scraped on the pavement as he pulled it aside. "Sorry for the inconvenience. Just doing my job."

"I understand," Ruth reassured him. "Thank you."

Skye sailed past the officer, her head held high. "Told you."

The girl wasn't nearly as cocky once they were beyond the barricade. She stared wide-eyed at all the trucks and cables and lights and equipment. "Jeeze, Grams—look at all this stuff!" Awed and silent, she stuck to Ruth's side, and let Ruth go first through the narrow doorway into the old bar.

The small, musty room was bright as the beach at midday, crowded with jeans-clad people and enormous cameras and lights. Ruth scanned the room, looking for Kate, and finally spotted her across the room, arranging old bottles behind the bar.

Skye dashed over and gave her mother a big hug.

"Hi, honey." Kate gave a surprised smile and hugged her back, briefly closing her eyes, as if she were committing the moment to memory.

A pang of poignancy shot through Ruth's heart. These instances of spontaneous affection from Skye were growing increasingly rare. More and more, Skye was pulling away from her mother. Ruth remembered it well—the heartbreaking sense that time was running out, that soon she would no longer be needed; the bittersweet mix of joy and loss as a child disappeared and a woman emerged; the pain and confusion of having a daughter go from biggest supporter and cheerful buddy to severest critic and moody stranger. It was all a part of the process, all a necessary step in separation as Skye grew toward adulthood, but knowing that didn't make it hurt any less. Ruth was glad to see her daughter get a momentary reprieve from Skye's sulky advance into adolescence.

The girl stepped back and looked around, her eyes as big and round as circus rings. "Wow, this is *cool!*"

"It is, isn't it?" Zack's amused voice rumbled over Ruth's shoulder. She turned around to find him standing next to a large camera, wearing a broad smile. "Hi, Ruth—Skye. Glad you two could make it."

A large, muscled man stepped out from behind the camera. Ruth's eyes fastened on him like a bug on flypaper and wouldn't let go.

He was tall, maybe six feet, and built like a Sherman tank— hard and bulky and solid. His gray hair was pulled straight back in a ponytail, his tanned face sported a thick gray beard, and his nose looked as if it had been broken a time or two. He wore a gold ring in one ear, a black T-shirt, and a pair of faded jeans.

He looked like a muscle-bound Willie Nelson—or a pirate, or an outlaw, or maybe a hit man. If he'd driven by her house, she would have reached for her camera. If she'd met him on the street, she would have ducked into a doorway until he passed. She ought to step back now, but her feet were strangely riveted to the floor.

He was standing disconcertingly close, so close she could see the odd green-gray tint of his eyes. Something about them— some spark or depth or intensity—made it impossible to look away. His gaze held hers like a pair of fur-lined manacles.

"I'd like you to meet Fritz Gibson, our director of photography," Zack was saying.

The man's eyes tightened their hold on hers. "Nice to meet you." His voice was a deep rumble, like the engine of an eighteen-wheeler. He stuck out a large hand. Ruth took it hesitantly. His grasp was gentle, but the callused warmth of his palm exuded a masculine strength that made her go weak in the knees.

He made her feel overwhelmed, overpowered, overcome, but not in the usual afraid-for-her safety way.

Sexually. This man's power was all sexual. Something about him resuscitated hormones that she'd thought long since expired.

The thought sent a shock wave pulsing through her. She was still reeling from it when she made another startling realization: Fritz was staring at her chest.

To her alarm, he gave a low, appreciative whistle. "Hey, that's real nice equipment you've got there."

Ruth's jaw dropped. She'd always heard that people in Hollywood were more open about sexual matters than she was accustomed to, but this was beyond the pale. The situation called for indignation, but all she could muster was shock. "I—I beg your pardon?"

He nodded at her chest. "That's an 'Eighty-four Nikon, isn't it?"

Ruth's fingers flew to her camera. *Of course.* Why on earth had she assumed he was talking about her breasts? She certainly wasn't herself this afternoon. "Why . . . why, yes. Yes, it is."

"It's a classic—a real beauty." His gaze tipped up and trapped hers again. "Just like it's owner."

There was no mistaking his meaning this time. Her face suffused with sudden heat. She would have thought it was a hot flash, except for the fact that she was hot in places that hadn't felt that way in a long, long time.

His eyes were doing that hypnotic, gravitational thing again. They weren't just eyes, Ruth thought hazily—they were a place to fall into. A place where the world was topsy-turvy and inside out, full of things she hadn't known she wanted but suddenly craved.

His gaze was positively penetrating. Penetrating and piercing—like arrows, or daggers, or bullets, or . . .

"So what do you like to shoot?" he asked.

Had they actually been talking about weapons? Ruth could have sworn she'd merely been thinking about them, but when Fritz looked at her like that, she couldn't be sure of anything. "Oh, I don't believe in carrying a weapon," Ruth told him earnestly. "It's too easy for a criminal to take it away and use it on you."

Laughter rumbled from Fritz's throat. "Hey, that's a good one!"

Ruth grinned nervously, not sure what she'd said that was so amusing but pleased at the way Fritz was smiling at her.

He stepped closer and lifted her camera. He was close, so close she could smell his faintly spicy, leathery scent. As he turned the camera and looked at the light setting, his knuckle accidentally grazed her breast. Her brain felt as if someone had turned on a fog machine. Oh, mercy, she felt nervous as a schoolgirl—as awkward as the time she'd smiled at her ninth-grade crush and accidentally shot a rubber band from her braces onto his forehead.

"So, what's your favorite subject?" Fritz asked.

He must be telepathic. How else could he know she was thinking about school? Or maybe she only *thought* she'd been thinking about it, when actually she'd been talking. Either way, he was looking at her expectantly, waiting for an answer. "Well, in high school it was social studies, but I majored in English in college."

Fritz threw back his head and roared. "I love your sense of humor, Ruth." He grinned at Zack. "She's one funny lady."

A dry smile tugged the corners of Zack's mouth. "You can say that again."

Ruth grinned uncertainly, once again not sure what had prompted Fritz's laughter but more than willing to be the cause of it. "I do my best."

"Sheeze, Grams. What's with all the dorky answers?" Skye rolled her eyes and turned to Fritz with a can-you-believe-how-weird-my-relatives-are, see-what-I-have-to-put-up-with look. "She mostly takes pictures of license plates."

Pictures. He was asking about pictures. Ruth would have wished the floor would open up and swallow her whole, except for the fact that Fritz thought she was witty.

He looked at her now with complete fascination. "Wow, what a coincidence. I collect plates myself."

Might as well stick with what worked. Ruth cocked her head at a coquettish angle. "Paper or china?"

Fritz's laughter filled the room. "You're really something, Ruth."

"I'll take that as a compliment."

"Good, because it's meant as one." He smiled at her, and she smiled back. They must have stayed like that for quite a while, because the next thing Ruth knew, Kate was discreetly clearing her throat.

"Do you have a lot of license plates, Mr. Gibson?" Kate asked.

"Call me Fritz. And yeah—a whole wall of my house is covered with them. I've got at least one from every state."

"So does Grams!" Skye interjected. "Not the actual plates, but photos of them. She's got books and books of license plate photos. And they're all from vehicles that drove down our street."

Fritz's eyes were full of admiration. "Hey, that's really cool."

Ruth couldn't resist shooting Kate and Skye a triumphant look. Here, finally, was someone who appreciated her efforts.

"I love the symbolism," Fritz was saying.

Skye's brow scrunched together. "What symbolism?"

"That the whole world is within reach."

"Ha! In Grams's case, it's more like the whole world is passing her by." Ruth felt as if she'd been slapped with a big bag of ice. The words skated through her mind, hard and cold and painful. Was that what Skye really thought? Did Kate think that, too?

Worst of all, was it true?

"Skye Marie Matthews." Kate fixed her daughter with a reprimanding glare. "That was rude and uncalled for."

"Sorry," Skye mumbled.

The exchange seemed lost on Fritz. He was still gazing at Ruth admiringly. "I'd love to see your photos sometime."

Ruth nodded numbly.

"What about tomorrow? We're only shooting two scenes, so I'll be free in the evening. I could come by around six, look at your pictures, then take you out to dinner."

Tomorrow! Oh, dear—he wasn't talking about an abstract sometime. He really wanted to come over! A wave of panic rushed through her. She wasn't comfortable with the idea of letting a man into her home—into her life.

Her mind starting piling up reasons like sandbags against a spring flood. She wasn't interested in dating. And she didn't really know anything about him, aside from the fact that he had amazing eyes and an incredible smile and an apparent appreciation for non sequiturs. He could be an ax murderer, for all she knew. Zack worked with him, but still . . . People had worked with John Wayne Gacy and never known what he was really like.

She shook her head. "I'm afraid I can't."

"Already got plans, huh?"

"Are you kidding?" Skye exclaimed. "Grams never has any pl—ow!" Skye rubbed her side and shot her mother an accusing look.

Fritz's gaze stayed on Ruth. "Don't tell me you're married."

"N-no."

"Seein' someone?"

"Oh, no, no. It's just . . ."

"Grams *never* goes out with . . . hey!" Skye rubbed her rib and glared at Kate. "Why do you do keep poking me?"

"Ruth is very cautious about who she sees," Zack said smoothly. "She doesn't usually go out with someone she's just met." He turned to Ruth. "I can vouch for Fritz. He's one of the most respected cinematographers in Hollywood, and I've known him for years."

"But Grams never—" Skye began.

"I'd be delighted," Ruth said abruptly, surprising even herself. "If Zack vouches for you."

"Great!" Fritz flashed that wide grin again, then hauled a small notepad out of the back pocket of his jeans. "I'll need your address and phone number . . . and think about where you want to go eat."

The notepad was warm with his body heat. A hot shiver scooted along her spine as she opened it and jotted down the information. Their fingers touched as she handed it back, and she felt a static shock.

"Hey, Fritz—ya want an uplight here?" a young man in a dingy white muscle shirt called from behind the bar.

Fritz gave Ruth an apologetic smile. "Duty calls. See you tomorrow."

"Tomorrow," Ruth echoed, wondering what on earth she'd done.

She was still wondering about it the following evening as she peered out the window, nervously smoothing the skirt of her long denim dress. Why, oh why had she agreed to this? She didn't consort with strange men—especially men who looked like pirates and made her feel all jumpy and addle-brained. She hadn't consorted with a man since Pete. And she had no intention of consorting with Fritz, either.

She was going to show him her photos, that was all, and then they were going to share a meal together. She'd put a roast in the oven. She hoped he wouldn't misinterpret the fact that she was cooking for him, but she simply couldn't deal with the stress of going out. Just the thought of leaving home at night made her short of breath. She'd explain to Fritz that she thought it was just easier to dine in than to hassle with a restaurant.

There was no reason to feel so jittery, she scolded herself. This was no big deal, just a platonic evening between two adults who shared a common interest in photography and license plates. There was nothing romantic or suggestive about it.

Nothing except for the way her body overheated at the thought of the man. Ruth fanned herself with one hand, fingering the camera around her neck with the other. The camera always calmed her. Looking through the shutter helped her focus her thoughts, helped her see things more clearly. When she was behind her camera, she felt in control.

The rumble of a car approached. She aimed the lens out the window, panning the vehicle as it drove by. It was the Bensons, who lived in the next block—no need to worry. She lowered the camera and watched the Chrysler's taillights fade in the distance.

"*The world is passing her by.*" Unbidden, Skye's remark rose in Ruth's mind and hovered like toxic fumes.

Why did the comment bother her so? Like any motor-mouthed kid, Skye said lots of smart-alecky things, and Ruth usually blew them off without a second thought. Why had this one gotten under her skin?

Because it is true. She stood at her window, watching other people going places while she stayed put. One day was much like another. She was just marking time, just letting days go by, waiting, watching, waiting, watching. Waiting . . . for what? For time to run out? For life to be over?

Ruth turned from the window and opened the oven to check on the roast. It wasn't as if she was sitting around twiddling her thumbs. She was helping Kate raise Skye. Without her help, Kate wouldn't have been able to get her education or her job.

But Skye was getting older. In a few years, she would be grown and gone. Hopefully Kate would meet someone and marry, and then Ruth would no longer be needed.

Then what? What would give Ruth's life meaning and purpose then?

The loud roar of an approaching vehicle jolted Ruth out of her thoughts. Closing the oven door, she hurried to the window, raised her camera, and looked through the lens. It was a motorcycle, and it was headed this way.

A wave of indignation shot through her. Motorcycles had no business on quiet residential streets like this one, making all kinds of noise and disturbing the peace. She didn't care for motorcyclists, anyway. Most of them were riffraff daredevils with no regard for others—loud, rowdy, uncouth troublemakers who traveled in packs and had no respect for the law.

This one was alone, but he looked more sinister than a dozen Hell's Angels. Dressed all in black and sitting astride a polished machine that gleamed like a dark diamond, he could have been the devil himself, prowling the street in search of lost souls. The blackened face shield of his helmet completely obscured his features, making him look like Darth Vader. A shiver crawled up Ruth's arms as she followed the cycle's noisy progress with her camera, ready to shoot the license plate as soon as it passed her house.

But instead of passing, the motorcycle slowed, turned into her drive, and stopped. The driver killed the engine. In the sudden silence, Ruth's heart thumped loudly in her ears. Oh, no—it couldn't be. . . .

But it was. Ruth's stomach did a weird flip as the burly man pulled off the helmet to reveal a gray ponytail and a grizzled beard.

She watched Fritz hang the helmet on the handlebar, then turn toward the house. His gaze honed in on her like radar. He smiled and waved at her through the window. Ruth waved back, then stood there, numbly staring, as he sauntered up the walk in a bowlegged stride. It wasn't until the doorbell rang that it dawned on her to scurry over to let him in.

He completely filled the doorway. "I'm a little early. Hope that's okay."

"Oh—that's, uh, fine." She stepped back and he strode in, bringing with him the scent of fresh air and faint aftershave. The smell did funny things to her pulse. He probably hadn't shaved in years, yet he wore aftershave. The thought intrigued and aroused her.

Lots of things about this man had that effect on her. She never would have thought that fitted black jeans and a Harley David-son T-shirt was an attractive outfit, yet on Fritz it looked pos-itively sexy. Another shiver shimmied down her arm, and her head got that odd, swathed-in-cotton feeling it had had yester-day.

"Wearing your camera again, I see."

Ruth's fingers flew to the Nikon. "I, uh, like to keep it handy."

Kate and Skye treated her as if she was nuts to always have her camera around her neck, but to her relief, Fritz nodded, as if the explanation made perfect sense. "The best shots are spontaneous. If you're not prepared, you miss them."

"That's exactly how I feel!" Ruth smiled at him. A long moment passed before she realized she was just standing there, grinning like a fool. "Oh, dear—where are my manners? Come in, come in." She opened the door wider and stepped back.

Fritz strode in and looked around the small foyer. "Nice place you've got here."

"Thanks." Ruth led him into the living room and perched on the green chenille sofa. He sat down beside her, his weight making the cushion sink so that she listed toward him. He'd no doubt do that to a mattress, too. A woman sleeping with him would end up flush against him all night. The thought made her cheeks burn.

"I couldn't help noticing the plaque on your porch. So this is a historic preservation home?"

Ruth nodded. "My late husband was an architect who specialized in restoring old buildings. This house was one of his first projects."

Fritz looked around. "He did good work." His gaze came to rest on her. "Have you been on your own for long?"

"Twenty-one years, five months, and . . ." Ruth did a fast mental calculation. "Twelve days."

Fritz grinned. "Not that you're counting."

"It's an old habit. Sorry."

"Nothing to be sorry about. It shows you loved him."

She wasn't sure what startled her more, his perceptiveness or the forthrightness of his comment. "You're right. I did."

"He was a lucky man."

A rush of heat coursed through Ruth.

Fritz's gaze fell on a silver-framed photo on the side table. He reached over and picked it up. "This him?"

"Yes." It was disconcerting, talking about Pete with a man who was so completely his physical opposite. Pete had been lean and slight, only a couple of inches taller than Ruth. Fritz was built like a professional wrestler and topped Ruth's height by a good half foot or more. Pete had been clean-shaven, with short hair that was always impeccably groomed. Fritz's hair and beard gave him a resemblance to Grizzly Adams. Pete had worn starched button-down shirts, pressed jackets, and polished wingtips. Fritz's clothing looked like it had been unrolled from a knapsack. How could she be attracted to two men who were so different?

She cleared her throat and tried to clear her thoughts. "I took that photo on Pete's thirtieth birthday. It's one of my favorites."

Fritz stared at it closely for a long, silent moment, then carefully put it back down. "Did you take these, too?" he asked, studying the other photos of Pete and Kate clustered on the table.

"Yes."

"Hey, you're a terrific photographer." His gaze shifted to her face, and the things she saw in those gray-green depths sent a thrill right through her skin. Admiration, respect . . . attraction. Heavens, no man had looked at her like that in a couple of decades.

She gave a tentative smile, and he smiled back. He turned his attention back to the photos, picking up one of Kate and Pete at the Audubon Zoo. "Great lighting, good angle, terrific composition. Best of all, you seem to have a knack for snapping the shutter at just the right moment."

"I got lucky on that one."

"Don't sell yourself short." He carefully placed the photo exactly where it had been. "Ever work professionally?"

"Oh, no. It's just a hobby."

"Well, you outshine ninety-nine percent of the pros out there." He picked up a photo of Pete, proudly holding an enormous catfish. "Where was this taken?"

"At our fishing camp. We used to go there just about every

weekend." Ruth grinned. "He caught that from our back porch. We ate off that fish for three days."

Fritz smiled. "Fishing, huh? Sounds like you and your husband had a lot of good times."

"We did." The conversation had taken an intimate turn at a disarmingly rapid pace. "So, what about you? Have you been married?"

"Nope."

"Why not?"

"Never met the right woman, I guess. I thought I had a couple of times, but it never worked out." Fritz gave a rueful grin. "Guess I came with too much baggage."

Oh, dear. That could mean anything from a criminal conviction to a penchant for cross-dressing. The image of this big, burly man in lace and garters made her smile. "This baggage of yours—was it carry-on or the kind that needs a skycap?"

Fritz laughed. "Damn, but I love your sense of humor."

Ruth grinned. "Flattery won't get you out of answering the question."

"Well, I'm afraid my baggage would have needed a forklift." Fritz slowly set down the photo, then leaned forward, his forearms on his thighs. "I had a younger brother who was a quadriplegic. I was the only family he had, so . . ."

Ruth's heart softened like a chocolate bar in the sun. "So you took care of him."

Fritz nodded. "He lived with me."

"That was very noble of you."

"I don't know about noble." Fritz's mouth twisted in a wry grin. "But it was sure a deal-buster when it came to women."

"You were dating the wrong kind. A lot of women would think a man that caring and compassionate was a real find."

"Yeah, well, I never ran across any like that—at least not any who stayed that way after they met Steven. I had someone who cared for him while I worked, but when I was home, I did it all myself. It wasn't a lifestyle most women were willing to buy into."

Ruth's throat grew tight.

"They all said I should put him in a home, but I couldn't do that. I just couldn't bring myself to store him away like he was some kind of vegetable. He was still the same person he'd always been, except he was trapped inside a wreck of a body. I figured, hey, his options in life have been limited enough as it was. He should at least get to live where he wanted."

"Was he in an accident?"

Fritz nodded. "One minute he was a healthy college student working a summer job as a roofer, and the next he'd taken a thirty-foot fall and severed his spinal cord. How tough a break is that?"

"Very tough."

"Damn straight. He was working that summer to buy a Harley." A flicker of pain crossed Fritz's face. "I wouldn't loan him the money, because I thought motorcycles were too dangerous."

"But you're riding one now."

Fritz's mouth turned up in a sheepish grin. "Yeah, well, I guess I'm kinda doin' it for him." He gazed at a brass sconce on the far wall. "He told me to live enough for both of us."

The knot in Ruth's throat doubled in size.

"I still miss him," Fritz finished.

Ruth nodded. "It's hard to lose a family member, especially if you've been caring for them for a long time."

Fritz's moss-green eyes fixed on hers. "Sounds like you've had some experience along those lines."

Ruth stared down at her skirt. "About thirteen years ago, my older sister's world fell to pieces. First her husband left her for some young co-worker, then she was diagnosed with terminal cancer. I convinced her to move here from Shreveport so I could care for her."

Fritz's gaze warmed her skin. "That had to be hard."

Ruth plucked at a loose thread in her lap. "You know, it's funny: I think she helped me as much as I helped her. Kate had just turned eighteen and run off to New York, and I was worried sick about her. I was going to go up there and find her and try

208

to convince her to come home. But my sister made me see that my overprotectiveness had driven her away. If I ever wanted to have a relationship with her, I had to back off and let her have her own life. Talk about hard . . . now, *that* was hard." Ruth smiled slightly. "It still is."

She looked up and found Fritz looking at her. He had the warmest, kindest eyes she'd ever seen. Not only kind but wise. And yet there was something risky about looking into them, something challenging and almost dangerous.

He was a threat to the status quo. If she kept looking into those eyes, her life would have to change.

The baritone gong of the grandfather clock in the foyer interrupted her thoughts. She jumped to her feet. "Oh, my—I'm giving Southern hospitality a bad name. What can I get you to drink?"

"Just water, please."

"You sure? I've got beer, or I could open a bottle of wine. And I've got some cheese and crackers."

"Water's fine for right now. We'll be going out to eat pretty soon. Did you decide which restaurant you want to go to?"

Ruth's palms grew damp, and her heart picked up speed. "I, um, hope you don't mind, but I'm cooking dinner here. I thought you probably eat out all the time, and it'll take a while to look through my license tag photos, and, well . . . I hope you don't mind just staying in."

"Mind? Are you kidding? A home-cooked meal sounds terrific. I can't think of anything nicer." He grinned. "But if you want to stay here because you're worried about getting to a restaurant in one piece, I wasn't planning to make you ride on the back of my Harley. I was going to call a taxi."

"Oh, that hadn't even occurred to me. But . . . thanks."

Fritz's smile widened. "Somehow, I didn't figure you for the motorcycle type."

"No? What type did you figure me for?"

Fritz studied her thoughtfully. "Witty. Intelligent. Artistic. Clever. Quirky." He grinned again. "Maybe even a little bit wacko. But fascinating." His gaze deepened and softened, and so did his voice. "Absolutely, positively fascinating."

"Really?"

"Absolutely."

A smile curved on Ruth's lips. Intelligent and witty? She'd never thought of herself in those terms. She'd always seen Pete and Kate as the ones with those attributes. She'd always been the supporter and encourager, the wife and mother, the keeper of hearth and home and domestic tranquillity. She'd occasionally suspected she was a little bit wacko—but artistic? Clever? *Fascinating?*

A thrill bubbled through her veins. She smoothed her hair self-consciously. "Well, I'd better go get your water. It's, um, in the kitchen. I mean, the kitchen is where I keep the glasses and ice, so . . ." She was babbling again. She clamped her lips shut, then smiled. "I'll be right back."

She fled the room, feeling flushed and giddy and more alive than she'd been in years.

Chapter Sixteen

Kate strode from the storage trailer to the set the next afternoon to find a familiar figure squatting in the corner, intently staring through a camera lens. "Mom?"

Ruth started and spun around. "Hi, Kate."

Kate regarded her curiously. "What're you doing here?"

"I, um, brought Skye down after school. She's off helping Deb with something. And I'm taking a few shots for Fritz."

This was completely out of character. Kate looked at her mother closely. Ruth was wearing makeup and earrings, and her hair was less unruly than usual. Kate grinned. "I guess that means things went well last night."

"We had a nice time." Ruth adjusted one of the camera settings and lifted it to her eye again.

"So, where did you go?"

A flash lit the room as Ruth snapped the camera. "Nowhere. We just stayed in. I cooked a roast."

"Sounds like a cozy evening." Real cozy—especially for a first date. Kate stared at her mother. "So what did you two do?"

Ruth squeezed off another shot. "Talked and looked at photos, mostly. Fritz said I'm a really good photographer. He said they usually hire someone to shoot still pictures while they're making a movie. He wants to talk to Zack about hiring me instead of bringing the usual guy all the way from California. Can you believe it?"

"Wow—that's terrific!" Kate had been urging her mother to get out more, but she'd always resisted. This was nothing short of astounding. "And you agreed?"

"Well, I agreed to take a few preliminary shots and see how they turn out."

"Sounds like you and Fritz really hit it off."

Ruth looked down at her camera again, the color rising in her cheeks. Kate stared in amazement. She was blushing. Her fifty-three-year-old mother was blushing!

"You don't mind, do you?" Ruth asked.

"Why should I mind?"

"Well, for one thing, I'd be working with you. And some-times . . ." She paused. "Well, some people get upset when their parents start . . . seeing someone."

Kate's mouth fell open. She abruptly closed it. "No, no, I think it's great. I'm just a little surprised, that's all." Boy, was that ever putting it mildly. The thought of her reclusive mother dating was shocking enough. The thought of her dating a man with a beard, a ponytail, and biker clothes was flat-out aston-ishing. "Where is Fritz?"

"He went to find an engineer. There's a problem with one of the cameras."

As if on cue, Fritz sauntered into the room. Ruth's face lit up. Fritz grinned and headed toward her.

Kate's cell phone rang. She pulled it out of her pocket and answered it, her attention riveted on the interplay between her mother and her unlikely suitor.

"Kate?" growled a rough voice.

She recognized it right away. "Mr. Goldman—hello! How are you today?"

"Just peachy," he replied. "Listen up, kiddo—you know that TV show 'Eye-To-Eye'?"

"The entertainment news show?"

"Yeah. They're gonna do a feature about *Ooh, La La!*, and they're sending a crew to New Orleans. You're gonna be their contact person."

"What does that mean, exactly?"

"You're gonna take them around, show them stuff, and make sure they do the story our way."

Kate's fingers tightened on the phone. "How am I supposed to do that?'

"I'm sendin' a media consultant down there to work with you. He understands just what I'm after, and he'll tell you how to get it."

"But I'm an expert on history, not media relations."

"Yeah, well, you're fixin' to become both."

"But . . ."

"No buts, sweetheart." His voice was cold and ugly as a slab of freezer-burned meat. "It's in your contract, so you'll damn well do it. Do we understand each other?"

A queasy feeling hit her stomach. "Y-yes. But I'm not sure exactly what you want me to do."

"Give 'em all that history mumbo-jumbo. An' just be yourself, sweetheart. I want you to just be yourself."

Just be yourself. Yeah, right, Kate thought the next week as she stared at herself in the wardrobe trailer mirror. That was a little hard to do, considering that for the last three days, the media consultant had tried to turn her into someone else.

An effeminate man with a toothpaste-ad smile and a propensity for overusing superlatives, the consultant had coached her on everything from body language to speech patterns. "You want to look super-serious, darling, so don't smile too much," he reminded her now.

As if she had anything to smile about. He'd spent hours coaching her on "spontaneous" answers to any conceivable question the "Eye-To-Eye" reporter might ask, drilling her on the importance of appearing scholarly and somber at all times.

He'd spent an equal amount of time huddling with the movie's wardrobe consultant, hair stylist, and make-up artist about how to give Kate the desired look.

Which apparently was the mud-ugly, homelier-than-a-frog's-hiny look. She hadn't had a makeover; she'd had a make-under. She now appeared to have no cheekbones, no lips, and no eyelashes, and her hair was pulled back so tightly in a bun that it felt as if her eyebrows were sitting on top of her head.

To add insult to injury, the consultant had insisted that she wear a pair of heavy black plastic eyeglasses to make her look more intellectual. He'd encased her feet in clunky three-inch platform shoes so she wouldn't have to look up at the reporter, and dressed her in a baggy beige suit so frumpy it looked like she'd borrowed it from the Queen of England.

The consultant clasped his hands together and beamed with satisfaction. "You look fabulous! Just terrific. You'll be marvelous."

Fabulous, terrific, marvelous . . . Oh, give me a break.

The consultant glanced at his wristwatch. "I've got to run or I'll miss my plane. Before I go, though, one more time—what's the core message we want to get across?"

"This movie is based on fact," Kate dutifully recited, "and we're going to great lengths to make sure that every detail is as authentic as possible."

"Wonderful!" He clapped his hands, his smile widening to show even more of his dazzling dental work. "You're going to be fantastic! I told Mr. Jackson just last night that he had nothing to worry about."

"He was worried?" Kate had only seen Zack once in the last week. Yesterday, as she and the consultant had done a final walk-through of the new set in the uptown mansion that was serving as the bordello interior, she'd felt Zack's gaze on her. It had been a physical sensation, a warming of the skin. She'd turned, and sure enough, there he was, looking at her across the room, his gaze intent, his expression inscrutable.

The consultant shrugged. "Oh, you know directors. They all worry about everything."

"What was *this* director worried about?"

The consultant's smile wattage rose to a placating level. "Nothing, dear. He was just concerned that you might make the movie seem a little, well . . . boring."

Kate felt as if she'd just been hit by a giant fist. "He thinks I'll be boring?"

She knew it shouldn't matter, but she hated for Zack to think of her that way. Boring meant dull, bland, colorless . . . uninteresting.

Uninteresting. Had Zack lost interest in her?

The thought made her heart sink like the *Titanic*. It was one thing for him to leave her alone because he was complying with her request. It was another for him to avoid her because he was no longer interested.

"Well, I'm off." The consultant pranced to the door. He raised a manicured hand and gave a beauty-queen wave. "Break a leg, darling!"

I'd rather break both of yours, Kate thought dourly as the door closed behind him. She turned back toward the mirror and frowned at her reflection. Zack thought she was boring, and he hadn't even seen her looking like this.

"And he's not going to, either," Kate muttered with sudden decisiveness. There was nothing in her contract that said she had to look boring. The history of Storyville was colorful. Why couldn't she be colorful, too?

Before she could change her mind, she pulled off the bulky jacket and strode rapidly to the draped changing area, where an assortment of other outfits that the wardrobe dresser had gathered from local stores hung in a neat row. Unfortunately, she discovered that all of them were dark, dull, and shapeless— all except one.

Kate grabbed it and pulled it out. It was fire-engine red and had a short, short skirt. A note was pinned to it: *For Lena. Shoes are below.*

Obviously it was meant for the movie's star, but Lena Brighton wasn't even in town yet, and the suit was Kate's size. Here goes nothing, she thought.

Peeling off the hideous blouse and skirt, Kate pulled on the red jacket and viewed herself in the dressing room mirror as she buttoned it. Tight, fitted, and cut low enough to show a hint of cleavage, it was designed to be worn without a blouse. Not bad. She stepped into the short skirt, slipped on the red snakeskin pumps she found beneath the clothes rack, and turned back to the mirror.

The slim skirt hugged her hips and stopped at mid-thigh. With the high-heeled shoes, her legs looked as long as the Yucatan Peninsula.

A smile crossed her face. Her friend Samantha had alway said she should raise her hemline to show off her legs. Maybe she should have listened to Sam's advice after all. From the neck down, she was definitely not boring.

From the neck up, though, she looked like a schoolmarm. Frowning at her reflection, Kate rapidly pulled all the pins out of her hair, then glanced at her watch. Just enough time to go back to the hair and makeup people and announce a change of plans. The plain-Jane look was out. Drop-dead gorgeous was in.

"Boring, huh?" Kate muttered to herself, shaking out her hair and gathering up her notes. "Well, we'll just see about that."

Chapter Seventeen

"Have you seen Kate since that consultant got through with her?" Fritz asked. He handed a cup of coffee to Ruth, who'd been shooting still photos of the bordello set; then he strode across the room and peered through the lens of a movie camera.

"No." Ruth took a sip from the steaming Styrofoam cup. "But when I talked to her last night, she was pretty upset about the way things were going. She said the consultant was making her look like a spinster librarian."

Zack kept his head down and tried to focus on the schedule he was making, but the sound of Kate's name had interrupted his concentration. From the corner of his eye, he watched Fritz lumber to the next camera.

"Well, he musta changed his mind, because she looks like a million bucks."

"Really?"

"Yeah. She could pass for a movie star herself. I saw her with that TV crew a few minutes ago and I had to look twice to make sure it was really her. The reporter was practically drooling over her."

Tension coiled in Zack's stomach like a rattlesnake.

"Is that right?" Ruth's voice sounded extraordinarily pleased.

"Yeah. His tongue was all but hangin' out. I think they're heading this way. You'll see for yourself in a minute."

Sure enough, the front door opened and Kate's voice sounded from the hallway. Zack stepped into a back room.

"And here we have the set for the *Ooh, La La!* main parlor," Kate said.

"Wow. This is really something." The voice had the practiced resonance of "Eye-To-Eye" 's main reporter, Stone Manning. "Ronnie, you ready to roll?"

Zack peered around the corner and saw a shaggy-headed man with a large video camera on his shoulder. The cameraman stepped to the side, giving Zack a clear view of the rest of the people in the hall. A sound man, a woman who must be the producer, Stone Manning, and a knockout blonde in a blazing red suit.

Holy Moses—was that *Kate?* Zack stared, his heart pounding hard. Fritz hadn't been exaggerating. Her hair hung to her shoulders in a smooth sweep, her legs went all the way to New York and back, and her face looked like a movie star's. He'd already thought she was gorgeous, but the makeup, hairstyle, and clothes kicked it up to a whole new level.

"Okay, Kate—stand over here." The reporter put his arm around her waist and guided her to a spot about three inches to the left. Anger sizzled in Zack's gut. Kate didn't need to move; the S.O.B. just wanted an excuse to put his hands on her.

"How authentic is this set?" Stone was asking.

"Authentic enough that a gentleman from the nineteenth century would feel right at home. The furnishings are based on Sophie's writings and a list of purchases made by the madame. Everything in here is an antique from the time period."

"Let's pretend I'm that nineteenth-century gentleman, and I've just stepped into the Ooh, La La bordello. What would happen next?"

"Well, you'd be greeted by the madame and ushered into the parlor, where you'd be entertained by a jazz pianist like Jelly

Roll Morton. The atmosphere would be that of a party. If it happened to be a Wednesday night, you'd be treated to a floor show. The madame would approach after a while and ask if a particular girl had caught your interest. You'd pay the madame, and the young woman would take you upstairs."

The reporter gazed at Kate in a way that made Zack tense. He just knew the S.O.B. was wishing he could take Kate upstairs.

"And this was all legal?"

"Absolutely. You see, the leaders of New Orleans realized they couldn't stop prostitution, but they could restrict it to one area of the city."

"Did it work?"

"Depends on your point of view. If you were a homeowner who didn't want a brothel in your neighborhood, Storyville was a great solution. If you were a sailor looking for a good time, it was Disneyland."

"So everyone was happy," the reporter said.

"Not everyone," Kate replied. "If you were a woman with no family and no means of support and nowhere else to turn, Storyville was a prison. Once a woman entered the 'sporting life,' her options were cut off. No decent person could associate with her without ruining his or her own reputation."

"So it was impossible for these girls to make a fresh start."

Kate nodded. "That was the predicament of the movie's heroine. Then along came a man who looked beyond her circumstances and saw her heart, and was willing to go up against incredible odds to free her. This movie is their story. It's the tale of an extraordinary love in an extraordinary place in an extraordinary time."

"It certainly sounds like an extraordinary movie, Dr. Matthews. It sounds like you have a hit on your hands."

"And . . . cut!" The TV producer gave Kate a thumbs-up, then turned to the cameraman. "Okay, Ronnie. Let's get some B-roll."

The reporter smiled at Kate as he took off his microphone.

"This is a fascinating topic. I'd love to hear more about it. Have you got plans for dinner tonight?"

"Tonight? Well . . ."

Zack tensed. No way was that slick-talking Romeo going to get Kate alone. He stepped into the room and craned his neck, as if he were looking around. "Oh, Kate—there you are. I need to get with you this evening and go over some details."

Her eyes grew wide. "On what?"

She *would* ask. "The, uh, swamp scene."

"Everything's all set on that. And that's not until next month."

Damn it, why did she have to be so blasted well-informed? "We've run into some problems, and they need to be settled tonight. There's going to be a meeting at six in the production trailer, and we need you there."

Stone smiled at Kate. "We can do dinner afterwards. I'll give you my cell number and you can give me a call when your meeting's over."

Zack shot him a dark look. "This will take a while. You'd better make other plans."

Stone's eyebrows rose. He looked from Zack to Kate, then gave Kate a smooth smile. "Perhaps another time." He turned back to Zack. "Mr. Jackson, while you're here, could I ask you a few questions?"

"Sorry, I don't have time." *And I intend to make sure Kate doesn't have time for you, either.*

Kate found the door to the production trailer slightly ajar at six. She tapped lightly on the door frame and pushed it open to find Zack leaning over a table spread with storyboards, scripts, and schedules. "Am I early?"

Zack straightened and turned toward her. "No, no. Come right on in."

Kate walked into the room and looked around. "Where's everyone else?"

He looked surprised for a moment. "Oh—It's, uh, just the two of us."

That was odd. He'd made it sound like a major meeting. She walked toward one of the chairs beside the table. "What did you need to discuss?"

Zack's eyes locked on her legs as she sat. She saw him swallow as he circled the table. "The, um, boat transportation for the swamp scene. Where are we on that?"

"It's all taken care of."

"Oh. Good." Zack sat on the edge of the table, his arms folded.

"Anything else?"

"The um, décor of the cabin. Are there any other items we'll need?"

This was definitely suspicious. "I've given the set designer a list." Kate narrowed her eyes. "What's this really all about?"

Zack pushed off the table and paced across the room. "Ah, hell. It's that reporter. He's got a reputation as a real ladies' man. I thought I should warn you."

Kate's heart gave a little leap. He was jealous! If he was jealous, he couldn't be indifferent to her. She knew her reaction was illogical, but it didn't keep her from feeling a burst of joy. Her mouth lifted in a wry grin. "Boy, that's the pot calling the kettle black."

He had the grace to give a sheepish smile. "Yeah, well . . . I thought I'd do you a favor and keep you from having to fight him off all night."

Kate couldn't resist baiting him a little. "What makes you think I'd fight him off?"

"Come on, Kate. I know how you feel about mixing sex and business."

"We're not talking about sex. We're talking about dinner."

"Same thing."

Kate's eyebrows flew up. "I beg your pardon?"

"He wouldn't have asked you to dinner if he didn't want to take you to bed."

"Just because that's the way *you* operate doesn't mean everyone else has such cheesy motives."

"This isn't about me. I'm trying to do you a favor."

"Well, thanks but no thanks." She rose from her chair. "Is that all you wanted?"

"No." His forehead gathered into a thundercloud of a scowl. "I want to know what the hell you're doing, all dolled up like that, anyway."

She looked down at her suit. "What do you mean?"

"I thought Goldman wanted you to look studious and scholarly and plain as toast. You look more like French pastry than toast."

A little thrill chased through her. "Yes, well, there was a change of plans."

Kate made a slow pirouette. "So, what do you think?"

"I think your skirt's awfully short."

Kate couldn't resist pressing him. "Do you like it?"

"Hell, yes," he snapped. "Any man with a pulse would *like* it."

"So you don't think it's boring?"

"Why would I ever think that?"

Kate lifted her shoulders. "The consultant said you were worried I'd be boring."

"You?" He stared at her. "I never thought *you* would be boring. I was afraid this publicity approach—focusing on history instead of action—might be boring." He slanted a grin at her. "You're a lot of things, Kate, but you're definitely not boring."

His eyes held a heat that melted her insides like an ice cream sandwich under a heatlamp. The basic fight-or-flight instinct kicked in, and she knew she had to get out of the room or she'd wind up in his arms. She drew a shaky breath and moved to the door. "Well, just for your information, I wasn't going to dinner with Stone anyway. Mom's got plans with Fritz, so I'm spending the evening with Skye."

Zack leaned against the doorjamb. "Your mom and Fritz seem to have really hit it off."

Kate nodded. "I never would have believed it."

"Me, neither, but I was glad to see it. Fritz is a bit of an eccentric, but he's a great guy. He single-handedly cared for his paralyzed brother for years and nobody even knew it. I only found out because Deb saw the brother's obituary and it had Fritz listed as sole survivor. He keeps to himself too much."

"Mom, too."

"Then they should be good for each other. Maybe they'll bring each other out of their shells." He moved closer. His eyes searched hers and his voice dropped, both in tenor and in volume. "You and I could be good for each other, Kate."

Kate's heart raced. His hands reached out and touched her arms.

"I'd love to be good to you. Very, very good."

Kate knew she should push the door open and leave, but her feet seemed embedded in concrete. "We've covered this before." Her voice came out high and thin, as if she weren't getting enough oxygen. "I don't think it's wise."

"What does wisdom have to do with anything?" His hands crept down and captured hers. "You're making me crazy, you know that, don't you?"

Kate's heart thumped like the wings of a caged bird. "Yeah, well, you're not exactly promoting my mental health, either."

His mouth curved ever so slightly. His eyes glittered with heat. "Well, at least that's something." He moved closer, his eyes on her lips, his intent unmistakable. "Kate, honey . . ."

God help her, because she couldn't help herself. He was going to kiss her, and she couldn't bring herself to stop him.

A knock sounded at the door, making them both jump. Fritz ducked his head in the doorway. "Oh, sorry." He backed out, closing the door.

"It's okay," Kate called. "I'm just leaving."

Fritz shot Zack a penitent look. "I, um, just wanted to let you know that the rushes are ready."

"Be right there," Zack said. He looked at Kate. "We'll finish this conversation later."

"It's already finished."

"Oh, no it's not." The determined light in his eyes sent a shiver down her spine.

"Not by a long shot."

*   *   *

"How was school today?" Kate asked later that evening as she cut into a boneless chicken breast.

Across the kitchen table, Skye helped herself to a huge serving of mashed potatoes. "Okay. I had an algebra test, but I'm pretty sure I aced it."

Kate never worried about Skye's grades. Learning was effortless for her, and she consistently brought home straight A's, even though she took advanced classes. The only thing that stumped her was interpersonal relationships.

"So . . . how are things otherwise?"

Skye shoveled a load of mashed potatoes onto her fork. "Okay."

The answer was a big improvement over the usual "they suck" response.

Kate took a sip of iced tea and looked at her daughter over the rim of her glass. "Does that mean things are better?"

Skye nodded, her mouth full. She swallowed and took a gulp of milk. "Everyone thinks it's awesome that I'm hanging out on the movie set. Mary Ann asked me to sit with her and some other kids at lunch, and they asked a lot of questions about it. They all want to come watch. I asked Zack about it this afternoon, and he said they could." She dug her fork into the potatoes again. "Know what he suggested? He said my whole homeroom class could come on a field trip." Skye's face was bright and childlike. "Zack is sooo cool, Mom."

Kate's heart went as soft as the mashed potatoes. Zack was cool, all right—not to mention perceptive and thoughtful and kind.

Kind. Kate's lips curled in a smile. He'd probably scowl at the description, yet it fit. She'd seen it on the set, in the respectful way he treated even his lowliest crew member. She'd seen him dig into his pocket every time he saw a homeless person, and she'd learned he donated all the leftover catered food to a local shelter. And she'd seen it in the way he treated Skye, finding ways to make her feel useful and included, always taking the time to listen to her and answer her questions. The more Kate was around Zack, the more things she found to love about him.

A fire-breathing dragon of panic roared to life in her chest. *Not love. Like.* She *liked* Zack, that was all.

Wasn't it?

She shifted in her chair, trying to block her thoughts from heading any further down that dark and scary path.

"Mary Ann said she's having a birthday sleepover next month, and she said I'm invited," Skye mentioned. "Her birthday is just a week after mine."

"I'm glad you're making friends," Kate said.

"Speaking of birthdays, I've decided what I want for mine."

As always, the mention of Skye's birthday shot a bullet of guilt through Kate. She'd already shipped a CD player and a birthday card signed "Love, Dad" to Samantha for her friend to mail to Skye from an overseas location. But this was the last time, Kate silently vowed again. When the movie was over, she would tell Skye the truth.

"What is it, honey?" Kate asked.

Skye's fork clattered as she set it down on her plate. She leaned forward, her eyes eager. "I want to find my father."

Kate's stomach plummeted like an elevator with a snapped cable. "Honey, that's not possible."

"It is!" Skye's voice was insistent. "With the Internet, you can find anyone."

Terror made it hard to ask the question that begged asking. "H-have you tried?"

"Yeah."

"And?"

Skye blew out a hard, frustrated breath. "No luck."

Relief flooded Kate's chest.

Skye's eyes held reproach. "Just because you don't get along with him doesn't mean I should be deprived. I think it's really selfish of you."

Selfish. She'd given her whole life to Skye, and she'd done her best to protect her from the pain of Wayne's indifference, yet Skye thought she was selfish. It was so ironic, it should have been funny, but Kate unexpectedly found herself blinking back tears. "Honey—I don't even know where he is."

"You could find out. Or you could just tell me the name of the foundation or company or whatever where he works, and I'll find it on the Internet."

"I can't. I—I don't know the—the—name of the organization. He's never . . ." *Don't lie anymore,* her brain warned. *The more you lie, the harder it will be later.* "I don't have any contact with your father," she finished lamely.

"Well, he always sends me something for my birthday. When he does this year, you can hire a detective agency to track him down."

Kate took another swallow of iced tea, trying to relieve her suddenly dry mouth. "Honey, detectives cost thousands of dollars."

"Not if you use one of those Internet services that advertise they can find anyone. They're not all that expensive. I've even got the names of a couple of them." Skye's eyes had that pleading look that was so hard to resist, the kind of look that made Kate willing to walk over hot coals in ordinary circumstances. "Please, Mom? Pleeease? You're always telling me how I should put myself in other people's shoes and look at things from their perspective. Well, how would you feel if you'd never known your father, all because he and Grams had some stupid argument?"

Kate's hand shook as she set down her glass. "Honey, it's not that simple. Some adult situations are too complicated for kids to understand."

"What's to understand?" Skye's eyes were hot and accusing. "I'm being punished because you hate him."

"Skye, honey . . ." Kate swallowed. She'd planned to wait, but this was the perfect opportunity. Maybe she should just tell Skye now. Her pulse raced. "Skye . . . I—"

The phone rang. Skye jumped up to get it. "That might be Mary Ann. She said she'd call me." She tossed Kate one last pleading look. "Don't say no, Mom. Promise you'll at least think about it."

Kate nodded numbly, not sure if she were relieved or disappointed, unsure if the call was a reprieve or a curse.

The buttery scent of popcorn wafted through Ruth's kitchen two weeks later as the fast rat-a-tat-tat in the microwave slowed to a few spastic, sporadic pops. Fritz opened the oven door and pulled out the steaming bag. "What do you want me to put this in?"

Ruth looked up from the lime she was slicing. She'd invited Fritz, Zack, Kate, and Skye over to watch the "Eye-to-Eye" show about the movie, and Fritz had come early to help with the refreshments.

"There's a large green bowl on the top shelf of the left cabinet." Ruth sawed through another slice of lime, watching Fritz from the corner of her eye. A soft smile curled the corners of her lips. My, but it felt good, having a man in her kitchen again. She liked the easy way Fritz moved about, as if he belonged here, taking on tasks as if he'd done them for years. It made her feel warm and cozy inside, like a cat curled up by a fireplace.

He pulled out the bowl and set it on the counter.

"Hold the bag away from your face when you open it," Ruth warned. "The steam in there is hot enough to burn off your beard."

Fritz shot a grin at her. "Would you be glad if it did?"

Ruth looked at him quizzically. "What do you mean?"

Fritz carefully pulled the bag apart, following Ruth's suggestion. "I was wondering if my beard bothered you."

"Why, no. Why would you think that?"

Fritz poured the popcorn in the bowl. "Some women don't like beards. They think they're too scratchy."

For a woman to think a beard was scratchy, she'd have to feel it. And the most likely way a woman would feel a man's beard would be . . .

Ruth felt her body temperature rise. Her gaze fastened on

Fritz's lips. They were nice lips, full and well shaped, surrounded by a thicket of salt-and-pepper whiskers. The thought of those lips on hers, the blunt edge of his mustache tickling her upper lip, the soft wiriness of his beard rasping her chin, sent a thrill-soaked shiver washing through her.

They'd been seeing a great deal of each other for nearly three weeks, and he hadn't yet kissed her. Oh, he'd kissed her hello and good-bye, soft pecks on the cheek or forehead that left her feeling heady and dizzy, but he hadn't yet *really* kissed her, not in a full-on-the-mouth, romantic way. Not that there had been much opportunity; ever since the movie's two stars had arrived on location five days earlier, the shooting schedule had left little time for socializing. Fritz began working before dawn and didn't finish until nine or ten. She saw him on the set every afternoon, but he hadn't been over for dinner in nearly a week.

She loved working alongside him, though. Fritz had convinced Zack to hire her to take the publicity photos. She didn't need to be on the set every single day, but since Skye wanted to visit the set every day after school, Ruth went, too. Between scenes, Fritz was teaching her lighting and angles and how many of the techniques of cinematography could also be used to shoot stills.

He might not know it, but he was teaching her other things, too—things about laughing and flirting and enjoying a man's company, things that she'd thought were all in her past. Ruth was attracted to him—wildly attracted, attracted on a raw, physical level, attracted to a degree that almost frightened her. Maybe he sensed her fear. Maybe that was why he hadn't yet made a romantic move. Maybe he'd sensed that she wasn't ready.

Would he sense it when she was? Would *she*?

Was she ready?

The prospect sent a ripple of fear racing through her. There were so many unknowns, so many things to learn all over again. Would she even remember how to kiss? She wondered how Fritz's lips would feel on hers, wondered about the sensation of his beard moving slowly across her face, then her neck, then her breasts, then down further, and . . .

She came out of her daydream with a start, a little shocked at how real it had felt. Boy, it had been a long time. She rapidly directed her attention back to the cutting board, afraid he'd guess what she was thinking. In the time that she'd known him, she'd discovered that he was disarmingly good at reading her.

Fritz shook the last kernel of popcorn into the bowl, then wadded up the bag and expertly tossed it in the trash. He lifted the bowl. "Where do you want this?"

"In the living room, please. The others should be arriving any minute."

Ruth glanced out the window to see if Kate and Skye were on their way. No movement from their house yet, but a block away, a beat-up white van slowly cruised toward her. Setting down the knife, Ruth rapidly wiped her hands on a dish towel and reached for her camera. She pulled off the lens cap, switched on the autofocus, then lifted it to her eye. As soon as the van passed her house, she clicked off a shot of the license plate.

"Out-of-state tag?"

Ruth started at the sound of Fritz behind her, and her face flamed with embarrassment. "Um . . . no." Ruth put down the camera. "That van looked like it might be casing the neighborhood."

"Maybe he was just looking for a particular address."

"And maybe he was up to no good. I thought I'd get a shot of his tag to help the police catch him if something happens."

Fritz looked at her, his brow knit. She'd never explained the reason she had so many photos of license plates, but he'd evidently just figured it out. Oh, Lord—what if he thought she was crazy as a rabid squirrel? An odd feeling of shame flushed over her. The corners of her mouth wobbled as she tried to smile. "I guess you think I watch too many crime shows, huh?"

Fritz's gaze was direct and somber. "I think you worry too much."

Ruth put the lens cap back on her camera, then set it down. "Our neighborhood watch committee is worse than useless. Someone's got to keep an eye out."

"Fretting about every slow-moving vehicle that goes by doesn't protect anybody."

"Oh, I don't just watch," Ruth said earnestly. "If I see something really suspicious, I call the police. Just the presence of a police car in the neighborhood chases them off."

"This seems like a nice, quiet neighborhood, Ruth."

"Yes, and I want to keep it that way. The very fact that we haven't had a crime in a while means the odds are, we will soon."

Fritz stepped close. His large, rough finger traced a path down her cheek, sending a shiver racing through her. His gaze poured into hers. "Why are you so afraid?" he asked softly.

"I-I'm not afraid. I'm just cautious."

The look in his eyes told her that he wasn't buying her story, but he was too much of a gentleman to call her on it. "Well, then, why are you so cautious?"

Ruth's heart bounded like a scared rabbit. How could she explain something she didn't really understand herself?

The doorbell rang. Relief flooded Ruth's chest. "That must be Kate and Skye."

Fritz dropped his hand, but his gaze never faltered. "We'll talk more about this later."

Not if I can help it, Ruth thought as she hurried out of the kitchen. Fritz made it sound as if there was something wrong with her, and there wasn't. There wasn't! She was cautious, that was all. If more people were more cautious, the crime rate would plummet. Why did everyone have such a hard time understanding that?

"Our very own TV star has arrived!"

Kate smiled at her mother, but she was wincing inwardly. The prospect of watching herself on television made her stomach twist like a pretzel. "Hi, Mom. Hi, Fritz." She stepped into the foyer and kissed them each on the cheek.

Skye trouped in right behind her. "Look—I made some brownies." She held up a foil-covered pan. "They're still warm."

"Yum!" Fritz patted his stomach. "You'd better hide those before Zack gets here or they'll disappear before we get a bite. He's a brownie junkie."

"Zack?" Kate turned questioningly toward her mother. "Zack's coming?"

"Why, yes." Avoiding Kate's gaze, Ruth took the pan from Skye and headed for the kitchen.

Kate trailed behind her, the knot in her stomach tightening. "You didn't tell me you'd invited Zack."

"You didn't ask." Ruth opened a cabinet under the kitchen counter and pulled out a large white platter, then cast Kate a sly glance as she straightened. "I hope it's not a problem."

As if she would admit that it was. The doorbell rang, and Kate's heart did a tap dance.

"Speak of the devil," Ruth said spryly. "Kate, would you mind getting that?"

"I'll do it," Skye said quickly.

Kate sauntered into the living room and watched Skye greet Zack with a big hug. Zack squeezed her back.

"Ask her," Kate heard Skye whisper as she led Zack into the living room. "Go ahead—ask her!"

"Ask me what?"

Skye prodded him with her elbow. Zack grinned down at the girl, then turned to Kate. "Well, Skye has been a really big help, running and fetching and generally gophering for us. I don't know what we'd do without her, so I'd like to offer her an after-school job."

"Please, Mom? Please?" Skye clasped her hands in a prayerful gesture and bounced up and down.

"What would she be doing?" Kate asked.

"Same thing as she's doing now."

"Only I'll be getting paid!" Skye added gleefully. "And I'll have

231

a real job title—assistant to the assistant of the assistant producer."

Kate quirked up an eyebrow as she looked at Zack.

He lifted his shoulders and gave a wry grin. "It has a certain ring to it."

"Please, Mom?"

It might be good for Skye, Kate silently conceded. Ever since she'd been volunteering on the set, the child's attitude had undergone a radical change for the better. She radiated a new sense of confidence and self-esteem. Not only was she more cooperative at home, but she was making new friends at school.

Making the job official would only reinforce those positive changes. So why was Kate so reluctant to accept Zack's offer?

Because every time Zack did something thoughtful, he stole another little piece of her heart.

Skye's eyes were desperate. "Please, Mom? Pleeeease?"

When the movie was over, he would leave. And then what would happen to all of them? Skye had no idea how badly it hurt to be abandoned by someone you loved.

But Kate couldn't let her own fears prevent her daughter from taking advantage of this opportunity. Forcing a smile, she reached out and stroked Skye's hair. "Sounds like an offer that's too good to refuse."

"Woo-hoo!" Skye victoriously pumped her arm in the air, then grabbed Kate in a rib-crunching hug. "Thank you, thank you, thank you!"

"Zack's the one you need to thank," Kate said.

Skye turned and threw her arms around Zack. "Thanks a million—a bazillion! I promise I'll do a really, really, really good job."

Zack lifted her off her feet, then set her back down. "I'm sure you will."

"Wait till I tell Grams!" Skye raced into the kitchen, leaving Kate alone in the living room with Zack.

She nervously smoothed her sleeveless black turtleneck over her jeans. "That was really nice of you."

Zack lifted his shoulders. "I need the help."

Kate shot him a dry grin. "You need a twelve-year-old assistant to the assistant's assistant about as much as I need a jock strap."

Zack smiled back. "I know you have exotic taste in underwear, but I thought your tastes ran to the lace variety."

To her chagrin, Kate felt her face heat. "It was kind of you."

He gazed at her intently for a moment. "You don't look particularly happy about it."

Kate strolled to the coffee table and picked up a handful of popcorn. "I have trouble dealing with you when you're nice," she admitted. "I was more comfortable around you when I thought you were just a jerk."

His mouth curved in an engaging grin. "I can regress, if you like."

Kate grinned back. "I'd know you were faking it. I'm afraid it wouldn't be the same."

She was afraid that nothing would ever be the same. She was trying her best to fight it; but bit by bit, Zack Jackson was capturing her heart.

Chapter Eighteen

"Hey, Kate—you looked terrific on TV last night!"

"Thanks, Joe." Kate smiled at the security guard as she stepped around one of the yellow barricades surrounding the house that served as the brothel interior.

"Great job on 'Eye-To-Eye,'" called one of the photographic assistants as she closed the heavy beveled glass door.

"Thanks, Martin."

From all reports, the TV segment had gone well. Kate had found it impossible to be objective. She'd hated watching herself on television, and she'd hated watching Zack watch her even more.

Zack and the others had cheered and whistled at the television. When the segment was finally over, they'd all gathered around and congratulated her.

"I hate to admit it, but Goldman was right," Zack had said. "It was a brilliant angle. You were fantastic."

"You were awesome!" Skye had exclaimed.

"You were gorgeous!" Ruth had said.

Kate had found a message from the university dean on her answering machine when she got home. "I just saw you on TV, and I had to call and congratulate you. You did a marvelous job. You're a real credit to the university."

So far, so good—but she hadn't yet heard from Goldman. She was more than a little nervous about what his reaction would be.

The call came an hour later. "Whaddaya tryin' to do, kiddo—give me a heart attack?"

Only one person in the world had a voice that sounded as if he gargled with broken glass. Kate's fingers tightened on her cell phone. "Mr. Goldman—good morning."

From across the elaborate parlor, Zack looked up.

"I swear, kiddo, when I saw you all dolled up like that, I nearly popped the caps off my teeth." Goldman's voice rasped in her ear. A bead of sweat formed on Kate's upper lip. Shifting the phone to her other hand, she turned her back, hoping to prevent Zack from hearing. "I can explain that, Mr. Goldman."

"That wasn't at all what I told that damn consultant I wanted. The little sonuvabitch defied my orders."

"Well, the consultant didn't actually . . ."

"Lucky for him, it worked," Goldman continued. "Yessir, it was a stroke of genius, pure genius. You were terrific. Beauty *and* brains, with a genteel, Southern lady kinda thing goin' there. Yessir, I gotta call that little twerp and thank him. It was brilliant."

Kate grinned. As long as Goldman was happy, she was more than glad to let the consultant take the credit.

"The phones have been buzzin' off the hook out here. 'Special Edition,' 'Entertainment Tonight,' 'Hollywood Insider,' even the History Channel—they're all wantin' to come do stories about *Ooh, La La!*."

"I'm glad to hear it, Mr. Goldman."

"You and me both. You're gonna be real busy the next few weeks."

"Good."

"My P.R. people will be in touch with you about all the details. Is Zack around?"

"Yes, sir."

"Put him on."

Kate crossed the room and handed the phone to Zack. "Mr. Goldman wants to talk to you."

"What did you do to him? He never used to make phone calls, and now he's a regular Chatty Cathy." Zack put the phone to his ear. "Hi there, Marvin." He paused. "Yeah, she *was* great." He flashed a grin at Kate.

She smiled back and turned away, pretending to adjust an antique vase and decanter set while keeping an ear on the conversation.

"No, no way," she heard Zack say. "Look—she's a professor, not an actress. That kind of publicity is frowned on by universities." A pause. "Forget it, Marvin. I'll talk to you later."

Zack folded the phone and handed it back to her.

Kate stared at him curiously. "What was *that* all about?"

"Oh, nothing." Zack casually shrugged his shoulders. "He just wants us to pretend to have an affair, that's all."

"*What?*"

"He says the movie needs a big, gossipy romance so the tabloids will have something to write about. Unfortunately, Lena and George are both married." He grinned at Kate. "Since you looked so good on TV last night and you're going to have lots of TV exposure, he wants you and me to pretend to have a hot affair."

"I can't believe he'd suggest such a thing!"

"You don't know Goldman. Anyway, it's done all the time. Get a press agent to drop a hint, let the paparrazi see you out a time or two, and presto—a bunch of free pre-release publicity."

Kate didn't know if she was more surprised at the concept or that Goldman had paired her with Zack. "It sounded like you refused."

"Damn right." Flashing a wicked grin, he leaned close and spoke in a conspiratorial tone. "I wouldn't dream of just pretending."

"Very funny." Kate tried to hide her fluttering nerves. "So, have you done this sort of thing before?"

"Are you kidding? More than half the stories printed about me are publicity stunts, and the other half are exaggerations."

For reasons that Kate didn't want to explore, the information gladdened her.

Deb strode up and handed Zack a sheaf of papers. "The accountant needs you to sign off on the weekly report. And someone named Mrs. Bennett called."

Kate's eyebrows rose. "Skye's teacher?"

"She wants to know if ten o'clock tomorrow will be okay for the field trip," Deb continued.

"Fine with me," Zack said. "Check the schedule and let her know where we're shooting."

Kate stared at Zack as Deb hurried off. "You arranged for Skye's class to come on a field trip?"

"Yeah. Skye said her homeroom teacher was interested, so I told her to call and we'd set it up."

It was bad enough that Zack was playing all too large a role in her life. Now he was wielding too much influence in her daughter's, as well. "You didn't ask me about this."

"Skye said she'd mentioned it to you."

"She said something about it, but I didn't know you were setting it up."

Zack lifted his shoulders. "We do this kind of thing with schools all the time."

"Not with my daughter's school, you don't." Her tone came out sharper than she intended.

He looked at her quizzically. "If it's a problem, we'll cancel it."

She was overreacting and she knew it. She just couldn't stand the thought of Zack taking over any more of her and Skye's lives than he already had. She didn't want him entrenching himself in their routines, becoming an element of their happiness, taking up space in their hearts.

237

Because the more he took over, the bigger void he'd leave when he left.

Still, this was just a field trip. There was no point in making a scene. "It—it's not a problem. It just surprised me, that's all. I like to be kept in the loop where my daughter is concerned."

"Sorry if you weren't. It won't happen again."

At ten o'clock the next morning, twenty chattering adolescents in navy blue school uniforms piled out of a school bus and trouped through the cordoned-off section of the French Quarter where the film crew was preparing to shoot a scene. After an hour's tour, they lined up behind a yellow barricade at the corner of St. Anne and Dauphine, behind the director's chair and the wide angle camera.

"They're all yours," Deb said. "I took them through wardrobe and make-up, and gave them an overview of the business, just like you asked."

Zack glanced at the slew of eager young faces craning toward him.

"Too bad Kate's busy with the 'Entertainment Tonight' crew," Deb said. "She would have made a better tour guide. I do better with animals than kids."

"Well, thanks for stepping up to the plate." Zack turned toward the group, which was being hushed by a stern-faced teacher.

Zack thrust his hands into his pockets and grinned. "As I'm sure Deb explained, we're about to shoot a street scene that shows a part of New Orleans in the late eighteen hundreds. I need you to be very quiet during the filming. All right?"

The heads all bobbed.

"Now look closely and you're likely to see someone you recognize in this scene."

"Is it Lena?" a freckle-faced boy asked. "Man, she's hot."

"I hope it's George!" said a girl with long blond hair.

"If it's George, I'm gonna faint," declared a girl with blue braces on her teeth.

"Well, if you faint, be sure you fall behind the barricade. And there's to be no waving or distracting the actors. Does everyone understand?"

The crowd of heads bobbed again.

"Good." Zack turned and started back toward the main camera. He gave a thumbs up to Skye, who was hidden from view behind a doorway, awaiting her cue. Grinning broadly, she stuck up her thumb in return.

A twinge of apprehension shot through him. He should have gotten Kate's permission to put Skye in this scene, but he hadn't had a chance to ask. The thought had only occurred to him this morning, and Kate had been preoccupied with the media. Besides, she'd already said that Skye could be in the movie. They just hadn't decided which scene she'd be in, that was all.

He didn't know why he hadn't thought of this earlier. What better way to make Skye look good in front of her peers than to turn her into a movie star right before their eyes?

When Skye had arrived with her class that morning, he'd taken her aside and asked if she was game. As if there was ever any question, he thought with amusement; Skye was always game for anything. She'd given him an excited hug, then dashed off to wardrobe and makeup like an Olympic sprinter.

An unexpected fondness had bloomed in Zack's chest as he watched her go. Skye wasn't just a breath of fresh air; she was a gale. He wondered how long she'd be able to hold on to her eagerness and enthusiasm. Maybe she'd be one of the rare ones who never lost her zest for life. He'd never known anyone so open, so genuine, so emotionally transparent. A person always knew where he stood with Skye.

If only he could say the same for Skye's mother. Zack sank heavily into his director's chair. The sexual tension between them was so thick it would take a chainsaw to cut through it, yet she claimed she didn't want to get involved. Why couldn't she see they already *were* involved? Hell, they were involved up to their eyeballs. The problem was, the relationship they were involved in was all in their heads.

239

"Looks like they're about to start filming," Kate said as she led the three-man crew from "Entertainment Tonight" to the French Quarter street corner. They stopped on the sidewalk in front of a two-story balconied building, about ten feet behind the camera.

"Can we tape this?" asked the producer, a tall man with thinning hair the color of his khakis.

"Sure," Kate replied. "As long as you do it from here."

The dapper reporter smoothed his dark hair and buttoned the jacket of his Armani suit. "What's this scene about?"

"We've tried to re-create a little slice of Storyville. This scene shows the seedier side of it, a few blocks from the elaborate brothels."

"Ready on the set," Zack called, rising from his chair. "Everyone in their places."

A dozen extras appeared on the street—men in working-class attire, a man in gentleman's clothing with his shirttail hanging out, and several heavily rouged women dressed as prostitutes sitting in windows and lounging in doorways. Most of them wore plain, low-cut dresses. One wore a tattered ballgown, and one decidedly plump woman was squeezed into a grimy corset that made her breasts bulge over the top like over-leavened bread dough.

But the person who drew Kate's eye was Zack. She watched him turn and pace, his arms folded, his face granitelike with intensity. He was wearing a headset and a red golf shirt, and he reminded Kate of a football coach calling the plays on the sidelines. He was in his element here, calling the shots, making it all come together. An unbidden shiver of attraction shimmied up Kate's spine.

"Hey—there's a class of kids back there," the reporter said, looking behind him.

Kate turned around. Her heart sank at the sight of the familiar navy uniforms. "Actually, it's my daughter's class," she said. "They're here on a field trip." She'd been so busy with the media lately that it had completely slipped her mind that it was scheduled for today.

"Oh, yeah?" The reporter craned his neck. "Which one is your daughter?"

"She's tall, and she's got long dark hair." Kate scanned the class, but didn't see her.

"Is this an appropriate scene for them to be watching?" the producer asked.

"I-I'm sure it will be fine," Kate said, but she was sure of no such thing. What had Zack been thinking, scheduling the field trip on a day when he was filming prostitutes soliciting customers? Why couldn't he have arranged it for a day when they were shooting the horse race or the fire or the scene at the banker's home—anything except this?

"Ready, set . . ." Across the street, Zack dropped his arm like the starter at a car race.

"Hey, they're about to start filming," the field producer told the TV cameraman. "Let's catch this."

"Let's roll!" Zack called.

Where the heck was Skye? Kate wondered as she turned to watch the scene. She must be running an errand for Deb or one of the assistant producers.

A young assistant held up a black-and-white clipboard. "Take one, Scene nineteen."

Zack spoke into his headset. "And . . . action!"

A horse-drawn cart filled with four rowdy, disheveled men clattered down the street, which had been cleverly painted to look like cobblestone. The men whistled, waved whiskey bottles, and made loud catcalls to the women, who preened, posed, and called back. As the cart rolled by, a girl wrapped in a tattered red robe trimmed with molting white feathers pranced out of a doorway. To get the men's attention, she did a series of Rockette-like high kicks, revealing gaudy red-and-black-striped stockings. The men hooted and hollered.

Her back to the camera, the girl opened her robe and flashed the men. The hoots rose to shouts and whistles, and a shoving match ensued as the men all struggled to climb out of the cart. They rolled into the street in a heap, then broke into a brawl over who was going to get the girl.

The girl, meanwhile, tied her robe and sauntered back to lean against her doorway, where she inspected her fingernails with an air of boredom, ignoring the men who were fighting over her. When the winning man staggered after her, she looked up. For the first time, she turned and faced the camera and the crowd. The girl's sad, resigned face was heartbreakingly young . . . and heart-stoppingly familiar. Kate's breath froze in her lungs.

Oh, dear heavens—it was Skye!

Kate stared, unable to believe her own eyes, as Skye led the man through the battered doorway, acting for all the world like a seasoned hooker.

"Cut!" Zack called.

"Wow," the "Entertainment Tonight" producer murmured.

Wow, indeed. Kate felt nauseated. Her baby, her beautiful, precious baby, was soliciting men on the street. Worst of all, she'd been good at it!

The kids behind them all talked at once. "That was Skye!" a young voice murmured excitedly. "Did you *see* her?"

"*That* was *Skye*?"

"Wow, I never knew she was so hot!"

"I thought she looked dumb."

"They know that girl?"

It took Kate a moment to realize that the producer was talking to her. "Umm . . . yes. That was my . . ." She swallowed, trying to moisten her arid tongue. "My daughter."

"How old is she?"

"N-nearly thirteen."

"Awfully young to be playing a hooker, don't you think?"

That was exactly what she thought. Outrage simmered in her chest, building like steam in a pressure cooker. What the *hell* had Zack been thinking? She couldn't wait to give him a piece of her mind!

"Did girls that young really work in Storyville?" the reporter asked.

Calm. She had to stay calm and collected. The consultant had warned her that reporters would seize on any hint of controversy and make it the focus of their story.

"I'm afraid so," Kate replied. "A girl who was orphaned or abandoned or whose reputation had been compromised had few, if any, alternatives."

"Your daughter really captured that. Her indifference, and that look of resignation and despair on her face . . . She was phenomenal!"

"Yeah," the producer said. "She summed up the whole plight of those girls without saying a word. She's got real talent. She's gonna go far."

The only place Kate wanted Skye to go right now was home.

How dare Zack cast Skye in such a role without her permission? How dare he put Kate herself in this position? Just who did he think he was, anyway? Kate's fingernails dug into her palm. She couldn't wait to get him alone and give him a piece of her mind.

She got the chance thirty minutes later, after she'd gotten the TV crew settled in to interview the two stars. Deb told her Zack could be found in the production trailer, so she headed there and marched right in, not bothering to knock.

She found him hanging up the phone. Kate stopped in front of his desk, her hands on her hips. "What on earth were you thinking?"

"About what?"

"About casting Skye as a prostitute. And in front of her class, no less!"

Zack grinned. "Hey, she was great, wasn't she?"

"Her acting ability isn't the issue here."

Zack circled the desk and sat on its edge. "Look, I know I should have gotten your permission, but you'd already said she could be an extra. When I realized her class was coming today,

243

I thought, hey—this is a great opportunity to let her shine in front of those kids."

"Did it ever occur to you that I might have a problem with my twelve-year-old daughter portraying a prostitute?"

Evidently not, from the expression on his face. "Oh, come on, Kate. She knows what went on in Storyville. Besides, you're the one who's always screaming about historical accuracy. You know a lot of those girls were her age, or even younger."

"That doesn't mean I want my child portrayed that way!"

"You've got it backwards. She was portraying a character; the character wasn't portraying her."

"She flashed those men!"

"She was fully dressed under that robe. She was wearing shorts and a tank top and striped pantyhose."

"It *looked* like she was flashing them. Didn't it occur to you that it would upset me? Do you have no concept of family values?"

"My dear," he snapped, "I have no concept of family, period."

The remark took her aback. She'd forgotten about his upbringing. He really did have no concept. Very likely it hadn't even occurred to him that the role was inappropriate.

"Come on, Kate. Skye wasn't hooking." Zack's voice was calm. "She was acting. And everyone here knows that."

"That doesn't change the fact that it was irresponsible of you to cast her in a role like that without consulting me. And to do it in front of her class . . ." Kate threw her hands in the air. "I'm mortified at the thought of facing her teacher."

"I spoke with her afterwards, and she seemed fine with it." He glanced out the window. "But it looks like you're about to find out for yourself."

A tentative knock sounded on the door; then, to Kate's embarrassment, Skye's teacher stepped into the trailer. A plain woman in her mid-fifties, and Kate had always thought that Mrs. Bennett bore an unfortunate resemblance to the witch in *The Wizard of Oz*.

"Mr. Jackson—and Ms. Matthews! I'm so glad to find you

together." The woman folded her hands in front of her stomach and gave a toothy smile. "This was the most fascinating field trip we've ever been on. Thank you ever so much."

Zack inclined his head. "You're very welcome."

She turned to Kate. "And Ms. Matthews—I was stunned at Skye's performance."

"You're not the only one," Kate muttered.

"I had no idea she had such acting ability. She was thrilling to watch. We absolutely *must* sign her up for drama club next year!"

Kate gave a wan smile.

"Well, I just wanted to stop by and thank you again, Mr. Jackson, before we left."

"You're very welcome."

"And it's extremely generous of you to invite the class to Jazzland for Skye's birthday."

"What?" Kate stared at Zack as if he were an alien creature.

"Oh, didn't you know? Mr. Jackson has invited the entire class to celebrate Skye's birthday at Jazzland. The boys and girls are thrilled about it." Mrs. Bennett opened the door. "Well, I'd better be going. Good-bye, and thanks again."

The door closed behind her. A flood of fresh outrage burst through Kate. "You've planned Skye's birthday party?"

"The invitation just kinda popped out." Zack looked down guilty. He picked up a stone paperweight and shifted it from hand to hand. "One of the kids said he'd seen a movie being made when he toured the MGM studio on spring break with his father. Another kid said her dad was going to take her to the new movie place in Orlando. Skye doesn't have a dad to take her places, and I knew her birthday was coming up, and someone mentioned to me yesterday that there was this amusement park east of New Orleans, and, well . . . it just came out."

"You had no right to do that without my permission. Just like you had no right to put her in that scene."

Zack's eyes flashed. "Yeah, well, if I'd asked your permission about either one, you would have just said no. You don't know

245

how to loosen up and go with the flow. To enjoy life as it happens. If you don't learn to lighten up, you're going to drive Skye away just like your mother did you."

Kate felt as if she'd been slapped in the face. "Oh, and you're such an expert on parenting?" She turned on her heel and strode toward the door.

Zack was right behind her. "Kate, wait."

She reached for the doorknob. His hand slammed against the door above her head, preventing her from opening it. He loomed over her, his face just inches from hers. He didn't touch her, but he was so close she could feel his body heat, see the gold flecks in his dark irises. They stared at each other for a long moment, eyes blazing, both of them breathing hard. And as they stood there, the anger changed to something else.

Zack drew a deep breath and stepped back, dropping his hands to his side. "Look—I butted in where I shouldn't have. I apologize. It's just that . . . dammit, I really like Skye, and I thought it would do her good to shine a little in front of those kids. And I guess I had a misguided notion that I could do something to kinda make up for her not having a dad."

Pain squeezed Kate's heart—pain that she wasn't able to give Skye all that she needed, pain that Zack wanted to try. He'd already had a profound effect on the girl. He'd brought spontaneity and self-confidence and a sense of infinite possibility to her life. The problem was, the more attached Skye became to Zack, the more she'd miss him when the movie wrapped and he was no longer a part of their lives.

Oh, dear—was Zack right? *Did* Kate need to learn to lighten up? She'd been so focused on being both a mother and father to Skye, a dutiful daughter to her mother and a ground-breaking historian at work, that she'd forgotten she wasn't always supposed to be in control. Her mother was always telling her she was too serious, that she needed to relax more, to smile more.

Kate's hand tightened on the doorknob, and her stomach tightened with regret. Zack and her mother were right. Somewhere along the way, she'd lost sight of a truth she'd learned with Skye's birth: The best blessings in life aren't always the things you've planned, or even the things you know you want.

"What I said was unfair," Zack was saying. "You're doing a great job raising Skye, or she wouldn't be such a terrific kid. And you're right." He shoved his hand through his hair and blew out another breath. "I don't know anything about families or kids or how to raise them."

Kate saw his Adam's apple bob as he swallowed. The chagrin in his eyes took the heat out of her anger.

"There is one thing I know, though," he went on, "and that's talent. And Skye has a boatload of it. She's a helluva an actress, but I have a feeling she'd be even better at writing or directing."

Kate stared at him. "Why would you think that? She hasn't done either one."

"Actually, she did a little of both this morning."

Kate pulled her eyebrows together.

"I didn't tell her to do that high-kicking, flashing number. I just told her to walk out and act like Madonna. She came up with all that other stuff herself." He gave a wry grin. "I was as surprised as you were. The kid's got a great instinct for drama."

"Don't I know it," Kate muttered.

Zack's grin widened. The next thing Kate knew, she was smiling back.

Zack's hands fell on her upper arms and slowly slid down the sleeves of her bright pink jacket. "Look, if it really bothers you, I'll reshoot the scene without Skye and use her somewhere else."

The offer melted the last of Kate's irritation, leaving her defenseless against the increasing affection she felt for this impossible man. "No. I don't want to clip her wings like that." Kate's mouth curved ruefully. "I named her Skye. I might as well let her reach for it."

Zack's eyes gleamed. "Atta girl."

"She was really good, wasn't she?" Kate asked.

"She was great."

Kate looked down. "I know it's silly, but I hate for her to

247

follow in Wayne's footsteps. You know, acting and all . . ."

"That kid's not going to follow anyone. She's going to forge her own path."

Kate nodded and turned to leave—before she forged herself a path straight into Zack's arms.

Chapter Nineteen

"Evenin'." Fritz's beard rasped Ruth's cheek as he kissed her hello at her front door, sending a shiver through her. She inhaled the special scent that was him, a delicious mingling of wind and leather and spicy cologne, and hugged him back, loving the solid warmth of his chest. Too soon, he pulled away.

Physical contact had been increasing, but things had not yet progressed to a full-out romantic level. Fritz had been holding back, and Ruth was waiting for him to make a move.

"Looks like there's quite a gathering across the street," Fritz observed, hooking a thumb toward Kate's brightly lit home. Several girls about Skye's age were pouring out of minivans and cars and traipsing up to the porch. Skye stood by the door, a huge grin on her face.

"Skye asked if she could invite a few girls over to watch the TV program she's featured on. Kate thought it was going to be just two or three." Ruth grinned. "Looks like the party list took on a life of its own."

"Looks like. Do we need to go help?"

We. The sweetness of the word poured over her. It had been so long since she was part of a *we,* part of a couple. It thrilled her and terrified her at the same time.

"I'm deliberately staying away," Ruth said. "Skye invited Zack, and I thought it would be best if I let Kate and him handle it."

Fritz followed her through the living room and into the kitchen. "I can't figure out what's going on between those two," he said.

"They're crazy about each other," Ruth confided. "But it's the classic romantic standoff. He's afraid of commitment, and she's afraid of getting hurt."

"She got burned bad in her marriage, huh?"

"It wasn't really a marriage."

Fritz's eyebrows rose.

Ruth pulled two tall glasses out of the cabinet. "I saw Skye's birth certificate. Kate had to get it out to register Skye in school, and the marital status box was marked single. She doesn't know I know."

"She's probably embarrassed to tell you." Fritz opened the freezer and pulled out some cubes of ice. They clinked as he dropped them into the glasses. "The longer a lie goes on, the harder it is to come clean."

Ruth nodded. She'd told Fritz all about how Kate had run away, and how her own overprotectiveness was to blame. "I don't know what the truth is, but I'm sure Wayne isn't quite the paragon of virtue that Kate's painted him to be." Ruth opened the refrigerator and took out a liter of Coke. "When she came back to New Orleans with the baby, she was in terrible shape—gaunt and ill and sad. It was like her spirit was broken. She didn't want to talk about it, and I was so glad to have her back, I didn't press her. I was afraid I'd drive her away again." The bottle hissed as Ruth unscrewed the cap. "I think she's afraid of getting involved with Zack because she doesn't want to be hurt again. I suspect that her feelings for him run a lot deeper than she wants to admit."

"She's not the only one who's developed deep feelings, Ruth."

The look on Fritz's face made Ruth's heart skip a beat. "What do you mean?"

Fritz stepped closer. He took the bottle from her hand and

set it on the counter. "My feelings for you are getting awfully strong, Ruth. I'm wondering where we stand."

Ruth's breath hitched.

He lifted her hands in his and looked deep into her eyes. "I'm not looking for a spring fling. I don't know where things might lead, but I care about you, and I want to take things to the next level. I want you to know that if we do, this isn't something I want to end when the movie wraps."

Ruth's heart pounded like a roofing hammer.

Fritz lifted her right hand and gently kissed her palm. "I've been taking things slow, Ruth, because I didn't want to spoil my chances."

Ruth watched him lift her other hand, turn it palm up, and plant a feather-soft kiss on the sensitive flesh. He looked into her eyes as if he could see right through her, into hidden spots that no one else had ever seen.

"I didn't want to scare you off."

His eyes were the color of deep woods. Her pulse roared in her ears as she looked into them, and then her fingers touched his beard in a soft caress. "I've been scared, all right, but not the way you think," she said. "I've been scared you'd never make a move."

His lips curved into a soft grin, and she smiled back—and then their lips were no longer smiling but pressed against each other. His mouth was warm and gentle, his beard a soft bristle against her skin. His big hands roamed her back, and one wound its way into her hair.

Sensation after sensation swept over her—his spicy leather scent, the heat and hardness of his body, the taste and texture of his mouth. Everything about him was so deliciously masculine, so thrillingly male. Desire sucked her down into a whirlpool where nothing mattered and nothing existed beyond the two of them and this moment.

When they came up for air, Ruth was trembling with desire.

"Ruth, honey . . ." Fritz smoothed a curl back from her forehead. "Let's go to your bedroom."

251

"No. Not there. Not where Pete and I—"

He put a finger to her lips to stop her. "I understand. Another room?"

"I—I turned the guest room into a study, and the only other bedroom was Kate's. It's Skye's room when she sleeps over, and I wouldn't feel comfortable there."

"Okay." His hands slid down her arms in a lingering caress. "Let's get out of here altogether. Come back to my place in the French Quarter. I've rented a little guest-house apartment there." His finger traced a tender trail down her cheek. "And when we get there, I'm going to stretch you out on the bed, peel off every scrap of your clothing, and kiss you all over."

The air evaporated from Ruth's lungs.

"I want to make love to you all night and wake up with you in my arms in the morning."

Ruth felt her passion give way to panic. How could she explain that she couldn't stand to be away from her house too long? He'd think she was crazy if she told him about the sharp cat claws of panic that ripped at her chest, the terrifying inability to breathe, the paralyzing fear that she was about to die. "I-I can't. I-I just wouldn't feel right."

Fritz's gaze was too deep and direct to avoid. "About being with me?"

"No!" The word erupted from her lips with a vehemence that made Ruth blush. She touched his cheek with a sheepish smile. "I want to be with you. I want to . . . to . . ." Words failed her, but this was too important to entrust to words, anyway. She drew his head down and claimed his lips in a kiss, a kiss that explained things more fully than words ever could.

"The sofa in the living room," she murmured long moments later.

"Are you sure?"

"Very."

Without another word, he lifted her off her feet and carried her to it, like Rhett carrying Scarlett up the stairs. Ruth clung to his neck, feeling small and feminine and utterly desired. He gently set her down on the soft cushions.

"It pulls out into a bed," Ruth whispered.

He tossed aside the back pillows to make more room, then leaned in for a kiss, a kiss as soft and warm as the look in his glade-green eyes. His beard riffed against her skin, setting her nerve endings on fire, sending hot rivers of pleasure shooting through her. "We'll fold it out later." His breath was warm against her ear as he kissed her neck. "Right now we have other things to do."

"It came, Mom! It came!" Skye burst into the storage trailer, parked on location at City Park, wearing an excited expression on her face.

Kate looked up from the boxful of antique harness equipment she was carefully unwrapping from protective tissue paper. "What came?"

"My birthday gift from Dad!"

A rush of guilt shot through her. "Really?" Kate stood and dusted off her knees, trying hard to act normal, hating the deception.

A workman carried another crate into the storage trailer and set it down on the floor. "That's the last one, Dr. Matthews."

Kate murmured her thanks, her eyes still on Skye.

"It came in today's mail," Skye chattered. "Grams had it in the car with her when she picked me up at school."

Normal. She needed to act normal. She forced a teasing tone into her voice. "I guess you want to wait until your birthday to open it."

"No way! I've already opened it."

"And?"

Skye pulled her bookbag off her shoulders, unzipped a compartment, and pulled out a headset. "It's a CD player. And guess where it came from?"

"Where?"

"Turkey. He's in *Turkey!*"

253

"Wow. That's pretty far away."

"No kidding. The opposite side of the world."

"So this CD player—do you like it?"

"Sure." Skye looked down at it. "I can play all my favorite music and you won't have to hear it."

"That is a nice gift."

Skye nodded, but her expression wasn't one of pure joy. Her eyes held a wistful light.

Kate's stomach tightened. "Is something wrong, honey?"

"He didn't really write anything this time."

Kate's heart ached for her daughter. She struggled to keep her features neutral, to think of something to say that wouldn't make the situation worse. Anything she said now would surely come back to haunt her once Skye knew the truth. "What did he write?"

"Just 'Happy birthday, Dad.' "

Kate dug into another box. "Well, I'm sure he's very busy."

"Yeah, I guess." There was a crestfallen, deflated look in Skye's eyes that made Kate's soul ache, and for a moment she wished she'd filled the card with all kinds of tender messages. But that would only make the truth harder to bear later.

Skye gazed down at the headset. "I wonder what kind of wildlife he's working with in Turkey."

Maybe humor would help. "Probably the endangered Butterballs," Kate suggested.

The comment brought a brief smile and a roll of Skye's eyes. Digging into her bookbag again, she pulled out a piece of brown wrapping paper and thrust it at Kate. "I need to send him a thank-you note. Here's the postmark. Can we try to trace the package, Mom? Please?"

"Honey, I don't see any way we're going to find someone in Istanbul."

"Maybe a detective could check with the government or something. There can't be that many American conservationists working there."

Kate swallowed nervously. There were times when having

such an intelligent child was a definite disadvantage. "Skye, sweetie, we'll have to talk about this later. Right now I have to get this carriage equipment cleared off to use in the next scene."

Skye's chin jutted out. "You're just stalling. You always say we'll talk about it later, and then you never want to."

"Honey, this is not the time or the place." To Kate's relief, the trailer door opened.

"Oh, there you are, Skye." Zack sauntered into the room. "I saw your grandmother, so I figured you had to be around here somewhere. How was school?"

"Okay," the girl answered sulkily.

"You sure? You look upset."

"That's not because of school. It's because of Mom."

"Yeah, she can be one upsetting individual, that's for sure." He shot Kate a wink, then turned back to Skye. "What did she do this time?"

"Well, I got this from my father for my birthday."

She handed Zack the CD player. Zack looked at it, twirling it in his hands like a football. "Nice gift."

Skye nodded. "I want to send him a thank-you note, but Mom won't help me find him."

"Hmm. Wasn't there a return address on the package?"

"No."

"I wonder why not?"

"He doesn't want Mom contacting him."

"Well, if he wanted *you* to contact him, he could have put a note in the package, couldn't he? Or he could pick up the phone. Or look you up on the Internet. You have your own Web page, don't you?"

Skye's eyes grew suspiciously full. Then she squared her shoulders, and her voice became defensive. "He doesn't contact me because he doesn't want Mom knowing where he is."

Zack handed the player back to Skye, then bent and inspected a bridle. "Skye, this may be none of my business, but sometimes when a father disappears, he doesn't want to be found. Usually it's because he doesn't want to pay child support."

"That's not the reason!"

"Are you sure?"

Kate's heart pounded. She saw Skye look at her, and she ducked her head, pretending to write down something on a clipboard.

"Mom has a good job. And—and I bet he doesn't earn hardly anything, 'cause he's doing it for the animals, not for money." Her tone was forceful, as if she was trying to convince herself.

Zack looked thoughtful, as if he was considering her words. "Well, if it were me, I'd still put my child first." He shifted his stance. "I don't know all the facts, but from what I can see, your mother has provided for you and loved you and raised you single-handedly all these years. A lot of kids would give anything to have someone who cares about them the way your mother cares about you. I know I would have." Zack put down the bridle, and picked up something that looked like a riding crop. From the corner of her eye, Kate could see that he was keeping his expression as neutral as his tone. "Maybe you should worry more about appreciating the parent who's always been there for you than tracking down the one who never has."

Skye's lower lip trembled, and her eyes filled with tears. Kate longed to pull her into her arms and comfort her, but she was afraid her daughter would push her away. This was one pain that Skye would have to come to terms with on her own.

Zack smacked himself on the forehead. "Oh, hey, I almost forgot the reason I came looking for you. Deb's been working on the details of your party. She needs the names and addresses of your classmates so she can send out invitations, and I think she has a few other questions for you. Go see if you can help her, okay? She's in the production trailer."

Skye nodded, apparently relieved to have a reason to escape the room, and hurried out the door.

Kate watched her go, her throat tight. She looked up at Zack, her heart full.

He held up his hands. "I know, I know—I should mind my own business. But when I walked in and heard her painting you

256

as the bad guy, I couldn't stop myself. She's been in denial about this father thing for way too long, and it's high time someone took the shine off that jerk's halo. Hopefully it'll make it easier for you to talk to her later."

Kate swallowed, trying to choke down the lump in her throat that felt as big as an alligator egg. "Thank you."

Zack looked surprised. "You're not mad?"

Would that she were. Anger might shield her from the dangerously warm, tender emotions filling her heart. "I should be, but I'm not."

Zack's mouth slanted into a sexy grin. "Probably because I'm so charming you just can't work up a proper snit, right?"

Kate grinned back. Fondness and something more, something deeper and more profound, was rising up inside her, refusing to stay unacknowledged any longer. "Don't overrate your charm."

"I'm glad you're not mad." His gaze burned into hers. "I just want to help."

The air between them was changing, like a weather front moving in. It was softening and warming, and it frightened Kate. She turned back to the box and lifted out a set of reins. "I appreciate it, but sometimes you go too far. Like with this party. I want to pay for it."

"Hey—I issued the invitation and it's my treat."

Kate shook her head. "It's not your place to pick up the tab for my child's birthday party."

"She's also one of my employees, remember?"

"Oh, right." Kate rolled her eyes in a more-than-fair imitation of Skye. "You expect me to believe you throw a big birthday party for every part-time gopher on your payroll?"

"Come on, Kate." He took a step toward her, his eyes questioning and wounded. "Why do you have such a hard time letting me do anything for you or Skye?"

Because every kind, considerate thing you do makes me fall more deeply in love with you.

Dear Lord. She couldn't fight it anymore. She was in love

with Zack! She'd tried to struggle, tried to deny it, but she'd fallen in love with him anyway. How could her heart be so foolish?

He took yet another step toward her.

She staggered back. "I like to pay my own freight. That way I don't feel beholden to anyone."

His mouth curved in a grin. "I'd like to be holdin' you."

"Very funny."

"You think that if I pay for Skye's party, you'll owe me?"

Kate gave an embarrassed shrug. "Something like that."

"Darn—you've seen right through me." His eyes were smiling. "I confess—I have an ulterior motive. Want to hear what it is?"

"Probably not, but go ahead and tell me anyway."

"I have this fantasy of you clinging to me, thrilled beyond words, screaming wildly in my arms. I figured the only way I'll ever get my dream to come true again is if I get you on a roller coaster."

He was impossible. Kate couldn't keep from grinning. "I feel like you've already got me on one."

It was meant to be a flippant response, but the minute his gaze met hers it became something else. "Good," he murmured. "Because you've got me turned upside down and inside out, too."

"I-I've got to take this stuff out to the horse trainer." She headed to the door.

"Kate?"

She stopped but didn't turn around.

"I want to throw this party because I care for you, and I care for Skye. So just let me do it, okay? No strings attached."

Kate's head bobbed in a nod, but her eyes were filling with tears. She opened the door and hurried across the grass, clutching the harnesses to her chest. *No strings attached*—that was a good one. Didn't he know that was the whole problem?

Chapter Twenty

"It's your own granddaughter's party," Fritz said. "Why on earth don't you want to go?"

The rain pounded on the green-and-white striped canvas roof of Café Du Monde the next day as Ruth stared down at her cup of café au lait, trying to avoid Fritz's intent gaze. He saw too much when he looked in her eyes, and if he looked at her now, he'd know how anxious she was. She always got a bad case of the jitters if she was in a strange place without Kate or Skye beside her. She was fine on the set because one or both of her family members were always there with her, but this afternoon's shoot had been delayed because of a downpour, and Fritz had persuaded her to come to the famous coffeeshop while they waited for the weather to clear. He had no idea how difficult it was for her to sit here with him. If he had, he'd think she was nuts.

He already thought she was odd for not wanting to go to Skye's birthday party. The truth was, there was no way she could spend an entire day at an amusement park. Just the thought of it sent a wave of terror chasing through her. She poured a second packet of sugar into her coffee cup. "I-I don't like amusement parks."

"We don't have to go on any rides that scare you."

"Well, I hate the idea of Kate or Skye being on any of them. I'd be worried sick if I was there." It was a true enough statement.

"Those rides are safer than the drive to the amusement park."

"Another reason not to go." She flashed a smile that she hoped would divert him.

It didn't. Fritz set down his cup and leaned forward, his eyes dark and troubled. "You never want to go anywhere, Ruth. You don't want to go to dinner or on a walk or to my room. I practically had to twist your arm to get you to come get a cup of coffee with me here." His eyes were hurt and confused. "Are you ashamed to be seen with me?"

"Oh, Fritz . . ." Ruth's heart broke. "You don't really think that, do you?"

"I don't know what else to think."

Tears welled up in Ruth's eyes. A familiar, panicky feeling welled up inside her as well.

She placed her hand over his. "I'm proud to be seen with you."

"Then, I don't understand. What's going on?"

"Nothing. I'm a homebody, that's all."

The look in Fritz's eyes clearly said he wasn't buying it. "It's more than that. You can tell me anything, Ruth, and I'll be okay with it. I can accept any problems you might have. If you're in the witness protection program, or if you've committed some kind of a crime . . ."

Ruth stared at him. "You think I'm in the witness protection program? Or that I'm a *criminal?*" Her voice rose with incredulity, making the people at the next table turn and stare at her.

Fritz lifted his hands, his palms up. "I don't know what to think, except that you're hiding something from me."

He was way too perceptive. Panic swelled in her chest.

"Whatever it is, Ruth, I can deal with and accept it. The one thing I can't accept is being shut out."

Oh, no, it was happening—that horrid stifling feeling, as if someone had put a plastic bag over her head. Her heart began to race, and a sweat broke out on her upper lip. She tried to draw a deep breath, but could only pull a tiny bit of air into her lungs. She tried again, then again—faster and faster and faster, the feeling of panic increasing.

"Ruth?"

She heard Fritz's voice as if from a distance. She panted, clutching her throat, trying to breathe. There was air all around, but none for her.

"Ruth—are you ill?" Fritz was out of his chair, kneeling in front of her.

The panic swirled around her like a tornado, sucking up her reason, spinning her around. She had to get away. Rising from her chair, she staggered forward, her eyes blinded by tears and terror. She had to get someplace safe, someplace where the air was thin enough to pull into her lungs.

She hurried forward, only to have something—someone— suddenly pull her back, jerking her with such force that it felt as if her arm were being wrenched from the socket. A horn blared beside her, and then everything went black.

"Ruth—Ruth!"

Ruth opened her eyes to see Fritz leaning over her, his eyes wide and worried. His face was dripping wet and framed by gray sky. Her hand felt something hard and rough and wet. "What . . . Where . . ."

"You ran into the street, and then you fainted. I managed to catch you so that you didn't hit your head."

Oh, dear—she was lying in the rain in a wet gutter, and Fritz was kneeling beside her. An awful sense of shame washed over her.

"Easy, honey. Take it easy." Fritz's arm came around her, supporting her as she rose to her feet. His chest felt hard and warm and safe. She gulped in a sweet lungful of air. "Does anything hurt?"

She shook her head.

"Let's go sit down." His arm around her, Fritz guided her through a throng of umbrella-toting people who were gawking at her as if she were a sideshow exhibit. He led her back to their table under the awning, pulled out her chair, and gently settled her into it. He unhooked his cell phone from his belt and sat down beside her. "I'm going to call an ambulance."

"No!" The word burst out in alarm. Embarrassed, Ruth modulated her voice. "I-I'm fine."

"You need medical attention, Ruth. You passed out and you're shaking like a leaf. You might have had a heart attack or some kind of stroke."

She ran a hand across her forehead. "I'll be fine. This always passes once I catch my breath."

His brows pulled together. "This has happened before?"

Oh, dear—how had she let that slip out? But there was no taking it back. Her head bobbed in a reluctant nod.

"Well, if you don't want an ambulance, I'll take you to an emergency room. You need to be looked at."

"I-I just need to go home."

"After you're seen by a doctor." The iron in his voice and the steely glint in his eyes told her that arguing was pointless.

Despair filled her soul. Once Fritz learned how crazy she was, he'd never want to see her again.

Ruth's bare feet dangled nervously from an examining table at Mercy Hospital as a young emergency room physician moved a cold stethoscope around her back. Across the room, Fritz sat in a blue vinyl chair against the wall, his eyes worried.

The doctor finally straightened, pulled the stethoscope from his ears, and gave Ruth a reassuring smile. "Your vital signs are good, your lungs are clear, and your heart sounds healthy. There's no indication you've had any kind of cardiac or pulmonary incident."

"Thank God." Fritz drew a relieved breath of the antiseptic-scented air. "So what happened?"

The doctor draped the stethoscope around his neck and

pulled a prescription pad out of the pocket of his white jacket. "I believe she had a panic attack. It's a common anxiety disorder, and it fits the symptoms you described." He looked at Ruth. "I'm going to give you a short-term prescription for an anti-anxiety drug, and I'd like you to follow up with a psychiatrist, Mrs. Matthews."

Ruth's heart pounded. "No. No way. I'm not crazy."

"No one is saying you are." The doctor drew a pen from his breast pocket. "You have a treatable disorder—one that is actually very common. A psychiatrist can evaluate you and decide on the best course of treatment."

"I don't need a shrink. There's nothing wrong with me that a little rest won't cure."

Fritz placed his hand on her back. "Ruth, let's follow the doctor's recommendations," he suggested.

She turned to him, her eyes pleading. "There's nothing *wrong* with me. The doctor just said I'm perfectly healthy."

The doctor frowned. "I said your vital signs are good. But you're exhibiting signs of anxiety."

"Well, of course I am." Ruth gave a nervous smile. "You'd be anxious, too, if you were sitting here wearing nothing but a paper hospital gown."

The doctor smiled.

"Can I get dressed now?"

"Of course. But I hope you'll consider my recommendation." The doctor went out the door.

"I'll wait for you outside," Fritz told Ruth, pulling the door closed behind him. He caught up with the doctor in the hall.

"You're pretty sure it's this anxiety thing?" Fritz asked.

The doctor nodded. "She has all the classic symptoms. And from the sound of things, she's got a pretty advanced case."

"What causes it?"

"It's hard to say. Sometimes it starts after a traumatic incident of some kind. Do you have any idea when this all began?"

"No. She was like this when I met her."

"Panic attacks often go hand-in-hand with other phobias. Does she have any abnormal fears?"

Fritz nodded. "She worries to death about crime. She constantly worries about her daughter and grandchild. And she doesn't like to go anywhere. She just wants to stay home."

"That last one sounds like a form of agoraphobia."

"What's that?"

"It literally means fear of the marketplace. People with it are afraid of leaving their homes or venturing out. Often they can only do so if they're going to a familiar place or if they're with a person who makes them feel safe."

That fit Ruth to a T. "How do I help her?"

"The best thing you can do is persuade her to seek professional help."

"What's the second best?"

"Get her to talk about whatever started all this. Sometimes getting it all out in the open can help."

Fritz nodded somberly. "Thanks, Doc."

"You're welcome." The doctor shook his hand. "Good luck."

Fritz steered Ruth's Camry into her driveway and killed the engine. They'd taken a taxi from the hospital back to Ruth's car in the French Quarter, and Fritz had driven her home. "Thanks for the ride," Ruth said.

"I wouldn't have wanted you to drive yourself."

"I'm feeling much better. I just got overtired, that's all." Ruth put her hand on the car door. "I imagine you need to be getting back. Do you want me to call you a taxi?"

"No. I'll walk to St. Charles and catch the streetcar."

Ruth nodded and opened the door. "Well, then, I guess I'll see you later."

"We need to talk, Ruth."

Her stomach did a nervous flutter. "Don't you need to get back to the set? The rain stopped."

"I called from the hospital. The shoot won't start until five."

Ruth fingered the necklace around her throat. She didn't want

Fritz hanging around and badgering her about seeing a psychiatrist. "I'd invite you in, but I'm really tired. I think I need a nap."

"We need to talk."

"This probably isn't a good time."

"We need to talk, Ruth." His voice had an edge Ruth had never heard before. "Now."

"Well, all—all right." Anxiety gripped her as Fritz walked her to her front door. Her hand shook as she unlocked the three deadbolts. Stepping into the foyer, Ruth turned off the burglar alarm and looked around. The anxiety was growing stronger. Oh dear—Fritz was sure to think she was nuts if he saw her check the house, but she couldn't bear not to.

She peered into the dining room. So far, so good. She opened the coat closet, then strolled through the living room, looking carefully behind the sofa, then the chairs.

Fritz watched her. "What are you doing?"

She ought to wait. Her brain told her that, but the odd, panicky feeling clutching at her chest overrode intellectual reasoning.

She tried for a breezy tone. "I'm just checking to make sure no one got in the house while I was gone." Ruth walked into the kitchen and checked the pantry, then the broom closet.

"Ruth, you have three deadbolts and a burglar alarm. How could anyone have gotten in?"

She flashed him a smile and tried to make her voice as offhand as possible. "Better safe than sorry, I always say."

"Do you do this every time you come home?"

"No." Ruth's spine straightened defensively. "Only if I've been gone a while and there's no one home at Kate's to keep an eye on the place." She strode into the half bath and pushed the door against the wall to make sure no one was hiding behind it, then headed into the study.

Fritz followed her. "Ruth, this is crazy."

Crazy. Ruth's spine went rigid at the word. "I'm a single

woman living alone. It's perfectly logical for me to want to make sure my house is secure."

"Ruth, honey—your concern about criminals is completely out of proportion. Surely you can see that your behavior isn't normal, can't you?"

Not normal. He thought she was a freak, a kook, a crazy lady.

Tears filled her eyes. Turning away from him, she blinked them back and headed up the stairs.

He followed her into her bedroom. "Oh, Ruth—don't cry. I didn't mean it that way." He put his hands on her shoulders and gently turned her around to face him. "I just want to help you."

"All I need is some time alone." She stared down, refusing to meet his gaze, until he dropped his hands. Turning away, she wiped a tear off her cheek, then marched to her closet. Yanking open the door, she patted down the hanging clothes, making sure no one was hiding behind them.

She headed to the master bath, where she yanked back the shower curtain and peered in, then looked in the cabinet under the sink. Fritz followed her in. He pulled a handful of tissues from the box on the counter, then stood in the doorway, blocking her path.

"Ruth, sweetie—don't cry." Ruth froze as he advanced toward her. Slowly, with exquisite gentleness, he stepped forward and wiped her eyes. Then he held a tissue under her nose. "Blow," he ordered.

Like an obedient child, she gave an inelegant blast. He tenderly wiped her nose, his eyes gentle and troubled. The intimacy of the simple act loosened something inside her. She sank back against the counter, all of her pride deflated.

He put his hands on her arms. "Something happened to make you this way, and I want to know what it was."

The tenderness in his voice set off a fresh round of tears.

"Were you or Kate attacked?"

She shook her head.

His voice dropped an octave. "Raped?"

"N-no."

"Burglarized?"

Panic welled up inside her, closing her throat. He immediately picked up on it.

"You were, weren't you? Was it recently?"

"N-no."

"When?"

"A-after Pete's death."

"Tell me about it, honey. Please tell me about it."

Tears fell unchecked down her cheeks, dripping off her chin.

Fritz grabbed another tissue and dabbed at her face. "Tell me, Ruth. Don't shut me out. I need to understand."

Ruth drew a ragged breath and turned her face away from him.

"I'm not leaving here until you tell me." His voice was soft, but it was filled with resolve. "Let's go sit down." Putting his arm around her, he guided her to the bedroom and eased her down onto the edge of her bed. He sat down beside her on the rose-printed comforter and waited, watching her twist a Kleenex in her fingers.

One minute became two, then three, then four or more, and still he waited. Something about the silence, about his willingness to just sit there, eased her anxiety. Before she knew it, the words came tumbling out. "When Pete died . . . oh, it was so awful. I was heartbroken. I could hardly function."

Fritz put his arm around her, lending sturdy support.

"After the funeral, I couldn't bear to spend the night here, to sleep in the bed where I'd—where we'd . . ."

Fritz pulled her against his chest and stroked her head. "It's all right to cry."

The words were so comforting that she found she didn't need to. She drew a deep breath and continued. "I decided to stay at a friend's house. I came by to pick up a change of clothes for Kate and me, and when I opened the door—oh, my heavens! You've never seen such a mess. Furniture was tipped over and stuff was all over the floor."

Robin Wells

She could still see it if she closed her eyes—the knocked-over lamps, the overturned armchair, the upended sofa, the contents of the kitchen drawers dumped out on the floor. "It took me a minute to realize I'd been burglarized. My first thought was that the house had been hit by a tornado." She drew a ragged breath. "I walked through the downstairs in a daze. Every room was a wreck. And then I went upstairs and went in Kate's room." Ruth closed her eyes.

Fritz patted her soothingly. "It's okay, sweetheart."

"A man grabbed me from behind." Her voice trembled. "He must have been hiding in the closet. He held a knife to my neck and told me not to move or he'd kill me. He told me to count to one hundred before I moved. And then I heard him call out 'Let's get out of here!' as he ran down the stairs, so there must have been others in the house that I walked right by."

"Good God, Ruthie." Fritz clutched her to his chest, as if he were shielding her. "You were lucky you weren't hurt."

"The police said so, too."

"Did they take much?"

Ruth nodded. "My grandmother's silver and all of my jewelry, and two TVs and a stereo. And our camera, which still had film in it from Christmas—my last Christmas with Pete. My last pictures of him."

She choked down a fresh sob. Fritz's fingers stroked her hair, calming her.

"They took other things, sentimental things. A silver frame with a picture of the three of us at Disneyland. Pete's fly rods. Even some of his clothes."

Ruth wiped her eyes. "The police said the burglars probably looked in the paper and saw the time of the funeral, then figured no one would be home. They said it happens all the time."

A cold rage reverberated inside Fritz. Anyone who'd rip off a widow attending her late husband's funeral should be charged with a double crime. He'd love to get his hands on whoever had taken such awful advantage of Ruth.

She dabbed at her eyes. "They went through everything. My lingerie, my medicine cabinet . . . Even my mattress was flipped over." She drew a shaky breath. "I can't describe how awful I felt. I felt so—so violated."

They'd taken a lot more than her possessions, Fritz thought. They'd robbed her of her peace of mind and her sense of safety. "How did Kate take it?"

"I never let her know. I didn't want her any more upset than she was. I kept her at my friend's until I got the place straightened up."

"Did the police ever catch who did it?"

"No." She was silent, a haunted, faraway look in her eye. "But I saw one of them."

Fritz's eyebrows shot up.

"It was months later. I was at the gas station down the street." She drew a deep breath. "I saw a man wearing Pete's jacket."

"You're sure?"

"I'm positive. I had it custom-made for him. It was brown tweed with leather patch elbows—I called it his Sherlock Holmes jacket." The tissue shredded as Ruth twisted it.

"What did you do?"

"I just stood there like an idiot and watched him climb into his car and drive away."

Ruth shook her head, her eyes filled with self-disgust. "Can you believe that? I just stood there. A few moments later, I was furious—at him, and at myself. How could I have been so stupid?"

Fritz rubbed her arm. "You might have gotten hurt if you'd tried to stop him."

"I should have written down his license plate number, or at least paid attention to what kind of car he was driving. All I remember is that it was white. I couldn't even describe the man, aside from the fact he had brown hair and a medium build. The police said there was nothing they could do without more information."

Ruth hesitated. "They said he might not even be the burglar, just someone who'd bought the jacket from the thieves. But I think that, even if he wasn't one of the thieves, he could have told the police who was." Ruth bit her lip. "I wanted to kick myself. If I'd had a camera, he would have been caught."

So that explained it. "So you started carrying a camera everywhere?"

Ruth gave him an embarrassed look. "That's how it started. After twenty years, I've pretty much given up on seeing him again. I got used to having it handy, though. It makes me feel like no one is going to get away with hurting me or my family again. It's kind of like a shield." Her mouth curved in a rueful grin. "Sounds kinda goofy, doesn't it?"

"Not at all." Fritz ran his hand up and down her spine. "Back when I started out, I was a TV news photographer. The camera gave me a sense of distance from whatever I was photographing. It made me feel more in control of things."

"That's it exactly." Ruth gazed him, her eyes surprised. "Wow—I've finally met someone who understands!"

"I want to understand everything, Ruth. Is the burglary the reason you're afraid to leave your house?"

She nodded. "I don't feel safe very many places. And if I leave home, I have to worry about coming back." Her voice grew small and sheepish, and fresh tears fell. "I've put in all sorts of security devices, but I'm still afraid I'm going to find everything trashed or someone hiding in wait."

"Aw, honey." Fritz hauled her back against his chest. The sympathy seemed to make something break loose inside her. She clung to him, sobbing, for long moments, while he held her and rocked her and murmured soothing things.

"Where do you feel safe?" he asked when her sobs subsided.

"Here, if I've checked the place thoroughly. And at Kate's house—I feel right at home there. And I can go to familiar places like the grocery store and the post office and church by myself. And I can go anywhere with Kate or Skye."

Fritz dropped a kiss on her hair. "You're too wonderful a woman to be living with all this. I want you to get some help."

She stiffened in his arms. "There's nothing wrong with my mind. I don't need a shrink." She pulled back and sat upright, smoothing her shirt. "I just need to work on breaking out of some ruts I've gotten into, that's all. If I put my mind to it, I'll get over this thing."

Fritz was afraid the ruts were way too deep for her to climb out of on her own, but it wasn't his call to make. It was her life and her decision. "I hope so, honey. I sure hope so."

Chapter Twenty-one

The late April sun was unseasonably warm as the roller coaster slowly clattered its way up the steep incline of the first steel hill the next Saturday. Gripping the metal bar in front of her until her knuckles ached, Kate closed her eyes and said a silent prayer.

"Are you okay?" Zack asked beside her. "You look a little green around the gills."

"I-I'm fine." Her voice came out in a thin, Minnie-Mouse squeak.

She felt Zack's amused gaze. "I thought you weren't afraid of roller coasters."

"I lied."

A chortle rumbled from the depths of Zack's chest as his warm, muscular arm came around her and pulled her close. She gripped his blue knit shirt with one hand and braced herself on the rail with the other as the roller coaster topped the summit and began a wild plunge to the other side.

For a breathless moment, she thought she was going to die. Then the coaster hit bottom and the force lifted her slightly off the seat as the ride careened up the next incline.

"That wasn't so bad, was it?" Zack said.

"No."

Kate opened her eyes, then squeezed them shut again as the ride plummeted down another hill.

Zack's arm tightened its hold on her. It was so comforting, so reassuring to be pressed against him, to inhale his scent. She closed her eyes and breathed it in as the roller coaster whipped up and down the curving track. The ride was so much like their relationship—dizzying heights, stomach-churning lows, and always, always, the desire to be close to him. When the coaster slowed and stopped at the gate, she regretted that it was already over. It had been worth the terror to be so close to Zack again.

Would it be worth it to be even closer? God help her, but she was considering it. Ever since she'd realized the depth of her feelings for Zack, she'd been wondering what she was going to do about it. Her love for Zack was far richer, more profound, than anything she'd ever felt for Wayne. She couldn't imagine ever caring this deeply for another man. Was she going to let this once-in-a-lifetime chance to be with a man she loved go by simply because she was afraid of how much it would hurt when it ended? Or was she going to go for it and love him with all that she had for the few weeks that were left?

Zack helped her out of the ride and onto the platform. They were nearing the exit when Skye bounded toward them, accompanied by a short blond girl. "Isn't this ride awesome? Mary Ann and I have already ridden it three times, and we're going to go again. Last time we rode in the last car with our hands in the air. This time we want to sit in the front." Skye and Mary Ann scurried off to get in line.

"She's fearless. I don't know how she could be my kid." Kate watched her go. "I'm so glad she's made some nice friends. I was a little afraid those kids were just using her to get access to the movie set, but that wasn't the case at all. She's gotten close to several of those girls, especially Mary Ann." Kate smiled at Zack. "She's having the time of her life today."

"So am I." Zack put his arm around her waist and gazed into her eyes.

Kate's heart skipped a beat. "What do you want to do next?"

"You mean, aside from kiss you?"

Kate struggled to keep her tone light. "Yeah, aside from that."

"Let's go on that Tilt-a-whirl ride again."

"The one that kept throwing me practically in your lap? I nearly squashed you to death on that one."

"That's why I liked it."

Kate playfully poked him with her elbow. "You're impossible."

"To resist?"

"You wish." Her amused tone belied her pounding heart.

"You're right. That's exactly what I wish." Zack tugged her off the main pathway, into the empty seating for the water-skiing show. "Because I find you completely, totally irresistible."

He was smiling, but his eyes held a deeper message, one that gave depth and weight to his words. Her heartbeat quickened, and all of a sudden the noise and bustle of the amusement park faded away as her gaze fastened on his lips. She didn't know if she made the first move or if he did, or if they simultaneously met each other halfway. All she knew was that suddenly his lips were on hers, and there was no place on earth she'd rather be.

It was a light kiss, tender and full of longing. He pulled back and gazed into her eyes, searching her face. Kate's arms wound around his neck. She stood there, lost in his eyes, holding the man who held her heart.

"Hey, Jackson—kiss her again!" called a nasal male voice.

Zack whipped around to see a man crouched about four feet away, a large camera obscuring his face, clicking off shots. His stomach sank to the pavement. Kate gasped and drew back.

"What the hell are you doing?" Zack demanded.

"My job, man. I'm with the *National Inquisitor.*" He clicked off another shot. "Give the professor another kiss, okay? Only this time turn around so I can get more of your face."

Zack struggled against a surge of anger. "Come on, now. You don't want to use this stuff. Give me the film and I'll get you something better. I'll set you up with Lena or George."

The man's mousy shoulder-length hair waved as he shook his head. "I was sent to shoot you and the lady professor."

"Sent by whom?" Zack demanded.

He shrugged. "My editor. He got a call from someone who said you two were an item and that you'd be here together."

A vein throbbed in Zack's temple. Goldman was probably behind this, but he'd never be able to prove it. He reached for his back pocket and pulled out a checkbook. "How much do you want for that film? I'll buy it from you."

The man's horselike face grew indignant. "Hey, what do you think I am?"

Zack's control snapped. "I know what you are," he snarled. "Bottom-feeding scum. Now give me that film."

The photographer backed away, wagging his finger as if Zack were a naughty child. "Uh-uh, uh-uh—that's no way to talk to the media. Besides, you know what they say—there's no such thing as bad publicity."

"There's no such thing as a pain-free broken nose, either," Zack snarled.

The photographer turned and fled. Kate grabbed Zack's arm as he started after him. "Don't!" she begged.

Zack hesitated. The photographer dashed into the crowd, his flak jacket flapping. A moment later, he disappeared around a corner. Zack blew out a hard sigh. "Hell, Kate—that photo's going to be in the next issue of that gossip rag."

"Yeah, well, if you'd attacked him, you'd be reading it from jail. It would be pretty hard to direct a movie from behind bars."

Zack raked both hands through his hair. "Damn it, the last thing I want to do is cost you tenure."

It was true. He gladly would have gone to jail rather than hurt her. When had Kate become more important than his movie, more important than his career? The thought sent a rush of alarm through him.

"I don't think that'll happen," Kate said. "The movie's as accurate as it can possibly be, so no one can fault me professionally. And the dean has called a couple of times, telling me how pleased he is with the positive publicity the university has gotten. He's practically assured me tenure."

Relief poured through Zack. He smiled at her. "Well, then, this does have an upside."

"Oh, yeah?"

"Yeah." He took a step toward her. "Since the whole world is going to think we're fooling around anyway, there's nothing to stop us from actually doing it, is there?"

He was right. Kate's heart skipped a beat. Did she dare?

Did she dare not?

When she was old and gray and rocking on her front porch, looking back on her life, would she prefer to regret loving Zack, or not loving him?

"Have dinner with me tonight," he urged.

Kate arched a brow. "You've already told me what a man is really asking when he asks a woman to dinner."

"So, what's your answer?"

"Yes." Her pulse was loud, but her voice was soft. "My answer's yes."

"They're back," Ruth said late that afternoon, peering out her kitchen window. "Wow, that's some bus Zack rented!"

Fritz joined Ruth by her sink and watched as two dozen adolescents bounded down the steps of a luxury tour bus. "When Zack does something, he doesn't do it halfway."

"Look—there's Skye! She's beaming from ear to ear. I don't know when I've seen her so happy."

"Looks like everyone had a great time. Especially Zack and Kate."

Ruth watched the couple stroll toward the house, their arms looped around each others' waists. A wide smile split her face. "Yes, indeed—and it's about time! I was beginning to wonder if those two were ever going to come to their senses."

She turned from the window and grinned at Fritz. "Looks like a red-letter day all around."

"Don't you wish we'd gone?" he asked.

Her stomach clenched with anxiety. "Oh, I had a wonderful time here with you. I love gardening. And I especially loved the afternoon 'nap'."

"That was my favorite part, too." The mention of the hour of passion on the sofa made him smile. "Listen, Ruth—I have to go back to L.A. to take care of some business next week. I'd love for you to come with me."

Panic jumped to life inside her. "Oh . . . I-I can't."

"Sure you can. It's just for a couple of days. Kate will keep an eye on your house."

"But Kate or Skye might need me."

"They'll be fine without you for two days."

Ruth shook her head. "I-I just can't."

He blew out a sigh. "These fears of yours are ruining your life, Ruth."

"I'm working on it. I'm doing better. We went out to dinner the other night, and I was fine."

"Fine? You were so tense and nervous you couldn't eat. You couldn't wait to get home—and then you had to search this place as if it were Jesse James's hideout, even though the burglar alarm was on and you had three dead bolts locked. In my opinion, that's not fine."

"I'm trying."

Fritz's eyes grew somber. "You need some help, honey. Why won't you get it? I don't understand why you're being so stubborn."

I don't want to discuss this anymore." She turned toward the cupboard. "What do you want for dinner—spaghetti or chicken?"

"Damn it, Ruth!" His voice was husky with frustration. "If you won't talk to me, this is never going to work. I'm trying to be patient here, but I'm at the end of my rope." He snatched his helmet off the kitchen table. "I'll see you tomorrow."

"B-but I thought you were staying for dinner."

"I've changed my mind. I'll catch a bite somewhere later."

Ruth watched him stalk toward the door, tears brimming in her eyes. Fritz was the best thing that had happened to her in the past twenty years. They'd talked about a long-term relationship, about the possibility of a future. But there would be no future if she couldn't get her act together. If she couldn't conquer her fears, she was going to lose him.

And with him, a real chance at happiness.

Twenty minutes later, Kate looked up to see her mother at her kitchen door. "Come on in, Mom." The automatic ice dispenser on the refrigerator door rumbled as she filled a glass with ice. "You're just in time for Happy Hour. What's your pleasure—Hawaiian Punch, Barq's, or iced tea?"

"Tea, please," Ruth said.

"Grams—you missed the best time ever!" Skye took a long swig of root beer and wiped her mouth with the back of her hand. "We went on this awesome roller coaster called the Wildcat, and then this cool ride called the Cajun Mixer, and there was this giant thing that drops you so fast you can't breathe. It was totally awesome. And everyone from my class came, and Mary Ann and I are becoming best friends!"

"That's wonderful, honey." Ruth patted Skye's hand, then grinned at Zack, who was leaning on the counter close to Kate. "Sounds like the party was a hit."

"It was great," Kate said, handing her mother a glass of tea. "Zack gets the prize for throwing the all-time best birthday party a kid ever had."

"I'm not a kid anymore," Skye piped up. "I'm a teenager."

"Don't remind me." Kate groaned.

"I got some great gifts, Grams—and a whole bunch of CDs. I can't wait to go listen to them!" She turned to Kate. "Can I take my drink upstairs? I'm thirteen now and I promise not to spill."

"Okay."

"Thanks!" Without another word, she bounded out of the room.

Ruth took a sip of tea. "That is one happy kid. Sounds like she had the time of her life."

Kate nodded. "No question. Did you and Fritz have a good day?"

"Um—yes. Very nice."

Something in her voice didn't ring true. Kate knit her brow. "So where is he?"

"He, was, um, tired. He's gone back to his room."

That was odd. Her mother and Fritz had become inseparable.

"Ruth, can I ask you a favor?" Zack spoke up.

"Sure. Just name it."

"Would you keep an eye on Skye tonight so I can take Kate out?"

"Of course."

"It's likely to be a late night."

Kate's heart pounded.

"I'll have Skye spend the night with me so you can be as late as you want." Ruth's eyes lit with all-too-familiar worry. "You'll take the flashlight, won't you? And be sure to stay in well-lit places? The later it gets, you know, the more dangerous it becomes."

Zack raised his hand as if he were making a solemn vow. "I'll protect Kate with my life."

"You've got to protect yourself, too."

"Why, Ruth—I'm touched that you care."

Ruth grinned. "Of course I care. If a crook gets you first, Kate's a sitting duck."

"Mom!"

"I'm teasing. But only a little bit." Ruth made a shooing motion with her hand. "Go on and get out of here."

Zack tightened his hold on Kate. "Come on."

She hesitated. "I-I really ought to shower and change . . ."

"Why don't you just grab your swimsuit? The Hyatt has a

279

great pool. We can swim, have dinner at the hotel, and just have a low-key evening."

Kate knew that swimming wasn't the only activity he had in mind. If she went back to his hotel, she'd be diving into more than water.

But her heart had already taken the plunge. She gave him a soft smile. "I'll just be a minute."

"If you pull me under one more time, you're really gonna get it," Kate warned.

"Oh, yeah?" Zack's teeth flashed in the moonlight. "What are you going to do?"

"This." Drawing a deep breath, Kate dove under the warm water and tackled his legs. Unfortunately, they were as immovable as tree trunks. She tugged and tugged to no avail. She finally came up for air to find him laughing.

"You don't have to work so hard trying to knock me off my feet, Kate. Don't you know you already have?"

Kate's heart did a flip. The romp in the deserted pool had been lighthearted and playful, but currents of serious attraction were growing stronger every moment. Zack moved closer and pulled her up against him. "Now, if I could just come up with a way to sweep you off yours."

The feel of his naked chest against the thin nylon of her lime green tankini sent heat pulsing through her. His hands went around her waist, pulling her flush against him.

"This is working," she murmured.

"Kate." Her name came out as a low, hungry growl. He tightened his hold on her and claimed her mouth in a kiss. The hard surge of his arousal pressed closer, setting off a hot ache deep within her.

She parted her lips and the kiss deepened. His tongue mated with hers, leaving her breathless and dizzy and weak with wanting. His mouth moved to the sensitive flesh of her neck. A shiver skittered down her spine.

"Let's go to your room," she whispered.

"You sure?"

"Yes."

He looped his arm under her legs and carried her to the side of the pool, where he hoisted her up on the edge. He climbed out after her, his obvious erection making the front of his swimsuit look like a tent.

Kate couldn't help but grin. "So, Chief Tight Britches—is that a teepee in your pants or are you just glad to see me?"

He grabbed his towel off the poolside chair and swatted her with it. "I'm *very* glad to see you. I just hope my gladness doesn't get me arrested on the way to the room."

He wrapped the towel around his waist, then held out another one for her. She folded it around her, tucking in the ends above her breasts.

The elevator was mercifully empty but cold. By the time they got to the room, Kate was shivering.

Zack noticed. "What do you say to a warm shower?"

"Sounds great."

Zack strode to the bathroom and turned on the water. He tested it with his hand, then bowed to Kate with a sweeping gesture. "Our shower awaits."

"*Our* shower?"

"Sure. What kind of a host lets his guest shower alone?"

Kate laughed and followed him inside. The bathroom lights were off, and it was lit only by the glow from the hallway. Feeling suddenly shy, she decided to keep her swimsuit on. Dropping her towel, she stepped into the glass shower and under a spray of deliciously warm water.

"Oh, that feels wonderful," she sighed as the water poured over her, enveloping her in heat.

Zack entered the shower behind her, closed the glass door, and pulled Kate's back tight against his chest. "It sure does."

Warm water sluiced down her breasts as Zack's hands slowly slid up toward them. She stood perfectly still, letting the sensations pour over her—the soft drumming of the warm water, the masculine solidity of Zack's chest, the exciting feel of his hands moving up her swimsuit.

"Are you starting to get warm?" he murmured.

She turned to face him. "Very warm."

"Well, then, let's go for hot." His mouth came down on hers, his lips both soft and demanding. She arched against him, fitting herself against his erection.

The water tumbled down, and so did her inhibitions. Zack slipped off a strap of her swimsuit, then lowered his head to kiss her shoulder. His mouth went lower, trailing kisses on the skin above the fabric. Slowly, slowly, with exquisite, agonizing slowness, he slid her top down, kissing each new inch of exposed flesh. Kate leaned against the wall of the shower, her head thrown back, as Zack finally eased the top all the way down and off.

"Good Lord, you're beautiful," he murmured.

Cupping a breast in his hand, Zack lowered his mouth and trailed a languorous kiss across it, burning a trail of pleasure. She gasped as he pulled a pebbled tip into his mouth. Her nipple swelled and hardened, causing her to moan with pleasure. His mouth slid to her other breast and he pleasured it as well, until it, too, was kiss-swollen and aching.

His lips moved up her neck, across her face, and back to her mouth, his erection pressing hard against her belly. Leaning back, she ran her hands down the soft/rough hair of his chest, down the hard horizontal muscles of his belly, down to the trace of hair that disappeared into his swim trunks. She tugged at the waistband.

His eyes held a hidden fire, a fire that thrilled her with its heat and intensity. He put his hands on hers to stop her. "Oh, no. Ladies first. Turn around."

She did as he asked. He pulled her back flush against his chest and slid his hands around to cup her breasts. His erection rested on the small of her back as his hands slid low, then still lower, down, down, down her belly. His fingers toyed with the top of her bikini bottom, then he slowly peeled it off.

Kate leaned back against him and closed her eyes, weak-kneed with desire. His finger moved down the center of her femininity, past the delicate nub that ached for his touch, past the spot that ached to be filled. The pleasure was acute and sharp, and a moan escaped her lips.

"You like that?" he murmured in her ear.

"Ohhhhh, yes."

He repeated the magical movement until Kate was writhing against him. The sensation of his finger sliding on her naked, aching flesh was almost more than she could stand.

She felt as fluid as the warm streams showering down upon them, wetter than water, as if her joints were turning to liquid.

Zack didn't stop. She moved against him, driven by a need so intense that it obliterated all thought, all awareness, all reality except the feel of his fingers. Her need grew to an unbearable peak, a peak that had her panting.

"Please—oh, please," she whispered.

Finally, finally he slid a finger inside her. She immediately convulsed around it, arching her back against him as spasm after spasm of unspeakably hot, sweet, pleasure-drenched sensation rocked through her.

His arm caught her as she sagged against him, her legs weak and trembling. His hands moved up to her waist, and she turned in his arms to face him.

She looked into his eyes, eyes that held an intoxicating mix of passion and tenderness, and her already full heart swelled to overflowing. She loved him—completely, thoroughly, without reservation. With all her heart and soul and mind and body, she loved him—loved him with a depth and intensity she'd never felt for another man.

It was not a love that would be returned. He didn't believe in love, didn't even believe in giving it a chance. He believed in expiration dates, in walking away before relationships soured.

The knowledge cut like a surgeon's scalpel, but it couldn't excise the love from her heart. It only made the expression of it more urgent. Winding her arms around his neck, she pulled his head down in a kiss, pressing herself against the hard ridge of his erection.

A groan hissed from his lips. Her hands skimmed down his body. She grabbed the waistband of his swim trunks and tugged them down. Impatiently he kicked them the rest of the way off, and hauled her against him. She stood on her tiptoes and wound one leg around his thigh. He lifted her off the ground, his hands under her bottom, and backed her against the wall of the shower. She wrapped both legs around his hips and gasped as he drove inside her, stretching and filling her, doing to her body what he'd already done to her heart.

Desire, white-hot and primal, flared again within her. His rhythm was as hard and insistent as a tribal drumbeat, and she matched him stroke for stroke.

They made love with a savage need. This was no sissy sex. It was wild and primitive and uninhibited, raw and frenzied, exciting beyond anything she'd ever imagined. Zack was a force of nature, powerful and unrestrained. He carried her like a tidal wave to a dizzying crest, to a height that left her breathless and stunned, and when he finally sent her over the edge, he followed right behind.

Chapter Twenty-two

When the bedside alarm clock jangled the next morning, Zack opened his eyes to find Kate gone.

He hit the OFF button so hard, the clock flew off the night-stand, then raised his head and looked around. She was gone, all right. Her clothing and purse had disappeared from the arm-chair across the room. He pushed himself up on his elbow, squinting at the intruding light of dawn creeping through the hotel window.

It hadn't been a dream. The drapes were open because Kate had pulled them back in the middle of the night to gaze at the skyline. The memory of the way she'd looked, naked and bathed in moonlight, her hair loose and tousled, her lips kiss-swollen and pink, made him want her all over again.

"What are you doing?" he'd asked.

"Admiring the view. You didn't give me a chance to look at it before you ravished me in the shower," she told him.

"That's because you made such an enticing view yourself," he'd replied, hauling her back to bed.

"Yeah, well, this time *I'm* going to ravish *you*."

And she had. The memory made him grin as he swung his legs off the side of the bed.

Robin Wells

He'd been like a teenager. He hadn't been able to get enough of her. She was incredible—passionate and giving, tender and taunting, naughty and nice. Very, very, very nice. They'd been so attuned to each other, so in sync, that they seemed to be in the same skin. He'd never felt so close to a woman. Their love-making had seemed to transcend the physical, to be more meaningful, more profound. Hell, it was almost as if they'd been making . . . well, love.

The thought made him scowl. He didn't believe in that schmaltz. Where the hell was she, anyway? She'd disappeared without so much as goodbye.

He sat up in bed, trying to fend off the cold, aching sense of emptiness sprawling through his gut. She'd disappeared, left, just like everybody else he'd ever cared about. This was exactly why he didn't allow himself to get attached to anyone. People always left. They always let you down.

And how the hell had Kate sneaked under the wire, anyway? He always cut things off before wanting someone became needing someone. Damn it, he thought he'd put this kind of bone-cold loneliness behind him.

His eye fell on a piece of paper on the nightstand. Zack snatched it up and stared at the neat, round handwriting.

See you at work.

The void in his chest shrank a little. He'd see her on the set; It wasn't as if she had left his life completely.

Still, what the heck did "See you at work" mean? In the cold morning light, he was afraid it meant she expected to go back to a platonic, all-business relationship. He scowled. If she thought he was going to pretend like last night never happened, she had another think coming.

The prop crew was hard at work setting up the flammable exterior of the bank when Zack arrived at the location for the day's shoot. It was eight-thirty, but Kate was nowhere to be seen. He tried to concentrate on all the things that demanded his attention, but his thoughts kept returning to her.

286

"Are you okay?" Deb asked, pushing her glasses up her nose.

"Sure. Why?"

"That's the third time you've asked me about the dialogue changes in Lena's next scene."

Hell. He'd never had a problem separating work from his personal life before. Mornings were dedicated to business. He usually began planning his day while he shaved. This morning he'd done nothing but think of Kate, and he'd nicked himself three times.

"Sorry," he said. "I've got a lot on my mind. So . . . are they ready?"

Deb looked at him cautiously, as if memory loss was contagious. "Yes."

"So, where are they?"

"In your right hand."

Jeeze. He was a real basket case. "Sorry," he muttered.

"Lena wants it changed again. She says she can't pronounce the word *constitutional.*"

Lena would probably have trouble pronouncing her own name if she hadn't rehearsed it for twenty-odd years. "Why the hell is that word in this scene anyway?"

"It's an old-fashioned term for taking a walk."

Zack's heart lurched at the sound of Kate's voice. He turned to see her behind him, and broke into a wide smile. "Maybe that's what we should do."

Deb's brow pulled down in an anxious frown. "But we still have some things to go over."

"Later," Zack said, not taking his eyes from Kate. Holy Moses—had any woman ever looked so beautiful? Her hair was loose around her shoulders and her face was unusually pink—abraded from his beard, he realized with chagrin. She was wearing blue jeans and a blue sleeveless turtleneck—but most importantly, she was wearing a smile.

"Good morning," she said.

Zack smiled back, his heart full of relief. "Great morning." He

put his arm around her waist and led her around the corner.
"When did you leave?"

"Around four."

"Why?"

"I wanted to be home when Skye woke up."

Of course. Why hadn't he thought of that? "How did you get
home?"

"I took a cab."

"You should have gotten me up."

Kate's grin was slow. "Again?"

Zack laughed. "Seriously, you should have let me take you
home. I hate the idea of you alone in a taxi at four in the morning."

"You sound like my mother."

"Well, in this case, she'd be right."

"Okay. Next time, you'll have to bring me home at a decent
hour."

Next time. It was ridiculous, the amount of relief he felt at
those two little words. "You've got a deal." He tightened his hold
on her. "So . . . can I see you tonight?"

Kate shook her head. "I've got a PTA meeting."

"And I have to go to California for a meeting the day after.
What about the weekend?"

"I promised Skye I'd take her and and her friend Mary Ann
to the fishing cabin for the night after school Friday. But on
Saturday, Skye's going to a sleepover." Kate's eyes took on a
provocative light. "That means you and I can have a sleepover
of our own."

"You're on."

"My place. Seven o'clock. Bring your toothbrush."

"I can't wait."

Fritz's face wore an unusually pleased expression as he snapped
his cell phone closed. Ruth smiled at him as he strode across
the set toward her. "You look like you just got some good news."

"I did." His gray-green eyes sparkled.

"So, are you going to share?"

"That was the cinematographers association. I'm up for an award for my last movie."

"That's wonderful!" Ruth threw her arms around his neck.

Fritz returned the hug. "I'm up against some pretty big names. There's no way I'll win."

"You can't know that. Besides, it's an honor just to be nominated."

"Yeah, I guess it is." He gave an embarrassed grin, but Ruth could see the pride in his eyes.

"When are they going to name the winner?" she asked.

"Next month. They're having a big shindig in L.A. If I go, I'll have to get a tux."

"What do you mean, 'if you go'? Of course you're going to go."

"You think I should?"

"Absolutely."

"Well, then, come with me."

The blood drained from Ruth's head. She took a step back. "Oh, Fritz—I—I can't."

"Why not?"

"Well, it . . . it's in California, for one thing."

"So? Last time I checked, they had planes flying there and back."

"It's so expensive."

"I'll buy you a ticket."

Ruth's mind raced. "I-I can't leave Kate and Skye."

Fritz's eyes lit with frustration. "Kate is a grown woman. She's perfectly capable of taking care of herself and her daughter."

"Well . . . still . . . What if something happened and Kate needed me?"

"Ruth, everyone needs to be needed, but you're carrying it way too far."

"But they need me."

"*I* need you." He leaned forward. "Know what I think? I think you're using Kate and Skye to cover up your own fear."

"I'm working on that," Ruth said. "I'm getting out more. I'm taking walks down the block. And . . . and yesterday I went in a video store by myself." No need to tell him it had triggered a full-scale panic attack. "I just need some more time."

"You need more than time. You need help, honey."

"I can handle this on my own."

"I had an uncle with a drinking problem who used to say the same thing; he was working on it, he didn't need any help. Know what happened to him? He got crocked, got behind the wheel, and smashed head-on into another car."

Ruth felt annoyed. "This is nothing like that. I'm not in danger of hurting anyone."

Fritz's eyes bore into hers. "Aren't you?"

She looked down. A tear dripped from her eye.

Fritz tipped up her face with his finger. His eyes were gentle yet troubled. "Ruth, I'm crazy about you. You're bright and witty and sexy and fun. I want you in my life. I want you to visit me in California. I want to show you where I live and take you to restaurants and go for long walks on the beach." He leaned forward. "But you have to want it, too. Enough to make some changes."

She looked up, her eyes pleading. "I'm trying. Please be patient with me."

She knew she was asking a lot. Too much, maybe. His whole life had been a long, patient wait.

He huffed out a long sigh. "I'm trying, too. But Ruth . . ." He took both her hands. "This movie's gonna wrap in just a few weeks. If we're going to continue seeing each other, you'll have to meet me halfway."

"I will. I promise." But how she'd manage, she didn't know.

Kate smoothed her hair in the hall mirror Saturday evening, then ran her hand down her low-cut black silk dress. Zack's plane should be on the ground, and he should be heading this way. A frisson of anticipation chased through her. He was taking her out to dinner, then they were coming back here for dessert.

She had a very special one planned. The thought made her smile. She could hardly wait.

The clunk of Skye's platform mules on the stairs stopped abruptly. "Wow, Mom—you look hot!"

Kate turned and grinned. "Thanks."

"Where'd you get the dress?"

"Samantha talked me into buying it a year ago."

"Well, you look really good. Maybe Zack'll even pop the question."

Kate's pulse faltered. "Honey, there's no chance of that."

"How do you know? The *National Inquisitor* said that you might be the one to make Zack settle down."

The mention of the full-page tabloid photo made Kate wince. "Oh, honey, you can't believe everything you read." Especially not about Zack Jackson settling down, she thought ruefully.

"Why not? Zack likes you, and you like him."

"It's not that simple. We come from entirely different backgrounds. We live more than fifteen-hundred miles away from each other, and our lifestyles are poles apart."

"If you fell in love and got married, you could work all that out."

"Honey, Zack isn't interested in getting married."

"Grams says no man ever is until he meets the right woman." *Thanks a lot, Mom.*

"I think Zack would make a cool dad," Skye continued.

Kate's heart tightened. "Oh, honey . . ."

"I mean it, Mom. I really like him. Most adults just kinda blow kids off, but Zack treats me like a real person—a person with thoughts and feelings and ideas and everything. So, if he asks you to marry him, I think you should say yes."

"Honey, he's not the marrying type."

"What do you mean? Why not?"

"It—it's complicated. But mainly it's because he's seen a lot of bad marriages and he thinks that sooner or later they all turn out that way."

"Oh." Skye seemed to absorb that for a moment. "Since your

marriage turned out lousy, I guess he thinks you're a pretty bad risk, huh?"

Kate's stomach clenched. "It's more complicated than that."

Skye looked down at her fingernails "So . . . did having me mess up your life or anything?"

The tightness in Kate's belly sharpened. "Of course not! Oh, Skye. Why would you ask a question like that?"

She lifted her shoulders. "A lady came and talked at my school about teenage pregnancy, and she said that having a baby when you're really young would wreck your life. You were really young when you had me, so I just wondered—"

Kate pulled her into her arms. "I wanted you and loved you from the moment I discovered I was going to have you, honey. Every day of your life, I've thanked God for you." She took her daughter's face between her hands and gazed at her earnestly. "You're the best thing that ever happened to me."

Skye's face split into a grin. It was amazing how bright her smile was, how it changed her appearance, changed the mood in the room, changed the outlook of anyone lucky enough to have it bestowed upon them. "You're pretty cool yourself, Mom."

The kitchen door opened. "Ready to go, Skye?" Ruth called. She made her way into the hallway, then stopped short and stared at Kate. "Wow!"

"Is the dress too much?" Kate asked worriedly.

"If anything, it's too little."

Kate fingered the spaghetti straps. "Maybe I should go change."

"Don't you dare!" Ruth grinned and gave her a hug. "I was teasing, sweetheart. You look wonderful."

Skye picked up her sleeping bag and backpack from the bottom of the stairs. "Let's go, Grams. I don't want to be late."

"Okay, okay." Ruth took the backpack from her granddaughter and hoisted it over her shoulder as Kate kissed Skye's cheek. "Have fun, honey."

"You, too."

"I'll be gone when you get back, Mom," Kate called.

"Okay. Be careful, honey."

It's too late for careful, Kate thought as the door closed behind them. She'd completely given her heart to Zack. She'd never felt this way about another man, and she was certain she never would again. This was her once-in-a-lifetime opportunity to experience full-throttle, with-all-her-heart love, and she was going make the most of it.

Zack braked the rented white minivan in Kate's driveway, killed the engine, and turned toward her. A shaft of moonlight gleamed through the windshield, making her hair look like spun gold. He reached out and touched a lock. "So, what's this special dessert you told me to save room for?"

"I can't tell you. It's a surprise." Her eyes held a seductive sparkle. "You told me to lighten up, though, so it's a light dessert."

He leaned toward her and touched her lips with his. *Soft.* Everything about her was so incredibly soft—her lips, her skin, her hair, her touch. He wanted to sink into her softness, to be enveloped by it, to let it soothe away all of the world's hard edges.

Her mouth opened under his, inviting him into its sweet depths. He groaned and deepened the kiss, trying to pull her closer, frustrated by the car's console.

"Let's go inside," he murmured.

"Okay. But you have to wait out here for five minutes while I get dessert ready."

"I don't think I can wait that long."

She touched his face and smiled. "I'll make it worth your while." She opened the door, causing the light inside the minivan to flash on. "Wait five minutes, then come in through the back door."

He watched her stroll around the side of the house, his eyes hungrily following her. The minutes passed slowly as he sat and stared at the minivan's clock. It was not his vehicle of choice, but the car-rental agency at the airport had been out of SUVs, and he needed a vehicle large enough to carry five or six crew members. He drummed his fingers on the steering wheel and wondered just what type of surprise Kate had in store. When the five minutes were up, he let himself in as she'd directed.

The kitchen was dark, except for a fat red candle burning in a hurricane glass on the rustic oak table. Next to it was a note in Kate's round handwriting:

> *Roses are red, violets are blue.*
> *Your dessert is waiting for you.*
> *Follow the candles to find your treat.*
> *They're sure to lead you to something sweet.*

A trail of votive candles led into the hallway. Grinning widely, Zack followed them into the dining room.

There, on the polished mahogany table, sat another candle enclosed in a lamp, with yet another note attached:

> *You're getting warm. If you want to get hot,*
> *Take off your shirt, your shoes, and your socks.*

"I hope you're not planning on getting me down to my skivvies only to have a bunch of people jump out and yell 'surprise,'" Zack called.

Kate's laughter wafted from the direction of the living room. "We're all alone. I promise."

Kicking off his shoes, he stripped off his shirt and socks, then followed the candles to the bottom of the stairs, where another note awaited.

> *If you're wondering where all this leads.*
> *Take off your pants and your BVDs.*

"You're *sure* we're alone?" he called.
"Very sure."

Ooh, La La!

"Well, in that case . . ." Zack hastily dropped his trousers and boxes briefs and followed the candles to the next stop, which happened to be the downstairs bathroom.

> *If you have followed each direction,*
> *You'll have no trouble passing inspection.*

"Inspection?" Zack called. "I'm standing here naked, and you're telling me I have to pass *inspection?*"

Kate's laugh came from the next room. "Keep reading," she called.

> *Your just desserts do now await.*
> *Follow the candles to learn your fate*

Zack's heart pounded. He hadn't felt this much anticipation in years. Trying hard not to look overly eager, he strolled into the darkened living room.

And there lay Kate, stretched out on a quilt in front of the candlelit hearth. She was propped on her side in a come-hither pose, one hand provocatively placed on her hip. A huge smile covered her face, but the rest of her was barely covered at all. She wore lace-topped black stockings, a black thong bikini, and dollops of whipped cream on each breast.

In front of her, on a silver platter, sat a bottle of chocolate syrup and a can of whipped cream.

She waved her hand. "Dessert is served."

Good heavens, but she was something. Funny, sexy, clever, adorable—a warm, tender feeling filled his chest, along with a rush of arousal. He sank to his knees on the quilt beside her. "Well, well, well. This beats Bananas Foster any day."

"As promised, it's light whipped cream. And it's the house specialty."

"It looks awfully special, all right." Leaning forward, he slowly circled her right breast with his finger, then held the whipped cream to her lips. Her pink tongue darted out to taste it.

295

He grinned. "It all looks so delicious, I don't know where to begin."

"The chef recommends the topping."

"Sounds like a good suggestion." He bent down and lapped up a tongueful from the tip of her breast. Kate stretched out and made a throaty sound that was half-purr, half-moan as his mouth moved over her. "Mmm," he murmured, pulling her nipple into his mouth, then freeing it to lick another spot of cream off the side of her breast. "This is the sweetest dessert I've ever tasted."

"There have to be at least five of them," Ruth whispered urgently into the phone. "There are flashlights moving all through the house."

"I have four police cars en route, Mrs. Matthews," the dispatcher said.

Fingering the camera around her neck, Ruth peered out her kitchen window at the eerie lights flickering inside Kate's house.

"Tell them to hurry! The burglars have already been in there for at least ten minutes."

"The squad cars are on their way."

Ruth was waiting outside when the police pulled up and stopped by the curb. She hurried toward them and spoke in a loud whisper. "They're over there, in my daughter's house." She pointed across the street.

"You're the person who reported the burglary?"

Ruth nodded. "I'm Ruth Matthews."

"I'm Sergeant Hutchins, and this is my partner, Officer Carter. Did you see the actual break-in, ma'am?"

"No. The thieves were already inside by the time I spotted the car. I went into my kitchen a few minutes ago, and I happened to look out the window." She'd been trying not to gaze out the window at Fritz's suggestion, but she'd been unable to resist. "I noticed a strange car in the driveway of my daughter's house, and odd lights moving around inside. My daughter's out for the evening and my grandchild is at a sleepover."

"Has anyone come out?"

"No."

"How many exterior doors does the house have?"

"Two. There's a kitchen door in the back."

"Okay." The sergeant turned to the other officers. "We don't know what we're walking into, so we'll have to assume they're armed. We've got the element of surprise on our side, so let's use it to the max."

The men all nodded.

"Carter, you come in the front door with me. Peterson, I want you and Ricketts to go in the back. The rest of you cover each side to make sure they don't escape out the windows." The sergeant turned to Ruth. "Are the doors unlocked?"

"Not usually. But I've got keys." She pulled two sets out of her pocket.

"Good." The sergeant handed one key to another officer. "Ready, men? Let's go."

Ruth started to follow. "Sorry, ma'am, but this is a police operation," the sergeant said. "You'll be safer in your house."

Ruth stopped, but she didn't retreat. She stood on her front lawn and watched the officers surround the house. Her heart hammered hard as the sergeant inserted the key in the door and drew his gun. "Now!" he shouted.

Guns drawn, he and his fellow officer burst inside.

"Freeze!"

The overhead lights abruptly burst on. Sergeant Hutchins stood spraddle-legged, his gun aimed at the alleged intruders. Officer Carter stood at his side, his gun drawn as well.

The sergeant took in the scene, his mind filing facts as if he were already writing his crime report. Two suspects lay sprawled on the floor, one male, one female. They both appeared to be naked.

The male suspect abruptly sat up, holding a silver tray in front of his groin. He was Caucasian, early thirties, with dark hair. He wore a dazed expression, and his face was covered with white foam. He and the woman quickly jumped behind a green wing-backed chair. The man stepped in front of the woman, apparently shielding her nakedness.

"Don't move!" the sergeant ordered. "Put your hands up!"

The male suspect complied. In his right hand, he held a canister of what appeared to be whipped cream. The woman peered out from behind his shoulder. She seemed to be hiding her body against the male suspect's back. From what little the sergeant could see, she was blond, late twenties or early thirties, and quite attractive—although it was hard to see nearly as much as he'd like. Her face, too, was splotched with white foam. A substance that appeared to be chocolate was smeared around her mouth.

Closer inspection revealed that a similar chocolatelike substance was dripping from the male suspect's chest.

"Hey, Sarge," Officer Carter said, talking out of the corner of his mouth. "Either this is a lot worse than we suspected, or we've made a big mistake."

Officer Ricketts and Peterson entered the room, their weapons drawn. They froze in the doorway, staring at the suspects.

"Did you find anything in the back of the house?" the sergeant asked.

Officer Ricketts appeared to have difficulty speaking. His eyes were transfixed on the suspects, particularly the female one. "N-no evidence of a break in. But we found a lot of candles and some notes."

"What kind of notes?"

Officer Peterson unfolded a pink piece of paper, cleared his throat and read in a stilted voice: " 'If you're wondering where all this leads, take off your pants and your BVDs.' " Here's another one: 'Roses are red . . .' "

Officer Ricketts snickered. "That's enough," the sergeant ordered. "This was no burglary. Apparently it was some kind of kinky sex thing—possibly a situation for the vice squad. "What are you two doing here?" the sergeant demanded.

"I-I *live* here," the female responded in a high voice. "What are *you* doing here?"

The sergeant's face grew warm. "Are—are you alone?"

"We *were*," the man growled.

Oh, hell—this wasn't a crime scene at all. They'd evidently interrupted a couple of citizens in the middle of a private moment.

And damn, but this was an elaborate private moment! His gaze swept the surroundings, taking in a plastic bottle of chocolate syrup, the whipped cream, and all the candles. He made a mental note to himself: Try this at home with Mabel.

The sergeant lowered his gun. The other officers followed suit. He cleared his throat in a loud harrumph. "It um, appears, um, that, um, there's been a mistake."

"No kidding." The male suspect—er, citizen—appeared agitated. "What the *hell* is going on?"

"We, um, had a report of a burglary in progress," the sergeant said sheepishly.

Ruth peeked around the door into Kate's living room. All she could see were the blue-shirted backs of four policemen, who apparently had the perpetrators cornered behind a chair. "Do you need me to call for back-up?" Ruth asked.

The sergeant turned toward her, his face as red as baked cherries. "Mrs. Matthews, we told you to stay home."

"But it's my daughter's house, and . . ." One of the other officers shifted his stance, giving Ruth a clear view of the perps. Her mouth fell open. She stood stock-still and stared, too shocked to comprehend what she was seeing.

"Zack?" He was shirtless, standing behind a wing-backed chair. Something brown and syrupy was smeared on his chest, and white foam festooned his face.

"Kate?" Ruth gasped.

Her daughter was peering around Zack's back, her face wide-eyed and streaked with what looked like chocolate. Her shoulders were bare, and globs of white foam hung in her hair.

"Kate, w-what are you two doing here? I thought you went out."

"We did. Then we came back." Kate looked from her mother to the police and back again. "What's going on?"

Ruth was wondering the very same thing. She frowned in bewilderment. A plastic bottle of chocolate syrup was on the floor, and Zack was holding a canister of something that looked like whipped cream in the other.

Chocolate syrup? Whipped cream? Candles everywhere, Zack and Kate undressed . . .

"Oh, my!" Ruth stepped back, her hand over her mouth. "Oh, *dear*! Oh, *heavens*! Oh, I'm so sorry!"

Mortification flooded her soul. "I-I thought you were being burglarized." Even to her ears, her voice sounded squeaky as a rusty hinge. "I thought you were gone for the whole evening. And then I saw a bunch of unusual lights, and a strange car in the driveway . . ."

"Christ, Ruth. Did you call these guys?"

She turned to find Fritz looming in the doorway, his face grim. He was looking at the police. Oh, dear—in all the hubbub, she'd forgotten he was coming over to watch the late movie with her. He must have seen the police cars and crossed the street looking for her.

She looked at him sheepishly. "I—I made a mistake."

"You can say that again." Fritz heaved an impatient sigh, then turned from Ruth to the cops. "Sorry we've wasted your time, officers. These folks are obviously not burglars. What do you say we get out of here and give them some privacy?"

The sergeant swallowed. "Um, yeah. Um, sure. Of course." He elbowed Officer Ricketts, who was still gaping at Kate. The officer jumped, then scurried from the room to follow the others. The sergeant paused at the door and gave an embarrassed nod to Kate and Zack. "Enjoy the rest of your evening."

The next thing Ruth knew, Fritz had her by the arm and was escorting her out of the house.

* * *

"I can't believe you did that!" Fritz shoved his hands into his pockets and glared at Ruth as the last of the police cars pulled away.

A chill passed through her despite the warm evening air. She rubbed her hands up and down her arms. "It was an honest mistake. Anyone could have made it."

"No, Ruth. Not just anyone would immediately jump to such an extreme conclusion."

"But it really, really, really looked suspicious. And it wasn't the black Navigator Zack has been driving."

"Of course it wasn't. Zack had just gotten back into town and the car rental agency gave him a different vehicle."

"Oh." Ruth hadn't thought of that. "Well, those candles looked like flashlights from across the street."

Fritz closed his eyes in exasperation. "If you were worried, why didn't you call Kate?"

"I didn't think she was home." Ruth looked at him pleadingly. "I was just trying to protect her house."

Fritz shook his head, sighing. "Ruth, you're ruining the lives of the very people you're trying to protect."

A tear ran down her cheek. "I don't mean to. I love them."

"And they love you. *I* love you."

She'd waited for him to say those words, waited and hoped and prayed. She'd imagined a dozen different scenarios when she'd hear him say those tender words, the very words that had been on the tip of her tongue for weeks. She'd never thought, though, that when he said them, they'd be tinged with such gray despair.

"Oh, Fritz—I love you, too."

He sighed and hung his head. "Ruthie, I just don't know if I can handle it."

"Wh-what do you mean?"

"How you are with the people you love. You watch them like hawks, hovering over them, constantly warning them of imagined dangers. It's like you're trying to clip their wings. You want everyone you care about to live in the same tiny box as you do."

The words entered her heart like shards of glass. "I don't! I want them to have full, happy lives. I'd love for Kate to get married and have more children. I-I just want her to be safe, that's all." A ragged sob escaped her lips.

"Oh, Ruth." He gathered her in his arms and held her close. "You mean well, I know you do. You have a kind, loving, giving heart. It's just . . ." He pulled back and looked down at her. "Nothing in this world is safe. Nothing. And no amount of worrying or warning or hovering will ever completely protect you or anyone else. It only limits you. All this fear and negativity is ruining your life and hampering the lives of others around you. And I . . ." He hesitated.

"What?"

He drew a breath and looked at her, his eyes filled with sorrow and something that looked suspiciously like pity. She was suddenly afraid to hear what he had to say next.

His hands slid down her arms and he took her hands. "I think you're great in a million ways. I'm crazy about you. But, Ruthie—you're scared of your own shadow. You're afraid to go to restaurants or on walks or to my room. You won't travel, and as soon as this movie's over, we'll be half a continent apart." He hung his head. "I love you, Ruthie, but I need someone who wants to be a part of my world. I don't know if this is going to work." His eyes were so sad it nearly broke Ruth's heart to look into them. "I wonder if we're only hurting each other by pretending it will."

"Give me a little more time."

"We're running out of time, Ruth. The shoot is nearly over. And if you don't make some major changes, I'm afraid we'll be over, too."

Chapter Twenty-three

Over the course of the next week, Kate and Zack developed a nightly ritual. At the end of the day, Kate would take Skye home, have dinner with her, help her with her homework, then head back to Zack's hotel, purportedly to watch the daily rushes on a screen set up in the parlor of his suite.

Most of the time, they actually managed to watch the film. Since Zack had already watched it while Kate at was home, though, it sometimes took a backseat to more compelling activities.

"Wow—that scene gave me goose bumps," Kate said Friday evening as they watched the last clip. She was lounging on the sofa, wrapped in a hotel robe and the contented glow that always followed making love with Zack. "Lena was incredible."

Zack turned off the projector, flipped on a lamp, and sank down beside her. "Even more incredible, we got it in only two takes." He looped his arm around her, his hand moving up under her hair to rub the back of her neck. "You bring me luck, Katie-girl. Things are going so well that it looks like we'll wrap a week ahead of schedule."

"And then you'll have to leave." The words were out before

she could stop them. *Fool,* she silently scolded. She'd promised herself she wouldn't complain, wouldn't speak about the future, wouldn't do anything to ruin the precious time they had left together.

"Come with me."

Kate's heart took wing like a startled sparrow. "What?"

"Come back to Hollywood with me. You've worked hard. You deserve a vacation."

Vacation. For a tiny, rapturous moment, her foolish heart had thought he was talking about a real future.

"It'll do you good to kick back for a week or so," he said. "You can see the sights, go shopping, laze around . . . do whatever you want."

A week. He was willing to give her one extra week. Which really wasn't extra, since the shoot would finish early. A lump the size of a lemon formed in her throat. "I-I can't. I'm expected back at work. And Skye needs me. And then there's Mom . . ." She forced a smile. "No reason you can't come back to New Orleans on weekends, though."

He shook his head regretfully. "I won't be able to go anywhere for a long while. I'll be up against the wall, editing this thing. And then I have to get moving on my next film. I've got an option on a terrific mystery novel, but it runs out in two months. I have to find funding or I'll lose the rights to it."

Kate jerked her head in a nod, the lump in her throat growing to the size of a grapefruit. When the movie ended, so would her relationship with Zack. He'd told her at the outset that he believed in expiration dates, not happily ever after. Why would she think he'd changed his mind? She knew he liked her, that he cared for her, even—but he didn't love her. Zack didn't believe in love.

She'd known that at the outset. She'd known their relationship would end, and she'd known it would hurt.

She just hadn't known how much, because she'd never loved anyone the way she loved Zack. Not even Wayne's sudden departure had hurt this bad.

Kate drew in a steadying breath. She wouldn't dwell on it now. There would be plenty of time to reflect later. She wouldn't let worries about the future ruin the present.

All the same, a lone tear escaped her eye. She looked down at her watch, letting her hair stream forward over her face to hide it, and surreptitiously wiped her cheek. "Oh, hey—I need to get home." She stood and headed for the bedroom, where her summer dress, underwear, and sandals lay at various places on the floor where Zack had taken them off of her.

"Kate—Is something wrong?" He followed her.

Zack took her by the shoulders and turned her around to face him. To her utter humilation, the tears welling in her eyes refused to stop.

"Kate, baby . . ."

"Sorry." She rapidly wiped her face, then bent down to pull on her sandals. "I just hate to think about you leaving."

His eyes were troubled. "I'm going to miss you, too."

Don't do this. Don't act all caring and devoted and sweet when we both know you're just going to walk away. Tears filled her eyes again. She drew a deep breath, determined to hold them at bay long enough to get out the door.

"Why are we talking as if this is good-bye?" she said bravely, trying for an upbeat tone. "We still have two weeks." She grabbed her purse off the corner of the chair, pulled the strap up on her shoulder, and gave him a quick kiss. He tried to deepen it, but she pulled away. She was too close to dissolving into tears. She quickly strode to the door and raised her hand in a casual wave. "See you tomorrow."

As she closed the door, tears streamed down her cheeks.

By the time she arrived home, Kate had pulled herself together, but her spirits were at an all-time low. "I'm home, Mom," she called as she pulled her key from the lock in the kitchen door.

She looked up and froze. There at the kitchen table sat Ruth, Skye, and a thin man who looked oddly familiar. His features were handsome and he was probably only a few years older than herself, but he had a weathered face that spoke of a hard life. His brown hair was shot with gray and thinning in front.

"Hello, there, Katie." He flashed a smile that had considerable charm despite the fact that it revealed yellow teeth, the kind that come from too many cigarettes and too much coffee. "Long time, no see."

Oh, God. Her knees started to buckle, and she gripped the doorjamb to steady herself.

"I see I surprised you," he said.

It couldn't be. He wouldn't be here in New Orleans, wouldn't be here in her kitchen. It just couldn't be.

But it was.

"Wayne?" Kate's voice came out in a tremulous warble.

"It's Dad, Mom! He came to see me." Skye's face was radiant, her voice excited. "And it's all okay. He says he's forgiven you for everything."

He forgives *me?* The words echoed so loudly in her head that for a moment, Kate feared she'd said them aloud.

And then the meaning of Skye's remark hit her. Oh, Lord—she'd told the child that the reason Wayne never came to see her was because he was angry at her over something she'd done. Skye must have somehow conveyed that to her father.

"Yeah, well, I figured might as well let bygones be bygones." Wayne gave her a wink, and a sickening sense of déjà vu washed over her. It was the same wink he'd used years ago, the wink that used to make her feel warm and special, the wink that had convinced her to empty her bank account and run away from home with him. Back then, she'd thought it was a sign of intimacy. It used to fill her heart with joy and anticipation.

Now it filled her with revulsion.

This couldn't be happening. It was just a bad dream. She'd wake up in a moment and it wouldn't be real. She briefly closed her eyes. But when she opened them again, he was still there.

"Where did you . . . When did you . . . What do you . . ." Her throat felt as dry as ashes. Too late, she realized that none of her questions were ones she'd actually want him to answer in front of Skye and her mother.

Wayne gave a harsh laugh that ended in a smoker's cough. "Guess we've got a lot of catching up to do."

Kate's gaze went to Skye's face, then to her mother's, wondering what he'd said, what they knew, what they thought.

Ruth glanced at her watch, then rose from the chair. "Oh my—it's nearly ten-thirty and it's a school night. You need to go to bed, Skye, and I need to go home."

"But Dad's here! I've waited my whole life to meet him. Can't I stay up a little longer?" She turned pleading eyes to Wayne. "Can't I, Dad? Can't I?"

"It's late. Better get to bed."

With an exasperated sigh, Skye rose from her chair. Wayne rose, too, and Skye gave him a big hug. "I can't believe you're really here. I'm so excited! Maybe you can come to my class and talk about endangered animals and stuff. Are you going to stay in town for a while? Will I get to see you tomorrow?"

"Sure."

"Great!" Giving him another hug, Skye turned and headed for the hall.

"Good night, sweetheart," Kate called.

" 'Night."

Skye had hugged Wayne twice but barely spoken to Kate. And instead of asking Kate's permission to stay up, she'd turned to her father.

A pang of alarm shot through Kate. They were small, silly things to worry about. The child was excited to meet her father, which was perfectly understandable. All the same, it seemed fraught with portent. If it came to choosing sides, wouldn't Skye go with the unknown, more exciting parent?

Kate's attention was pulled to her mother, who was grabbing her flashlight from the counter and moving toward the door. "Well, Wayne, it was nice to finally meet you." Ruth paused at the door and looked at Kate, her eyes full of concern. "If you need anything, I'm just across the street."

"Thanks, Mom." Unfortunately, the thing she really needed—a magic wand that would make Wayne disappear—wasn't something her mother could provide.

The kitchen seemed close and cloying now that she was alone with Wayne. The stench of stale cigarette smoke radiated from his navy knit shirt and fitted jeans. He curled his lip in a smile and looked her up and down in a way that made her flesh crawl.

"You look great, Kate. You've come a long way from the mousy little girl I remember."

Mousy? He'd thought she was mousy? She'd figured out years ago that he never meant to marry her, that his early proclamations of love had only been to get her to cash in her trust fund and finance his trip to New York. All the same, learning that he'd considered her mousy added insult to injury.

She turned abruptly and headed for the door. "Let's go talk on the deck."

"Whatever you say, darlin'." Instead of following her, Wayne opened the refrigerator. "Got any beer?"

Kate stiffened at his gall. "No."

"Oh, right—I forgot. You never *could* drink, could you?"

"As I recall, you did enough of that for the two of us."

Wayne's chest rattled as he laughed. Jerking open the door, Kate walked outside and drew a deep breath, trying to calm herself.

Wayne followed her out. He pulled a pack of Camels from his shirt pocket, along with a plastic lighter.

"What are you doing here?" Kate asked.

"I came to see my daughter." He tapped the pack on his hand and extracted an unfiltered cigarette. "Named her Skye, huh? Pretty name."

"What prompted your sudden interest?"

He lit the cigarette and inhaled. In the flash from the lighter, she saw a crafty look in his eyes. He blew out a puff of smoke. "I saw a picture of you and Zack Jackson in one of those supermarket newspapers. I wouldn't have recognized you, but it gave your name and said you were in New Orleans at your daughter's thirteenth birthday party. I did a little math and figured out the girl must be mine." He picked a piece of tobacco off his tongue. "Until I saw that article, I never knew whether you actually had the kid or not."

"If you hadn't stolen my money and abandoned me, you would have found out."

"Hey, now—no point in getting into all that." His teeth showed as he grinned. "From what Skye told me, seems like you've been sendin' her gifts and sayin' they were from me all these years. An' you told her I travel the world savin' endangered species?" He gave a congested chuckle.

The thought of Wayne talking to Skye made Kate sick to her stomach. "I had to tell her something. She wanted to know where her father was and why he didn't love her."

"Works for me. I played along." He took a drag of his cigarette. "Sounds better than saying I was in the joint."

Anxiety clutched Kate's heart. She gazed out at the backyard. "What exactly did you tell her?"

"Nothin'. I let her do all the talkin'. The minute she heard my name, she started huggin' me and callin' me daddy and talkin' nonstop. She was full of information." He inhaled and blew out a smoke ring.

Kate stiffened her spine. "What's the real reason you're here?"

"I told you, to meet my daughter." The acrid scent of cigarette smoke assaulted her nostrils as the ring of smoke floated past her face. "Besides, I always wanted to be in the movies, and I thought you could help me break into the business, now that you're boinkin' a big-time director."

The crudeness of the remark felt like a slap. She knotted her hands at her side.

"Why on earth would I want to help you?"

"For our little girl's sake."

"I don't want you in her life."

"Too bad, 'cause here I am." His cigarette had burned down to a mere stub. He held it between his thumb and first finger and took a final drag, giving her a calculating look. "If you were gonna tell her a fib, why didn't you just tell her I was dead?"

"I wish I had."

"So, why didn't you?"

A memory flashed in Kate's mind. It was the day after Skye's fourth birthday party, and Kate had found her sitting on her bedroom floor, her elbows propped on the pink plastic roof of her new Barbie dollhouse, her head in her hands. A tear had splashed on Barbie's chimney.

"What's the matter, honey?" Kate had asked.

Skye had peeked out through her fingers. "I wished for my daddy when I blew out the birthday candles, but he didn't come."

"Oh, honey!"

"Why doesn't he love me?" She'd looked up, her pink chubby cheeks wet with tears. "Did I do something bad?"

Kate turned away from Wayne now, her heart heavy. "Believe it or not, I kept thinking you might decide to come back and play a role in her life." A bitter taste rose in Kate's throat. She swallowed it back. "Just like I kept thinking you'd come back to me in New York."

He lifted his shoulders in a shrug. "I wasn't ready to be a dad."

As if that were an excuse. Kate strolled to the far side of the deck. "I planned to tell her the truth about you as soon as the movie was over."

"When's that gonna be?"

"A couple of weeks."

"Only two weeks left? Sounds like I got here just in the nick of time."

Kate bristled. "I'd say you're about thirteen years too late."

He tossed the cigarette stub on the deck and stomped it with his scuffed work boot. "Okay, so I've been a lousy father. I'm here now. Maybe I can change that."

"I told you: I don't want you in Skye's life."

"She wants me in it. She said so. And, hey, I'm her biological father. I've got rights."

A cold chill chased up Kate's spine. "You're an ex-con."

"So? I'm still a parent. And if Skye tells a judge she wants to live with me part of the time, well . . ." He grinned. "Who knows? Maybe I could even get child support from you, since you have a fancy degree and a good job and all."

Kate froze. "You'd try to get custody of Skye?"

Wayne lifted his shoulders. "Maybe I will, maybe I won't. But I could sure mess up your life, couldn't I?"

Kate's blood ran cold.

Skye's father's eyes took on a sly gleam. "On the other hand, maybe we could work a little deal here."

"What kind of a deal?"

He pulled a cigarette out of his pack and tapped it on his palm. "Get this director boyfriend of yours to give me a part in the movie, and I won't cause you any problems."

So that was it. After all this time, he still had delusions of grandeur.

"The movie's almost over. All the roles are cast."

"I'm sure he could find me something if you ask him real nice."

"You're not here to see Skye at all, are you?"

"Hey, there's no law that says I can't kill two birds with one stone. She said she's workin' on the movie. If I get a part in it, I can see her on the set."

"She won't want to see you if I tell her the truth about you."

Wayne's eyes grew hard and cold. "You tell her the truth and I'll tell her some lies. I'll make you out to be such an evil bitch that she'll never speak to you again."

The vitriolic tone of his voice made her draw back.

"She already thinks you did something so horrible that I couldn't bear to see you for years." He grinned as Kate's jaw dropped. "Oh, yeah—she let that slip, too. So tell me, Kate— how likely is it she's gonna believe *you* when she learns you lied about me all those years?"

Oh, mercy. If she talked to Skye now, the girl would confront her father, and he'd put a sinister spin on Kate's every word. As Wayne had just pointed out, Skye already believed her mother had somehow wronged him.

Besides, Skye had spent her entire life putting her father on a pedestal. She wasn't likely to easily accept having him knocked off of it. Fear skulked up Kate's spine, gripping her gut with clammy fingers.

Wayne's voice sharpened to a coercive wheedle. "Come on, Katie-did. All you've got to do is talk your boyfriend into giving me a part, and I'm out of your life in a few days. Otherwise, I might just decide to move back to New Orleans, where I can see my darlin' daughter every day."

He cared nothing about Skye, except how he could use her to get what he wanted. Kate wanted to slap him so bad her palms itched.

A few days and he'd be gone. More than anything, she wanted him gone. "I-I'll see what I can do."

He gave a satisfied smile. "I thought you'd come around."

"Tell me where you're staying and I'll give you a call after I talk to Zack."

He ran a hand through his greasy hair. "Gee—I was kinda hopin' I could stay here."

"*What?*"

"I just hit town and I don't have a place to stay. And to tell you the truth, I'm busted. I thought I'd just crash here."

"No. No way."

He gave an evil grin. "If you don't have a spare bedroom, maybe I could just bunk with you."

The thought sent a fresh wave of nausea coursing through her. He was a worm, a subterranean parasite, and there was no way he was staying in her house. "I'll give you some money for a motel room. There are some inexpensive ones on Airline Highway."

He scratched his head again, this time with the hand that

held the cigarette. Kate found herself wishing he'd go up in flames.

No such luck.

"If you're gonna put me up in a motel, it needs to be a nice one. A successful biologist wouldn't stay in a cheesy flophouse, would he?" His mouth smiled, but his eyes were cold. "And let's see . . . if I'm not gonna be a guest here, I'll also need cash for food and transportation. And I really ought to buy some new clothes, too, if I'm going to carry off this biologist gig."

He was scamming her, and she was helpless to stop it. Not if she didn't want him poisoning Skye's mind against her. "How much?"

"Oh, gee . . ." He looked up at the sky, as if he were deep in thought. "I suppose two thousand oughta cover it."

"You want me to give you two thousand *dollars?*"

He lifted his shoulders in a careless shrug. "Hey, New Orleans is an expensive town."

A few days. A few days and he'd be gone. Two thousand dollars was a bargain if it would get him out of her life, away from Skye. And then she'd tell Skye and her mother the whole story.

"I don't have that kind of money sitting around the house. I'll have to give you a check." Which would be proof she'd paid him off, in case she ever needed it.

"I suppose that'll do."

He'd planned this all along. The smug look on his face made her angry and sick all at the same time.

She drew her shoulders back and looked him square in the eye. "You'd better not do or say anything to hurt Skye in any way."

"Why would I hurt my own kid?"

Because you're heartless, mercenary, and completely self-centered. "Wait here," she said curtly. "I'll write you a check and call you a cab."

"Okay. Better give me some cash to pay for it, though." His lips turned up in a self-satisfied grin as he huffed out a mouthful of smoke. He couldn't have looked more like a cat who'd just eaten a canary if he'd had feathers coming out of his mouth.

"You've made a wise decision, Kate. You won't be sorry about this."

You're dead wrong, she thought, heading into the house. *I already am.*

"He just showed up on your doorstep?" Zack stared at Kate incredulously. She looked wan and pale in the morning light. They were standing at Jackson Square, waiting for the police to clear the artists, fortune-tellers, mimes, and tourists away so they could shoot a scene in front of St. Louis Cathedral. "After all these years and not a word to Skye, he just appeared out of the blue?"

Kate nodded.

Zack stared up at the Disneylike spire on the historic church. "What the hell does he want?"

"He says he wants to get to know Skye. And he wants a part in the movie. He's always wanted to work in show business, and he thinks this is his big break."

"Oh, he does, does he?" A nerve worked in Zack's jaw as a maelstrom of dark emotions swirled inside him. "How is Skye handling all this?"

"She's thrilled beyond words."

"How's she dealing with the fact that he's not a biologist?"

"She doesn't know."

"*What?*"

Kate sighed. "You know how talkative Skye is. From the questions she asked and the way she babbled on, Wayne figured out she thought he was a regular Doctor Doolittle. He played right along."

"Oh, hell. Kate, you've got to tell her."

"I know, I know. But I want to wait until he's gone."

"For God's sake, why?"

Kate looked down at the pavement. "He—he wants a chance to get to know her before she learns what a jerk he is."

"Why the hell should you give him that chance?"

Kate sighed. "Because he wants it. And . . ."

"And what?"

Kate hesitated.

"Come on, Kate. Tell me."

"Because Skye thinks I did something horrid to him, and he's threatened to make up a story that will turn her against me."

"The lousy S.O.B. Why, I ought to . . ."

Kate put a hand on his arm. "He's threatened to try to get custody of her."

Zack gave a disdainful snort. "No judge is going to give custody to an ex-con over a devoted, loving mother."

"They might give him joint custody if Skye says she wants that. You know she's always idolized her father. And Wayne will tell her anything she wants to hear." Kate turned pleading eyes on Zack. "Please, Zack, I don't want to make any waves. I don't know what Wayne's capable of, or how Skye is likely to take it when she finds out I lied to her all those years. She's built her father up in her mind to be almost a superhero. You should have seen her with him. I think she'd rather think ill of me than him."

She tightened her hand on his arm, her eyes imploring. "Please. I want to just ride this out. If we give him what he wants, he'll be gone in a few days. And once he's out of the picture, I'll tell her the whole story."

"What he's doing is called extortion, Kate. It's illegal."

Something about the way she averted her gaze deepened Zack's frown. "Is there something else going on, something you're not telling me?"

"Don't you think this is bad enough?"

"Hell, yes."

"Then help me out, Zack." Her eyes pleaded with him. "Give him a little part."

Zack hissed a sigh through his teeth. He didn't like this, not one bit, but he couldn't refuse her. "Damn it all."

"You'll do it?"

He gave a reluctant nod.

Relief flooded her eyes. "Thanks, Zack." She raised up on her toes and kissed his cheek. He pulled her close, inhaling the scent of her hair, absorbing the warmth of her body.

He hadn't even met Wayne and he hated his guts. The man had conned Kate, stolen her money, and abandoned her when he'd gotten her pregnant. He'd never even tried to contact his daughter, much less support her.

The man was the lowest of the low, and a convicted felon to boot. But of all the crimes he'd committed, one stood out in Zack's mind as the most heinous of all: He'd once stolen Kate's heart, then thrown it away.

"Hi, Dad!" Skye sprinted toward Wayne as soon as she arrived on the set after school and gave him a big hug. "Where were you last night? I waited up until eleven o'clock, and then Mom made me go to bed."

"I, um, got tied up," Wayne said.

Tied up? More like tied one on, Zack thought darkly. The man had shown up on the set for three days in a row reeking of beer and whiskey. Zack had to fight the urge to deck him every time he saw his face.

"Why didn't you call?" Skye asked. "I was worried about you."

"Oh, um—because I was on the phone until really late. I had a—a conference call."

Skye cocked her head quizzically. "At night?"

"It was long distance. From, um, overseas. It's not night there."

Jeez, this joker was pathetic. You could practically hear the rusty gears in his head creaking as he made this stuff up.

And Skye—hell, it was heartbreaking, the faith she put in him, the way she just unquestioningly accepted whatever he said. She acted as if this guy were the greatest thing since spring break. "Were you discussing an endangered species?"

"Yeah. Some, um, monkeys. From Nigeria."

"Wow! What kind?"

"The, um, Kahlua monkey. They're very rare."

Really rare, Zack thought, his mouth twisting into an expression of contempt. *As in nonexistent.*

Skye's eyes brightened. "Maybe you could come to my biology class and talk about them."

"Um . . . sure."

"I'll talk to my teacher. I'll bet she'll be thrilled."

Zack couldn't take any more. He strolled around the corner and into the room. "Hi, Skye. Deb's been looking for you. She needs some help in the wardrobe trailer."

"Okay." The girl gave Wayne a kiss on the cheek. "See you later, Dad."

Zack waited until she'd scampered out of earshot. "You're laying it on pretty thick, don't you think?"

He lifted his shoulders in a shrug. "I'm just playin' along." He gave Zack a sly grin. "And showcasin' my actin' skills for you."

"Yeah, well, you're overplaying the role." Zack leveled a hard look at him. "Don't make any promises to that girl that you're not going to keep."

"I won't."

"If you hurt that kid, I'll make you pay for it. You hear me?"

Wayne held up his hands, his teeth bared in a feral smile. "Hey, don't take it wrong, man. I'm not the one who made up this cockamamy story."

"But you're doing your best to keep it going."

"You've got it all wrong. I just want the chance to get to know my daughter."

Zack took a step toward him. "What the hell do you really want, Wayne?"

"Whattaya mean?"

"Well, it's kind of hard to believe you're here because you're motivated by paternal love."

The man's eyes widened in a patently phony attempt at innocence. "I don't know what you're talkin' about. I just want to

317

get to know my kid, and while I'm at it, I'm hopin' to break into acting."

"I gave you a role as an extra."

"What I really need is a speakin' part. Somethin' to put on my résumé to help me get other roles." He hitched up his baggy jeans. "I just need one good break."

A muscle twitched in Zack's jaw. "As far as I'm concerned, Wayne, you've had your break. Several of them, in fact. You had Kate, and you abandoned her when she needed you most. Now you've got a wonderful daughter, the kind of kid any man would be proud to have, a kid who just wants a little of your time, and you're too busy partying on Bourbon Street to pay any attention to her."

"I told you, man, I've been busy. But I'll go see her tonight."

"Don't tell her you will and then not go."

"I'll be there." He gave Zack a cagey grin. "So, what do you say? If I turn into a world-class dad, will you give me a speaking part?"

Zack blew out a hard sigh. Damn, but he hated doing anything for this sleazebag. The idea of bribing him into behaving like a decent human being was repugnant, but if that was what it took to keep him from hurting Kate or Skye, he'd do it. "Treat the kid decently and I'll find you a line or two in the last brothel scene."

Wayne grinned. "I'll be so good you'll wish you'd given me a major role."

You've already got a major role—pretending not to be the jackass you are. Zack bit back the words and stalked away before his temper got the best of him.

Chapter Twenty-four

"Why are we parking here?" Ruth asked nervously.

Fritz manuevered Ruth's car into a parking spot along the curb of Esplanade Avenue. "It's as close as we can get. There's no parking outside my place."

"But it's four or five blocks away!"

"It's a beautiful night, Ruth. You'll enjoy the stroll."

Ruth's heart pounded. "It-it's not a safe part of town. There's been a lot of crime in this area."

"We'll be fine. You'll be with me."

"Maybe we could take a cab."

"It's only four blocks, Ruth. We'd have to walk that far to find a cab."

A raggedly dressed man staggered past. Ruth started to quake inside.

"Come on, Ruth." Fritz opened his door and climbed out. "It'll be all right."

Why, oh why had she agreed to this? Ruth watched Fritz circle the car to open her door, panic mounting in her throat. It hadn't seemed so terrifying when she'd first agreed to come to his rented apartment. She'd thought she could handle it, thought it would be a good way to convince Fritz that she was making progress on overcoming her fears.

"Come spend the night with me," he'd said. "I want to hold you all night and wake up with you in my arms."

It wasn't something they'd been able to do at Ruth's house. Fritz had a bad back and was unable to sleep on the sofa bed.

Fritz opened her door and Ruth cautiously stepped out of the car, gripping her flashlight.

Fritz took it from her hand and placed it back on the seat. "You don't need that thing. We'll be fine." Putting his arm around her, he escorted her down the sidewalk.

The quaking inside her intensified the farther they got from the car. Ruth gripped Fritz's arm as they neared the open door of a bar. Music spilled out into the air.

"It's all right, honey."

"I—I want to go back."

"Come on, Ruth. It's just a little farther."

A wave of panic rose in her throat. "I-I can't."

"You can't, or you won't?"

"It-it's too risky. I want to go back to the car."

"Ruth . . ."

She tugged on his arm. "I can't do this. It's unsafe. Take me back to the car."

Fritz blew out a lungful of air. His mouth took on a hard set, but he turned around and strode back to the car. Ruth nearly had to run to keep up with him. He unlocked the car, jerked open Ruth's door, then rounded it and climbed inside.

"I-I'm sorry," she said in a small voice.

Fritz started the engine and jerked it into gear.

"I just don't want to be mugged."

Fritz didn't say a word. He backed up the car, put it in forward and peeled out of the parking spot.

"That's a rough section of the French Quarter," Ruth said nervously.

Fritz stared straight through the windshield, his face like granite.

"You're not from here, so naturally you wouldn't be familiar with the neighborhoods, but there have been some terrible crimes committed around here over the years."

Fritz continued to drive in stony silence.

They were just a few blocks from Ruth's house before she ventured another remark. "Just a couple of months ago a man was mugged just a few blocks from where we were."

Fritz never took his eyes off the street. "You're not afraid of being mugged, Ruth."

She looked at him in surprise. "Why, of course I am. Mugged or raped or assaulted or kidnapped or murdered."

"Those aren't the things you're really afraid of."

"Why, of course they are."

He pulled into her driveway, killed the engine, and turned to her.

"You're not afraid of being a victim. You're afraid of being happy." His face was hard and impassive. Something about his expression was so fixed, so final, that it chilled her blood.

"W-why do you say that?"

"Because it's true. You're afraid to let yourself experience joy, because you're afraid you might lose it."

"That—that doesn't make any sense."

"You're right. It doesn't." He climbed out of her car and walked her to the door, unlocked her front door's three locks, then handed her the key. "You need help, but you refuse to get it. If you want to live in fear and misery and loneliness, that's your business. But you'll have to do it without me." He turned to go.

"Fritz—wait!"

"You made your choice, Ruth. Good-bye."

Ruth stood in her doorway and watched him stalk away toward the streetcar. Loneliness, deeper and more profound than any she'd ever known, swept through her like a desolate wind. She watched his receding back until he disappeared around the corner. Then she went inside and locked the door behind her, locking herself in, locking the world and all its dangers out. She

321

listlessly headed to the sofa where she and Fritz had made love, plopped down on it, and wept.

It wasn't until a couple of hours later that she realized she hadn't even looked under it to see if a burglar was hiding there. And the funny thing was, she didn't even care.

The grandfather clock in Ruth's hallway solemnly gonged twelve times. Midnight. One day had ended and another had begun. It was funny, how the beginning of a new day happened in the dark of the night.

The last note hung in the air, echoing off the walls. As it faded, Fritz's words reverberated in her mind.

"You're afraid to let yourself experience joy, because you're afraid you might lose it."

Was it true? Was she deliberately pushing him away because she was afraid of losing him? It made no sense. If she was afraid to feel love and happiness because it might end, she'd never feel happy or loved at all. Was that the convoluted logic of her heart?

"If you want to live in fear and misery and loneliness that's your business. But you'll have to do it without me."

How could those things be a choice? They weren't things she wanted. They were things she simply endured. She had no other option.

Or did she?

"You need help."

Ruth covered her face with her hands. She was ashamed of her silly fears, ashamed of being weak, ashamed of lacking gumption or guts or courage. If she were a stronger, better person, she'd be able to deal with these ridiculous problems herself. It was humiliating, having people think she needed mental health care.

Humiliating, and terrifying. If she closed her eyes, she could still hear the gate clink shut at the Baton Rouge sanatorium, still see the zombie-faced patients in the sunroom, still smell her aunt's urine-soaked clothes as a nurse led her back from shock treatment.

"We don't talk about Aunt Helen outside the family, Ruthie," her mother used to caution. "Mental illness runs in families, and we don't want people to think we're crazy, too."

Ruth knew that mental health care had changed a lot since the fifties and sixties, and she knew people's attitudes had changed as well. Dr. Phil was always on Oprah, lots of celebrities went to shrinks, and antidepressants were advertised on TV as if they were breath mints. She knew all that, but none of that knowledge alleviated her gut-deep sense that mental illness was shameful. Even worse than the sense of shame was the secret terror that had haunted her since girlhood: What if she became like her aunt?

Was she becoming like her aunt? Fear was restricting her, just as surely as a straight jacket.

You need help. Dear Lord, maybe she did. She'd had no success conquering her fears alone. She'd tried, and she'd failed. The failures were just one more source of shame.

Here she sat with everything to live for—a wonderful daughter, a terrific granddaughter, a new career, a second chance at love. Was she going to give it all up because she was too proud and scared to admit she needed help?

"No." Ruth abruptly sat up straight and swung her feet to the floor. "No!"

By Jove, she'd rather be murdered by a maniac than die cowering in this house, locked in by fear. Heck, she'd even prefer to be labeled a maniac herself.

Life was a risk. It came with no guarantees. The only guarantee she had was that she'd end up all alone if she didn't make some major changes.

Starting right now. She stood up, setting her mouth in a determined line. Without giving herself a chance to change her mind, she grabbed her camera and her flashlight and headed to her car.

It was nearly one o'clock in the morning when she angled her car into a parking spot in the French Quarter, near the one

323

where Fritz had parked a few hours ago. Killing the engine, she slung her camera over her neck, pulled her purse strap onto her shoulder and grabbed her flashlight. Lifting her chin in defiance of her fear, she set out for Fritz's apartment. He'd driven her by it once, so she knew exactly where it was.

She hoped she wasn't too late. She hoped Fritz would forgive her. She hoped he still loved her, hoped he still wanted her, hoped he'd give her another chance.

She was so wrapped up in her thoughts that it took her completely by surprise when she felt a sharp tug on her purse.

Reflexively tightening her grip on the strap, Ruth turned around to see a thin man in a red-and-black ski mask trying to yank her purse off her arm. She gasped and put up her arm. He made a dive for her bag. His head hit her hand, and she snatched at his mask. It came off in her hand.

He was a youth, probably no more than seventeen, with bloodshot eyes and stringy dark hair.

Anger shot through her. How dare this punk slow her down when she was on her way to straighten out her life? "You ought to be ashamed of yourself," she hissed.

He shoved her to the sidewalk. Ruth fell hard, but managed to land on her purse.

"Give me your pocket book, lady, or you'll wish you had."

She grabbed his foot, pulling off his sneaker, which caused him to fall to the sidewalk beside her. He tried to wrestle her purse away from her, but she kicked him in the groin.

"Owww!" he yelped, holding his crotch.

Ruth jumped to her feet, backed into the street, and raised her camera.

"Hey! Whaddaya think you're doin'?"

Ruth flashed off a shot in his face. The boy struggled to his feet and started after her. Standing her ground, Ruth stomped her heel into the instep of his shoeless foot. The youth fell back to the sidewalk, clutching his foot and groaning. Ruth smacked him upside the head with the flashlight, then took off running. She didn't stop until she reached Fritz's doorstep three blocks later. It was an old Acadian town house made of stucco and brick with green shutters and a large door. The lights were off. Ruth knocked on the door, her heart pounding. *Please, God— don't let it be too late. Please let him forgive me. Please let him still want me.*

It seemed to take forever for him to answer. Finally, at long last, the door swung open. Fritz, wearing a pair of sweat pants and nothing else, appeared in the doorway. His eyes widened in disbelief. "Ruth?"

"Oh, Fritz, I'm so sorry. You were right." She was out of breath from running, and the words tumbled out between pants. "I've been letting fear run my life. I've let it make me a prisoner in my own home, and I've tried to take you and Kate and Skye prisoner, too. Fritz, I want to change, and I'm willing to do whatever it takes. I've had a hard time admitting I need help, because I had an aunt in an institution when I was a girl, and visiting her every month used to terrify me. But I do need help, and I'm going to get it. Because I love you and I want to be with you. In your world, not just in mine."

"Oh, Ruth. I love you, too." Fritz dragged her into his arms and hugged her close. After a long moment, he held her at arm's length and looked her up and down, his eyes worried. "But— what happened to you? You're all bruised and dirty and out of breath, and your shirt is torn . . ."

Ruth looked down. She hadn't even noticed what the scuffle had done to her appearance. "Some punk up the street tried to steal my purse, but I wouldn't let him. It turns out this flashlight and camera are good for something after all. I busted him in the head with the light and took his picture."

"*What?*"

Ruth patted her camera and smiled proudly. "When I take this to the police, I bet they'll be able to nail the little bastard."

Fritz stared at her, openmouthed. "Are you okay?"

"Well, it depends." She stepped forward, drew a deep breath, and gazed up at him. "Will you forgive me?"

"Of-of course."

"And did you mean it when you said you loved me?"

"Absolutely."

"And you don't mind that I'm a mental case?"

"Ruth, you're not. But you need some help."

She gave a big grin. "Well, then, I'm fine. I'm better than fine. I've never been better."

"Don't you think we should report this mugging to the police?"

"Later." Ruth reached her arms around his neck. "Right now, we've got more important things to do."

It was the same thing he'd said to her the first time they made love, and the words made him smile. She pulled his head down and fitted her lips to his, relishing the taste of his mouth, the scent of his neck, the solid heat of his body, the soft scratch of his beard. As Fritz wound his arms around her, she kicked his door closed, and she didn't worry about whether it was locked or not.

Kate's legs wound around Zack's hips, pulling him closer. He was buried deep inside her, and every stroke pushed her higher, closer to the pinnacle, up to the peak where earth ended and heaven began.

His mouth was at her ear. She heard a throaty murmur of her name, felt a warm rush of his breath, inhaled the scent of his skin—and then she was there, in that hot, sweet world where only Zack could take her, a world where boundaries dissolved and souls had wings and the time was always now.

Gradually, slowly, she floated back to earth, back to an awareness of the mattress beneath her. Zack rained kisses across her face as she opened her eyes.

He was looking at her with such tenderness that her heart ached. The words I love you welled up in her throat, but she swallowed them back. Those were not words he would want to hear, not words he would say in return.

"Kate." He said her name softly, almost reverently, grazing her lips with his. "That was amazing."

Kate smiled. "It always is."

But it wouldn't be for much longer. They only had two more days of filming left. The wrap party would be held the day after tomorrow, and then Zack would head back to California. When the shoot ended, so would their relationship.

The fact lay in bed with them like a slab of ice, hard and cold and impossible to ignore.

Zack dropped another soft kiss on her lips, then rolled onto his back, folding his hands behind his head and staring up at the ceiling. Kate curled beside him, her head on his chest.

"What are you thinking about?" she asked.

"The night we spent together in the swamp."

Her heart picked up speed. If he was thinking about their beginning, then maybe, just maybe, he was thinking about a future as well.

"You know we're shooting there tomorrow." Zack gave her a lazy grin. "Funny, how art imitates life. Lena and George will be doing their big love scene in the very place you and I first made love."

Kate lifted her head. "Did that scene get rewritten?"

"What do you mean?"

"You know—so that Joe and Sadie sleep together but don't have sex."

"Oh, Kate—come on. Not that again."

Kate sat up and leaned against the headboard. "We talked about this when I signed off on the script, Zack. Joe insisted on waiting until Sadie left the Ooh, La La."

Zack leaned up on an elbow. "The diary was ambiguous about that. Since we don't know for sure what happened, it's open to interpretation. This isn't an issue of historical accuracy, Kate. This movie needs a love scene. The audience expects it."

"They can have a love scene. Just don't make it a sex scene."

"It's all one and the same."

"What a typically male thing to say!" Sitting up straighter, Kate pulled the pillow into her lap and gazed at him. "It's not—at least not in this case. Joe wanted their lovemaking to be special and beautiful and on a whole other level than anything Sadie had ever known at the brothel. He wanted it to be the start of a whole new life."

Zack hauled himself to a sitting position beside her. "That's not the way it's written, and Rich is back in L.A. I couldn't change it now if I wanted to."

"Yes, you can. We have the diary. The dialogue is just a couple of lines. Lena's been reading it, and she agrees that the scene would have more emotional impact if Joe and Sadie just hold each other."

Zack blew out a hard breath. "So, now both you and Lena are directors?"

"No. We just think this makes Joe look more committed."

"Sadie was a *hooker*, Kate. She was putting out for anyone who had five bucks. Joe was going to pay three thousand dollars to free her and not get any? I think it makes him look like a fool."

Anger spurted out of her like blood from a cut artery. Kate swung her legs around, grabbed her clothes off the bedside chair and began yanking them on. "You just don't get it, do you?"

"Don't get what?"

"What Joe was *feeling*. You don't even know what your own movie is about." She yanked on her panties, fastened her bra, and pulled her red knit shirt over her head. "Well, that figures."

"What figures?"

"You don't know anything about love, so it figures that you wouldn't have a clue what it looks like. Well, let me explain it to you, Zack." She faced him, her hands on her hips. "Love doesn't worry about looking foolish. It looks at the big picture, not just the moment. It's not a transaction, and it doesn't keep score. It's a leap of faith, an all-or-nothing, no-holds-barred commitment to cherish another person, and that means putting the other person's happiness and well-being before your own." She snatched her skirt off the bed. "It makes no sense to someone who's never experienced it, because love's not logical. It just *is.* It doesn't have an escape clause, and it darn sure doesn't have an expiration date."

"We're not talking about the movie any more, are we?"

"We're talking about the nature of love, which was the basis of Joe and Sadie's relationship." She stepped into her short denim skirt and zipped it up as she struggled into her sandals. "Unfortunately, it's something you'll evidently never know anything about." She strode toward the door.

"Kate, wait."

She stopped, her hand on the door, breathing hard.

"Kate, I care about you. I really, really do. But these things never work out for long. There's either a big argument or the feelings just gradually fade away. I don't want us to go through that."

She turned and faced him. "What makes you so sure we would turn out that way?"

"History. Face it, Kate—I'm a bad risk."

"Isn't that a decision I should make?"

"It's a decision that's already been made." His voice was sad, his eyes troubled. "We still have a couple of days, honey. Let's not spoil them."

Too late, she thought, blinking back the tears. *They're already spoiled.*

He ran his hand through his hair. "Look—if it means so much to you, I'll shoot the scene both ways and decide which one to use later."

He was only doing it to appease her. His mind was already made up. But Kate's throat was too tight to tell him there was no point in bothering, so she simply nodded, tried to muster a smile, then fled before she broke into tears.

"It's hotter than Hades out here," George grumbled the next morning as the make-up girl patted a fresh layer of powder on the actor's sweating forehead. "It's bad enough to have to shoot this scene once. I don't see why we have to shoot it two ways."

I don't, either, Zack thought darkly, slapping a mosquito on his neck. Especially since Kate hadn't even shown up. She'd called Deb and said she wasn't going to be able to make it, but that Jean-Pierre would have the cabin ready and the set designer had all of the props.

"We wanted to have a couple of options," he told the movie's star. "We'll see how they look and decide which one to use later."

Not we. He. This was his movie, by damn, and he'd make that decision. Hell, he'd already made it.

Just like he made all his own decisions. The same way he'd made the one about whether or not he and Kate had a future.

Alone.

Zack took a swig from the water bottle in his hand, wondering why the thought didn't give him the usual sense of satisfaction. He'd always taken pleasure in the fact that he was in control of his own destiny. At the moment, however, being in complete control didn't feel like freedom. Instead, it felt like loneliness.

Hell, there was no reason *that* should bother him. He'd always been alone. Even when he was with other people, he usually felt somehow isolated, somehow disconnected. It was as if he didn't send or receive signals on the same frequency as everyone else.

Everyone except Kate. Kate had somehow fine-tuned the dial. She'd made him feel understood and accepted and cared about. She somehow fed the hunger that had always gnawed at his soul.

It was probably because he knew Kate wasn't with him because of his name or job or money. She wasn't interested in the trappings. She was interested in *him*. She saw things in him that were good and kind and decent. She brought out qualities he never knew he possessed. When he was with her, he was a better man.

"You okay?" the actor asked. "You look kinda weird."

"Yeah, I'm fine, George. Just ready to wrap this baby up."

What the hell was the matter with him? The movie was nearly

finished, and from all indications he had a hit on his hands. That was what he'd wanted. That had been his goal. That had been his sole reason for coming to Louisiana. By all rights, he should be the happiest man on the planet. So why the hell did he feel so miserable?

It was all Kate's fault. He hated the way she'd left last night, hated the look of pain on her face, hated the way she'd tried to hide it with that goofy, lip-quivering excuse of a smile. He especially hated the fact that she hadn't shown up today. And it didn't help matters that he was here in the cabin where they'd first made love, with memories of Kate floating around in his head like water hyacinth on the swamp water. The scent of her hair, the sound of her sighs, the way she'd looked in the lamplight, all naked and mussed and gorgeous . . . Damn it, she was driving him crazy.

"Ready when you are, Zack," Fritz called.

"I'm more than ready," he growled. "The sooner we shoot this, the sooner we can get out of this godforsaken place."

And back to California, where he could finally get back to normal.

The funny thing was, he could no longer remember what normal was like.

Chapter Twenty-five

The Creole Queen plowed the waters of the Mississippi, churning up waves in its wake, casting the sounds of the wrap party into the night air. The wail of a sax, the high peal of a woman's laughter, the clink and clatter of glasses and plates, the dull roar of conversation . . . all of it drifted out the open windows of the boat's ballroom and floated on the river-scented air.

The noise flowed over and past Zack as he stood on the lower back deck, watching the paddlewheel spin uselessly in the water. It was unconnected to a drive shaft or engine, a purely decorative ornament put there for tourists who wanted to believe they'd ridden on a real paddle wheeler.

It was not historically accurate.

Zack muttered an oath under his breath. That term belonged to Kate's vocabulary, not his. He'd never cared if things were authentic or not, as long as they looked or felt good.

But then, a lot of nevers had entered his life since he'd met Kate. He'd never felt so close to anyone. He'd never enjoyed a woman's company so much. But most of all, he'd never had a woman get inside his head the way she had. Without knowing it, he'd started seeing things differently, processing them in a new way, thinking about them from a new perspective.

From *her* perspective.

He scowled out at the churning water. Where the hell was she, anyway? It ate at him that she'd just disappeared without as much as a good-bye phone call. She'd had a bellboy deliver a note to his hotel room, saying how much she'd enjoyed working with him and how she hoped the movie would be a big success. She was sorry to miss the last two days of filming and the wrap party, but she had to attend a higher education conference in Baton Rouge. She'd asked him to tell everyone good-bye for her, and she wished him a pleasant trip back to California.

Hell. Zack wasn't buying that lame-tailed conference excuse for a minute. She'd run away. She hadn't wanted to tell him good-bye.

His fingers tightened on the metal railing. Well, fine. Just fine. He certainly hadn't been looking forward to a big, emotional farewell scene. When things were over they were over, and sloppy, weepy good-byes had never been his idea of a happy ending.

Still, it stuck in his craw that she'd just left, without telling him good-bye in person. She'd missed the swamp scene and Wayne's big speaking debut. Zack had thought the scene was the perfect revenge. He'd cast the man as a pickpocket who was first punched in the nose by the madam and then tossed down a flight of stairs by the bordello bouncer. His big line had been, "Ouch, that hurt." Even though the first take was perfect, Zack had insisted they do it ten more times. By the last take, Wayne's nose was broken, and his "Ouch, that hurt" had the ring of authenticity.

Zack's thoughts were interrupted by voices approaching behind him. He turned to see Ruth and Fritz strolling the deck, their arms around each other. The older woman wore a glowing smile and a long red dress with a flowing scarf.

Zack kissed her on the cheek. "You look beautiful. Fritz, even you cleaned up well. Are you two having a good time?"

333

Ruth nodded. "Wonderful. This is a terrific party."

"I'm glad you made it," Zack said.

Ruth looked up adoringly at Fritz's face. "I wouldn't have missed it. I want to spend every moment I can with him."

Zack smiled, but his stomach coiled into a knot. Evidently Kate didn't feel the same way about him.

Fritz's hand moved up and down Ruth's back. "Ruth is coming out to California as soon as her therapist says she's ready."

Zack's gaze swiveled to Ruth. "So . . . you're seeing a therapist?"

She gave a sheepish nod. "She's got me on anti-anxiety medicine, and I'm already doing a whole lot better. And I'm going through de-sensitization therapy to get more comfortable being away from home."

"Hey, that's terrific. Glad to hear it." He searched for a not-too-obvious way to find out what he wanted to know. "So, when you come out West, are you coming alone?"

"Yes."

"Oh." Disappointment socked him in the gut. He did his best not to show it. "So . . . how long do you plan to stay?"

Fritz beamed down at her. "Only the rest of her life."

Zack's mouth fell open. *"What?"*

"We're getting married!" Ruth blurted.

Another fist felt like it had slammed into his stomach. "Oh, hey—that's—that's great." He sounded more shocked than pleased, but Fritz and Ruth didn't seem to notice. They were looking at each other as if they'd simultaneously won the lottery and an Academy Award.

Zack cleared his throat. "Wow. What does Kate say about all this?"

"She doesn't know yet. We just decided."

"Just now?"

Ruth's curls bobbed as she nodded. "Fritz just proposed on the bow of the boat. He said it was the perfect place to ask me, because I made him feel like the king of the world, and he wanted to know if I'd be his queen. Isn't that romantic?"

Romantic? More like astounding. It was hard to imagine big, burly, ponytailed, motorcycle-riding Fritz acting so sappy.

"Very romantic," Zack agreed. "But I'm having a hard time picturing Fritz as Leonardo DiCaprio."

"That's because Fritz is so much sexier."

Zack rolled his eyes and poked the cinematographer in the ribs. "Aren't you worried that your bride-to-be has such poor eyesight?"

Fritz smiled down at her. "I think it's one of her best features."

Zack laughed. "Well, hey, this is great." He slapped the man on the shoulder and held out his hand. "Congratulations, buddy."

Fritz shook it. "Thanks."

"You ought to think about taking the plunge yourself," Ruth said slyly.

Zack took a step back and shook his head. "Oh, no. I'm not marriage material."

"How do you know if you haven't tried it?"

"I haven't tried cyanide, either, but I know it's poison."

Fritz pulled Ruth closer to his side and gazed fondly down at her. "Well, all I can say is, if being with the person you love is poison, what a way to go."

The way they looked at each other made a lump form in Zack's throat.

"*There* you are!" Skye hurried across the deck toward them, her face creased in a worried frown, her friend Mary Ann by her side.

Zack turned toward her. "Hi, Skye—Mary Ann. What's wrong?"

"It's Dad."

Zack stiffened. He hadn't wanted to invite Wayne to the party, but because of Skye, he had. "What about him?"

"He's acting weird."

"Weird, how?"

"He's drunk," Mary Ann said flatly. "And he's hitting on Lena."

"Oh, no." Ruth groaned.

Tears formed in Skye's eyes. "Can you help him?" she asked Zack.

I'd like to help him, all right, Zack thought sourly. *I'd like to help his sorry tail land in the middle of the river.* But he couldn't resist the imploring look on Skye's face.

"The bartender's mixing extra-strong drinks." It stuck in Zack's craw to make excuses for the jerk, but he hated seeing Skye so upset. "He probably had more than he realized."

Ruth's eyes silently thanked him for downplaying Wayne's behavior. Zack pushed off the rail. "I'll go see what I can do."

"I'll come too," Fritz said. "You might need a hand."

Skye started after them.

"Skye, honey, why don't you and Mary Ann stay with me?" Ruth called. "I've got some exciting news to tell you."

"Wayne was loaded, all right," Fritz told Ruth ten minutes later, after he and Zack had returned to the deck and Zack had taken the girls back into the ballroom. "He was critiquing George's performance in his last picture and trying to get Lena to sit in his lap."

"Oh, dear!"

"Zack handled him well, though." Fritz grinned. "He told Wayne he wanted him to do a screen test, and told him that the infirmary was wired with a hidden camera. He said the part called for him to lie on the cot and pretend to be asleep." Fritz chuckled. "Wayne lay down, closed his eyes, and passed out."

Ruth laughed. "Zack is some kind of clever."

"I could tell he would have much preferred to punch Wayne's lights out."

"Zack's not the only one." Ruth said. "I can't stand him, and Kate avoids him like the plague."

"How long do you think he's going to hang around?"

"He's promised Skye he'll take her to a Britney Spears concert

Thursday night. I hope he'll leave town right after that."

Fritz hoped so, too.

Zack was gone.

Kate stared into her refrigerator on Wednesday afternoon, trying to make a grocery list, but her mind kept going blank, circling back to the one thought that kept edging out all others.

Zack was gone. He'd flown out on the same flight as Fritz last Saturday morning. Ruth had gone to the airport to say good-bye to her fiancé, and she'd hugged Zack farewell, too, just before the two men headed down the concourse.

He was gone. It was over. It was time to get on with things, to concentrate on her child and her job and all the little mundane details that comprised her so-called life.

At least her future at the university looked secure. The dean had called her again to congratulate her on her latest appearance on a TV news show. Tenure, he'd told her, was virtually assured. He'd even wanted to know—strictly on the QT, of course—if she would be interested in co-chairing the history department. The board of regents was concerned that Dr. Compton's approach to history was outdated.

Outdated history. A couple of months ago, the non sequitur would have made Kate smile. So would the thought that the administration was finally seeing through Compton's pompous facade. But now she just didn't care. In fact, aside from Skye and her mother, she didn't care about much of anything. Zack was gone, and all the joy in her life had gone with him.

She slammed the refrigerator door and turned to the pantry, chiding herself for feeling so blue. She wasn't stupid or blind. She'd known this was coming. She'd known it was inevitable. The problem was, somewhere along the line she'd begun to hope that Zack would change his mind.

Hope—what a cruel thing it could be. It left her longing for things that were unattainable, craving things she had no business wanting. That old saying was wrong. It wasn't better to have loved and lost than to have never loved at all. If she'd never loved, she wouldn't know what she was missing, and she wouldn't feel so bad right now. . . .

The doorbell rang, startling Kate out of her thoughts. She strode to the front door and saw Wayne on the other side of the beveled glass, wearing a large white bandage on his nose. She barely suppressed a groan as she opened the door.

"What do you want?" she asked. She didn't care enough to ask how he'd gotten injured.

Wayne made a tsking sound as he strolled into the house. "Now, now, now—is that any way to greet the father of your child?"

Kate folded her arms across her chest and sighed. "What do you want?" she repeated.

"Well, I'm running a little low on funds."

"Too bad."

"Yeah, well . . ." Wayne picked up a china vase on the narrow foyer table. "I need some money to get out of town and make a new start."

"Sorry. That's not my problem."

He turned the vase upside down and looked at the bottom of it. "It is, if you don't want me to tell your kid some wild and wooly tales about her dear sweet mama."

"You make me sick, you know that?"

"Save it for someone who cares." He set the vase back down. "I figure I'll need ten thousand dollars."

It was so ludicrous, she almost laughed. "Forget it."

Wayne's face turned pink. "I'll tell her you're a pathological liar. I'll say you banged half of New York. I'll tell her you were a drug addict and a prostitute. I'll tell you wanted to abort her and I talked you out of it."

The last remark made Kate see red. She pointed to the front door. "Get out before I call the police."

"You don't have anything on me."

"Do you want me to call the police and ask? I think this fits the definition of blackmail and extortion."

"Why, you little . . ."

He took a step toward her, his face menacing. Alarm shot through Kate. She didn't know him anymore. Apparently she'd never known him at all. There was no telling what he was capable of. She raced out the door and onto her porch, and was relieved to see her pudgy neighbor, Mr. Hendrix, trimming his shrubs. Kate waved to him, just to let Wayne know they were being watched.

Wayne followed her outside. "I have a right to see my daughter, and I'll tell her anything I damn well please. Where is she?"

"At a friend's," Kate said. And she wasn't due home anytime soon, thank heavens. She was spending the night at Mary Ann's.

"Well, then, I'll wait for her."

Kate decided to try a bold bluff. "It won't do you any good." She spoke with a confidence she didn't feel, stretching herself to her full height and looking him dead in the eye. "I already told her everything—how you stole from me, how you abandoned me, how you never tried to contact her, how you've spent the last seven years in the pen. She knows I sent the gifts and cards, and she even knows you've already extorted two thousand dollars from me. She never wants to see you again."

Kate stepped back inside, leaving Wayne on the porch. "And neither do I. You're never going to get another dime out of me, so I suggest you hit the road and find a new mark to prey on."

With that, Kate slammed the door. From the living room, she heard Wayne utter a string of vile curses. She stood by the side of the window, out of sight but not out of hearing. After several long, tense moments, she heard footsteps retreating down the porch stairs, then receding into the distance. She peered out the window and sighed with relief as Wayne disappeared down the sidewalk.

Kate sank into a chair, her knees suddenly weak. She had to tell Skye the truth. She couldn't wait any longer.

Kate was a nervous wreck the next morning as she helped Skye load her sleeping bag and backpack into the Camry in Mary Ann's driveway. She'd always found it easier to talk to her daughter in the car than anyplace else, so she'd decided to tell Skye the truth about her father on the drive home.

" 'Bye, Mary Ann!" Skye yelled from the car. "Maybe I'll see you tonight at the concert."

Kate inwardly winced. She'd called Ticketmaster last night and tried to buy tickets, but the concert was sold out. She knew how much Skye had been looking forward to going with her father. Now that Wayne knew he wasn't going to get any more money from Kate, he'd probably left town.

Kate glanced over at her child as she drove through the residential area. "Did you and Mary Ann have fun?"

"Yeah! We did our nails and ate pizza and watched a movie. And guess what? She's going to the concert, too."

"So I gathered." Kate braked for a light and drew a deep breath. Her hand trembled as she pushed a strand of hair behind her ear. "Skye, honey, we have to talk."

"Uh-oh." Skye plopped her head back against the headrest. "What did I do this time?"

"You didn't do anything. It's—it's about your father."

Skye looked at her, her expression guarded. "Yeah?"

She would try to ease into this. "Your grandmother told me how he acted at the wrap party."

Skye shrugged her shoulders and stared down at her fingers, which were painted pale blue and decorated with little flower decals. "It wasn't Dad's fault. Zack said the bartender mixed the drinks too strong."

"Honey, Zack was covering for him. He didn't want you to be embarrassed or angry at your dad. And, Skye—I've been covering for him, too."

The car behind Kate honked. Startled, she looked up and saw that the light had turned green. She took her foot off the brake and steered the car through the intersection. Kate drew a deep breath. "I—I haven't been entirely honest with you about your father."

From the corner of her eye, Kate could see Skye's eyes grow large. "You mean you haven't told me what you did to him."

"Honey, the truth is, I didn't do anything to him."

"Yeah, right."

"It's true. I told you that to spare your feelings when you were little. I figured it was better for you to think it was my fault that he didn't come around instead of thinking that . . . thinking that . . ." *That he didn't love you.* Kate swallowed, still unable to get out the words.

"That what?"

"That he didn't care."

Skye stared at her. "But he *did* care. He sent me cards and presents from all over the world."

Kate swallowed miserably. "He didn't send you that stuff. I did."

"What?" Skye's eyes got huge, then narrowed. She shook her head, her mouth firmed into a tight line. "You're lying."

"Honey, I'm not. Let me—"

"You couldn't have sent them," Skye interrupted. "You were right here, and they were postmarked from all over the world."

"I had Samantha send them. I'd give them to her, and she'd mail them to you when she worked overseas flights."

Skye stared at her for a long moment. "Why would you do such a stupid thing?"

Kate pulled into her driveway. She was glad to be home, because she was too upset to be driving. She shut off the engine and turned to Skye. "Because I love you. When you were little, you asked me why your father didn't love you. I couldn't stand to see you so heartbroken, so I . . ."

"But he *does* love me," Skye cut in. "He came here to be with me. And he's taking me to the concert tonight."

"Honey—I know how hard this must be to hear. I've put off telling you because I dreaded making you feel bad. All these years, you've thought your father was this great guy with an important job . . ."

"He is!"

Kate shook her head. "He's not a wildlife biologist. I made

341

that up. I know it was wrong of me, but you were so little and you wanted to believe so badly—"

"I don't believe you!" Skye opened the car door and climbed out, her hands over her ears.

Kate got out of the car and followed her into the kitchen. "Sweetheart, I know it's a shock."

Tears ran down the girl's face. "He told me about his job! He said he's going to Nigeria to save the Kahlua monkeys. And he's worked with hippos and tigers and parrots . . ."

"Sweetheart." Kate touched her shoulder, longing to somehow connect, but Skye yanked away, her arms folded around herself. "He was lying," Kate continued. "He hasn't been in Africa or Asia. He's been in prison."

"No!" Skye whipped around, her eyes blazing with anger and belligerence. "No! You're making all this up because you hate him!"

"I wouldn't hurt you like this if I didn't have to."

"You just told me you've been lying to me for years." Her jaw jutted forward in stubborn denial. "How do I know you're not lying now?"

"I can show you a newspaper clipping about his conviction. Or we can call the New York Department of Corrections. There are court records, and the D.A.'s office would have papers on file. There are lots of ways of proving it."

Skye stood still for a moment, apparently absorbing the information. "Well, innocent people go to prison all the time. It must have been a mistake." She wiped her nose with the back of her hand. "What was he in for?"

"Theft, grand larceny, and credit card fraud."

"They must have gotten the wrong person."

"Honey, he was caught red-handed."

"He was framed. The cops set him up." Her chin went up higher. "I'm sure he'll explain it all to me tonight."

Kate's heart ached. "Honey, you won't see him tonight."

"I will, too! He's taking me to the concert."

Kate had known this would be difficult, but it was worse than she'd ever imagined. "He came by yesterday and tried to extort ten thousand dollars from me. I threatened to call the police. Sweetheart, I don't think he'll be back." Kate took a step toward her.

Skye stepped back. "No! You're making up all these lies because you're—you're jealous. You don't want him in my life. You don't want me to have a father."

"You're upset right now, Skye. You know that's not true."

Skye put her hands over her ears. "I won't listen to you anymore." She fled the room and bolted up the stairs.

Kate stared after her, her heart heavy as a concrete block, wishing she could take back all her well-intentioned lies. She'd meant to help her child, not hurt her. She hadn't realized Skye would grow so attached to her imaginary father.

Tears of sympathy formed in Kate's eyes. She knew how hard it was, losing the belief—however false—that someone you loved, loved you back.

Skye didn't come downstairs until seven o'clock. When she did, she was dressed in her best jeans and a sparkly blue top, and her hair was carefully blow-dried.

Kate's heart felt as if it were being cut in two. "Oh, honey . . ."

"I don't want to talk to you." She went to the front door. "I'm going to wait on the porch for Dad."

"Sweetheart, he's not"—the door slammed in her face—"coming."

Kate waited an hour, then carried a turkey sandwich out to the porch. "I thought you might be hungry."

Skye stared straight ahead, as if her mother were invisible. Kate set the plate down on the porch railing and leaned against the post. "Honey, he's not coming."

"He will! He's just running late, that's all."

Kate sighed and went back inside the house. She returned to the porch forty-five minutes later. "You've been out here an awfully long time. How long are you going to wait?"

"As long as it takes."

343

"Do you want some company?"

"No! You'll just scare him off." Skye glared at her. "That's what you did, isn't it? You ran him off."

"Sweetheart, I didn't do anything. I just refused to give him any more money."

"Any *more?*"

Kate nodded reluctantly. "I gave him two thousand dollars when he first arrived."

"Oh, yeah, sure." Skye rolled her eyes. "That's pretty lame, Mom."

"It's the truth. I can show you the cancelled check."

Skye's eyes flashed with belligerence. "How do I know you didn't just owe him the money? You've lied to me all these years. Why should I believe you now?"

Kate blew out a deep breath. "Sweetheart, I couldn't stand for you to think it was your fault that your father had abandoned us. When I first started sending you the cards and gifts, I didn't think it was any worse than letting you believe in Santa Claus or the Tooth Fairy."

"But it *was*. Way worse. Not even in the same league." Skye looked at her accusingly. "Fathers are real. And mothers don't lie to their kids." Tears welled in her eyes. "You know the worst part? I don't know what to believe. I used to trust you. And now I can't, and you're telling me Dad's a crook, and nothing's like I thought it was . . ." Tears ran down her face. "I don't even know who I am anymore."

Skye's words sent a dagger into Kate's heart. "Oh, honey." The swing creaked as Kate sat down beside her and pulled her into an embrace.

Skye jerked away. "Don't touch me. Just leave me alone!"

"All right, sweetheart." Kate rose slowly. "I'll be inside if you need me."

"I don't!" Skye sobbed. "I don't need anyone I can't trust!"

Kate softly closed the door behind her, Skye's words echoing through the lonely chambers of her heart.

She picked up a pillow from the sofa and carried it to the

living room rocker, the one where she'd rocked Skye as a baby. Cradling the pillow against her chest, she leaned back and set the chair in motion, wistfully remembering the days when she'd been able to provide for Skye's every need.

It took all Kate's self-restraint to wait forty-five more minutes before going back out to the porch. She knew she needed to give Skye time and space to accept the truth, but she was anxious to provide comfort.

The door creaked on its hinges as Kate pushed it open. She stepped out and stared at the porch swing.

Empty. The chains that suspended it from the porch beam were straight and silent, as still as the warm night air. Alarm shot through her.

"Skye?" she called. Only the rhythmic swell of cicadas answered. Kate stepped farther out on the porch. "Skye, where are you?"

Silence. Kate hurried down the porch steps to the sidewalk and looked up and down the street but saw no sign of the girl. She went in the backyard, then checked both sides of the house. Nothing.

Stay calm, Kate ordered herself. *Stay calm and think.*

Perhaps she'd gone on a walk. Or maybe she'd gone to Mary Ann's house—it was only about a mile away. Kate rushed inside, pulled out Skye's school directory, and looked up the phone number, then hesitated. Mary Ann would be at the concert. It was unlikely Skye would go to her house knowing she wouldn't be home.

Still, it was worth a try. Kate got an answering machine. She left a message that she was looking for Skye and wanted to be contacted if she showed up or called.

She hung up the phone, trying to tamp down the panic rising in her throat. Maybe Skye had taken the streetcar to the Superdome. After all, she'd taken the streetcar the day she went to the French Quarter.

Kate was tempted to get in her car and race downtown. But

the Superdome was huge, and she wouldn't know where to start. Kate needed to be home in case—no, not in case; *when*—Skye returned home.

Another thought hit her. Oh, Lord! Could Wayne have come by and taken Skye out of spite? The thought sent a cold chill racing through her. Grabbing the phone, she called the motel where Wayne had been staying. A brief conversation with the desk clerk revealed that he had checked out the day before.

Kate hung up the phone, more alarmed and confused than ever. Just because he'd checked out didn't mean he'd left town. It only meant she had no idea where he might be.

Kate paced the living room. She longed to talk to her mother, but Ruth had gone on an overnight trip with her therapy group as part of her treatment.

At eleven-thirty, Kate gave in and called the police.

A squad car pulled up five minutes later. Kate was relieved that the policeman wasn't one of the officers who had responded to her mother's false burglary report.

The officer listened to her story, making notes as she talked. "We'll put out an A.P.B. for the girl's father on a possible domestic kidnapping. From what you've told me, though, ma'am, it sounds like she's run away."

Kate swallowed.

"In most cases, teens who run away—especially younger ones—return within forty-eight hours. But, if you like, we can go ahead and file a missing persons report. We don't have to wait twenty-four hours with minors."

"I want to file one."

"I'll need a recent photo and a full description of your daughter."

Kate strode to the back of the sofa, where a collection of silver-framed pictures adorned a narrow table: Skye as a baby, giving an enormous toothless grin; Skye sitting in front of a Christmas tree, hugging her grandmother; Skye and Kate on a visit to Disney World. Her heart ached as she looked through this photo gallery of her daughter's life. She picked up Skye's most recent school photo and handed it to the officer, then answered a long series of questions.

"What will happen now?" she asked as he finally closed his notebook.

"We'll distribute her photo and this information to local and state police, and get this info on a national hotline for missing children. Since she's gone to the French Quarter before, I'll call the French Quarter precinct and ask them to keep an eye out for her."

"Is that all?"

He rubbed his chin, his eyes apologetic. "Well, we'll be looking for her father, as well. And we have extra patrols around the Superdome, keeping an eye out for unsupervised teenagers." He rose from the sofa. "There's a good possibility she'll show up later tonight. In the meantime, make a list of all the places she might be. Call all her friends and see if any of them have heard from her or have any idea where she's gone. Check all of her hangouts. You might even check the hospitals." He hesitated. "Do you happen to have a set of her fingerprints?"

"No."

"How about dental records?"

A chill cut through Kate. "I-I can get them from her dentist."

"It's good to have them on hand."

In case she shows up dead. Tears sprang to her eyes as she walked the officer to the entry way.

The officer paused at the door. "I sympathize with you, ma'am. I've got two little ones of my own."

Kate nodded, fighting back the tears.

"Chances are, she'll come back soon. Most young teens do."

"I hope you're right," Kate said, her fingers clutching the door as he walked away. *Please. God. Please, please, please, bring my baby home safe and sound. And soon.*

347

Chapter Twenty-six

Ruth burst through Kate's kitchen door at ten the next morning, her face beaming, her voice happy and excited. "I did it! I spent the night away from home and didn't have a single panic attack!"

Kate tried to smile. "That's great, Mom."

Ruth froze in her tracks, her expression abruptly shifting to one of concern. "My heavens, Kate—what's wrong?"

Kate hesitated. She hated to give her mother such bad news just as she was starting to conquer her fear. It might cause a setback. But she had to tell her.

"It's Skye." Tears streaming down her face, Kate sank into a chair at the kitchen table beside her mother and poured out the whole story. "I don't know where she's gone," she finished. "I've called everywhere."

Ruth tightened her grip on Kate's hand. "Have you called Zack?"

Kate looked up.

"She really bonded with him. She might try to go to California."

"But how? She can't have more than twenty dollars on her."

"Maybe she'd try to hitchhike."

The two women stared somberly at each other, their unspoken fears darkening the room.

"You need to call him," Ruth urged.

Her mother was right. Drawing a deep breath, Kate rose from the table and went to the phone.

The film editor clicked off the projector, plunging the dimly lit edit booth into near total darkness. "Which take do you want to use?"

"Let me see them again," Zack said.

"All seven?"

"Yeah."

With a long sigh, the heavyset man hit the rewind button.

Zack scowled into his Styrofoam cup of coffee. It was irritating as hell, the way he couldn't keep his mind on the movie. For the umpteenth time this morning, his mind had strayed back to New Orleans, to a woman with hair the color of spun gold and a heart made out of the same substance. Instead of making decisions about what footage to cut, he'd found himself daydreaming like a lovesick schoolboy. What was Kate doing? What was she thinking? Was she back at her job at the university? Did she miss working on the movie?

Did she miss him?

He took a punishing sip of coffee. It bothered the bejeezus out of him that she'd sent him that damned note instead of telling him good-bye in person. Everything in it had sounded so blasted reasonable, so damned sensible, so friggin' *cheerful*.

Kate had made things easy for him, and he resented the hell out of it. He knew his reaction made no sense, but knowing that irritated him all the more. If she'd wept and wailed and begged him to pledge his undying love, he'd have been eager to leave her. At least that's how it had always worked with other women.

But Kate was unlike any other woman he'd ever known. Everything about her was special. She was smart and funny and enthusiastic. She was ethical and kindhearted and fair. She was the most caring, most giving, most alive person he'd ever met. And when it came to sex—hell, the chemistry between them blew the bedroom door off its hinges.

All the same, it was darned inconsiderate of her not to say good-bye. Nobody liked good-byes, but they provided a sense of closure. There was unfinished business between them, and it was affecting his work.

At this stage of a movie, he usually didn't care about anything except getting it finished. Like a man possessed, he'd skip meals, forgo sleep, and forget to shave, pouring all his energy into sculpting the footage into a movie. The editing process was tedious and excruciatingly slow, but Zack had always thought it was the most creative, exhilarating part of the process, the part where the story all came together. While he was editing, he usually came the closest he ever got to actually being happy.

He sure wasn't happy now. He was skipping meals and losing sleep and sporting a growth of beard, all right, but it was because he was miserable and distracted. This was the most important project of his life, and he couldn't concentrate on it. It was a good movie—maybe even a great movie—yet it seemed somehow lacking, somehow unsatisfying.

Hell, his whole life was lacking and unsatisfying. For the first time, work was letting him down. In the past, it had filled up all the crevices and low spots in his life, like high tide over a rocky shoal. Now it had receded, leaving nothing but jagged edges and broken shells.

Something was missing. No, not some*thing*; some*one*.

Damn it, he didn't need this. He'd always taken a secret pride in the fact that he didn't *do* emotions. He stayed on an even keel. He used logic. He didn't moon or pine or regret the past. He dealt with what was in front of him, did what needed doing, moved on.

But he couldn't seem to move past Kate.

The editor snapped a switch. "Okay. Here we go."

Zack shifted in the chair, trying to gather his concentration as the image of the swamp filled the screen.

A shaft of light intruded from the back of the booth. "Thought I'd stop by and see how this puppy's coming along," came an unmistakable rasp.

Goldman. Sure enough, Zack looked up to see his grotesque Humpty-Dumpty form standing in the doorway.

Zack attempted a congenial expression. "Come on in, Marvin. We're looking at the raw footage."

"Hell, if I wanted to see raw, I'd go to a meat market." Goldman rotated the cigar in his mouth. "Show me what you've laid down."

"We're still going through the rough stuff. You know what they say—you can't hurry perfection."

Goldman muttered a particularly crude obscenity. "You damn sure can, and you damn sure will. I want this in front of a test audience in two weeks."

"Two *weeks?*"

"You heard me."

Post-production usually took two, three, even four times that long. Goldman was asking the near impossible.

But maybe it was just what Zack needed. A near-impossible challenge would force him to concentrate. "It'll mean working around the clock," Zack warned. "I'll need another editor."

"So get one. And send some clips to promotions ASAP. They needed them yesterday." Goldman chomped his cigar. "Got any footage of Lena naked?"

"Sorry, Marvin."

"No outtakes? You didn't shoot some film when she wasn't watchin'?"

Zack shook his head.

Goldman gave a phlem-rattling cough. "You disappoint me, Jackson."

A young assistant popped her head in the booth, her expression apologetic. "I hate to interrupt, but you've got a call, Zack."

"Take a message."

351

"I tried to, but she said it was an emergency."

"Who?"

"Kate Matthews."

Zack rose from his chair so fast he almost knocked it over. "I'll take it outside."

He brushed past Goldman and followed the assistant to an empty cubicle. The office chair squeaked as he simultaneously sat down and pushed the flashing light on the phone. "Kate?"

"I'm sorry to bother you, but something's happened." Her voice sounded strained and thin.

His heart kicked into high gear as his mind seized on a possibility. Was she pregnant? Hope, irrational and excited, rushed through his veins. "What is it?"

"It's Skye." Kate's voice wavered. "She's missing."

His blood froze in his veins. He gripped the phone as if it were about to take flight. "Since when? What happened?"

His chest grew tighter and heavier as Kate explained the situation. "And she was gone all night?" Zack asked when she finished.

"Yes. I was wondering . . . has she called you?"

"No."

He heard a quick intake of breath, as if Kate were stifling a sob. "If she does, will you let me know?" Her voice cracked on the last word.

"Of course." He rose, unable to sit still. "What are the police doing?"

"N-not a whole lot. They're looking for Wayne, but they're pretty much treating this as a typical runaway case. They told me she'd probably come back in forty-eight hours."

A lot of horrible things could happen to a young girl in forty-eight hours. He prayed none of them already had.

"We need to get Skye's picture on TV and in the newspapers," Zack said decisively.

"The officer told me dozens of teens run away from home every day in Louisiana. The media can't publicize them all."

There were times when having a well-known name could be

useful, and this was one of them. "Listen, Kate—I'm going to call my publicist. I'll have him phone your local news media and say that you're my girlfriend. Better yet, my fiancée. We'll say we're afraid Skye's been kidnapped and we're asking the public to keep an eye out for her. That ought to get things moving."

A long silence followed.

"Okay, Kate?"

"O-okay."

"I'm coming back to Louisiana." He wasn't aware he'd made the decision until he heard himself saying it, but he was immediately certain it was his only possible course of action. To hell with Goldman and his damned deadline. "I'll get there as soon as I can."

"Thanks, Zack."

The tears in her voice did something funny to his throat. "Hang in there, honey. We'll get her back."

It was amazing what a difference Zack's name made.

Within an hour after her conversation with him, a TV news crew had appeared at Kate's front door, wanting to tape a story about Skye's disappearance.

Within two hours, police detectives were processing Kate's porch as a possible crime scene and gathering further information from her.

Within four hours, the state police called to say that Wayne had been taken into custody in Texas. He was alone and claimed to know nothing about Skye's disappearance. The authorities believed he was telling the truth. They were holding him, however, because he had two other people's wallets in his back pocket.

And within seven hours, Kate opened her front door to find Zack standing on the porch. She stared at him for a long moment, her heart pounding. He took a step toward her, and the next thing she knew, she was in his arms, bawling like a baby.

Zack held her close. "We'll find her," he murmured. "I promise we will."

All of the pent-up fear and worry came pouring out of Kate as Zack embraced her. He murmured to her softly, stroking her hair, as she soaked the shoulder of his navy shirt. He felt warm and solid and strong, and his presence gave her hope.

Ruth greeted Zack warmly, then went to answer the phone. She returned a moment later. "Kate—it's the detectives. They think they have a lead."

Kate rushed to the kitchen phone, Zack and Ruth right behind her.

"Ms. Matthews, we might have something," said a deep baritone voice.

"What?"

"We had a couple of calls after the five o'clock news aired. Both reported a girl matching Skye's description hitchhiking on I-Ten."

"Which direction was she going?"

"West. Which matches up with another call we got."

Kate couldn't breathe. "Yes?"

"A girl with long, dark hair wearing a shiny blue shirt was spotted getting out of the cab of a semi-trailer truck."

"That's Skye! Where?"

"Outside Houma. The lady who called us said the girl seemed fine," the detective said. "She saw her wave to the driver as he drove off."

"Oh, thank heavens," Kate breathed.

"What?" Ruth asked. She and Zack were standing beside her, their expressions anxious.

Kate put her hand over the receiver. "A girl who sounds like Skye evidently hitched a ride to Houma."

"The cabin," Zack and Ruth simultaneously murmured.

"We have a fishing cabin about ten miles southwest of Houma," Kate said into the phone. "It's only accessible by boat."

"Where, exactly?"

"The launch is about two miles west of the highway, a couple of miles past Theriot."

"Do you keep a boat at the launch?"

"Just a rowboat. We always get a ride from a friend who takes care of the place. His name is Jean-Pierre Vacherie. I'll get you his number. He can take you there or give you directions."

Kate set down the phone and darted across the room to retrieve her address book from a desk drawer. "While you're giving him numbers, give him the one to your cell phone," Zack said. "And tell him you and I are on our way."

It was dark when Zack turned onto the dirt road that led to the boat launch. The sky was an unrelenting black that seemed to go all the way through Kate's soul. There was no moon, and the stars were obscured by clouds. To make matters worse, a dense fog was creeping in, gathering in a thickening veil over the bayou.

As Zack braked at the road's dead end, the headlights of his rental car gleamed on two sheriff's deputies standing beside a patrol car. The musky scent of swamp water filled Kate's nostrils as she climbed out of the car.

"Hey, you're Zack Jackson! Wait'll my wife hears I met you," one of the officers said, sticking out his hand.

Zack gave it a single shake, then put his arm around Kate. "This is the girl's mother. Do you have any news?"

The other officer stepped forward. "There's been another development."

Kate tensed. "Yes?"

"A sport fisherman outside Theriot said he saw a girl run into the woods today about five miles north of here." The officer looked down. "He said it looked like she was running away from some men in a dirty white pickup truck."

Kate's hand covered her mouth.

"How many men?" Zack asked.

"Two were pursuing her. Two more were in the cab."

The cloyingly humid air condensed on Kate's skin like a film on cold gumbo. "Oh, dear Lord."

Zack's arm tightened around her. "This fisherman—what else did he say?"

"That's it. He called us tonight after he saw a news report."

"Did he stop to help her?"

"No. He said he didn't think it was any of his business."

Zack muttered a curse. "When was this?"

"Today. Around noon." The officer hitched up his blue uniform pants by the belt. "We've got some men out searching for her, but the woods turn into swamp pretty fast, and the trees are too dense to use a motorboat or airboat. With this fog, we don't expect to be able to do much until morning."

Panic swelled in Kate's chest. "There are alligators and water moccasins and cottonmouths in that swamp."

"Well, now, ma'am. We're not really sure that's where she is," the other officer said.

If he meant to reassure her, he missed the mark by a mile. Kate stared at him. "Are you saying you think those men caught her?"

He gazed down at his boots. "We don't know, ma'am. You know all we do. We've got an A.P.B. out on the truck, and we're searching the swamp near where she was last seen, but this fog is slowing things down."

Despair seeped into Kate's heart like swamp water into a leaky boot. Zack's arm steadied her. "Let's find Jean-Pierre," he suggested. "He knows this swamp backwards and forwards."

Dawn found Kate sitting at the rough-hewn kitchen table in Jean-Pierre and Marie's rustic home, drinking strong, chickory-laced coffee, her spirits as gray as the fog that still hovered over the swamp waters out the window. It had been a long, confusing night filled with a lot of activity and little progress. Zack and Jean-Pierre had taken off in a pirogue in search of Skye, while Kate had talked to local police, state police, the sheriff's officers, and even two FBI agents.

She'd finally been dropped off here, where she'd sat up the rest of the night, awaiting word.

Marie fussed over a pot of gumbo on the stove, then turned to Kate, wiping her hands on a ragged blue dish towel. "You need to eat somezing, *cherie.*" Worry lines marked Marie's round face like latitude lines on a globe. "You're skin and bones, and you'll need your strength for when Skye returns."

If Skye returns. It was the thought she'd been trying to keep at bay ever since this nightmare began.

"You can't go on with no sleep and no food."

"Neither can Skye." The thought of her child, scared and hungry and exhausted, chilled Kate's soul. How could she eat when Skye was starving, or sleep when Skye was lost and wet and shivering? The swamp was no place for a child to spend the night.

But the alternative was worse. If Skye wasn't in the swamp, that meant the men had caught up with her, which could mean . . .

Kate's mind refused to go any further. She checked her watch for the umpteenth time that morning, then rose from the rickety chair and paced the worn plank floor. "It's driving me crazy, just sitting here," she said.

"The police are looking, along with Jean-Pierre and your Zack. Zey will find her."

Alive, Kate prayed. *Please, God, let them find her alive.*

"Marie, I'm so scared."

The plump woman crossed the room and put her arms around her. *"Pauvre petite,"* she murmured. "Why don' you call your *maman?* She's been where you are, you know."

Oh, heavens—is this what her mother had felt when she'd run away with Wayne? She'd been older, and she'd left a note telling where she was going, but still . . .

Kate's heart ached as she pulled out her cell phone and punched in the number.

Ruth answered midway through the first ring. "Yes?"

"Mom, it's me. There's no word yet."

"Oh, honey, I'm so sorry."

"Mom—I'm so scared."

"I know."

"I know you know." Her voice cracked. "Mom, I'm so sorry I put you through this when I ran away. I . . ." Tears clogged her throat, making it impossible to continue.

"That all worked out, dear, and this will, too." Her mother sounded sure. It helped some.

Kate drew a ragged breath. "I love you, Mom."

"I love you, too."

Something melted inside Kate, some tiny, hard, residual bit of hurt that had been lodged in her heart for years.

It was impossible to be a perfect parent, to give a child exactly what she needed, exactly when she needed it. It was impossible to always know when to protect your child and when to set her free, when to shield her from pain and when to make her face it. Kate was making mistakes with Skye just as her mother had made them with her, just as Skye would no doubt make them when she had a child of her own.

They could only do their best and hope it was enough— praying that time would caulk the gaps, that forgiveness would sand down the rough edges, that love would cover the flaws like a shiny new coat of paint.

Nothing further needed to be said. Love, accepting and unconditional, flowed through the silent phone line.

"Hang in there, Kate," her mother said softly. "Hang in there and pray."

"You, too." Kate clicked off the line and gazed out at the water. Her eyes must be playing tricks on her, because it looked like a ghost was emerging from the fog, gliding across the water. She blinked hard, but the ghost was still there.

"Marie!" she called. Her heart began a fast, erratic skitter as the older woman wiped her hands on an old dish towel and hurried toward her. Kate opened the squeaky screen door that led to the long wooden pier. It was no ghost—it was Jean-Pierre, sitting low in a pirogue, wearing a white rain poncho. The boat disappeared briefly behind a large cypress tree then reemerged closer than ever.

Kate's heart pounded hard. She could make out Zack in the back of the boat, holding something that looked like a large sack of potatoes. Oh, dear God—it was still and unmoving, wrapped in an old blanket. It looked like a body.

Kate's knees started to buckle. Marie grabbed her arm. The boat was getting closer now, but Jean-Pierre's rain slicker was pulled low over his face, and Kate couldn't make out his expression.

"Zey're docking at zee end of zee fishing pier. I'm going to give zem a hand."

The pier was several feet above the water, and the boat disappeared beneath it. The pier creaked as Marie hurried down it, but Kate couldn't move. Her heart was frozen with dread, and her feet along with it. *No. No. Please, God, no.*

She held her breath as Jean-Pierre climbed up the short ladder onto the pier. She closed her eyes as he turned back to pull something up.

And then she heard a voice that sent her heart into orbit.

"Where's my mom?"

The feet that had been frozen a moment ago suddenly had wings. She flew to the end of the pier and grabbed Skye so tightly that they were both in danger of tumbling into the swamp. "Skye! Oh, honey—you're back! You're back!"

Skye gripped her tight and sobbed.

"It's okay, sweetheart. Everything is going to be okay." Kate held her child, stroking her hair. She looked up a moment later to see Zack stepping onto the pier. Kate held out an arm, and he joined them in a three-way hug, squeezing mother and daughter as they clasped each other in a joyful, tearful embrace.

The story spilled out of Skye in a torrent as she sat on the bench on the pier, wrapped in a blanket. Kate's arm was around her. She'd hitchhiked from New Orleans to Houma, then walked along the two-lane highway south, looking for the dirt road to the boat launch.

"A white pickup pulled over and asked if I wanted a ride. There were four really creepy-lookin' men in it and they were all drinking beer. I didn't like the way they looked or the way they were yelling at me, so I said no and kept walking. But they wouldn't leave me alone. The truck drove real slow beside me, and then the two men in the back climbed out."

Kate suppressed a shudder.

"I ran into the woods. I could hear them behind me. The biggest one was huffing and puffing and calling me names and yelling out threats. I was really, really scared. I ran and ran, even though I was in water and it kept getting deeper and sometimes I had to swim. I finally found a tree with branches low enough to climb, so I did that, and I sat there for a long time. I wanted to make sure they were gone.

"After about an hour, I figured it was safe to come down. I tried to go back to the road, but I guess I went the wrong way. I was all turned around, and I didn't know which way was which. Everything looked the same. And then I saw an old rowboat. I got in it, but it had a hole in the side and it was leaky on the bottom and it kept filling up. So I dragged it over to a clump of cypress knees sticking out of the water, and I put it on them and climbed in. And that's where I stayed until Jean-Pierre and Zack found me."

"Oh, honey." Tears of relief and gratitude ran down Kate's cheeks.

Skye looked up at her with wet, remorseful eyes. "Mom, I'm so sorry. It was stupid of me to run away. I was just all upset and confused and angry, and I didn't know what to think or who to trust or even who I was anymore."

"Sweetheart, you're the same wonderful girl you've always been."

Fresh tears burst from the girl's eyes. "I love you, Mom."

"I love you, too, honey. And I'm so sorry I didn't level with you about your father from the very beginning."

"I've had a lot of time to think about that, and Zack talked to me about it on the boat ride back. You just didn't want me to feel bad that my dad was a jerk, right?"

Kate pulled her close, her heart brimming with relief and sadness—relief that Skye understood, and sadness that she needed to. It was difficult to accept that any man could be so indifferent to his own child. At the same time, it was heartwarming to see that Zack could be so caring to a child in need of a father figure. Heartwarming and heartbreaking.

Kate's fingers sifted through Skye's hair. "I promise you, honey, that from now on I'll always be truthful with you. Even when I'm afraid the truth will hurt, I'll trust you enough to handle it."

Skye looked up at her, her eyes the color of robin's eggs, and just as full of life. "Can you tell me the truth about something else?"

"Sure."

"Is there any way I can get something to eat? I'm *starved!*"

Everyone laughed. "There's the old Skye we know and love," Zack said, ruffling her hair.

"Come weeth me, *ma petite,*" Marie said, putting her arm around Skye as the girl rose to her feet. "We'll get you food an' a hot shower an' dry clothes."

While Skye showered and plowed through a huge bowl of gumbo, Kate called Ruth with the news, and smiled at her mother's jubilant yelp of joy. It took a while for the police to take Skye's statement and wrap up their paperwork, and then the media descended.

By the time everyone had cleared out and things had settled down, Skye had fallen asleep on the sofa and Kate didn't have the heart to wake her. While Jean-Pierre and Marie watched TV to see all the news stories about Skye's recovery, Kate and Zack strolled out on the pier.

The sun had burned off the fog, and the sky was so blue it

could have been lifted from a van Gogh painting. The swamp looked entirely different now than it had just a few hours earlier.

Life looked entirely different than it had just a few hours earlier.

"I don't know how to thank you," Kate told Zack. "If you hadn't stepped in and gotten all the news coverage about Skye's disappearance, she might still be out there."

"I'm glad you called me." Zack looked at her, his eyes as dark and warm as espresso.

"And I'm glad you came." Now that the crisis was over, an awkwardness stretched between them, along with a tension as strong as a ten-gauge fishing line. Kate stuck her hands in the pockets of her jeans. "So . . . How's the editing going?"

"Lousy. I've had trouble concentrating."

A frog jumped off a lily pad, disturbing the still water, creating an ever-widening circle on the surface. A ripple of something—fear? hope? anticipation?—spread through Kate as well.

"I was looking at the swamp scenes when you called," Zack said.

"Yeah? Have you decided which one you're going to use?"

He nodded. "The one where they don't make love. Where Joe tells Sadie they've got forever."

It wasn't just the words but the way his eyes went all soft and sincere as he said them that made her soul tremble. Hope rose up inside her, lifting her to a dizzying, heart-shattering height. She tried to tether it, to keep it low enough that she could survive the fall if she was wrong, but it refused to stay earthbound. "What changed your mind?"

"I was looking at the wildlife footage, and thinking about what you said about how things in the swamp aren't always how they seem—how alligators look like logs and brown pelicans look like tree stumps, how you have to look beyond the surface to see what's really there."

Kate watched a blue-black dragonfly skitter along the water, and her pulse thrummed like its wings.

"And then you called, and I realized that nothing is as I thought it was. There's nothing in the whole world more important to me than you. You are what's beneath my surface. You're what matters, you're what's real."

His hands slid down Kate's bare arms. He lifted her hands to his lips and dropped a kiss on each one, right above her knuckles. His gaze poured into hers, as dark and sweet as hot chocolate.

Kate's heart sped like the fan blades on an airboat.

"You've changed the way I see things, Kate. I used to think that commitment was a trap, but now I realize the trap was pretending I didn't need you. I used to think it was impossible for a couple to live happily together for a lifetime, but now the thing that seems impossible is ever living without you."

Kate's soul soared to the heavens.

"Now I understand where Joe was coming from, because that's where *I'm* coming from." He tightened his grip on her hands. "I want to take that leap of faith you talked about. I want to make that no-holds-barred commitment, with no reservations, with nothing held back, and with no expiration dates."

He stepped closer. "What I'm trying to say here is . . . I love you."

"I love you, too," she whispered.

His eyes were full of emotion. In their dark depths, Kate saw her heart's desire. "If we're going to do this commitment thing, I want to do it right." He tightened his grip on her hands. "Kate, will you marry me?"

Kate's heart was so full, she felt it would burst. Her legs trembled as she stood on tiptoe and pressed her lips to his—and then she was in his arms and he was in hers, and the kiss grew warm and deep and heartfelt, full of joy and promise.

"Is that a yes?" he asked at last.

Her throat was too tight to speak. She could only nod.

"I like the way you express yourself." He smiled down at her, his eyes warmer than the midday Louisiana sun. "Tell me yes again."

As their lips met and their hearts merged, a brown pelican took off from a knobby stump, soaring straight and high and unafraid, his wings dark against the clear blue sky.

Epilogue

One year later, the following item appeared in the "Holly-wood Gossip" column of the *National Inquisitor:*

ZACK JACKSON GETS LUCKY MAKING OOH, LA LA!

The stork paid a visit to Academy Award-nominated director Zack Jackson and his wife, Kate, last Thursday, leaving an eight-pound, five-ounce bundle of joy named Zeke Matthew.

"Mother and child are both doing great," the attending physician told this reporter.

"I've never seen a more devoted husband," gushed a delivery-room nurse. "Zack stroked her hair, held her hand, and whispered words of encouragement. They're obviously very much in love."

Baby Zeke's birth is the latest in a string of happy events resulting from the filming of the hit movie *Ooh, La La!* The film not only generated great reviews and huge box office returns, but two marriages, four Academy Award nominations, and an adoption.

Once considered one of Hollywood's most elusive bachelors, Jackson surprised everyone in Tinsel Town by marrying Kate Matthews, the historical consultant on *Ooh, La La!* eleven months ago. He met the attractive blonde during a location shoot in New Orleans and tied the knot in a private ceremony at a rustic cabin deep in the Louisiana bayou. Shortly afterwards, he adopted Kate's thirteen-year-old daughter, Skye.

Zack wasn't the only Academy Award nominee bitten by the love bug during the making of *Ooh, La La!*—and Kate wasn't the only Matthews woman. Alert *Inquisitor* readers will recall that Kate's mother, Ruth Matthews, married *Ooh, La La!*'s Oscar-nominated director of photography, Fritz Gibson, in a ceremony at the groom's license-plate-covered home last June. The photo of the fifty-four-year-old bride beaming on the back of her husband's Harley, her wedding gown billowing in the wind as they set off on a cross-country motorcycle tour, appeared in the *National Inquisitor*'s special "Wacky Hollywood Weddings" issue.

In addition to Oscar nominations for Best Director and Best Cinematography, *Ooh, La La!* is up for Best Picture and Best Screenplay. When asked how many gold statues he hopes to take home, Jackson gave his characteristic grin and replied, "All of them, of course. But even if I go home empty-handed, I've already won the most important thing in the world—the heart of the woman I love."

Aww! Makes you want to go out and make a little Ooh, La La of your own, doesn't it, folks?

"Craig's latest will DELIGHT . . . fans of
JANET EVANOVICH and HARLEY JANE KOZAK."
—*Booklist* on *Gotcha!*

Award-winning Author

Christie Craig

"Christie Craig will crack you up!"
—*New York Times* Bestselling Author Kerrelyn Sparks

Of the Divorced, Desperate and Delicious club, Kathy Callahan is
the last surviving member. Oh, her two friends haven't died or anything. They just gave up their vows of chastity. They went for hot sex
with hot cops and got happy second marriages—something Kathy
can never consider, given her past. Yet there's always her plumber,
Stan Bradley. He seems honest, hardworking, and skilled with a tool.

But Kathy's best-laid plans have hit a clog. The guy snaking her drain
isn't what he seems. He's handier with a pistol than a pipe wrench,
and she's about to see more action than Jason Statham. The next
forty-eight hours promise hot pursuit, hotter passion and a super
perky pug, and at the end of this wild escapade, Kathy and her very
own undercover lawman will be flush with happiness—assuming they
both survive.

Divorced, Desperate and Deceived

ISBN 13: 978-0-505-52798-1

Tracy Madison

A Stroke of Magic

You know how freaky it is, to expect one taste and get another? Imagine picking up a can of tepid ginger ale and taking a swig of delicious, icy cold peppermint tea. Alice Raymond did just that. And though the tea is exactly what she wants, she bought herself a soda.

ONE STROKE OF MAGIC, AND EVERYTHING HAS CHANGED

No, Alice's life isn't exactly paint-by-numbers. After breaking things off with her lying, stealing, bum of an ex, she discovered she's pregnant. Motherhood was definitely on her "someday" wish list, but a baby means less time for her art and no time for recent hallucinations that include this switcharoo with the tea. She has to impress her new boss, the ridiculously long-lashed, smoky-eyed Ethan Gallagher, and she has to deal with her family, who have started rambling about gypsy curses. Only a soul-deep bond with the right man can save her and her child? As if being single wasn't pressure enough!

Available July 2009!   ISBN 13: 978-0-505-52811-7

JANA DeLeon

"DeLeon is excellent at weaving comedy, suspense and spicy romance into one compelling story." —*RT Book Reviews*

Everyone in Mudbug, Louisiana, knows that when Helena Henry shows up, no good will come of it. Especially now that Helena is dead. And more meddlesome than ever.

Sabine LeVeche needs to locate a blood relative fast—her life depends on it. Her only ally is the smart-mouthed ghost of Helena Henry. Until Beau Villeneuve agrees to take the case. The super-sexy PI is a master at finding missing persons—and all the spots that make Sabine weak in the knees. But as they start to uncover the truth about the past, it becomes clear that someone out there wants to bury Sabine along with all her parents' secrets. And she realizes what they say is true: family really can be the death of you.

Mischief in Mudbug

A
Ghost-in-Law
Mystery Romance

ISBN 13: 978-0-505-52785-1

"Kate Angell is to baseball as Susan Elizabeth Phillips
is to football. Wonderful!"
— *USA Today* Bestselling Author Sandra Hill

KATE ANGELL

WHO'D BEEN SLEEPING IN KASON RHODES'S BED?

The left fielder for the Richmond Rogues had returned
from six weeks of spring training in Florida to find someone
had moved into his mobile home. That person was presently
in his shower. And no matter how sexy the squatter might be,
Kason wanted her out.

He had his trusty dobie, Cimarron; he didn't need anyone
else in his life. Not even a stubborn tomboy who roused all
kinds of wild reactions in him, then soothed his soul with
peace offerings of macaroni & cheese and rainbow Jell-O.
The bad boy of baseball was ready to play hardball if need be,
but with Dayne Sheridan firmly planted between his sheets,
he found himself . . .

SLIDING HOME

ISBN 13: 978-0-505-52808-7

To order a book or to request a catalog call:
1-800-481-9191
Our books are also available at your local bookstore, or you
can check out our Web site **www.dorchesterpub.com**
where you can look up your favorite authors, read excerpts,
glance at our discussion forum, and check out our digital
content. Many of our books are now available as e-books!

CHRiSTIE CRAIG

Macy Tucker was five years old when her beloved grandfather dropped dead in his spaghetti. At twelve, her father left his family in the dust. At twenty-five, her husband gave his secretary a pre-Christmas bonus in bed, and Macy gave him the boot. To put things lightly, men have been undependable.

That's why dating's off the menu. Macy is focused on putting herself though law school—which means being the delivery girl for Papa's Pizza. But cheesier than her job is her pie-eyed brother, who just recently escaped from prison to protect his new girlfriend. And hotter than Texas toast is the investigating detective. Proud, sexy…inflexible, he's a man who would kiss her just to shut her up. But Jake Baldwin's a protector as much as a dish. And when he gets his man—or his woman—Macy knows it's for life.

Gotcha!

ISBN 13: 978-0-505-52797-4

Who's coming down your chimney tonight?

SANTA, Honey

Ho, Humbug, Ho
KATE ANGELL

Forced into a scratchy white beard and a red velvet suit two sizes too small, hotshot ballplayer Alex Boxer knows his goose is cooked when the woman supervising his community service turns out to be cute as a Christmas elf but channelling the nutcracker.

Naughty or Nice
SANDRA HILL

Anyone can hold up a convenience store on Christmas Eve. But to do it impersonating Santa Claus, on behalf of a nun, handcuffed to a gorgeous hostage—that takes brass . . . bells.

Christmas Unplugged
JOY NASH

Two sisters, plus two brothers, plus one romantic Christmas weekend at Dutch Lodge with zero electricity. It all adds up to a sleigh load of mix-ups, breakups and happily-ever-after hookups.

ISBN 13: 978-0-505-52753-0

☐ **YES!**

Sign me up for the Love Spell Book Club and send my
FREE BOOKS! If I choose to stay in the club, I will pay
only $8.50* each month, a savings of $6.48!

NAME: _____

ADDRESS: _____

TELEPHONE: _____

EMAIL: _____

☐ I want to pay by credit card.

☐ VISA   ☐ MasterCard.   ☐ DISCOVER

ACCOUNT #: _____

EXPIRATION DATE: _____

SIGNATURE: _____

Mail this page along with $2.00 shipping and handling to:
Love Spell Book Club
PO Box 6640
Wayne, PA 19087
Or fax (must include credit card information) to:
610-995-9274
You can also sign up online at **www.dorchesterpub.com**.
*Plus $2.00 for shipping. Offer open to residents of the U.S. and Canada only.
Canadian residents please call 1-800-481-9191 for pricing information.
If under 18, a parent or guardian must sign. Terms, prices and conditions subject to
change. Subscription subject to acceptance. Dorchester Publishing reserves the right
to reject any order or cancel any subscription.